THE HIGH WHITE FOREST

THE
HIGH
WHITE
FOREST

by RALPH ALLEN

DOUBLEDAY & COMPANY, INC., GARDEN CITY, N.Y., 1964

All of the characters in this book
are fictitious, and any resemblance
to actual persons, living or dead,
is purely coincidental.

To Birdeen Allen

THE HIGH WHITE FOREST

CHAPTER ONE

The attack was not to begin for another seven hours and twenty-three minutes, but already the last of the medium guns were coming into position on the slopes and in the clearings and the first of the tanks were creeping out of the heavy, dark, snow-burdened woods to start forming up their columns. Although a heavy mist lay close to the narrow roadways and the thick pines and firs drew it in like blotting paper, a partial blackout was being enforced. There was no danger of air observation and from the foremost tip of the foremost panzer to the foremost American outpost the distance was believed to be at least seven kilometers, but it was important to establish a pattern of discipline at the outset. Smoking was permitted and officers were allowed to use hand flashlights to confer this final time over their map cases, but none of the vehicles, not even the tortured and sorely laboring artillery tractors and panzers, used headlights. Occasionally, fighting and snarling and clawing its way through a muddy cut-up ditch, one of the panzers flung a trail of angry sparks from its exhaust, and then, drawn in briefly from the fog and the dark edge of the woods, the half-faces of two, three, or a dozen of the quarter of a million waiting soldiers became half visible, like wicked wood-cutters or honest charcoal burners or lost children staring out of one of the night forests of the Brothers Grimm.

SS Hauptscharführer Franz Koerner had brought his jeep into place, as scheduled and in good order, at the rear of the Sixth Panzer Army's main column. "You can get out and stretch now if you like," he said in English. "But don't go far away. I've got a hunch we might move up a mile or so more before the jump-off." It sounded all right to him; a lot better after five years than it might have been.

Unteroffizier Tannenbaum, sitting in the other front seat, beside him, rotated some of the stiffness out of his shoulders. "It's drier here," he said, also in English.

"Drier here what?" Hauptscharführer Koerner asked quickly.

"Drier here *Captain*," Tannenbaum answered with a trace of weary patience.

"Or drier here *sir*," the *Hauptscharführer* reminded him relentlessly. "And don't you damned well forget it."

"Yes, Cap'n-boss, sah. Ah sho' 'nuff reads y'all loud en' cleah. *Oui, mon capitaine. Jawohl, mein Hauptsturm—*"

"Sergeant Foster!" Franz would have liked to laugh, just for the hell of laughing again; Erich was forever almost making him laugh and he was forever having to check himself. He made his voice hard and menacing; in deference to the tacit understanding that had grown between them during the last seven weeks the *Unteroffizier* straightened in his seat and spoke now with full military solemnity.

"Sir?"

"What's your first name, Sergeant?"

"Roger, sir. Full name Roger Harding Foster."

"Serial number? Quick now."

"One one eight nine six four four seven."

"That's up in the eleven millions. Let me see your dog tag." Franz paused a few seconds. "You sure got in late, didn't you, Sergeant? Where'd they find you? In the canebrakes?"

"Look soldier, I don't have to take—"

"What's your home town?" Franz snapped.

"Philly."

"Where's Independence Hall?"

"Sixth and Chestnut."

"Who's your most famous citizen?"

"I guess you'd have to say old Connie Mack."

"What's your outfit?"

"Artillery Observation, Forty-Second Infantry Division. Attached to First Battalion, Nine Twelve Regiment."

"Whose artillery do you expect to observe back here? Don't you know you're thirty miles behind the front?"

"I got news for you, soldier. I'm two thousand yards behind the front and so are you. Half an hour from now the front will be right here. They've overrun everything up there. There's a general order to retreat. Our regiment's wiped out. The last order we got was every man for himself."

"Come on, come on." Hauptscharführer Koerner half scolded

2

and half coaxed. "You're supposed to be scared shitless at this point."

"Quite." Unteroffizier Tannenbaum, alias Sergeant Foster, slumped down in the seat again, thrust his hands into the pockets of his GI combat jacket, and lapsed defiantly into the mildly sardonic tone he had been using when the conversation began. "Quite. The funny thing is that if we do get to that point, I *will* be scared shitless." Then he said in German, though the use of German was now explicitly forbidden, "Look, Franz, I can't promise much. But I won't forget my lines. I promise that."

"Well, that's something." Franz spoke in German also. He could not see the round, intelligent cynical face of his companion, but it warmed him strangely to think that a flicker of unaffected anxiety must have crossed it just now; the whisper of the confessional was clearly audible in Tannebaum's voice.

"How about you, Corporal Christianson? Do you want to stretch?"

The perfectly disciplined voice of SS Rottenführer Lemmering responded at once from the seat directly behind. "I think I'll just stay here a while, sir."

"PFC Lachaise?"

"He's asleep, sir," Rottenführer Lemmering said, disposing only momentarily of that particular problem. It was hard enough to think of Grenadier Gotthold Preysing being mistaken for anyone in the world but Grenadier Gotthold Preysing of Hamburg; the weird lottery that had designated him as PFC Henri Lachaise of New Orleans and wiped away the last trace of an excuse for his incurable Gotthold Preysingness was like piling one impossible accident on another. When Preysing, with innocent pride, had displayed the dog tag in the barracks at Grafenwöhr, Hauptscharführer Koemer had stridden to the orderly room to see what could be done. "Sir," he had tried to explain to the busy Wehrmacht major in charge of documentation and orientation, "if we could just find a Germanic name for Grenadier Preysing. Or at least an Anglo-Saxon one. There are lots of German accents in America. Where I come from sir, in Yorkville—"

"I don't care where you come from, *Hauptscharführer*." The Wehrmacht rarely had so rich a chance to pull rank on the SS. "I'm busy with more important matters and can do nothing."

"*Jawohl, Herr Major*." Franz's impeccably correct salute admitted defeat.

3

But the problem of Grenadier Gotthold Preysing, the putative PFC Lachaise, could not be dismissed so simply. At that stage, before they had even heard the code words Operation Greif and Operation Einheit Stielau, the only two things they knew for certain were that they were to function as a four-man unit with Hauptscharführer Koerner in charge, that they would be using American weapons and American vehicles, that they would in due course be issued American uniforms, and that they had only a very short time to bone up on or learn the American language as spoken by the American GI. The strongest rumor, and the one that gained the easiest passage through their sealed and closely guarded assembly camp, was that they were to be part of a swift-striking fifth column whose assignment, no more, no less, was to dash into Paris, seize General Eisenhower himself, and spirit him back through the American lines to Berlin. That this was feasible no one doubted. Was not their commandant the great Oberst Otto Skorzeny, to whom nothing was impossible? Was it not Skorzeny who, at the Führer's personal order, had dropped with a handful of men on an Italian mountaintop and snatched Mussolini from his captors of the Carbinieri? Was it not Skorzeny who had swooped into Budapest to kidnap the son of the wavering Regent of Hungary? Was it not Skorzeny who, as much as any other man, had snuffed out the treasonable plot of July 20 against the Führer's life?

Watching Skorzeny stride across the parade square, long, lean, and bursting with blond Nordic energy, Unteroffizier Tannenbaum turned his round face from the window of their barracks room. For once the perpetual little curve was gone from the corner of his mouth; for once he did not seem too wise for his twenty-three years; for once his manner was as boyish and eager as it should have been.

He and Franz were in the little hut alone; they could, provided Franz didn't object, pretend that they were back in real life again, that they were fellow-sergeants respectively of the Wehrmacht and the Waffen SS, and that there was no need for the time being to go on play-acting at something else.

"Look at the big bastard!" Tannenbaum invited admiringly. "Whatever it's going to be it's no wonder they've called it Operation Greif." They were talking English for practice, even though the order to talk nothing else had not yet come down. "The son-of-a-bitch *looks* like a *greif*."

"What's a *greif?*" Franz was a little envious of Tannenbaum's unflagging erudition and seldom encouraged him to display it. But he was genuinely curious.

"I guess the English word would be griffin. Half lion and half eagle. Well, I'll be damned!" he exploded. "Of course it's Paris. What a fool! It's been staring us in the face right from the start."

"What do you mean?"

"You remember *Paradise Lost*, of course?" The wise little curve had reappeared and Franz knew he was about to be needled, gently and with mild affection, but still needled.

"Of course I remember *Paradise Lost*," Franz said, feeling for once he was getting just a shade the best of it. "Back at dear old Winchester they wouldn't give us our crumpets until we recited the whole God-damned thing backward."

The trouble was that Tannenbaum *had* been at Winchester, for six years, and then at Oxford for two before his father packed up along with the rest of the German Embassy in London. He knew something about everything. He'd even studied theater, and when he remembered he was perfectly capable of transferring his donnish accent to any known region from Yorkshire to Alabama. It was unlikely, Franz had decided, that he'd be worth a damn as a soldier, but if he did turn out to be a soldier he'd be a magnificent asset on a mission like this, no matter where the mission might lead them.

"Of course it's Paris!" Tannenbaum refused to allow his excitement to be dampened. "This Skorzeny is the greatest military ham since Hannibal. I'll bet right now he's gnashing his teeth to think that Hannibal beat him to the elephants. He's also supposed to be an intellectual. You can bet the griffin was his idea and you can bet he was thinking of Milton. Listen! *Paradise Lost!* Part Two!" Unteroffizier Erich Tannenbaum flung his arm wide, commanding silence.

> "As when a gryphon thro' the wilderness,
>   With wingèd course, o'er hill or moory dale,
>   Pursues the Arimaspian, who, by stealth,
>   Had from his wakeful custody purloined
>   The guarded gold."

"Get it, Franz?" Erich's eyes were fairly prancing now.

"No." Franz was back on the defensive, where Erich always forced him when they got away from soldiering.

5

"Well, you do get the business about the gryphon—the *greif*, that's us and the *Oberst*—pursuing with wingèd course o'er hill or moory dale?"

"Go on, Professor."

"The Arimaspian! There's the rest of your key! You know who the Arimaspian is?"

Franz refused to be drawn into any further admissions.

"It's Eisenhower!" Erich shouted. "That's who the Arimaspian is. It's Eisenhower. How could I have missed it!"

"And why is it Eisenhower?" Franz could not avoid one last question, but he made it easier by edging it with his heaviest sarcasm.

"The Arimaspians were the people who used to raid the griffins' gold mines, just to make wreaths and garlands for their hair. What are the bloody Yanks doing, what's Ike doing but raiding Germany, raiding all Europe, grabbing its gold for a crown of glory?"

"Ike's got no hair to put it in," Franz pointed out. Nevertheless he was impressed.

Tannenbaum had already rushed on past him. He was striding up and down between the bunks.

"I wouldn't be Eisenhower for all the tea in China. *Here we go, through the wilderness, o'er hill or moory dale. Allons, les enfants de la pa-ha-trie, lala lala tum-tum-tum* TUM." He stopped in mid-flight. "You've been to Paree?"

"No," Franz said. "They chased my outfit right on past."

"Ah, yes," Erich said sympathetically. "You are of the fighting forces. An enviable distinction. For my part I was forced after the blitz and conquest of France to spend almost two years in Paris. They exiled me to a demeaning existence as chief steward of an officers' club on the Rue des Italiens. There were of course compensations. In return for certain unscheduled favors to certain high-ranking officers I was able to obtain fairly frequent leaves to Berlin. And of course the rations, even when I was confined to the veritable hell of Paris, were at least bearable. Yes, one might say very bearable."

Franz listened with growing interest. "Then of course, if one was fortunate one might find companions—though not always, regrettably, of the highest moral character. There was a girl named Yvette. While you and the *Herr Oberst* and the others are putting the snatch on General Eisenhower, I might just—but no. No, I guess that would be impractical."

6

Franz lay back on his bunk. In the SS you didn't make jokes about military affairs, even obliquely. You seldom felt the desire to, for the SS was an iron inner priesthood within the larger priesthood of the Reich. Still, a break from habit was sometimes a good thing in itself and there couldn't be any real harm in listening awhile longer to this bubbling, unabashed, and outrageously, illogically likable young scoundrel from the soft and bumbling Wehrmacht.

"I find myself, like old Kaspar in the sun, groping for ancient memories," Erich went on lyrically. "It seems to come to me faintly, as though from a great distance, that there was also a girl in Berlin. A girl in Berlin named Else. Ah yes, it becomes more distinct by the moment."

Franz threw him a cigarette. Tannenbaum fielded it expertly in mid-air and put a lighter to it without losing more than a breath or two. "Now that the details come back I remember it as a most practical arrangement. My girl in Paris supplied me with perfume and silk, which I took to my girl in Berlin; my girl in Berlin supplied me with *Bratwurst* and goose liver, which I took to my girl in Paris. I would not have dreamed such days could come back so soon."

"Weren't the girls jealous?"

"Indescribably. Ferociously. That is why I did not trouble their pretty heads with an excess of needless information."

"And tell me." In spite of himself Franz entered the spirit of jovial irony. "During all this international trade in love and goose liver and *Bratwurst* and perfume did no money change hands?"

"Providence, as I have indicated, does provide certain compensations," Tannenbaum admitted. "There was usually a little money for Yvette in Paris and a little for Else in Berlin and sometimes, God willing, a bit left over for me. Quite a bit when I was able to squeeze a few cigarettes into the equation."

"In other words," Franz said, ashamed to be discussing so monstrous a matter so casually, but still half spellbound, "you were working the black market."

Tannenbaum sprang to attention. "*Herr Hauptscharführer*, if you will repeat that remark on our return to Heidelberg, you may expect a call from my friend Prince Scharnhorststauffel. In the meantime the answer is yes. *Ah, Paris! Allons les enfants de la—*"

"God! What a cynic!"

"*Au contraire, mein lieber freund.* Just the opposite. I am a

7

fanatical and devoted idealist." He sprang to attention again and raised his arm in salute. "*Heil Yvette! Heil Else!*"

Franz was almost stunned. "Cut that out!" he shouted. But the black rage he should have felt sputtered out in semispeechless shock. "If they catch you at that—if anybody else catches you at anything like that—*kaput!* curtains!"

"Alas, how true, *mein lieber freund*. If anybody catches me at anything the result will be a most unhappy one. If the police catch me at the black market it's assuredly curtains. If the Gestapo catches me displaying my deepest and most exalted feelings for Yvette and Else in the deepest and most exalted manner at my command, it is of a surety *kaput!* If the *Schweinhund Englisch* or the *sales Americaines* or the debased Canadians catch me in my incarnation as Sergeant Roger Harding Foster it is both curtains and kaput. And if, by any hideous misfortune Yvette should catch me with Else, or vice versa, it then would be not only curtains and *kaput* but *zut! zut! zut!*"

"Tell me one more thing," Franz said, "before we get back to work. How in the name of God did a *Kleinlich* like you ever get into an outfit like this? You must have volunteered like the rest of us."

"Ah," Tannenbaum reflected, "yet another story, equally sad. You remember the wording of the appeal for volunteers?"

"Pretty well," Franz said. "My company commander read it to me in private."

"For my part," Tannenbaum said, "I remember to the letter, as any man granted an advance look at it would remember his own epitaph. No, no, don't take that literally. I fully intend to survive our forthcoming adventure, whatever it may be and wherever it may lead us. The epitaph I refer to applies not to the corporeal Unteroffizier Tannenbaum but to the part of him that is forever Yvette, forever Else, forever the fine ripe burgundies of the officers' club on the Rue des Italiens. Do you have another cigarette to spare?"

He sat down on the bed across the narrow hut from Franz and swung his feet up from the floor until he was half reclining.

"I would perhaps never have heard of the call for volunteers except for what I must regard as the most disastrous single mistake of my entire military career. We, that is to say, the management of the officers' club in Paris, had by now been driven all the way back to Paris along with the other, er, civilizing agencies of the Wehrmacht. However, my fighting spirit unimpaired, I had plunged back into the fray as chief steward of another officers' club on one of those excellent little streets off the Kurfürstendamm. In view of the somewhat altered fortunes of war, it was not a bad little club at all. Better, let us be fair enough to concede"—Tannenbaum paused to regard their bare dormitory—"than this."

"It was there," he continued, "that I made my critical error. One quiet morning I allowed my ravishing Yvette to visit me there. My superior, a dreadful fat pig of an *Oberleutnant*, chanced upon us in the hallway and insisted on being introduced. The next thing I knew—it couldn't have been more than a day or so afterward— there I was standing at attention while he read the message from headquarters. Remember, my dear Franz, up to then I had been indispensable to this swollen, comatose head of *Blumenkohl*. But here he was now, having filled his fat *Blumenkohl* head with sinful and illicit thoughts of my fair Yvette, plotting to get rid of me at once and altogether."

Tannenbaum paused. "If you find this too painful, my dear Franz, pray stop me. I know you have an intense sense of justice and the rest of the story may be more than you can endure."

"Go on," Franz said.

"Well, there I was standing before this unspeakable *Abzugskanal*. As I have said, every syllable is burned eternally on my soul. 'One,' the fat pail of *Abfall* read, 'The Führer has ordered the formation of a special unit of a strength of about two battalions for employment in reconnaissance and special tasks on the Western Front. The personnel will be assembled from volunteers of all arms of the Army and Waffen SS, who must fulfill the following requirements:

" ' "A.," ' the bloated tub of *Eingeweide* read on, ' "physically A-1, suitable for special tasks, mentally keen, strong personality.

" ' "Paragraph," ' the indescribable *Entsetzen* continued, ' "B. Fully trained in single combat.

" ' "Paragraph," ' the obscene *Geschwulst* concluded. ' "C." ' Knowledge of the English language and also the American dialect." ' "

Tannenbaum paused again. "Then this decaying *Venusmuschel* peered at me out of his crafty little eyes and said, 'I shall not, of course, stand in your way, Unteroffizier Tannenbaum.' I tried vainly to explain that although I did, indeed, have a knowledge of the English language, my knowledge of the American dialect ended

9

with the last Hollywood pictures of 1941. The grinning *Ungeheuer* said a man of my intelligence would have no difficulty in bringing myself up to date. Then I hinted that I was not only not fully trained in single combat but that I was not trained in single combat in any manner or degree whatsoever. 'There will no doubt be facilities,' the mound of *Teig* assured me. 'And there is no question that you are mentally keen. As for your strong personality—well, we hardly need to go into that, do we?' The loathsome *Spinne* had the nerve to laugh out loud, thinking out loud of my lovely Yvette.

"I saw, however, that I was defeated. I decided at least to give the monstrous *Kröte* something to think about. 'That leaves only the question of physical fitness, doesn't it, *Herr Oberleutnant?*' I asked.

" 'That's the general idea,' he said, grinning evilly.

" 'I regularly run a thousand kilometers in three minutes and chin myself a hundred times without missing a breath,' I said, fixing him with a dignified and manly stare. 'There's not a gram of fat on my entire body,' I added for good measure. The overstuffed *Klumpen* did not even have the decency to blush. And that, my dear Franz, is how you find me foursquare at your side, a fellow volunteer in Operation Greif."

"You know." Franz got to his feet after a few moments' silent contemplation. He stood before the *Unteroffizier*, half a head taller, visibly leaner and harder. In spite of the ease with which Tannenbaum had dominated the conversation there was not the slightest doubt of who was in command, in fact as well as in rank. "You know, there's only one thing that encourages me about you, Erich. I think even your phoniness is a little phony. I think you may be all right, or anyway you'll do your best to be all right. If I had any real doubt you know, of course, I'd turn you in. If I thought you meant real disrespect to the Führer, if I thought your attitude to this coming job was as impossible as you make it sound—"

"You'd turn me in."

"All the way in," Franz said evenly. "All the way in to the Gestapo, Erich. You shouldn't have forgotten I'm a member of the Schutzstaffel. I shouldn't have forgotten either."

"Well," Erich said, solemn for the first time, not visibly frightened but wholly solemn nevertheless, "since you've been frank with me, I'll be frank with you. I'm not a traitor and I don't intend to become one. If I have to give this war my blood, I'll do so; I won't give it my reverence." He looked straight up into Franz's still-appraising blue eyes. "I told you my father was in the diplomatic service. I didn't tell you he was killed just before I reported here."

Franz started to murmur something.

"No, no. Please. There was nothing heroic about it. A bomb jettisoned on one of the safe suburbs; naturally my father had found a safe suburb as soon as they called him back from England. He's only worth a little mourning; I can provide that myself and still have plenty left for later uses."

Franz stirred uneasily. "My father was of the Junker class," Tannenbaum went on. "He had a good record in the first war. As a staff officer, of course. Nothing so grubby or dangerous as this. Naturally he was against the Führer from the outset, considered him a hideous, vulgar little upstart. Now sit still, Franz. I'm not going to subject you to another display of sedition. The fact is I always considered the Führer right and necessary for Germany. I still do."

"I'm sure the Führer would be relieved," Franz said coldly. "Then we don't have to go any further, do we?"

"Please let me finish, Franz. It's important to me, at least, that you tolerate my eccentricities, and you can't tolerate them unless you understand them."

"I find it growing harder to do either." Franz still kept his voice firm and distant.

"My father joined the National Socialist party in 1934 and had a safe and moderately successful career in its service until that purely accidental bomb hit him late last month. In 1933 my father was a proud and charming man, full of sparkling lively talk, bursting with ideas, and incidentally the best fly fisherman I ever saw. In 1943 he was nothing, less than nothing. He spoke in nothing but party clichés; since the Reichstag fire he made a career of fawning on his natural enemies and betraying his lifelong friends."

"Perhaps he was merely doing his duty." Franz was vaguely aware that this was a party cliché too. He was also aware that clichés weren't necessarily untrue.

"Terror has broken better men than my father," Tannenbaum reflected forlornly. "But what a cruel joke to make the bargain of Faust and then have the devil go back on his end of it. My father was so afraid of death that he allowed his life to lose all meaning and then he lost that, too."

11

"That's a tragedy," Franz said shortly. "Wars are full of tragedy."

"Granted," Tannenbaum said more cheerfully. "I merely wanted to explain why, although I'm more or less resigned to fighting this one, I can't pay homage to it."

"Just watch it from now on." Franz was friendly again. "We'll both be better off that way."

Tannenbaum, his spirits apparently restored in full, began whistling "*Auprès de ma blonde.*"

"What are we going to do about Gotthold Preysing?" Franz was now wholly businesslike.

"What indeed?" Tannenbaum whistled a bar or two of the song.

"Don't forget you're deputy leader of this detachment," Franz reminded him. "If anything happens to me you take charge. What are we going to do about Gotthold Preysing?"

"Treat him as a shellshock case," Tannenbaum counseled. "If anybody intercepts us, tell Gotthold just to roll his eyes and start gibbering."

"I don't know whether you're serious or not. It's a damned serious matter. We may really *be* in Paris capturing Eisenhower. Or God knows where else doing what. If we're stopped I can get by. So can you if you'll quit trying to be so God-damned clever. Lemmering's accent isn't perfect but with a cover name like Christianson he can pass for a Danish-American. But Preysing with the cover name of Henri Lachaise—"

A shadow passed over Franz's lean, tough, wind-burned face. Tannenbaum spoke in alarm. "Look, Franz! He'll be all right. You're not thinking—"

Franz looked at him without expression and spoke in the stiff careful language of an SS marching order.

"Nothing that can be prevented will be allowed to jeopardize our mission."

"He's such a nice little bastard." Tannenbaum was on the edge but not quite across the edge of desperate earnestness, as though desiring to plead something but half afraid to plead, lest in doing so he magnify the danger he was pleading against.

"Where the hell did he get what he thinks is his English?" Franz was no more willing than Erich to spell out the harder, ultimate question.

"You've never really talked to him, have you, Franz?"

"I'd like to, but he seems scared of me."

"Well, he is. He's scared of both you and Lemmering. He's heard so many stories about the SS. I guess that's why he talks to me so much. He shows me pictures of his family—two plump little buck-toothed daughters, one son old enough to be in the Luftwaffe."

"How did the Army let him in for this?"

"The poor little guy fought his way in. He was an interpreter for Cunard in Bremen for nearly fifteen years. That's where he got most of his English, the rest came from school. He never had any complaints about it before."

"Gotthold would be perfect," Franz conceded sourly, "if we were running steamship excursions to New York. But I doubt if that's what Oberst Skorzeny has in mind."

"Anyway, Gotthold, unlike me, is a one-thousand-per-cent, dyed-in-the-wool, honest-to-God volunteer." Tannenbaum went on. "Originally he was in one of the stomach divisions. Leaving the state of his innards aside, just being in a stomach division was like being in hell. Poor Gotthold wants to be a hero even worse than I don't. Well, the diet helped his ulcer quite a bit and between that and the shortage of reinforcements he got transferred a couple of months ago from the stomach division to a Volksgrenadier division. They used him there on PW interrogation. His Cunard-line English was fine for that and he got quite a reputation for it. So when Greif came up they told him about it; naturally he leaped at the chance. Who can guess how he got through the final screening here? Somebody must have been drunk."

"But what do we do with him?" Franz repeated stonily. "They won't let me replace him. If we could even get him another name, another identification tag, if we could make him a Cincinnati Dutchman named Schultz—but my God, Henri Lachaise!"

"Look, Franz, don't give up on him yet," Tannenbaum said quickly. "Let me see what I can do. He keeps showing me those God-damned pictures of his wife and kids and then hinting that we Wehrmacht men must stick together or you SS bastards will throw us to the wolves and—"

"All right," Franz cut in curtly. "Do what you can with him. But remember what I said. Preysing starts out with us, I have no control over that. But nothing I can prevent will jeopardize our mission. Nothing, Sergeant Foster. Nothing at all."

Franz still had a last-minute hope that they'd weed Gotthold Preysing out in the daily classes of English instruction and review. But the officer in charge, a former language professor from Westphalia, had a schoolmaster's ear for words and no ear at all for sounds. He asked Grenadier Preysing one question only.

"State your rank and name."

"Brivate Virsst Klass La Dgjass, Ennrig," Gotthold replied.

"*Jawohl*," the professor said absently. "Not bad. A little too hard on the consonants. Practice in your barracks room the consonants. Next man. State your rank and name."

The professor yielded to the professor's old temptation to lean on his star pupils, and Gotthold was called on for no further performances in public. When Oberst Skorzeny or one of the other senior officers dropped in to see how things were going, the professor focused the drill on Franz or Erich or on the former merchant seaman from Baltimore, the former mechanic from Montreal, the former bus boy from Cincinnati, and the dozen other pupils whose English had not come solely from books and classrooms.

"*Achtung!*" the professor would shout, bringing them to their feet.

"*Kommando zurück*," the visiting officer would order companionably. As the class sat down again, the professor would ask, "Shall we proceed, *Herr Oberst*?"

"By all means, and you might as well call me Colonel."

"Yes, sir." The professor would pretend to survey the class at random and then he'd point, perhaps, toward Erich. "That man in the third row, translate the two commands you have just heard and acted on."

Erich would be on his feet, poker-faced. "*Achtung*: Attention. *Kommando zurück*: As you were."

"Good. What is *Weitermachen*?"

"Carry on."

"*Gewehr ab!*"

"Order arms!"

"*Weggetreten!*"

"Dismissed!"

"*Stahlhelm?*"

"Helmet."

"You may sit down. Now we try some military slang. German slang into American slang. We place great stress on this part of the course," the professor would explain to the visiting officer, trying to suppress a beam of self-satisfaction. "Ah, let me see. We'll try the man over there at the left of the second row." This would probably be Franz or the bus boy from Cincinnati.

14

"*Horchkussus maken?*"

"Hit the sack."

"*Arschloch?*"

"Bloody fool."

"*Frikandellenfriedhof?*"

"Belly."

"*Wuhling?*"

"Snafu. Foul-up."

"*Getrankeobervormann?*"

"Lush. Drunk. Soak."

"Good." The professor might turn to the officer again, smiling with a fellow-officer's delicacy. "Do you mind, sir, if we—er—"

"No. No. I've had a certain amount of experience, Major."

"The man on the aisle in the fourth row. *Blech?*"

"Balls."

"*Scheisse?*"

"Crap."

"*Puff?*"

"Cat-house."

"*Pinkeln?*"

"Piss."

Most of their time on parade was spent on heavy PT, in practicing maintenance on their jeep, and in dismantling, reassembling, and firing their American small arms. Franz was issued a Tommy gun and Erich and the other two members of their squad with M-1 rifles. In addition Franz was given a complete set of millimeter-to-the-kilometer maps of the entire Western front from Arnhem on the north to Colmar on the south. "I don't know our sector yet myself," the *Sturmbanführer* who handed them out said. "When they tell us they'll give us other maps. In the meantime study these carefully."

They were, of course, confined to their heavily guarded barracks area and weren't allowed to send mail out. Sometimes there was a moving picture in the recreation hall and on one improbable Saturday night the wet canteen struck a swift, brief gusher of Löwenbrau (whether it was wholly genuine, pre-1942, pre-Stalingrad, pre-Alamein, pre-Pearl Harbor, pre-Second Front Löwenbrau was a subject of much debate; the young soldiers had never known real Löwenbrau and the old soldiers were no longer sure they could trust their memories). Most evenings the four men lounged around their little squad room in a state of domestic informality.

The wood stove—for the first time in months there seemed to be no shortage of either fuel or rations—glowed reassuringly between the two double-tiered bunks. Rottenführer Lemmering, who had once worked in the Ford assembly plant at River Rouge, Michigan, spent hours studying the manual on the jeep and breaking down, cleaning, and oiling the Tommy gun and the M-1s. Franz studied his maps. The Eisenhower rumor fitted the maps and the mysterious preparations as well as any of the other rumors fitted. Franz dismissed the one that said they were to make a dash for the Channel coast and liberate the German garrison imprisoned at Calais, nor could he make much of the one that insisted there was to be a full-scale multiarmy drive for Antwerp to slice the Allied forces in two and cut off their best supply port. The first seemed to offer too small a prize, the second too impossible an effort. He was on the verge of agreeing with Erich that they were indeed making ready to pursue the Arimaspian.

While Franz proceeded with these private speculations, Unteroffizier Tannenbaum devoted most of his spare time to an equally doubtful project. Erich was making a desperate and oddly chivalrous attempt to get Gotthold Preysing ready for *Der Tag*. Preysing accepted his help reluctantly. Having been at first so full of cheerful complacency, he was now deep in gloom and self-mistrust; everybody made fun of his English, even the illiterate ex-convict from St. Louis who'd been discovered in the Todt labor organization and the suspected pansy who'd once been a clerk for American Express in Vienna.

"I don't think we're getting anywhere, Sergeant Foster." Gotthold was at least growing accustomed to his own and the others' *noms de guerre*.

"Of course we are, PFC Lachaise. Don't forget, for all we know *Der Tag* may be still a month away, perhaps two months away. Now, just try to remember the three things. Watch my mouth when I form the words before you. Soft always on the consonants. Try to get the sound more through the nose and less from the throat."

Gotthold kept glancing nervously toward Hauptscharführer Koerner, busy with the maps, and Rottenführer Lemmering, busy with the guns. Quite clearly his apprehensiveness was growing by the day. It added to his demoralization to have his weakness constantly on parade before the two frightening SS men. It could be sensed that he'd gladly have forefeited his fading dream of glory to be back in the puny sanctuary of the stomach battalion.

"Now, slowly," Tannenbaum would coax him. "I say the German. You say the English. Ready?"

"Hchreddy."

"First word. Now think carefully. *Frass.*"

"Jow?" Gotthold would venture hopefully.

"Chow. Try it again."

"Jow."

"That's better. *Flutterluke.*"

"Mouth."

"Perfect! Damn' good work, PFC Lachaise. *Angst.*"

"Zgaredt."

"Scared." Tannenbaum was as gentle as a mother.

"Zgaredt." By now Gotthold was usually sweating.

"Now here comes the big one again. Take your time, PFC Lachaise. *Figgen.*"

"Fock."

"Not quite. Watch me while I say it and listen carefully."

Then Gotthold would try again.

"Fugg."

"Not quite. Listen again, PFC Lachaise."

Gotthold would listen again, think again, bring a desperate frown to his desperately concentrated face and say carefully:

"Fogck."

A knifelike sleet began driving in across the treetops. It smothered the farthest gusts and gleams of light, but closer in, where the troubled panzers threw orange sparks against the roadway and flashlights flickered on and off, the sleet acted as a lens and pulled the dark shapes in closer and made them twice as large as life. The noise had grown, swollen by a background chorus of half-shouted demands, orders, and questions. Where the guns and tanks and other vehicles had come to rest their crews began dismounting, taking what shelter they could from the sleet and stamping their feet, slapping their sides, and muttering therapeutic curses against the deepening cold.

Franz got out and walked a little way down the convoy. At a narrow crossroad an NCO of the *Feldgendarmerie*, trying without much success to control the local traffic, picked him up with a flashlight and ordered him to halt. The field policeman was not

17

suspicious, merely curious. "So you're one of the Yanks?" he said after Franz had answered his challenge. "They told us to watch out for you fellows. Is it true you're going to be across the Meuse by nightfall?"

Franz hesitated. Everybody knew by now where the armies were headed, and the temptation to share the excitement with someone new was very strong. But you had to be careful with the *Feldgendarmerie*. They could be as dangerous as the Gestapo itself sometimes; for all he knew this was some childish security trap. "I'm not allowed to discuss those things, *Gefreiter*," he said, and began walking back to the jeep.

Gotthold Preysing was still sound asleep on the back seat and the other two men were dozing too, huddled into their combat jackets with their helmets pulled down sidewise in the path of the driving sleet. Franz looked at his watch. Still more than an hour until midnight. Nearly six hours until the barrage began. If they went on sitting here like this they'd be half paralyzed by morning.

He manhandled Preysing awake and shook Tannenbaum and Lemmering erect.

"Out!" he said. "Start digging in." He had never quite grown accustomed to giving apparently senseless orders without explaining them, but one thing he'd learned was that once you started explaining orders there was no end to it. That was one of the crucial differences between the Wehrmacht and the SS. The SS neither apologized for anything nor justified anything; even a lowly *Rottenführer*, passing down an order he didn't understand himself to an even more lowly *Sturmmann* who didn't understand it either, almost never violated the unwritten rule that every order explained itself, simply by reason of being an order. Franz's men were capable of reasoning it out for themselves that they were better off digging useless trenches than sitting uselessly in the falling snow, growing more numb and useless by the minute.

He remembered the sense of outrage and anticlimax with which he himself had first heard the gospel of the shovel. This was on his very first day in the Army, more than a year before he had won his transfer to the SS. Because of the technicalities over his American citizenship—America was still neutral then—it had taken almost a year and a half before he was accepted. Amid the swift, sure triumphs of 1940, with Western Europe in collapse and Russia lying stupefied, awaiting the Führer's pleasure, the Army could afford to be as choosy as it wanted. But soon afterward it was reaching out hungrily for every able-bodied man in sight. Franz hadn't minded his job monitoring the BBC for the Foreign Ministry, and his boss kept assuring him that nothing he could do in uniform could possibly be of greater service to the Reich, but that wasn't what he'd come for. When his call-up arrived at last he felt utterly sure that he had at last found his place in the grand design, not only of the Reich, but of the world and the universe.

Since then he had become accustomed to the physical realities of war and had made the much more difficult and shocking adjustment to its moral and philosophical disappointments. He still remembered his first lecture in his first training camp. He was then twenty-three, two years younger in time than he was now and perhaps forty years younger in experience, and he had fully expected his indoctrination to begin with a Wagenerian flourish of trumpets. But in this German lecture hall, as of August 1941 at any rate, they were doing things far less dramatically and with far less emotion than the Bund had done them even before the war began and even as far away as Camp Siegfried, Long Island, and Camp Nordland, New Jersey.

A very old *Oberstleutnant* strode in and ordered them at ease. He must have known that it was an entirely new draft and therefore an intensely keyed-up one. Most of them had been civilians not more than two days earlier, and only a few of them had as yet even drawn all their equipment. But without a single word of greeting or preamble the old officer launched into a long and immensely detailed dissertation on what he termed their most vital and previous single article of equipment. Was this the rifle? Was it the light machine gun? Was it the heavy machine gun? The grenade? The hard, killing bayonet? The mortar? Or was it perhaps something more abstract he was leading to; perhaps the sense of duty and of destiny, the sense of unity and faith between them and their new comrades. No. Indeed no. Nothing so fancy or poetic. Their most vital piece of equipment, the old *Oberstleutnant* was telling them, was the shovel. The shovel.

"An infantryman without a rifle is no soldier," the weary old officer announced. "An infantryman without a shovel is a suicide. The shovel belongs to the modern infantryman as the horse to the rider or the bullet to the rifle."

He went into a lengthy aside on the *Hochloch* and its uses. Momentarily confused, Franz found himself groping back toward his English. *Hochloch?* What was a *Hochloch?* He knew he ought to know and he looked around him uneasily, wondering if anybody in the room could guess he was sitting there grubbing around in the debris of his alien American youth. Foxhole! The context supplied the definition before he had time to feel really guilty; with a sense of relief he retransferred his thoughts to German.

"In modern war," the *Oberstleutnant* had explained, "the infantryman does not have to build an intricate system of positions. He merely has to be able to build a *Hochloch*. He must be able to build it in any terrain, in any posture and at any time of day or night."

Franz was older than most of the other recruits. He saw by their faces that they felt just as cheated and let down by this prosaic stuff as he did. They were all too green and timid to stir or cough, but the *Oberstleutnant*, perhaps because he had faced so many similar audiences before and had said precisely the same things to them and had seen them receive it with precisely the same expressions, sensed that their thoughts were wandering from the *Hochlochen* and called them back with a sharp and threatening: "*Achtung!*"

"The *Hochloch*," he proceeded, "must be deep and narrow. Deep enough to provide full cover for the rifleman, yet enabling him at the same time, to find a proper aiming position; in addition narrow enough to provide protection for the rifleman against enemy tanks. The *Hochloch* must be large enough to afford room for two riflemen, for in combat two riflemen form a group. The *Hochloch*, therefore, has to be fifty by eighty centimeters in width and length and one meter deep. Whether its long or its short side should face the enemy depends on the terrain, the enemy situation and the assigned mission."

When they scattered afterward to their billets, it was the consensus among the men of the new draft that this was just something someone on the General Staff had shoved into the training syllabus to keep old colonels on the payroll and young privates out of mischief. They'd surely pass this threadbare, 1917 ante-blitzkrieg nonsense down to the labor battalions, where it belonged, and start getting the fighting men ready for the fighting.

But the *Oberstleutnant* must have been a man of greater influence than it appeared, for the warnings he had given them all came true. "The training of the recruit in the use of the rifle and the shovel has to be given equal attention from the very first day," he had announced. They began training in the use of the shovel on the very first day thereafter; they did not begin training with the rifle until the very eleventh day. "Young and old soldiers, of all grades, officers as well as enlisted men, must not allow a single day to pass without having practiced with the shovel," the old officer persisted. Not a single day did pass without practice with the shovel, although the sweating young recruits agreed sourly that their preceptor must be doing his own daily practice on some private, hidden field reserved for officers. The *Oberstleutnant* took out a dog-eared manual and read from some even higher authority: "The use of the shovel at night, already neglected in daytime, is generally thought to be superfluous. This conclusion is wrong, for the night offers the soldier just the right opportunity to make himself invisible and invulnerable for the day." They went on trenching exercises at night, crouching low under the pale autumn stars while underofficers lay listening a hundred yards away for telltale sounds and firing live tracer bullets two feet above the ground.

Franz was an expert with the shovel before he left his training camp; he did not become a convert until he left Normandy. He left Normandy through the Falaise gap with the last blackened, broken, stumbling remnants of the 12th SS Panzer, the young and undefilable division that had gone into battle bearing the proud name of the Hitler Jugend. The Hitler Jugend had survived in name at least, and now, having spent four months in reassembling and training its reinforcements, it was going back into battle somewhere in this very column. The Hitler Jugend, Franz had often told himself while he was helping to build it up again, had lived only because it refused to die. In his less romantic moments he also reminded himself that he, Franz Koerner, had lived because he had truly learned the holy writ of the shovel, because he had clung to his shovel as faithfully as he had clung to his rifle, clung to his shovel after his last bullet was gone, after his water was gone, after his rations were gone, after his helmet was lost, after one shoe was torn off by the concussion of a twenty-five-pounder and the other worn through to the naked, bleeding flesh. During his two months and sixteen days and nights in Normandy—days and nights of attack, counterattack, defense, and the ultimate reeling retreat— Franz's life had been saved perhaps a dozen times by his Schmeisser, at least twice by hand grenades, and at least once by a Canadian artillery barrage that miraculously fell short and chopped up an attacking Canadian battalion just as Franz's company seemed certain to be overrun. But his short trenching spade had saved him many more times than that. Only twice—once during a blissful three-day lull in front of Caen and another time when his regiment was pulled back a few kilos for a five-day rest—did Franz have an opportunity to dig the geometrically perfect *Hochloch* fifty by eighty centimeters in width and one meter deep. Often his *Hochloch* was no more than a hastily scrabbled furrow in a soft Norman wheat field, a rut just deep enough to offer refuge from the rising shrapnel of a ground burst or the illusion of refuge from a descending air burst. (For all his wisdom, the old *Oberstleutnant* had missed the essential point, the Archimedes principle of the infantry: In battle any hole in the ground displaces its own weight in fear.) Often Franz's hastily created fortress was barely deep enough to let him burrow, pulling in his stomach and breathing shallowly, an inch or two below the trajectory of a Canadian or English machine gun or the spray of a mortar; sometimes he inhabited it only during the ten or fifteen minutes while his platoon gathered itself to dash the fifty or sixty yards from one apple orchard to another, from a farmyard to a house, from a roadside to a church, from a graveyard to a stone fence where a line of khaki helmets rose and at last there was no place of sanctuary for any man of either side.

Digging, or the exercise of digging, could be an end in itself. "Come on, get moving," he ordered sharply now. "Get well back among the trees or one of these damned tanks will run over you. Sergeant Foster, make your *Hochloch* big enough for two; have the others help you. I'm going to stay in the jeep and study the map." He put his flashlight on the now familiar square of paper beneath the square of transparent talc and tried again to visualize what kinds of road went with the red and blue lines stretching to the west, what hills and valleys with the brown contour lines, what distances lay between the black grid lines, how thick the trees would be in the deep green shaded areas, how large and important the towns ahead would be, what arguments there were for trying to rush straight through them, what arguments for taking the side roads and circling around. Forty-eight hours ago the names had all been totally unknown to him; now they were almost as familiar and full of meaning as the two great cities from which he derived his very marrow, his two home towns, Manhattan and Berlin.

Monschau, Krinkelt, Malmédy, St. Vith. He must be ready, depending on where the first break came, to push his jeep beyond the tanks and by-pass any one of these beckoning new towns of his and proceed thence into the rear area of the Amis. Any one of these new towns and a hundred others between here and the Meuse. And if no break came here on the northern flank, he must be ready to wheel south, if necessary all the way into the sector of the Seventh Army, beyond the tiny dark lines of print that read Clervaux, Noville, Wiltz, Longvilly, and Bastogne.

Once they reached the territory held by the Amis, the options were many and open. The written order, long since memorized and destroyed, had listed these: to conduct reconnaissance in depth east and west of the Meuse; to detect enemy tank, artillery, and other movements and report back on them by radio, in person, or by any other means that offers itself; to give false commands, when possible, to enemy units in the Allied sector; to reverse road signs; to remove the tapes from enemy-held roads that are mined; to place tapes on enemy-held roads that were not mined; to cut enemy telephone wires; to spread panic and confusion. There was no specific mention of General Eisenhower or the Arimaspian, but Tannenbaum insisted even that possibility was included in their last oral briefing. "And finally," the *Oberst* had added with a sweeping wave of his arm and a hugh, delighted laugh, "to give the bastards any and every kind of bloody hell you can possibly think of."

A dispatch rider, creeping warily along the heaving line of the forming tanks, pulled his motorcycle up beside the jeep. "What outfit's this?" he asked above his idling motor.

"What outfit's yours?" Franz asked him in return.

"Keep your shirt on. Divisional signals, Panzer Lehr."

"Reconnaissance Group, Special Commando Unit, Operation Einheit Stielau." Let the smart bastard figure that one out.

The dispatch rider pulled a notebook from his belt and turned a light on it. "Look, Kamerad," he said in exasperation. "Don't play games with me. I've got a lot of ground to cover. Who the hell *do* you belong to? Tell me in language I can understand."

"Try Operation Greif," Franz suggested more helpfully.

"Well, for God's sake, why didn't you say so?" The dispatch rider spoke now with a mixture of resentment and respect. "Hey! Have you seen Skorzeny yourself? Have you talked to him? What's he like? Is it true he nabbed old Musso with less than fifty men? They say he gets all his orders direct from the Führer, right over the heads of the High Command."

Franz made no reply. He felt a tiny swelling of pride at the other man's eager, admiring curiosity, but he felt it best to remain silent.

"All right, then, all right," the dispatch rider said in the hurt tone of a small boy who has just been refused an autograph. "But you have to tell me one thing whether you want to or not. Have you seen the field marshal's special order of the day? Or has it been read to you?"

Franz hesitated again.

"It's the field marshal's personal order that every man on the front receive his message before dawn," the soldier on the motor-cycle said.

"I don't know anything about it."

The dispatch rider drew off his gauntlet, blew on his fingers, reached inside his leather jacket, drew out a sheaf of papers, and handed Franz the top copy. "Here," he said. "You're to see that it's read to or by everyone in your command or traveling in your vehicle." He rode off down the edge of the column. "Well anyway," he called back, still a trifle aggrieved, still a trifle awed, "Good luck."

Franz read the paper twice, once hurriedly to see if it required any action on his part, the second time translating it into English, wondering how it might sound ten years from now in the history class at P.S. 77 at the corner of Eighty-sixth Street East and First Avenue in Manhattan, how it might sound at some future anniversary service of the German-American Bund.

It would ring forth again, he knew at once, as pure and hard and strong as the first *"Sieg Heil!"* Whatever doubts, whatever interventions, whatever interruptions, whatever unhappy compromises had been forced in upon it, this was still the untouched distillation of a faith, the clean etching on the blade of a clean, unstained dagger: *Blut und Ehre, Blut und Ehre,* blood and honor, blood and honor.

His tough blue eyes had not felt the sting of tears since the summer morning in 1939 when he'd looked back from the Hudson River toward the receding docks, looked at the stony palisade of skyscrapers that shut his vision off, perhaps forever, from the place where he was born; looked a final time and then gone below to sit alone until the land was out of sight.

Now he felt tears again, but these were not tears of melancholy.

They were tears of simple devotion and an almost unbearable exultation. The paper banner cried:

Soldiers of the Western Front! Your great hour has come. Strong attacking armies are advancing against the Anglo-Americans! I do not need to tell you more than that. You yourselves feel it! We gamble everything! You bear in yourselves the holy duty to give all and to achieve the superhuman for OUR FATHERLAND and OUR FÜHRER!

Commander in Chief West
VON RUNSTEDT
Field Marshal

CHAPTER TWO

Perhaps, David Kyle reminded himself again, it might have turned out differently if his home town had had another name. But how could you say in one breath that you were a conchie and in the next that you came from a place called Battle Creek? Some had, of course, and endured whatever extra torment it involved, but few of them could have been already reeling, as he had been doing, under a prior burden of other incongruities, other contradictions, and other doubts and convictions so finely balanced that they sometimes changed places overnight.

"Camel?" The man slumped beside him in the steamy, twilit but oddly cheerful cellar was a three-day-old reinforcement. "Oh, I forgot," he said. "One of the guys told me you never even tasted one. That can't be right, can it?" The man beside him—David remembered now that his name was Jones—drew back the bayonet attached to his M-1 rifle to inspect the damp sacks he'd been drying over the damp, rebellious remnants of the fire in the middle of the floor.

"No, thanks," Dave said. That tiny indiscretion, mumbled in a moment of bored gabbiness away back on the other side of the

Seine, came home to rest at the most unexpected times; not precisely to haunt him or embarrass him but rather to remind him, in a dull, stale, repetitious way of a whole complex of matters he'd rather have forgotten for now at least. Murchison, to whom he'd first made the disclosure, had left the company long ago, on his way to the hospital. Almost two hundred others had gone after him and another two hundred had come to take their places. Of his own platoon only he, Henry Whelan, Carmen (the Hood) Ruiz, and Sergeant Kennebec were still there now. Pretty soon, Henry Whelan had once prophesied, the two of them would be like his great-grandfather's old ax that had had nine new handles and four new blades but was still the oldest store-bought ax in the United States of America, the selfsame original ax that *his* great-grandfather had bought in Boston about the time of John Quincy Adams. Yet though David Kyle had never voluntarily discussed the subject of his never-smoking with anyone again, this one muttered, utterly trivial boast or confession or whatever he had intended it to be at the time had been kept alive in the platoon and handed down from each of its generations to the next, like some priestly secret or family heirloom. Perhaps before this was over he would blunder into a Congressional Medal of Honor or be sentenced to life imprisonment for cowardice in the face of the enemy, or simply disappear into the limbo of an ambulance jeep, but the thing he'd still be best and solely and surely remembered for in the annals of Number Three Platoon of Able Company of the First Battalion of the 957th Infantry Regiment was that he was the one who'd never, not only even as a kid or even for curiosity, tasted tobacco. Not a single drag, no sir, not even one single drag. "I offered him one more than once myself. He didn't like to talk about it much. In most other ways he was pretty much the same as the rest of us. No, I don't know what happened to him. I saw him last in some kind of a stone cellar in Belgium or Luxembourg or one of those countries; the winter of 1944, I guess."

He moved away from the fire and felt in a corner for his blanket. He squatted down and unlaced his high combat boots but did not take them off. His feet were almost dry and warm, the blanket above him was almost dry and warm, and with his scarf folded on top of his pack it was soft and easy beneath his head. They'd eaten abundantly and well, and hot, from the field kitchen. The air of the cellar, thick and gently rustling with the yawns, belches, sighs, scratchings, and reassuring smells of a dozen companions, offered a further invitation to repose. There was no reason to expect a short or interrupted night, but even though he was certain he'd heard it somewhere else, he had learned to respect and, whenever possible, to follow Sergeant Kennebec's First Law of the Infantry: Never miss a chance to eat, sleep, or go to the can.

But he couldn't sleep after all. The business about the cigarette had got him going a little again. Not in an unduly remorseful or self-pitying way, just going a little, mainly for the rare pleasure of employing his mind from the surface down in some wholly nonutilitarian, optional, and harmless pursuit, like plucking daisies or counting watch ticks in the dark.

Now, if they'd called the place Utopia, or Kingdom Come—but Battle Creek! No, this line of speculation was too retroactive. He'd have to watch it. These post-facto rationalizations could drive a man loony as surely as the shelling, the cold, the wet, the clock and the calendar, and the absence of any visible boundary to any of them. It had never occurred to him *before* he joined the shooting army that names had anything to do with it. Whether his decision had been good or bad, it had been already taken for altogether different reasons; this grabbing and grubbing around for extra reasons after it was over and done with might easily become habit-forming. Soon he'd be telling himself that he'd enlisted because of the look on young Harvey's face when the floodlights caught him between two shell craters in the advance toward St. Lô and Harvey knew and David Kyle, miraculously safe in one of the craters, knew, too, that the Spandau had young Harvey in its sights and young Harvey had a tenth of a second left to live.

The fact he mustn't lose sight of was that he was already in long long before he'd known young Harvey. The only thing he hoped to win any longer, aside from his survival, which he cherished and believed in, was some sort of clarity; if he got out even fuller of confusion and self-deceit than when he'd got in, he'd have lost on all counts.

"Aw right! Off those merry asses! Out!" The high voice of Sergeant Kennebec, sharpened to a tone of perpetual defensiveness by months of ridiculous demands, unappreciated apologies, and almost unheeded—almost but never quite—threats, came down to them from the kitchen like a voice from the top of a well.

Kennebec's long legs now appeared on the wooden ladder leading downward from the wooden trap door. He had to bend anyway to keep his head below the six-foot beam-and-plaster ceiling, so he bent all the way and warmed his hands above the damply floundering fire.

"Is it an alert, Sergeant?" Henry Whelan knew the answer as well as any of them. He put the question with innocent venom. But Whelan was already on his feet, moving briskly toward the ladder. The company hadn't had a casualty in a week and all the contact they'd been able to get from his patrols indicated that the enemy was, for the moment, as thin on the ground, unbloodyminded, and even companionable as they were. Six nights ago, Whelan and Carmen (the Hood) Ruiz had found themselves staring down across a row of snow-covered sandbags into the barrel of one big machine gun and at least three Schmeissers. They hadn't even had a chance to lift their M-1's, but had done the next best thing and turned and run for the trees. The Krauts hadn't fired a single shot, just shouted gleefully and mockingly, and when Whelan and Ruiz were two hundred yards out of sight one of the Krauts was still hollering after them, half-choked with laughter, "*Raus! Raus!* Yankee jerk! Jerk Yankee!" Two nights later, in an almost exactly reversed situation out beyond the BAR emplacement that they called the Northwest Haystack, two men from Seven Platoon lined up a solitary German who'd lost his patrol along with his way, gave him a yell of warning, and peppered him with frozen cow turds they'd gathered to take back to the fireplace at company headquarters. Perhaps the Germans had caught the same scuttlebutt about an already-arranged ending before Christmas, and Christmas was less than two weeks off. Certainly nobody seemed to be trying to make any kind of a major move, or getting ready to make one, not in this sector at least. But they all knew you couldn't count on anything at all, and no matter how gratifying it might be to know that another alert at this time and place represented a brand-new pinnacle in stupidity and useless mortification of the flesh, you couldn't do much but go on complying with and secretly reveling in the continued mindlessness of the Great God They. Henry Whelan, blaspheming only mildly, was halfway up the ladder, closing up his field jacket and hauling on his gloves. David was right behind him. Suddenly remembering that you never knew how long you might be out there, he darted back and scooped up his blanket before he went up and through the kitchen and out in the yard, where it was now thick night.

He had only two or three hundred yards to go. Other dark figures flitted ahead along the line of the wire fence before the barnyard and groped, disappearing one by one, toward their forward foxholes in the trees. No one kept particularly low or made any particular attempt to use the shadows. A cold wind was swinging down the frozen roadway and it felt all the colder because of the abrupt transition from the fetid, stagnant, lovely air of the cellar. Everybody was hurrying to get back beneath the hostile crust of the essentially friendly earth.

David Kyle slowed a little when he came to the edge of the small clearing covered by their platoon's main sentry hole. This hole was far more than just another man-sized excavation. Compared to other sentry posts that they'd dug, maintained, and swiftly left behind in their comparative dash across Northwestern Europe, this one had grown, during the last ten days, into a veritable Fort Knox. As much as anything to relieve the boredom and thaw their stiffened limbs, its rotating tenants had fallen into the habit of making gradual improvements during each of their four-hour terms of occupancy. On one particularly bright and shiny and peaceful day half a dozen men from the platoon had come out voluntarily and all had begun digging together, driven by some sudden obsessive impulse to create the deepest, longest, widest, most spacious and splendid foxhole in the annals of the U. S. First Army. It was almost six feet deep and twice that long and half that wide before Sergeant Kennebec, drifting up in the late afternoon to see what was going on, commanded them to desist. "Yah, you smart bastards!" he shouted over their angry protests. "She looks great in broad daylight while you got a convention going and a jug of schnapps to pass around. Wait till you're all alone in her, rattling around in her all alone in the middle of the night." They had an uneasy premonition that Sergeant Kennebec, as frequently turned out to be the case, knew what he was talking about. "Wait till the screaming meemies start floating in," he demanded as a clincher. "What do you do then—start diggin' foxholes in the foxhole?" Muttering, they'd filled it partly in with the earth they'd already taken out. They found some old timbers around the farm and made a kind of catwalk along the front and tore a big piece of rusty corrugated sheeting off a storage bin and made a roof to protect the rear half from air bursts.

Unwilling to give up the notion that they were creating something special and even moderately historic, the instigator of the project, a squad leader named Williamson, had found a coil of fencing wire, strung it out along the bases of the trees on the far side of the clearing, and at considerable personal risk fastened three half-unpinned hand grenades to the wire with loops of finer wire borrowed from the signalers. It was very delicate work, but, as Williamson kept shouting back over his shoulder to the fascinated spectators gathered in the shelter of the foxhole, it was a very delicate war. It was Williamson's perfectly sound theory that any Kraut who came in contact with the wire would shake the pin loose from at least one of the grenades and complete the mechanism's intended cycle, thus killing or at the least wounding himself and any nearby companions. When the sergeant objected that Williamson had created a hazard almost as dangerous to their own night patrols as to the enemy's and demanded that the apparatus be dismantled forthwith, Williamson flatly refused. The sergeant backed away a little, knowing full well that Williamson had already used up all his luck in getting the grenades planted. It would have been easy enough to explode the grenades with a rifle from the giant foxhole. The grenades were all quite visible, hanging from the wire, but the sounds of war had grown so rare during the last few days that the sergeant was unwilling to take the responsibility of starting them up again.

They compromised by laying out a white tape halfway across the clearing and posting an old German sign someone had thrown into the rations truck for a souvenir away back in Normandy. Every time a sentry mounted the catwalk in the big foxhole to peer across the clearing, the stenciled black-on-white death's-head hit him in the eye: beside it the two familiar cried-out words "Achtung! Minen!"

David Kyle paused a moment in the trees, trying to calculate who would be standing sentry in the big trench now. Somebody, somewhere on the forward positions, must have got the wind up; otherwise in the absence of an enemy barrage there'd have been no reason for the general alert. If the panic had happened to begin in this particular place, then it could be important to know who was there.

It wasn't necessarily the new and inexperienced men who were the trigger-happy ones. The new ones might start playing Glorious Fourth or, on the other hand, they might still be so full of their drill and lectures that they'd never think of shooting until they were absolutely sure what they were shooting at. The older men, particularly the Normandy men like Henry Whelan and Carmen (the Hood) Ruiz—or, if it came right down to it, Sergeant Kennebec—could not be counted on to be quite so finicky. Out there alone and with an unrecognized and unexpected form moving toward them—it didn't matter much from what direction—they were apt to shoot first and ask the questions later.

It was an admitted fact—admitted even by Ruiz—that when Carmen (the Hood) Ruiz shot Charley Bernstein through the leg last September there had been at least some doubt in his mind even before he pulled the trigger. "Of course I didn't *know* it wasn't one of our guys," Ruiz explained logically and with a certain resentment at his conduct's being questioned. "If I'd a *known* I'd a shot the son-of-a-bitch through the head. Now on when you send anybody to relieve me an hour ahead of time, tell him either to come up a hell of a lot louder or a hell of a lot quieter or I might make another mistake." The matter was dropped and Charley Bernstein was evacuated as a normal battle casualty and awarded a Purple Heart. There were half a dozen others in the platoon—Dave Kyle wasn't sure what he'd have done himself—who'd said they'd have done the same thing as Carmen Ruiz.

There was always another possibility, of course; the possibility that the man he was about to join in the darkness ahead might be asleep. This was by no means out of the question, but Dave excluded it from his calculations because, although there were at least three known sleeping sentries in their company and he knew their names, he'd never thought to ascertain whether they were light sleepers or heavy sleepers and without this detail the basic information would be meaningless. (Everybody who knew about them, and this included practically all the privates and corporals, kept nagging at the sleepers to stay awake out there, and threatening to turn them in, but nobody ever did; some people might have attributed this to misguided chivalry, but the fact was that the Krauts had never tried anything serious without dropping in at least a few mortars or eighty-eights ahead of the infantry, and it was largely felt that the only lives the sleepers were risking were their own. It was, besides, no minor thing to take any man's sleep away from him.)

Dave Kyle's own foxhole was about twenty yards to the right of and a little behind the giant foxhole. He stood in the shadow of the trees for a moment, wondering whether he should just slip into his own hole unnoticed. But he had no way of telling whether the sentry in the big trench had been told about the alert or not; probably he hadn't. In that case he'd better announce himself

31

somehow. The clouds were low and there was no moon or stars; all he could see was the little rise of the big foxhole's half-roof and beyond that the dark edge of the clearing. There was no sound anywhere. He stood still for a moment and then whistled a few bars of "Are You from Dixie?" into the flat, cold night air. Almost at once a low, hand-cupped half-call came from the edge of the sentry post. He did not recognize the voice. It must be one of the new men, he thought. "FDR," the half-voice half-called.

"This is Dave Kyle." He bent down, hissing across the few feet of ground between them.

"FDR," the half-voice repeated, now a trifle anxiously.

"All right for me to come in for a minute?" Dave hissed. "I'm setting up over on your right."

"FDR," the half-voice repeated, rising and close to fright.

"FDR?" He heard a rifle barrel scrape against the upper part of the roof. Then in a swift flash of memory it came to him. "Eleanor! Eleanor, for Christ's sake!" He seldom swore except in moments of extreme stress.

"Advance," the half-voice commanded in a tone of relief.

Dave crouched lower, ran the few steps to the edge of the big trench and vaulted down inside.

"Hey, what about that FDR-Eleanor crap?" he whispered, angry at his own instant of fear. "That's two weeks old."

"Well, it's the last password anybody gave me," the sentry whispered self-righteously. Dave finally recognized him; a new man, as he'd suspected, recently arrived all the way from England.

"Well, listen," Dave whispered. "Most of the time the people back there forget to give us the new one and when they do most of the people up here forget it. And even then another half-forget the countersign. You've got to use your head up here, boy. This is no place for playing games."

"Who was playing games?"

"I heard you aiming at me, even after I whistled and told you who I was," Dave answered accusingly. Then as an afterthought, "Hey! You got your safety back on?"

The other man groped at the stock of his rifle.

"God damn it, you *still* got it off," Dave said. The momentary excitement had warmed him a little and he sought to keep the warmth alive with a glow of wrath.

"All right, all right." The sentry sounded aggrieved and still far from complete understanding. Dave dropped it. "What's been going on?" he whispered.

"All I saw was one flare, about a quarter of a mile ahead and to the left. I figured one of their patrols might have hit one of our trip wires."

"Nothing else?"

"Not a thing that I saw."

"Oh, Christ. It was probably only Bed-Check Charlie. Did you hear anything that sounded like a small plane?"

"Who's Bed-Check Charlie?"

"Guy that does a low-flying recon most nights when there's any weather at all for him. He drops a flare or two and disappears."

"I didn't hear a plane." The other man, who had been whispering, now spoke aloud too, but less querulously; it was always good to have company up here. "Hey, you say your name's Kyle. Mine's Colhurst."

"That's all right." Dave spoke grudgingly, as though making a concession. He was still pretty indignant, but more so now at the ubiquitous, unfailing thickheadedness of Them than at the casual and just possibly amendable thickheadedness of his companion.

"Say, why don't you stay in here?" Colhurst suggested.

"No. I'm supposed to go over to my own foxhole and cover you from there." He was aware of sounding very soldierly, very stiff and pretentious, and unduly respectful of authority. With Whelan or Ruiz he'd simply have told the truth: "This place gives me the creeps." The sentry Colhurst sensed it anyway.

"Why the hell didn't we fill this thing in and be done with it?" Colhurst asked. "It seemed like such a hot-shot idea when that bastard corporal had us up here digging. But holy God, it gives you as much privacy and shelter as Piccadilly Circus. You been there lots of times, I guess?"

"Lots."

"Once I laid a broad in the blackout right beneath that round little platform where they say the statue of love used to be. Another broad stumbled across us and started counting."

Dave said nothing. "Of course," the other man added hastily, "they were both hookers and I was drunk."

"Lots of funny things have happened," Dave responded vaguely, trying not to sound priggish.

"Well, anyways," the sentry said, "this is one son-of-a-bitch of a lousy foxhole. Look out in front and you see that sign with the skull on it. Look out either end and you hear noises in the other end. A whole platoon of the bastards could crawl into one side of it and cook their breakfast while you were watching the other side."

Dave thawed a little more. He laughed faintly. "What we should do is declare it an open city. Well, see you later."

"Sure you don't want to stay here? You could cover one end and me the other."

"No. I'll be over there. You watch to the left of the mine field and I'll watch the right. It's a false alarm anyway."

"O.K., then. Want to split a cigarette before you go? God knows we can get down far enough so nobody will see. We could take turns."

"No, thanks."

"Hey, you're the guy that doesn't smoke at all, aren't you? That never even tried it."

"That's right."

"How come?" the sentry asked, genuinely puzzled.

"No particular reason," Dave said. "I just never got around to it."

"I bet you took one of those pledges when you were a school kid," Colhurst speculated sympathetically. "They bullied me into signing one. I was never going to taste tobacco or liquor or shack up with anybody I wasn't married to. But what the hell! they caught me when I was eleven years old, away under the age of consent and I figured it wasn't legal."

"Go ahead and grab a couple of drags," Dave said. "But don't be long." The other man disappeared beneath the roofing and was back within a minute.

"Thanks."

"O.K. I'll be over there."

Alone in his own well-fitting little box of earth, he squatted on the empty ammunition box he had brought up earlier, checked his rifle, and prepared to sit there until some authority or some event should permit or require him to stop sitting and do something else. His resentment of the unnecessary alert and the unnecessary discomfort it had caused had not been forgotten, but he pushed it aside for the time being. Back there in the cellar before the rude advent of the sergeant he had been on the verge of one of those mellow little inner dialogues that, once broken up—as they almost always were before they got anywhere—could take days or weeks to get going again. Conversation in the Army, even conversation with yourself, was hedged with its own special rules and handicaps. It was something like a Berlitz school, where the French class spoke only French, the Russian class spoke only Russian, the Spanish class spoke only Spanish, and the newcomer to the class was never allowed to speak or hear a single word in any other language that he might already know. Throw them in and they'll swim. In the Army you spoke Army. Maybe if you got off into a corner with some other expatriate from your part of the universe of words, you could risk a few sentences in something besides Army. In these circumstances books, theater, and music were permissible, but if there was any danger of being widely overheard, it was dangerous to go past *Gone with the Wind* or Raymond Chandler or, at the most extreme, Hemingway or the relative sleepability-with of the pinup girls. Philosophy was absolutely out, except as a semiunderground affair preferably pursued in a dark corner of a dark pub while on leave. Religion O.K. so long as you stuck to exalting God's name whenever ordered, instructed and led by a chaplain and profaning it whenever not; arguing about religion forbidden at any time. Politics permitted but only under the headings Democraticwayoflife, Fascistoppressors, Toughrussianallies with Formercommunistmenace in strict abeyance and Republicans vs. Democrats clearly labeled Dangerous, especially in the presence of officers. If you were particularly discreet and unshowy, the Army Berlitz system permitted partial, though not total, abstinence from the standard obscenities. But these set the normal form of conversation just as the subject matter was set by baseball, boxing, movies, radio, sex, food, leaves, the digestive system, and the professional shop talk of life and death. One of the advantages of talking to yourself was that you could choose your own topics and your own vocabulary.

At the time of the original charter, Elder Morgan had once told him, their ancestors had decided momentarily to call the new city Wopikisko. But hotter heads prevailed—the elder smiled indulgently—and Battle Creek it was. Even the strife-bearing name was born in strife, the elder's words reminded him; the essential challenge of strife, the smile added, was the need to rise above it.

One of the minor disappointments—well, not so minor, either, because in a sense it crowned all the others—was the mounting evidence that the elder meant more or less what he seemed to mean. It had been hard in those first few months in the Army to forgive Elder Morgan for having forgiven him. The elder's refusal to treat him like a betrayer had left David feeling betrayed himself.

Elder Morgan's Christmas card, postmarked November 14, had reached him early in December, a week before either his father's or Mary Egan's. There wasn't the slightest hint of churchliness about it; indeed the lopsided red and green type conveyed a note of jocularity. The hand-written note below was conventional and gossipy and it would have taken a great deal of touchiness and imagination to read any special ecclesiastical significance, much less an implied rebuke, into the elder's closing "God bless you, David."

But Mary and his father had both been more dependable. Their cards were identical, a photograph of the new temple on Washington Street. His father's message had been a few anguished sentences. "All our love is with you, as always, David. I will not burden you with all my thoughts. But remember always that, even though it may be too late to change your mind in the sight of the world, it is never too late to change your heart. Whatever you do or do not do, I have always known that the truth has always been there, there in your heart, and has never left and never will."

It was not possible to be bitter in the face of such passionate, single-minded sincerity, but at least it gave you something to come to grips with, as Elder Morgan had not done. So, in a way, did the longer letter that accompanied Mary's card. This was some new, shy Mary he was hearing from. He'd mentioned in one of his letters to her that his letters had to be read and censored by an officer; she must have thought the rule applied to those he received as well as those he sent, for she was altogether too splendid, sturdy, and aloof. Perhaps, on the other hand, it was his own response she was nervous of; maybe they *had* gone a little far on that last night.

I manage to keep fairly busy. We're still far understaffed at the office and I'm now rolling bandages four nights a week instead of two. We bring sandwiches to choir practice and hold it now at suppertime and I'm still helping teach the brass section in the band at the academy. It did not come naturally to Mary to be so mousy and undramatic and resigned. No memory of her could ever eclipse his first one: a nine-year-old and sweaty redhead, shouting and squalling and punching at big Hortense McGraw in a corner of the open-air playground one summer afternoon, so consumed by her anger that it took two boys to haul her off and a third boy to help the first two boys escape when she turned her rage on them. David had been the third boy. Ordinarily he wouldn't have been on this corner of the ground at all, for he was much bigger than any of the other parties involved, bigger even than big Hortense McGraw; he had been making a detour from the big boys' baseball diamond on a short cut home for lunch. When this panting red-haired captive saw who he was, her ingrained respect for age and for their mutual commitments caused her to stop trying to bite him and he felt safe enough to release his hammer lock.

She appeared to take his sympathy for granted. "She called me a Holy Roller!" she panted, not caring whether the other kids had dispersed beyond hearing range or not. "You'd have hit her yourself, wouldn't you? And I'll hit her again, the next time I catch her."

"No, you won't," David had said. He remembered now that he'd seen her, or someone like her, waiting at Sabbath School last week for the new boy in his class, Gustav Egan.

He saw then that she was better brought up than you'd have thought at first, for she did not contradict him, even though she was still shaking with indignation.

"What *would* you have done?" she asked.

"I'd have paid no attention," he said, very likely truthfully. There was, of course, no way of being certain, for Hortense McGraw would never have said anything like that to him to begin with. It was one thing for Hortense to try out her insolence on a newcomer of her own age and sex and a good deal less than her own size, but the Kyles had been here for three generations, almost as long as the Kelloggs and far, far longer than Mr. Post. There had been at least one Kyle up at the Health Center ever since the Health Center began, on terms of mutual esteem with two generations of movie stars, maharajahs and millionaires. Great-Uncle Richard Kyle had been head of cardiology for eighteen years, and David's father had recently been appointed to the almost equally prestigious position of supervising attendant of the men's bath department. Mrs. Tillie Woolaston, née Kyle, had been assistant dietitian until she retired to raise a family. Even the family's one black sheep, a cousin named Hubert Sorensen, had gone to his downfall with a certain raffish élan—caught red-handed smuggling in a pound of smoked ham, a carton of Luckies, and a bottle of Old Grand-Dad to a famous producer from Broadway. The Kyles were as solid as the Sanitarium itself, as solid as Corn Flakes, as solid as Battle Creek.

"How did this fight start?" David asked her. They had begun to walk away from the playground together, the disheveled, pugnacious girl of nine and the tall, serious boy of eleven.

"She started it."

"But how?"

"Well, she asked me to come and play scrub on Saturday."

"That sounds friendly. She meant well."

"No, she didn't. She was looking at me the way they do. She already knew."

"But that wasn't enough to start a fight."

"Of *course* not," she said impatiently. "I *told* you she started it."

"Well, then what happened next?"

"I said I wouldn't."

"Not couldn't?"

"No, wouldn't. I wasn't going to let her sneak anything in and start pretending she was sorry for me, the way they do."

"And then what did she say?"

"She asked me why."

"And what did you say?"

"I said I wouldn't porfane the Lord's day and—"

"Profane."

"And I saw her getting her big mouth ready to say something smart and so I said if she wanted to be destroyed in the lake of fire it was none of my business and one of those two boys started giggling and egging her on and she came right out and called me a Holy Roller and then I gave her a good big shove and she shoved me back. I told you she started it."

"Well, let me tell you something," he said severely. "I don't know where you came from but—where do you come from?"

"Busby." She looked up at him in a tentative, guarded way, challenging him to pretend that he'd never heard of Busby.

"That's in the Upper Peninsula, isn't it? My father and I went camping near there once."

"The schools there aren't much good. There's no Adventist school at all. So when my father got this chance of a job at Post's he thought we'd better move now. My brother and I will be going to the academy in the fall. I guess you go there, don't you? I've seen you at church."

"That's the thing I was going to tell you," he said.

"What?"

"Well, I don't know what it was like in the Upper Peninsula, but here you don't need to carry a chip on your shoulder. It's not needed and it's not—not dignified."

"You mean you should let them call you a Holy Roller and just not do anything about it?"

"They know better," he said. "They don't mean it at all. And maybe they're a little bit jealous, too."

"Jealous?" Her still-smoldering gray-green eyes widened. "Nobody in Busby was jealous," she said candidly. "In Busby they didn't just pretend to look down on us. They really did."

"Well, here they don't." He'd been instructed a hundred times not to be vain or boastful about spiritual matters, but this was more in the line of dispensing Christian comfort.

"Oh." The momentary eagerness had disappeared. Her voice had grown wary, as though getting ready for the disappointment to come. "You mean they're jealous about us going to heaven and them not."

He'd been warned, too, about not falling back on the worldly arguments, but she was too good an audience to waste. "Well, partly that, but just as much for other reasons. Except for us would Battle Creek be famous all over the world? Would famous people come to Battle Creek from everywhere, from New York and India and Detroit and Chicago? Except for us would there be a San at all? All that marble and the fountains and movie actresses? Henry Ford and Eddie Cantor coming right here and as friendly with Dr. John as he'll let them be? Would there be Corn Flakes, or Bran Flakes, or Postum or Post Toasties or Grape Nuts? Would there be Nuttose or Protose or Savita? Would there be a Kellogg's or a Post's?"

In the strict theological sense he was conscious of having strayed far off course, but in this summer noontime, they both found the words voluptuous and exciting, like the Songs of Solomon stumbled upon during a search for the Book of Obadiah. *How beautiful, my beloved, upon thy—*

"Have you ever been in the San?" she asked him. And in the next breath, "Is it true it doesn't belong to the church any more?"

"It doesn't belong in the dollars-and-cents and bricks-and-mortar sense." He was quoting his father exactly now. "Sometime when you're older you'll be able to understand everything that led

Dr. John away from the church and Mrs. White. But don't forget a mistaken man can still be a good man. Dr. John hasn't allowed the San itself to drift away. There's still no meat allowed. No tobacco. No strong drink. No tea. No coffee. Christian prayers every day. Christian thanks at every meal. No steam baths or gym classes on Saturday. Full observance of the true Sabbath, the Seventh Day."

"In Busby"—it was plain that she was asking him only for further reassurance—"they used to say it was Sister White who burned down the old San. Of course, nobody believed them for a minute."

"Well I *hope* not."

"And they used to say whoever burned down the old Tabernacle did it because Sister White told them to."

They had turned the corner off Van Buren. They might have been actors in a pageant; straight ahead was the clean-columned bulk of the new Temple, rising above its tall, wide stair like a vision of ancient Greece, and then, almost directly behind, the majestic, block-long San itself, with its block-high tower soaring up above the winding driveway. At that very instant a chauffeur-driven Packard disgorged a plump and elegant lady who might as well have been a duchess as not. The busy, opulent breakfast-food factories across the river were not in sight, but they were no less a part of the general presence and emanations of this summer day. There was no need to reply to Mary in words.

"You'll like Battle Creek," David said nevertheless. He was grateful to her for helping him to summarize his blessings. "Don't ever worry about what anybody says." *As one whom his mother comforteth, so will I comfort you; and ye shall be comforted in Jerusalem.* Isaiah something.

When school started that fall, Mary's older brother Gus was in David's class. Soon the two boys became best friends and soon after that, since the Egan children had no mother and David Kyle's mother had no daughter, Gus and Mary became ex-officio members of the Kyle household.

When Hannah Kyle discovered they were getting their own midday meal, she persuaded their father to allow them to come home with David; there was of course an unobtrusive arrangement about payment and the arrangement continued until David went to Ann Arbor to study pharmacy, Gus joined the design staff at Kellogg's and, two years later, Mary began her nurse's training at the San.

David's father liked but never fully trusted the father of the Egan children. His name was Martin Egan. The Martin was for Martin Luther and Egan made no attempt to keep it a secret that except for the prompting of his late wife he'd never even have given a second thought to the real truth and prophecies about the Advent, much less found the sense to follow them. Even now, Samuel Kyle sometimes suspected, Egan only discharged his religious duties as an example; anybody with eyes could see that Adventist children were almost automatically healthier, happier, better-mannered, better-schooled, better-nourished, and in better company than other children.

One day at lunch—Samuel Kyle took all his meals at home as part of his duty to his family—young Gustav Egan let it slip that he knew the taste of bacon.

A little clean meat now and then, especially living on that lonely little farm and with the woman gone to her rest and waiting—a little clean meat was probably no worse than eggs or milk, if you came right down to it; but bacon! pork! specifically forbidden in the Bible. Samuel's frown was so eloquent that young Gus dropped his eyes and went scarlet with shame and Gus's sister Mary burst out with a loyal explanation. "It was only once. A neighbor lady brought it over when Father was out haying. As soon as he found out he made us throw the rest away." Samuel would have felt more certain, nevertheless, except that, on three successive foot-washing Sabbaths, Martin Egan had had impeccable excuses for being absent: twice a sick sister in Flint, once a cold that kept him in bed all day Saturday but did not prevent him from going back to work as usual on Sunday. There was never enough for a direct confrontation, but Samuel discovered all too quickly that the two fine new children at his table were all too urgently in need of instruction. He seized on every possible pretext and, if no pretext came forward, invented one, to introduce some essential article of Scripture or one of the interpretations or canons of Sister White.

"I spy with my little eye." Mary soon was starting the game herself. Everybody taught children, but nobody sat on them. In the Temple—even in the middle of the most portentous messages from the pulpit or the mightiest anthems from the choir—three-, four-, and five-year-olds as scrubbed and dainty as wedding china romped, tottered, shrieked, cried, and floundered down the aisles without noticeable let or visible hindrance. The noisiest cases were sometimes gently exiled to and allowed to run down in a cubicle called the cry room, but this was very rare. In general it was held that children were better off to have the law sink in on them by degrees rather than have it smother them all at once. So Mary could speak without being spoken to.

"I spy with my little eye, something—"

"Something what?" David's mother asked.

"Something red."

It was Gustav's turn. "Your hair."

"No."

"Be more systematic," Mr. Kyle suggested, balancing a morsel of vegetarian steak.

"Is it on the table?"

"No."

"Is it on one of us?" David asked.

"No."

"Is it on one of the walls?"

"Yes."

"Red and on a wall," Gus summarized. "Is it the red flower in the picture?"

"Oh, you got it!"

"Your turn, Gus," David might say.

"Ah, red," Mr. Kyle might break in. He'd more than likely say, so sure of the need and value of saying it that there was no trace of self-consciousness, lifting his proud and gently certain head and smiling, "Red is for redemption."

And then, by whatever contrived route he'd led them in by, Mr. Kyle would be giving them a quiet lesson in their faith. David didn't need it; for him it was solved and settled and timeless, but his kinship with his father was so perfect that he pretended he was hearing for the first time, so that Gus and Mary wouldn't know they were learning things they should have learned long long ago. Samuel kept a much-annotated and book-marked Bible on an oaken side table beside his oaken chair, and there were always several volumes of the Testimonies as well as the other works of Mrs. White.

"Here, now, let me read it to you," he'd say. "Go on with your Protose, Mary. Now I'm reading this from Mrs. White's own writing." In spite of his injunction, Mary put down her fork. "Now, then," Samuel read. "No one has yet received the Mark of the Beast. The testing time has not yet come. There are true Christians in every church, not excepting the Roman Catholic Communion." At this there might be a faint stirring of unrest from David's mother. "None are condemned," Samuel would read on quietly, "until they have had the light and have seen the obligation of the Fourth Commandment. But when the decree shall go forth exploring the counterfeit Sabbath, and the loud cry of the Third Angel shall warn men against the worship of the Beast and his image, the line shall be clearly drawn between the false and the true. Then those who still continue in transgression will receive the Mark of the Beast."

Samuel spent countless lunchtimes over the prophecies, explaining and quoting exact authorities for the 2300 Days of Daniel 8 and the Seventy Weeks of Daniel 9. Gustav was a placid boy and David was long accustomed, but Mary often squirmed and there was never any positive way of knowing whether it was through boredom or excitement. One Friday she let it drop that some of the kids from down the street were thinking of going fishing tomorrow in the Kalamazoo River, let it drop in such a way that it didn't appear whether she'd been asked to go with them or not and Samuel had one of the Books open again: " 'If thou turn away thy foot from the Sabbath, from doing thy pleasure on my holy day; and call the Sabbath a delight, the holy of the Lord, honourable; and shalt honour him, not doing thine own ways, nor finding thine own pleasure, nor speaking thine own words: then shalt thou delight thyself in the Lord; and I will cause thee to ride upon the high places of the earth, and feed thee with the heritage of Jacob thy father; for the mouth of the Lord hath spoken it.' "

"You can't go fishing tomorrow, Mary," David translated.

One time when they were talking about the flawless way in which Charlie Gehringer played second base for the Detroit Tigers, young Gus was suddenly and unexpectedly full of fire and conversation and started telling them about an article he'd read in *The Saturday Evening Post* about another, greater Tiger, Ty Cobb; a minotaur, a swift and killing bull moose, all hoofs and thudding shoulders and bone-hard thighs. Samuel quickly calmed him down. He did not have to consult the Books, for it was ready to his mind.

"With all power to Mr. Cobb," Samuel said, "let's not lose sight of Matthew Seven."

"Yes, sir," Gus said, meek and horrified at his departure from meekness.

"All things whatsoever that men shall do to you, do ye even so to them. And then of course thou shalt love thy neighbour as thyself."

Gus was speechless with shame, but Mary, characteristically, came to his defense.

"We had this awful teacher up in Busby, Mr. Kyle. A real mean teacher, always hitting kids and giving them bad marks. One day this teacher forgot to bring his lunch and do you know what Gus did, he gave the teacher half his lunch."

Gus blushed even worse.

Samuel sighed approvingly, "Ah, Gustav."

"You see, Gustav," Samuel smiled, "when it is your heart you follow, it is not this unfortunate Mr. Cobb you follow. It is the Book you follow. You know the Book before you've heard it." He had the Bible open on the table. He leafed it and caressed it with his tender hands and gentle eyes.

"See now in John," Samuel said. " 'These things I have spoken unto you, that in me ye might have peace. In the world ye shall have tribulation: but be of good cheer; I have overcome the world.' "

"Mr. Cobb was only trying to steal third base," David interrupted daringly. If Mary and poor Gus were being lectured, he did not want them to go through it alone.

His father emitted a half-chuckle, as David had hoped he might. But then he was stern again. "That will do, David. We are just recovering from one terrible war and perhaps getting ready for another one. Now I'll read to you. You may put down your fork, Mary.

" 'Ye have heard that it hath been said,' " Samuel read, " 'Thou shalt love thy neighbour and hate thine enemy. But I say unto you, love your enemies, bless them that curse you, do good to them that hate you, and pray for them which despitefully use you and persecute you; that ye may be the children of your Father which is in heaven: for he maketh this sun to rise on the evil and the good, and sendeth rain on the just and the unjust.'

"That's, of course, Matthew." No one ever interrupted when the Bible was being read. It was permissible to go on eating, though quietly, when it was Mrs. White, but they were all quite still while Samuel turned a few chapters ahead.

"This is Romans," Samuel said. "See how durable are the things that must endure. 'Recompense to no man evil for evil. Provide things honest in the sight of all men. If it be possible, as much as lieth in you, live peaceably with all men. Dearly beloved, avenge not yourselves, but rather give place unto wrath: for it is written Vengeance is mine; I will repay, saith the Lord. Therefore if thine enemy hunger, feed him; if he thirst, give him drink: for in so doing thou shalt heap coals of fire upon his head. Be not overcome of evil, but overcome evil with good.' "

None of this was lost on David, but he had other things to think of too. It became his intention, at the age of fourteen, to make Mary his bride and live with her in unceasing vast felicity, as his father Samuel lived with his mother Hannah. He did not mention this personally to her. He was never shy with Mary. She was his firmest and far least inhibited friend, not at all like Gus, who was often too careful and pious to be wholly companionable with. But for all her confidence, Mary had a streak of scariness too. The reason he didn't mention their ordained nuptials to her was that he'd read somewhere, in one of the forbidden books he was always reading, that the Wedding Bed was painful to Young Brides and he feared that if he gave her too much warning she might try to sneak out of it.

Then a sterner truth appeared. He'd gone to the monthly band concert at the academy. Mary went ahead, of course, because she had to be there for tuning up, and there was no specific understanding that he'd wait for her afterward. He was in the twelfth row of the audience and Mary was in the fourth row of the band. Her wild red hair was partly plastered down—he'd lent her his own Sultan's Pride liquid brilliantine—but an untamed swatch of it careened down over her left eye and David could see her other eye concentrated, as sparkling and proud as John Philip Sousa's or Evangeline Booth's, on the collapsible tin music stand in front of her. They never let Mary play solo cornet or even first or second cornet. An outrage, and no use pretending that it had nothing to do with being a newcomer from the Upper Peninsula. Mary was allowed to play only third cornet—a community instrument with rusty valves and two gobs of beeswax sealing its ancient wounds. Pause pah pah; pause pah pah. If they gave Mary a chance, she'd play *Over the Waves* as high and sweet as it was ever heard. But there she was with the cluster of red hair over her eye, there in the fourth row going pause pah pah on the old and ruined third cornet, pause pah pah. His heart went out like the swelling of an ocean.

Being sorry for her was, however, a mistake. David waited for her outside the auditorium. She must have seen him sighing with his unwelcome compassion, because she had consented to be walked home by a trombone player and she walked on past with her hand on the trombone player's arm and pretended not even to see David standing there.

He had his own pride too and it was nearly a week—even though they continued to have lunch at the same table with Gus and David's father and mother—before they exchanged an unnecessary word. Suddenly one noontime, with a burst of womanhood and wisdom, she asked him, "David, would you please help me with my arithmetic?" He said he would and they were friends again.

There were three definable shades of cold—cold, *vrai* cold, and *formidable* cold. He'd borrowed it from the grades of calvados. "*Oui, monsieur, j'ai du calvados.*" If they said it just like that, without an adjective, the calvados was a pale, weak vinegar. A *vrai* calvados had a bite to it, but it was raw and harsh, the mashed apples of last spring. But when they promised you a *formidable* calvados, they dug it out of haystacks or manure piles or fished it up from the bottoms of their wells; a *formidable* calvados was a pre-German calvados, ten years old, twenty years old, thirty years old perhaps, as ripe and mellow as the Norman fields.

So it was with cold. There was just plain ordinary cold, the kind that began in October, the organic cold, the nine-tenths of cold that never showed above the surface, the cold that was with you night and day, not quite freezing you, not quite numbing you, not quite stinging you awake, not quite clubbing you to sleep, not quite turning your blood to jelly, not quite turning it to fire, not a Nirvana, euphoria cold, not a gangrene, cut-his-green-foot-off-and-send-him-home cold; just cold, steady, unspectacular, and always there.

The *vrai* cold, the true cold hit you very hard. You didn't want to do anything but get through it and find a fire or another blanket somewhere. The one good thing about a *vrai* cold was that the Krauts didn't like it either; in a *vrai* cold there was very little unwarranted shooting anywhere.

The *formidable* cold was another matter again. On the big guns, away back of the infantry lines, the ammunition numbers slapped their flanks and pounded their fists into their open palms. Ammunition numbers were notoriously peaceable and unenterprising. They had none of the satisfaction of laying a gun or commanding it to fire or causing it to fire, and every time they fed another round into the breech it increased their chances of betraying their position to the equally miserable and congealing enemy and goading him to search them out and blow them all to hell. In a *formidable* cold, when a man caught, say, a piece of shrapnel in his leg and started losing blood, or got pinned down all night in a ditch or maybe even left his damp socks on—in a *formidable* cold and in these special circumstances, more than one man had been turned to a rock-hard statue. Nevertheless the shooting seemed to step up when it was desperately cold rather than just abjectly cold. Perhaps in a *formidable* cold some death wish communicated back to the commanders far and snugly away in Brussels or Berlin and bounced back to the frigid occupants of the gun pits.

This was merely a *vrai* cold tonight. Perhaps twelve above, perhaps even fifteen. David looked across to the big foxhole, saw a sign of movement there, checked the dimly visible death's-head on the *"Achtung! Minen!"* sign out in front and resumed his vigil over the frozen strip of ground and the frozen line of trees, the whole of his frozen universe.

He'd arrived here on his own; there was no way of going back. Ann Arbor had been a crucial error. Right into his sophomore year he'd been full of unassailable truth; as a junior he was a shipwreck of doubt. His roommate was not so crude as to laugh at him, but he did smile. They were too fast for him at Ann Arbor, altogether too swift and knowing. He wrote home to Samuel in anguish and supplication. "I know the Bible says we're right, but this friend of mine and this girl of his keep asking how I'm sure the Bible's right."

"My son," Samuel wrote back to him, "it's the Bible."

And then he was left and lonely. He explored the roots of his being time and time again. He was only nineteen; Samuel had never encouraged reading except the Bible and Mrs. White, and David could only grope.

Suddenly all the articles of his faith, all that he had grown up with, all that gave him meaning and a place to go were in total jeopardy. He wrote Samuel again. "It's all there in the Bible," Samuel answered.

He'd stopped talking religion at all, stopped going to chapel, cut out philosophy, changed roommates, stared blankly past his former roommate's girl when they passed on the campus. But the more he'd tried to reinforce himself the more difficult it became. There was no one but Samuel to reassure him.

Christ did live, Christ did die, Christ would return, at his Advent the righteous would be borne to eternal bliss and the unrighteous would be devoured in flames. This was the soul of all his belief, and Samuel, as staggered as the boy himself before his son's dawning apostasy, had no true help to give him.

He went home at Easter and here he found a disappointment far worse.

"Mary, I'm in a God-awful mess," he said. Now Mary was eighteen and David was twenty. They no longer held hands naturally, as a brother and sister would, but David touched her just the same and felt the touch returned. Physical attraction was not supposed to count with decent people. Mrs. White had given at least tacit approval to the bloomer girls in an earlier day, but then she had relented. The doctrine was mixed. "The dress question is not to be our present truth. To create an issue on this point now would please the enemy. He would be delighted to have minds diverted to any subject which might create division of sentiment—I beg of our people to walk carefully and circumspectly before God. Let our sisters dress plainly, having the dress of good, durable material, appropriate to this age. Our sisters should clothe themselves in modest apparel, with shamefacedness and sobriety."

Walking down the street with Mary, under the tall elm trees and with their hands together, shyer than they had been before, David could not for the life of him find the slightest sign of shamefacedness or sobriety in whatever it was she wore. He couldn't think of the color of it or the texture or the length or breadth. All he was sure of was that Mary's radiant red head was above the dress and the rest of Mary was curving and rippling and creating fantastic arcs and emanations beneath it and he needed her love and help as he'd never needed anything in all his life.

"Mary," David said, "my draft number's come up."

"Oh, David!"

"I wasn't going to tell you until I got back to school and started packing. I wasn't going to tell my father and mother, either."

"I'm glad you told me now."

"But Mary, I've just started to tell you. This is where the real mess comes in."

"Are you afraid, David?" Her touch was closer. "I guess everybody's afraid. I'm afraid and I don't even have to go."

"No, I'm not afraid. At least I don't think so. That will come later, I suppose."

"David." Mary stopped and turned him to face her, squaring him with her hands on his shoulders. She had guessed without his telling her. "David, you mustn't. You mustn't even think of it."

"I've thought of it."

"How long?"

"Oh, years. Maybe since that day I saw you first and hauled you out of the Holy Roller fight."

"David, I'm not like that any more. You mustn't get like that."

"I haven't got guts enough to be a coward."

"David," she implored him. "David."

"They've put my number up. That means I'm eligible for getting shot at. All right. I claim the right to shoot back."

"Oh, David, join the medical corps, join the ambulance corps. You can't go killing people. It's your right to stay out of the killing. It's the law. You'll be in as much danger as anyone. It's—"

"I'm not taking my exemption, Mary."

"Your father—"

"Yes, my father. How I'd like to have his infallibility, but I haven't and that's more or less that. That's the mess I was talking about."

"So you'll go and fight this war. It will be a sin against your father, it will be a sin against yourself, it will be a sin against God and the church, but nobody will ever be able to say you were afraid. All you've believed in, all you've been taught, it's all gone, but you're still most highly brave." She drew away from him in the springtime night.

He was a traitor, but what else could he be? "You cannot possibly change the heart," Mrs. White had written. "There are many things that will come to try and test these poor deluded spiritually dwarfed, world-loving souls."

Mary Egan, please don't be so sanctimonious. Mary Egan, I love you, deluded, spiritually dwarfed, world-loving, and trial-haunted as I am. If you won't love me in return, who will? He didn't say it aloud. They walked on down the street and crossed the bridge across the Kalamazoo, Mary still in her good durable dress appropriate to this age, but her hand no longer in his.

"Mary Egan. Mary Egan."

Now the cold was truly *formidable*. The sentry in the big fox-hole was pounding his hands on the frozen earth, kicking at the timbers. "Hey," he sobbed across at David, "when's our relief coming?" David did not reply, and for perhaps ten minutes everything was still. He guessed the new man was sitting on the timber in the big foxhole with his boots off and his rifle put aside, trying to rub some life into his feet. He was about to start doing the same thing himself, when there was an unbelievable interruption in the black and bitter night. Two new shapes half-lurched, half-crouched across the clearing, big bucket helmets halfway down to their hunched-up shoulders. Somehow they'd missed the mine field, not even seen it. Each of them carried a rifle, or rather dangled it. There was no caution in their movements, they just plodded ahead, waiting for what the next step might bring, half comatose, not caring much one way or the other. The sentry in the big foxhole hadn't seen or apparently even heard them. David hoped they might somehow stumble past or turn around or do anything but keep coming on toward him as numb and beaten as he was himself, trailing their useless guns. But they kept coming. Now the death's-head sign *"Achtung! Minen!"* was right behind them. David lost a second praying that the man in the big foxhole would miraculously come to life and do it for him. Then he put the M-1 on the first German, but by a miracle almost equal to the one he'd desired the two of them suddenly turned and stumbled away in the direction from which they'd come.

At last Sergeant Kennebec came up with another new man to relieve both him and Colhurst. "Panic's off," he said. David told him about the two Germans. "For God's sake," Kennebec said. "Maybe it's true after all."

"What's true?" David said. "Look, get me out of here. You'd better get him out, too." He waved his rifle in the direction of the giant foxhole and the invisible sentry Colhurst.

"I came to get you out," Kennebec said. "But I may have to bring you back."

Suddenly Colhurst pulled himself from the other foxhole. It was a slow, painful performance; his stiff legs buckled underneath him and he fell headlong on the snow-covered ground. But he got up again.

The relief sentry slid into the big foxhole.

"I heard you, Sergeant," Colhurst said. "Maybe you'll get *him* back here." He turned painfully toward David's faint shadow for some sign of joint rebellion. "You won't get me back. Nothing, nobody will get me back." He was almost shouting.

"Shut up," Kennebec said. "It may be true. It came down from regiment."

"What came down?"

"They're attacking."

"They'll have to find somebody else to attack. They're not attacking me. I'm going to get warm."

"They got a talking PW. He said it's a very big attack and it's coming at first light."

David walked her home that night and they parted silently. There were three more days of total silence, but on the fourth day he had to go away and he knew he had to see her, whatever the cost.

His favorite song ran through his head, a note of it in time with every step toward her house.

> *Where is the one*
> *Who will mourn me when I'm gone,*
> *When the dogwood is in bloom who will sigh?*
> *If the robin won't sing*
> *At the first sign of spring*
> *I'll know that my darling don't cry,*
> *I'll know that my darling don't cry.*

He rapped timidly on the door. "Come in, David," Mr. Egan said. "Gus is at work. Mary's upstairs. I'm home looking after her."

"Can I talk to her a minute, Mr. Egan?"

"No, you can't. You're a good young man but you've upset her far too much."

"Can I sit down, Mr. Egan?"

"Yes, of course."

"I know Mary doesn't read a lot."

"No," Mr. Egan said dryly. "None of us read much, do we? I used to read more before I joined the church."

"She knows *Götterdämmerung*."

"The twilight of the gods."

"Yes," David said. "And my gods are all in twilight. Can't I tell her that?"

"No, David. You just go on away. You and your father got Mary built up on this business. Your father got me built up on it again just about when I was ready to go away. Now you've gone away, leaving Mary stuck with it. All right, David. Stay away from your church if you must. But stay away from Mary, too."

Until the last night that whole last week as a civilian was full of torment. Martin Egan's scorn and Mary's sad rejection swung the pendulum again and called back into doubt the honesty of his doubts. Was he yielding to impulses that even he, somewhere beneath some protective sheath of hypocrisy, knew to be cruel, false, selfish, and craven? Was it an admissible argument—and if so, on which side?—that in most places his impulses would be taken to be straightforward and manly?

It was only now that David began to realize how little he understood his father. He had dreaded the ordeal of telling him, but only because he always dreaded the ordeal of telling his father that he had broken a rule. He had expected Samuel to feel shamed, and perhaps even—though he'd never seen him that way—angry. He had been ready for thunderous reproaches and even fearful prophecies. But he had grown so accustomed to thinking of Samuel Kyle as a man securely rooted in and insulated by his religion that the idea of his being strongly affected by any purely earthly disappointment had not entered his calculations at all. A man who believed in his religion as firmly and held to it as unwaveringly as Samuel Kyle could be offended, but he could not be damaged. He was beyond the reach of tragedy. The only tragedy that could ever touch him lay beyond the grave; and if silence dwelt there in spite of all the promises, he would never know.

It came as a totally unexpected, totally shattering discovery that his decision to enlist for combat duty was not a mere defeat for his father, but a cause of aching sorrow. For the first time he perceived that his father neither saw nor leaned upon his gospel of salvation as a gospel mainly of self-preservation; it was a gospel of pity and concern, and Samuel's concern now was not for forms and observances and rules and his own unflawed performance of his duty, but for the immortal soul of his only son.

Samuel sat for ten minutes without speaking. David had expected him to bring out the marked Bible and attempt to overwhelm him with the literal Word, as he had done so often and so easily before. "I can see I've gotten away behind you, Son," Samuel said heavily when he was ready to speak. "I've failed you. I've asked you to take too much on faith and go on taking it on faith too long."

He crossed the room and opened the lower drawer of the long

chest in which the silverware and table linen were kept. David's mother sat, white-faced, in the other corner of the room. After one smothered gasp of disbelief at David's first announcement she had not spoken either.

"I'd almost forgotten," Samuel said. "I'd almost forgotten these. I'd almost forgotten I needed them once myself." He began sorting out a stack of pamphlets. "Here you'll find all the important reasons all the important rationalists have given for not believing in the Bible. You'll also find the reasons why their reasons don't stand up, why they all ultimately refute themselves. You'll find—" The old man looked into David's miserable, set eyes and stopped himself in midsentence. "Oh, I guess it's old stuff to you anyway," he said sorrowfully.

"I've thought about it so much, Father," David said. "It's just that there's no time left to think any more. I've had to make up my mind, that's all—and, well, I have and I'm sorry."

"David," his father said, "I'm sorry too and I'm not going to pester you about this. But you do know that no one's asking you to put your church ahead of your country?"

"I haven't been thinking of it that way, Father. All I've thought is that if I'm going to be in the war at all, I'm going to be all the way in. The excuse I could use doesn't fit my case any longer, that's all."

"We declared ourselves at the time of the Civil War, David." Samuel was determined to make his point. "The Adventist declaration was accepted by the Government and it was accepted again in 1917 and it's still accepted."

"I know, Father."

Samuel read from one of the pamphlets. "Our declaration was this: 'That we recognize civil government as ordained by God, that order, justice, and quiet may be maintained in the land, and that the people of God may lead quiet and peaceable lives in all godliness and honesty. In accordance with this fact, we acknowledge the justice of rendering tribute, custom, honor and reverence to the civil power, as enjoined in the New Testament. While we thus cheerfully render unto Caesar the things which the Scriptures show to be his, we are compelled to decline all participation in acts of war and bloodshed, as being inconsistent with the duties enjoined upon us by our divine Master toward our enemies and toward all mankind.'"

There was no reply that David could think of.

"Son, if it's a question of not wanting to evade danger, your mother and I would both be proud to think of you driving an ambulance."

"Maybe that *is* the question, Father. I can't be sure. But I'm going to enlist in the infantry."

"I think I'll go for a walk," Samuel said. "You stay here and talk to your mother for a while. Oh, and there's one thing. Will you come to church with us on Saturday?"

"I'd like that," David had said. That was their last discussion on the subject. Samuel and Hannah Kyle entered quietly and obediently on the most difficult test of their mortal life: accepting the fearful ordinance that when heaven opened to receive them they would look in vain for their only son.

The night before David left, Mary came to say good-by to him. She gave no indication whether it was with her father's knowledge or not. She asked him to go for a walk with her. Instead he borrowed his father's car and they drove a few miles into the country. At first they were both self-conscious and uncommunicative.

The black Plymouth coach ambled past a neon-lit roadhouse and a few bars of jukebox music ushered them on down the moonlit roadway. "Turn around," Mary said abruptly. "I want to go back there and dance."

He put on the brakes. "Dance?" he asked incredulously. "You can't dance, Mary." He paused and added anxiously, "Can you?"

"Can you?"

"Well," he admitted, "I tried it two or three times at Ann Arbor. I'm no good at it. There was nothing wrong in my doing it; or anyway, nothing any more wrong than the whole business."

"I don't think it would be wrong for me either."

"Yes, it would, Mary, and you know it." He was talking to her again in the severe, uncomplicated, unsophisticated, almost technologically precise language of the tracts and the Sabbath School. This was exactly the tone in which he'd first met her and begun filling in the more urgent gaps in her instruction. Perhaps it was only imagination that the pugnacious set of her red head had come back again and she once more seemed to be squirming free to resume her assault on some new oppressor, some new mocker, some larger and more troublesome Hortense McGraw. He had not seen her in this fully redheaded mood since the night she'd walked home, treasonably, with the trombone player.

54

"I don't know anything of the kind."

He listened in alarm and bafflement. Mary was not always as easy a girl to figure as she seemed. There did not seem to be any bitterness in her voice or any taunting, either. He'd have felt easier if he could be sure that she merely was taking some oblique way of paying him back or offering him some reckless dare. *All right, Gus,* she'd said to her brother one late-May morning, *if you and David are going swimming in your birthday suits, so am I,* and she'd made them back down and resume their search for mushrooms. *All right, David, if you're going to hell I'm going too.* In her first mood of shock and reproof and pious incredulity she had left him full of guilt and haunting second thoughts, but in this abrupt claim to a share in his folly and his sin it was almost impossible to define her, much less to cope with her.

"Mary"—having forfeited the right to fall back upon the church, her church still, no longer his, he floundered for the unassailable argument—"I can't go dancing with you. Your father would never forgive me."

"He'll never know," she said coolly. "Look, David, I've made a new dress." She opened her fawn trench coat and slipped her bare arms through the sleeves and reached forward and turned on the dash light. It was a green dress with a startling intermediate neckline and—if David had heard right from his former roommate's girl at Ann Arbor—a high waist and a full, fringed bust. It was not a fast dress, per se, but it was a fast dress to see on Mary. "At first," she said before he had a chance to comment, "I just went up to my room and started bawling and Father thought I was going to stay there bawling forever and for a while I thought so too. But then I heard you at the door the other night—yes, I heard you all right, David—and I decided there were more constructive things I might be doing, so I made this dress. Father hasn't seen it of course and there's no need for him to see it. I didn't make it for him. I made it for you and I want you to take me dancing in it."

"I can't do that, Mary," he said. "I've got enough to answer for as it is."

She stirred impatiently. Could it be—no it must be some flowering bush along the roadside—she couldn't be wearing perfume.

"It's perfectly all *right,* David," she said. "If it's the dress you're thinking of anyway. I just knew you'd be like this," she said reproachfully. "So I borrowed one of Father's Mrs. White books. Do you know what she said?"

"Sure." David's reply was light, almost bantering. He wanted to hit a note mixed of tolerance, wry humor, and the very gentlest confession of the very gentlest feeling of surprise. "Mrs. White said our sisters should clothe themselves in modest apparel with shamefacedness and sobriety. I don't think she'd object," he said, forcing himself into a lie that did not deceive her for an instant.

Mary's response again was beyond the range of prediction. She giggled. "She also said," Mary added, "and don't bother contradicting me because I memorized it for you: she said to enter into no controversy in regard to outward apparel, but be sure you have the inward adorning of a meek and quiet spirit. Now tell me, David, have you ever been able to deny that I have a meek and quiet spirit?"

"Only sometimes, only about ninety-five per cent of the time." David reached across the seat and took her hand.

"Mrs. White also said," Mary informed him, "'We are a spectacle to the world, to angels and to men.'"

He grinned and looked at her squarely and wholly for the first time since she'd removed her coat. "I don't know about Mrs. White. I thought she wore bloomers. But you qualify all right."

"False prudence," Mary continued, "mock modesty may be shown in the outward apparel, while the heart is in great need of inward adorning. Take me dancing in my new dress, David."

"All right," he said, and reached for the starter.

"No," she said in alarm. "Good heavens, David, I'd just fall all over your feet. I'd be scared anyway. I only wanted to see if you would."

He had never been so close, since the unfortunate night of the trombone player, to bringing up the matter of their marriage. But David was a creature of convention and, having strayed from the conventions of the church, he had all the greater need of abiding by the conventions of the outer world. Fighting for His Country had become the chief of these; Not Asking a Girl to Wait was an almost equally compelling one. But he did kiss her, long and sweetly, before the long, sweet night was over. When at last she turned to go in, his pulse was pounding hard and he knew that hers was pounding too. "Put the dress away until you see me next," he commanded.

"I will," she whispered, and left him easily and confidently, with nothing so mean as tears.

56

When they got back to the cellar, Henry Whelan and Carmen (the Hood) Ruiz were already there. Whelan had a big can of coffee going on the smoking bonfire in the middle of the stone floor and Carmen (the Hood) had a mixture of K-ration cheese, K-ration meat, biscuits, and bouillon cubes mixed into an iron pot along with a half-pound can of lobster he had been bragging about for several days as the very early Christmas present of a very early lady friend. Out there during the last four hours, Ruiz said, he'd made up his mind that he'd never feel anything hot again, see anything hot again, or eat anything hot again. From now on any time he discovered a fire, anything within reach of it was going on it.

Colhurst, the new man, acquired the prestige of six months' battle service by producing a full bottle of cognac. It was just a little past midnight and nobody was ready to try the sack again for a while. Kennebec came back in and sat down. After a while he asked David to tell him some more about the two Germans he'd seen. Did they look as if they were on an organized patrol or did they just look lost? David had decided to say nothing about them because he knew it would revive an old and pointless argument with Henry Whelan and Carmen (the Hood) Ruiz, and after the bad beginning it had turned into too comfortable a night for arguing.

"Hey!" Ruiz had been working over the last of the lobster and picked up the conversation only at the tail end. "You mean you had two of the bastards lined up and let them go? What the hell *is* this?"

"Isn't that what they did for you and Henry the other night?" David asked.

"That's been evened up once already," Ruiz's dark head swung around and he scowled across the fire, getting ready to get worked up. "From now on I don't want nobody paying back no favors for me. To nobody. Never. Christ!"

"What do *you* say, Sarge?" Whelan invited the sergeant to join the discussion as an equal. "Is it time to start the war again or not?"

"You God-damn' right it is," Carmen (the Hood) said. When they were discussing ethical matters, large matters, affairs in general, the affairs of politics, human behavior, and the world as distinct from military and local matters, Ruiz had something of the status of an elder statesman. It was clear from the tone and context and the whole atmosphere that Henry Whelan had meant his question in the larger sense. Therefore, Ruiz was perfectly free to break in ahead of the sergeant, and he did so.

Three or four other men gathered around to listen. Back in Jersey and indeed up to a week before they had gone aboard their convoy ship, nobody had done much listening to Carmen Ruiz. A gulf of nearly fifteen years separated him from most of the GI's in their battalion, and to men in their early twenties that meant a whole generation. Ruiz made it worse by being at first too polite and deferential, too obviously eager for friendship and respect. And then he'd made matters worse by letting it drop—too clumsily for it to be taken as an accident—that his draft number had been nowhere near in sight. When one or two skeptics began harassing him, he'd got off some highly embarrassing claptrap about democracy and wanting to fight for the country that had been so good to him; and when somebody demanded, "How do you mean, good?" he'd started throwing in pompous hints about leaving a 1940 Cadillac and a 1941 blonde behind him. "To hear him tell it, you'd think the son-of-a-bitch was a cross between the chaplain and John D. Rockefeller," Henry Whelan announced in disgust, and pretty soon nobody at all was listening to Carmen Ruiz and scarcely anybody was talking to him.

Then a man from Buffalo showed up in the last draft before they sailed. "Good God!" he announced in awe. "That's one of the biggest gangsters in Western New York." At first nobody would believe him and quite a few of the more contemptuous anti-Ruizists were trapped into making sucker bets. The man from Buffalo sent back home for some newspaper clippings and photographs. Carmen's darkly amiable scowl was always identified, with full civic honors, as that of Carmen (the Hood) Ruiz. The enterprises mentioned in connection with his name were always carefully described as alleged; they included lotteries, slot machines, labor organization, and prostitution. Confronted with the evidence by a small and respectful committee of losing bettors, Ruiz was more than happy to confirm his eminence. The boldest of the interviewers, Henry Whelan, came right out and asked him how a man with a record like his could be accepted by the Army. "What record?" Ruiz asked, making use of his newly established right to be a little haughty. "Outside of one hot-car rap when I was a punk, I never done a day." Even Henry Whelan wasn't so presumptuous as to delve more deeply into Carmen's real reason for beating the draft board by so sensational a margin. The theories were divided: maybe income-tax trouble; maybe some crazy desire for kicks; maybe some rival hood had a light burning in the window for him; maybe he even meant all that about democracy; certainly nobody could deny that his country had been good to him.

"You God-damn' right it's time to start the war again," Carmen repeated. He looked across the fire at David. It was a severe look, but a fond one, too, a look of avuncular, reluctant disapproval. "We got too God-damn' many pacifists around here."

David wasn't being led into it again. He and Ruiz and Whelan had covered all the essential ground that long night outside St. Lô, and although they'd touched on it again two or three times since, they'd always ended up where they'd started. Their division came in through Omaha Beach on D Plus Five. The men they met from Omaha assured them that nobody anywhere would ever run into anything quite as rough as Omaha even if the war lasted forever. But St. Lô was rough enough. The hedgerows were like walls of barbed wire three feet thick, the Germans had their armor in behind, the U.S. division on their right kept falling apart, the Limeys on their left weren't moving an inch, the artillery behind them and the planes above them proved infallibly unable, by widespread agreement among the infantry, of hitting a cow in the ass with a handful of buckshot, and they fought for eight straight days and nights just to stay alive. A surprising number of them did and an appalling number didn't. Casualties in the battalion were 33 per cent and in their company 39.

When the German armor pulled out, David Kyle and Carmen Ruiz were lying close together in a shell hole they had discovered and deepened under the one corner still left standing of what not long ago had been a crossroads church. They'd had no orders from either their platoon or company since the night before, and as the queer silence of the morning gathered volume they'd had no idea what they should be doing next. Then, halfway through the morning, before the reaction had had a chance to set in, Henry Whelan limped into view, dirty, groggy, splattered with the dried blood of other men, and full of a bitter, new-earned hate.

He sat down in the open, too weary to think of taking cover. "They sent me out from company to see who I could round up," he said. "Come on. We're moving back."

"My Christ, boy, where you *been?*" Carmen Ruiz asked him.

"The dirty bastards," Whelan said. "The dirty bastards."

"What's new about that?" Ruiz asked with a mixture of curiosity and concern. "Where you been, Henry? All that blood can't be yours or you'd be dead." If Ruiz felt any relief at the news that they didn't have to go on fighting, it was too early to show. His voice, too, was groggy, though not so groggy as Whelan's. Dave Kyle closed his eyes and tried to imagine that the strange silence around them was not another of the many tricks of his drugged and spongy mind and that Henry Whelan had really said they were moving back. But all he could imagine was that Henry Whelan wasn't even there and that what he mistook for silence was only the lull before another salvo from the *Nebelwerfer* or another counterattack by the Panthers.

"The dirty bastards," Henry Whelan said again. He looked around the cluster of gravestones in what had been the churchyard. Three dead GI's and four dead Germans, their red-white-purple-black-and-belly-white grab bag of gaps, incisions, and absent members still gleaming wetly in the morning sun, lay within twenty feet of the shell hole. "I see they got in here too," Henry said.

"Yeah, they were in here all right." Ruiz looked out among the broken gravestones. "One shell got them all," he said with a note of proprietary interest in the seven visible corpses. "One of our guys is Herbie Witherspoon. Dave was going along right beside him, we were trying to get across the road when the Krauts jumped out of their foxholes and the shell hit all at once. Dave stayed out there a good five minutes trying to patch Herbie up. He told me to get down and cover him and I don't God-damn' care who knows that's exactly what I did. I got down. One of the other GI's is that fellow Casey or Ryan from company headquarters; I don't know how he got over here anyway." Ruiz made it sound as though he was objecting to an act of trespass. "We can't figure out who the other one is. Dave thought it was you at first. The crazy bugger wanted to go and look but I wouldn't let him."

"The dirty bastards," Henry Whelan said once more. "They got in on us over there too. They killed every God-damn' medic in the company. So finally the captain put me and that little Johnny Meyers fellow on medic and we were on it all night. We brought in eleven and all but four of them are gone already. Finally just after daylight they got Johnny Meyers. He was wearing an armband, the dirty bastards."

"Well, let's go, then," Carmen said. "Come on, Dave."

"Sure." David realized that it wasn't an illusion after all and they were really supposed to leave. He pushed himself to his feet, using his M-1 as a cane, but careful to keep the barrel uppermost and free of dirt.

A rifle bullet thwacked against the stone corner of the church behind them and sang off like the twang of a breaking wire. Then another thwacked into the ground. Henry Whelan threw himself over the edge of the crater. In the first movement they all punched themselves absolutely flat, driving their bellies into the earth, but without breaking the continuity they rolled back up in a half-crouch, like gymnasts bouncing down and up again under the same momentum. Whelan and Ruiz shoved their eyes above the edge of the crater to the front. David scrambled in behind them and looked the other way, expecting to see another cluster of gray-green figures fanning in against the wiry hedgerow.

"Nothing here," he said over his shoulder.

"Two at ten o'clock. On their bellies at the base of those trees." Henry Whelan's voice was shaking. "The dirty bastards!" he said once more, talking himself out of the shakes. He raised up a little more and took two quick pot shots. "Bastards!" His composure had returned. Now there was a quick, rippling burst from the other side of the ground that Whelan and Ruiz were watching. "Light machine gun at one o'clock," Ruiz said.

It was quite a while before they were satisfied that there were just the three enemy weapons. Nobody, neither they themselves nor the Germans, was getting up high enough or staying long enough to take a real aim or offer a real target. There'd be a round or two from the Germans, a quick wild shot by Ruiz or Whelan, a very short burst from the machine gun, then nothing at all for five or six minutes from anywhere. The Germans were as wary of moving in or moving back as they were themselves.

Another hour went. "The dirty bastards aren't keeping me here forever," Henry Whelan announced. "I'm going out there."

"No," Carmen said.

"You God-damn' right I am," Henry Whelan corrected him.

"Wait a minute," David said. There was no bravery involved in this, just bad luck. For the last while he'd been studying a tiny fold in the ground directly in his line of vision and on the opposite side of the shell crater to Whelan and Ruiz. He'd decided not to say anything about it, but since Henry Whelan was forcing the issue he had no choice. "I've got a nice little draw on this side,"

61

David called softly over his shoulder. "Keep them down and I think I can get around them. When I say go, give them a couple of rounds and I'll go too."

Since they were all of equal rank, there was no one in command. But since they were also used to each other, any idea put forth with special emphasis and conviction by any one of them had always attained the force of a command unless someone else challenged it with still greater emphasis. Henry Whelan had been emphatic enough and his idea would have had to be accepted if no one had offered a better one. But even he had known it was a foolish idea.

"Go!" David shouted, and in the quick flurry of shots he made a dive for the grassy slope outside, crawled ahead four or five body lengths, and then rested. "It looks good," he called back softly. "I'm going around to the right for the machine gun."

He had been reasonably sure that if he could get the machine gun first the two riflemen would chicken out, and, after an hour's slow and painful stalking, that was precisely how it happened. His cover ran out when he was still fifty or sixty yards from the machine gunner, and he had to hurry his shot because there was a chance one of the riflemen might see him if he took too long, but he got the machine gunner on the side of the thigh, spinning him away from the gun in a sidewise sprawl. Fast though it happened, this was one Kraut who knew what hit him, because he was on his feet at once with his arms held high, bawling, *"Kamerad! Kamerad!"* at the top of his lungs and looking wildly around him to see whom he was surrendering to. In the next second the two riflemen heaved their Mausers out into the clearing and jumped up with their hands held even higher. David lay still for a moment or two, taking in their bewilderment and making certain there were no others left. Then he got to one knee with his rifle across the other knee and waved the three Germans in toward him. He signaled them into a triangle and started off behind them to the shell crater where Henry Whelan and Carmen (the Hood) Ruiz were on their feet and waiting. The machine gunner's leg had not been broken and he was able to hobble along with help from one of the riflemen.

When they were thirty feet or so away, Henry Whelan shouted, "Stand aside, Dave." David saw at once what was in Henry's mind and he shouted to the three prisoners to halt. "Put it down, Henry,"

David said. "Like hell I will!" Whelan shouted. "Get out of the way, Dave!"

Carmen Ruiz had his rifle up too. "Get out of the way, Dave!" Carmen shouted.

One of the Krauts sank to the ground and for a moment the only sound was the curiously embarrassing noise of his slackening bowels. "*Bitte! Bitte!*" another of the Krauts whimpered. "*Kamerad!*" the machine gunner cried more strongly, reminding them that everything was already solved.

"Come on, Henry, put it down," David urged. "Come on, Carmen."

"All right, Dave," Henry said with the measured venom of a man who is determined to show that he is patient and then to let his patience go. "I'll saw off with you. Let's go over and look at their guns."

"Yeah," Carmen Ruiz said, emerging from the shell hole. "Let's do that."

They marched the three captives back. Ruiz picked up the two rifles on the way and then the six soldiers went to the upturned machine gun. The three Germans held their hands very high while Carmen Ruiz inspected their bullet pouches. "Empty," he said when he'd finished with the first. He picked up one of the rifles, broke it open at the breech, and took off the magazine and looked into it. "Empty," he said. "This yours?" He thrust the empty rifle under the nearest German's nose. "*Bitte!*" the German wept. "Is it yours, God damn it?" Carmen shouted.

"*Ja,*" the German wept. "*Bitte.*"

Carmen went through the same procedure with the second rifleman. His bullet pouches and his rifle were empty too. "No bullets left?" Carmen asked pleasantly. The German understood. "*Nein,*" he sobbed with sudden, radiant hopefulness. "No bullets." Ruiz stepped over in front of David so that he was between David and their captives. "All right, Henry," Ruiz said. Whelan brought his rifle up. He shot the first German through the heart from a foot away and shot the second through the head as the German turned to run.

The machine gunner sank to his knees shouting, "*Kamerad!*" again. The sound was muffled and hopeless. He had already buried his head in his arms.

David threw himself to the ground before the machine gunner. Henry Whelan had lost a few seconds reloading his rifle. David stood up and grabbed the rifle by its muzzle. His eyes wavered on the new-dead riflemen, stopped at the machine gunner, now a crouching bundle of terror, and then brought Henry Whelan back into focus. Henry was panting. His mouth was wide open and his eyes gleamed with a wild, perfervid joy. "Out of the way, you bastard!" Henry commanded, and struggled to wrench his rifle free.

"No!" David started to say, but at first he could bring out no sound. He wet his lips, while he and Henry wrestled for the rifle. "No!"

Carmen Ruiz threw himself in between them. "Henry!" he shouted. "Cut it out, Henry!" Whelan was cursing wildly now. He tried to drive David off with a knee to the groin. Carmen Ruiz aimed a chopping, side-handed blow at Whelan's neck and Henry let go the rifle and floundered to the ground. He got up shaking his head, dazed and suddenly much calmer.

"It's O.K., Henry," Carmen Ruiz said. "This one's O.K. He's got a whole magazine left."

"Sure," Henry said, feeling the side of his neck. He was quite easy now and mildly rueful, as though he'd lost his wind in a football scrimmage and was glad to take a breather. "Sure, that's O.K., I guess."

"Dave did a good job with these bastards," Carmen said.

"I know he did," Henry Whelan agreed, his excitement worn away, anxious to be fair. "You did a good job, Dave. I'm sorry I got sore at you." He looked at the two dead riflemen. "I did a good job too."

Carmen Ruiz kicked the half-paralyzed machine gunner to his feet. "*Raus!*" he commanded, "*Raus!* you lucky Heinie pisspot. Consider yourself a prisoner of the Boy Scouts of America."

They were driven back in trucks to a schoolhouse just outside Bayeux. With short interruptions for food, a visit to a mobile bath and delousing unit, and an extremely unpopular but compulsory service of prayer for the dead and missing, they did nothing for the next forty-eight hours but sleep. David, Ruiz, and Whelan were the last ones in and they drew a small storage cupboard to themselves. They did very little talking until just after dusk on the second night, when, as though by some radar signal, they all came fully and luxuriously awake again.

Dave had hoped there'd be no more said about the way their part of St. Lô had ended. Nothing was going to be clarified or amended by conversation. Ruiz didn't seem to want to discuss that subject either, and while they were reasserting their quiet satisfaction in each other's presence he told them easy, not unduly interesting stories about his mother's Spanish cooking, his beautiful sister's thwarted romance with a young man who went into the priesthood, and his own brief, much-regretted career as a semi-professional shortstop. But Henry Whelan kept skirting around the edges of the other topic, obviously needing to talk it out and establish the justness of his position. When he got no encouragement he went into it head on.

"Dave," Henry Whelan said. "I want to get something straightened out. Why didn't you want me to shoot those Krauts?"

"Let's not go into it, Henry," David said. "The less talking there is the better."

"That's right," Carmen Ruiz said. "We better just forget it. A thing like that gets around and the first thing you know some pressed-pants prick of an officer has you up for a court of inquiry and God knows what else. Well, I wasn't ready for the Bisons or anywhere near, but they were always looking out for local talent and they offered me this tryout. I shouldn't have taken it. I wasn't even eighteen. The batting practice pitcher they started me out on was a sour old crock of a southpaw on the way down from Cincinnati. The miserable s.o.b. would never think of giving a break to a kid on the way up. He threw me nothing but the same fat-looking slider and I spent a whole morning breaking my back on it and—"

"It doesn't have to go past us three," Henry Whelan interrupted. "I just want to know why Dave was against it."

Carmen tried again, anxious to forestall an argument. "It's these pricks in pressed pants, Henry," he said. "There was a guy on the ship whose buddy was in Italy. This guy's buddy helped shoot up a tank crew after the bastards lost their tank and tried to pretend the war was over just because they didn't have anything left to shoot with. And do you know what the U. S. Army tried to do to this guy's buddy? They tried to send him to Leavenworth, for Christ's sake. To Leavenworth."

"I know, I know," Whelan said with mounting disgust. "I heard about a captain in North Africa that got knocked down all the way to private. Not even PFC. I just want to know what's wrong with Dave."

"There's nothing wrong," David said. "No two people look at everything exactly the same."

"If I thought it was just a nervous gut I wouldn't care," Henry Whelan persisted. "But it's not that. I'll admit I was pretty excited but I noticed what was going on. You looked at me damn' funny, Dave. As if there was something horrible about me, a hell of a lot more horrible than anything about those bastard Krauts. As if I was a criminal."

"Come on, Henry," Carmen broke in. "Let's just drop it, kid."

"Do you go for that crap about the articles of war and the Geneva Convention and all that other crap, Dave?" Henry Whelan put it as a direct accusation. "Do you?"

David had no idea how to answer. So far as he was able to analyze the sickness he had felt when Henry Whelan shot the two Germans, laws and regulations had had nothing to do with it. He'd only had a short time to work it over. Most of the time since then he'd been either dreamlessly asleep or asleep and dreaming of pleasant waterfalls and snow in the woods and handsome women and almost everything else *but* fresh-dead men of any nationality, fresh-dead of whatever cause.

"Now listen, Dave." Henry Whelan was a year younger than David and a dozen years younger than Carmen Ruiz but he had taken charge. He stood up in the center of the floor, blinking down at them, dominating them both by the stronger force of his feelings. "Everybody around here isn't stupid. You don't smoke. That's your business but how come you *never* smoked, never even tasted it? You hardly ever swear. But you've got guts, more guts than most of us, more guts than I've got. Then why, for Christ's sake—"

"I don't know, Henry," David said.

"You a philosopher or something? You belong to one of those funny churches, like those guys in the medical corps?"

"Drop it, Henry," Carmen Ruiz broke in.

"I think it *is* something like the Geneva Convention that was eating your ass back there," Whelan announced. "Well, to avoid any more misunderstanding in the future, let me now proclaim the Henry Whelan Convention. Under the Henry Whelan Convention anybody who discharges dangerous weapons in the direction of Henry Whelan will find Henry Whelan, God willing, discharging dangerous weapons right back in *his* direction. And when and if this other party decides to stop discharging dangerous weapons he better not count on Henry Whelan stopping too."

"Now you're getting around to the Ruiz Convention." Carmen's awakened interest overrode his desire to head off a dispute. "Under the Ruiz Convention any Kraut who puts down his gun and puts his hands up in the air is Carmen's friend. Carmen will treat him like those other conventions say he should. Carmen will treat him like a brother. With one exception."

He looked at David, waiting for a question. "Henry knows what the exception is, and why," he said to David. "I don't think you understood it. Two of those bastards were out of ammo; the two I told Henry to give it to. How *about* that? They throw everything at you that they've got, then when they got nothing more to throw they want to be friends, they want to call the war off. I say no. If they surrender to old Carmen they better surrender while they still got some bullets. That's the Ruiz Convention."

"Now tell me what's wrong about that, Dave?" Henry Whelan demanded. "What the hell is wrong about that?"

"I didn't say there was anything wrong about it, did I?" All David wanted to do now was to get back to his private thoughts and see if there *was* anything to be extracted from what had been done and said. He could not get much meaning here and his weary mind kept leading him back to the simpler, surer universe he thought he had renounced forever. His mother hadn't spoken much when his father left them alone that evening. "I know you're confused, David," Hannah Kyle had said gently. "I can understand a boy like you wavering on a lot of things. You always did do so much thinking. But leaving the Bible out of it, if you must, how can you waver on a thing as true as 'Thou shalt not kill.'"

For all he knew, David brought himself to admit, it might be even more elementary—to use the Ann Arbor word, more fundamental—than that. For all he knew he'd failed, after all, to discard the deep and bottomless terror of the lake of fire. As Henry Whelan had conceded, he had already established his temporal possession of a full temporal share of temporal courage. His life was filled with desperate, uncluttered temporal fear, but he hadn't run from it. Moreover he had proved that he could kill men when he had to. The machine gunner was the first German he knew, to his certain knowledge, that he'd ever hit with his rifle, but at the start of the battle for St. Lô he personally, he David Kyle and he David

Kyle alone, had put a bazooka through a Tiger tank and seen the tank burn slowly with its turret sealed as tightly as a tomb. He could kill men, in their uncapitalized, lower-case, collective state. But could he kill a Man—a Man close up and identifiable and individual, a Man he could see and sense and pity and, if the temptation overcame him, even shelter and protect?

Carmen Ruiz, having dispatched the last of the lobster, signaled PFC Colhurst to pass the cognac. "Too God-damned many pacifists," he repeated, looking indulgently at David across the fire. "Time to start the war again."

It was Sergeant Kennebec's judgment, not Ruiz's, that had been sought in the first place, and he felt obliged to make his own pronouncement. "Don't worry," he counseled. "It will start again all right. It always does, doesn't it?"

CHAPTER THREE

"Well, here we are." Two trucks had been drawn up beside the road, their headlights showing the way along the ruts in the fresh snow. Young Haig Ballantyne dragged a crosscut saw that had fallen off another truck ahead. He patted down the ear flaps on his khaki melton hat and blew through his mitts to warm his fingers. He kicked his feet through the thin layer of snow on the flinty ground and waved at the dark, enveloping pine trees. "We really *must* be in the rear echelon." George Ballantyne, struggling along beside his brother, looked at his watch. "Nearly twenty-one hundred hours. I guess we just forget the blackout away back here."

Haig ignored him. "Another part of the forest," he said. "The lovely forest of Arden. I never thought we'd make it."

"It's the forest of Ardennes, Haig, and you damn' well know it."

George scowled slightly. The vapor of his breath trailed up through the pale wash of the headlights and disappeared over the cliff of total darkness at the side of the roadway.

"I prefer the Bard's version," Haig said.

The jeep behind them turned its lights on too and a sergeant shouted, "O.K. Let's keep moving." A corporal on foot drew abreast of them.

"I'll stick with Arden," Haig insisted. "We did the whole play two years ago in the Drama Club, you know. I tried out for Oliver but the tights wouldn't fit and I ended up as a mere duke."

George moved over beside him. His overshoes creaked against the untouched snow between the ruts. "Want me to carry for a while?"

"No, thanks, it's fine. I had a few good lines at that. 'The icy fang and churlish chiding of the winter's wind, which, when it bites and blows upon my body, even till I shrink with cold, I smile,' et cetera! Do you get the feeling that this is a churlish *wined*? They kept after us to pronounce it 'wined'!"

"Well, let's just settle for chiding."

"Of course," Haig pointed out, "the Bard did temper his whinging. 'Heigh-ho! sing, heigh-ho! unto the green holly.'"

"All right, let's keep moving," the corporal beside them said.

"I happen, Corporal," Haig said, "to be giving my elder brother here, a fellow serviceman after all in His Majesty's Royal Canadian Forestry Corps, a few pointers on the local terrain and climate. These might well prove of immense military value in their proper time."

"I could have you up for dumb insolence," the corporal said.

"Except that I'm talking," Haig said. "Only one more stanza, Corporal.

> "Freeze, freeze, thou bitter sky,
> That dost not bite so nigh
> As benefits forgot;
> Though thou the waters warp,
> Thy sting is not so sharp
> As friend rememb'red not.
> Heigh-ho! sing, heigh-ho! unto the green holly."

At the last his voice rose in a mimic serenade and he looked around once more at the winter trees.

The corporal laughed, saving face. "I think you got a point there after all. Heigh-ho unto the green holly. Let's keep moving, though."

The little convoy turned down a side road and groaned up a hill, the muddy rabble of vehicles seeming to curse in sympathy with the men on foot. They halted in the middle of a gray and weath-ered village square, where an advance party had set up a search-light and reinforced it with the headlights of another jeep. Most of the village was empty and the rest of it pretended to be. There was no one on the streets, no smoke coming from the chimneys, only here and there the ghostly frightened face of a woman, a child, or a very old man looking out through a gap in the shutters. The steeple had been blown off the church and two of the other main buildings were black shells.

In the middle of the half-lit square the adjutant was already trying to cope with the task of directing them to billets. The adjutant, a short, immensely likable man, had rather obviously been taking comfort from the unit's small store of rum. As they passed, George heard him reporting to the company commander.

His voice, thick with rum and then thinned with the raw night air, created, George thought, one of the oddest sounds he'd ever heard, a little like a female impersonator impersonating a hoarse old man.

"I don't know what we can expect here, sir." The adjutant's thick-thin voice carried its shrill rasp almost all the way across the square. "I talked to the priest. He's sore at everybody including us. The mayor's not available; the people on our side think he was collaborating with their side and the people on their side think he was collaborating with our side. Anyway he seems to have taken it on the lam. The chief of police got killed in the last bombard-ment. The woman who ran the hotel got knocked up by a Ger-man warrant officer and was last seen getting aboard a train east."

"All right, Captain Earnshaw," the major said. "Let's try to confine it to the essentials."

"Well, sir, as near as I can make out," the adjutant elaborated, "this town has been either liberated or captured at least fourteen times each by everybody from Genghis Khan and Charlemagne right down through Wellington and Rommel. Possibly Stonewall Jackson and Byng of Vimy too; the priest seemed a little uncertain on that point."

"Slow down, Captain," the major ordered. "What arrangements have you made for billeting?"

"Well, sir," the adjutant said, "that's what I was coming to. It doesn't look too promising. I think if we just buggered off out of here there would be no vast burst of civic outrage."

"Now look. You've had a two-hour start on us and it's damned near twenty-hundred hours. What billeting arrangements have you made?"

"I'd recommend anywhere, sir," the adjutant said, waving around him again.

George and Haig found a little cubicle together in a house just off the square. They were lucky. It had a small bed. "You sleep on it, Haig," George said.

"No, you. I'm O.K."

The orderly sergeant came around, floundering through the darkness.

"All right here?"

"Sure," Haig yawned from the floor.

"Sure," George yawned from the bed.

A stray Dornier throbbed above them and one bomb dropped a few hundred yards away. It shook the little house. Haig sat up and started groping for his gear. "Take it easy," George said. "It's just another drunken driver."

The sergeant was still standing in a corner of the dark room.

"Sure," he said, "nothing."

"I guess," Haig said from the floor, "I guess it wouldn't count if one of those nothing things hit you by mistake."

"In that case," the sergeant said, "I'd let someone else do the worrying."

"Nobody's worrying around here, Sergeant," George said.

"Anyway, what I came to do, besides chasing the women out, was to tell you about tomorrow. Sleep as long as you want. But then get ready for work. We're going to set up the mill here and start logging off right away. We've got a big forest ahead."

"The forest of Arden," young Haig yawned.

"No," the sergeant corrected him. "Ardennes."

"Ardennes," George confirmed.

"Have it your way," Haig said.

Halfway through the night, George was awake and he heard Haig stirring on the floor below him.

"You all right?"

"Is anybody?"

"Haig, you never did tell me much."

"About what?"

"Well—"

"About why I signed the papers? About why I'm here?"

"Yes."

71

"George, if I had a hundred and ninety-seven brothers I'd want you to be all of them."

"And you still won't tell me about the other thing?"

"You know it anyway. No, I don't want to talk about it, even to you."

"You're so God-damn' bitter, Haig."

"That's the most preposterous thing I ever heard. I'm not bitter. What have I got to be bitter about? Some stranger is dropping strange bombs at me. I am hemmed in by officers and gentlemen giving me clearly idiotic orders. My tiny career as a scholar is over. I am in some danger of freezing to death. I am far from home. To-morrow I'll get up and start chopping down the forest of Arden, a place I love with all my heart. Why should I be bitter?"

"You won't tell me what went on back in Canada, will you?"

"I guess not."

There was another silence between them.

"I'll say one thing, George. Being a zombie was pretty bad. Being an ex-zombie is worse. An honest slacker has at least got his standards. A slacker who lets himself be bullied out of it ends up kind of empty and sheepish, like a cured drunk."

"Oh, come off it, Haig, and go back to sleep."

"That's all I wanted to do in the first place." George was left alone again.

"Ha! Ve zoon zee!" Mr. Massinov's huge brown baseball glove of a hand hurled forth the ten of hearts and struck it and the table beneath it a thunderous ultimatum. "Dake it! Dake it now ze hearts or dake it next ze pisser!"

An earlier, civilian, version of George Ballantyne underplayed with the nine of hearts. "Not through me, Mr. Massinov," he said. He could just as well have said Boris, or even Massy, but habits weren't that soon changed. His father had taught him that you always called older men mister, no matter how intimate you might seem to have become with them; it was not an optional matter and it was not subject to amendment or review.

Mr. Massinov's thrust head was as vast and playfully mysterious as a stone monument on Easter Island. His large brown eyes re-treated behind a film of simulated wrath and his stainless-steel front teeth emerged in a menacing smile. "Hokay!" he growled vindictively. "Liddle Geortchie wants it to dake it ze pisser."

The sports editor, Mr. Malloy, dropped the king of diamonds.

The city editor, Mr. Gundarson, played the eight of hearts. Mr. Massinov now focused his attention on the fifth player in the game, the football lineman, Joe Wilson. Joe was, to be sure, five or six years older than young George Ballantyne, but after all he *was* a lineman and he sold life insurance on the side as well; to be mistered, George had recognized from the start of their acquaintance, would only have confused and hurt Joe Wilson and made him feel more insecure than ever.

"Dake it, Choe!" Mr. Massinov demanded in sudden alarm. "Duck it and *you* dake it ze pisser!"

Joe Wilson's frank, open, dishonest countenance fixed itself momentarily in a lineman's scowl and then sidled into the oily smile of an insurance man. As all the players in the hearts game knew, Wilson had been trying for several months to work out a floating group-insurance scheme to cover the dozen wrestlers Boris Massinov was rotating between Winnipeg, Minneapolis, and Duluth; both the underwriters and Massinov kept torturing him with demands for more details, and Wilson was disintegrating under the strain. Watching him at grips with this new dilemma, George Ballantyne was torn between sympathy and avarice. In the noble cut-throat game of hearts every man was an island and moreover an island under siege; any scrap of misfortune that came to anyone, however cruel or ill-deserved, was a blow for the common good. If Joe Wilson now obeyed Massinov's injunction to take the trick, he would thereby relieve Massinov of the liability of four hearts at a nickel a heart and generally rearrange the fulcrum of disaster. If Joe Wilson refused the injunction, he would save himself an immediate twenty cents and risk the ill-favor, real or simulated, of his leading and indeed his only business prospect. Of course Joe Wilson knew down deep that Massinov was only pretending to be a prospect; things being what they were, all over and all the time, nobody was really buying insurance and nobody was really selling it, either, but if Boris Massinov ceased to pretend that he was capable of and on the verge of buying and if Joe Wilson therefore had to cease pretending that he was capable of and on the verge of selling, then both men would be subtly but palpably diminished. It was demoralizing enough to lose your last genuine prospect—an experience that had befallen Joe Wilson some eleven months earlier, when his brother-in-law was laid off at the packing plant —but to lose your last phony prospect would be unendurable.

Joe Wilson stared out the window at the roof of the Acme Tool and Die Works. "You, Joe," the city editor said accusingly. Joe removed his gaze to the wall above the sports editor's desk and the framed and autographed photograph of Mike Gibbons, the St. Paul Phantom, not to be confused with Tommy Gibbons, the man who fought Jack Dempsey. "Holy Jesus!" he said. What's more, if he didn't take the four hearts right now, Massinov, who almost certainly held the queen of spades, would likely retaliate by sticking him, instead of George Ballantyne, with it, and that would cost thirteen points, or sixty-five cents. "Come on, Joe," the sports editor encouraged him. "Play. It's only money." Joe played the ace of hearts and drew the trick toward him, full of rectitude and sorrow. Then he got out with the seven of hearts.

"Vell, vell." Boris Massinov's carved and mighty Easter Island face curved upward in a mighty beam. "Comes now, ze lady. Comes now ze secret black and midnight hag. Comes now," he declaimed, "ze concubine of Rameses and ze scanted whore of Babylon. Comes now, in short," he held the card aloft, exposing at first only its red back and then by degrees its darkling face in a crescendo of pageantry and suspense, "comes now, in short, ze pisser!"

The queen of spades lay on the table, whispering like an ebony Venus, taunting and squalling like a fishwife. "Dake it, Geortchie!" her sponsor roared. George Ballantyne played the six of hearts.

"Sonnomavitch!" Mr. Massinov cried. "Oh, sonnomavitch!" The sports editor showed out again and the city editor, Mr. Gundarson, played the two of hearts. "Vicked," Mr. Massinov stated. "Vicked, corrupt, debased, debilitatinck, calamitous, cas—vait a minute—cas-cas-castatrophic. Bad."

"That's all for me," George Ballantyne said. "I go."

It always had to be after five. Degrading but holy God! Put the hand upon the silken thigh, let love stay here and stay and stay forever.

"You're such a funny boy," she said.

"Oh, I'm as funny as they come." She stretched and drew him near. "Close. Close. Close."

He was sated, full, therefore, of grace and vengeance.

"You're fantastic," he said to her. "What's *he* think?"

"I won't answer."

"But what *does* he think?"

"Oh, then I'll tell. Put your warm head on my cold breast. Put your cold head on my warm breast. Stay, my dearest, stay."

"I can't. Worse luck, I can't." He had completely forgotten his impulse to be overwhelming and mean.

"Well, then, if you insist. He thinks I'm tall and undefilable. He thinks I'm clean and smooth and harmless like the Winged Victory."

"It's no use. No one ever stays and I can't stay either."

"Now you're thinking about the war again."

"Maybe."

"My hero."

"Not hero. Just around."

Around August 1939. "Listen, Sylvia." He orated like some pompous damn'-fool elocutionist. She had given him three stiff drinks and he'd never been particularly good at holding drinks. "I don't want to fight their war but if they're going to have it anyway I've got to see it. If there's loving to be done I'll love; if there's hating to be done I'll hate; if there's singing I'll sing, if there's crying I'll cry, if there's living I'll live, if there's dying I'll die."

She seemed to recoil a little and beckon him all at once, rather like the queen of spades. "Honest to God, Sylvia," he apologized, following her across the bed, "it's not something I rehearsed. It just came out just this minute."

"You know," she said, "just because I'm eight years older than you dosen't necessarily mean I'm eight years dumber. Just because you're twenty-three and I'm, let's say it, over thirty." She stretched again and yawned. "You asked about him. Well, I'll tell you about him. Little does he realize. There he is running the paper, running the country, keeping you in a job, keeping me in clothes he won't even take the trouble to help me off with. Winged Victory, for heaven's sake, Venus, for that matter, with men like him they'd never get their girdles off. Not that I don't love him and respect him. But as long as we're going to be dwarfed by monuments I've got a monument for him. Mount Rushmore, great yacking faces with their balls invisible in uncut stone."

Quickened again, he was betrayed into another confidence. "Once," he said, "I wrote a poem."

"Oh, tell it to me." She drew near him once more on the wide, clean bed.

"It's not really very good," he said, and put his arms around her.

75

"Oh, but tell it."

"All right.

> "*The mind is lonely and the questing heart*
> *Moves unwanted in the unwanting crowd;*
> *But they are not and cannot be apart—*
> *Affinity shines stubborn from the most neglected shroud.*"

"No matter," she said. "Andrew took the tape recorder to the cottage anyway."

"The thing I like about you," he said, "is that you have such a kindly sense of humor."

"Yes," she said. "Go to sleep, my darling. Go to sleep loving, go to sleep hating, go to sleep singing, crying, living and dying, go to sleep whatever way you said, I'll still be here when you wake up."

"But I wonder if I'll be. Oh, sure I will," he reassured himself. "You've got to quit feeding me drinks," he said. "They make me self-important and maudlin."

It was only four months since he'd ferried his father across the bleak and misty straits between Saltspring Island and Victoria. He stood in the drenching rain and the fog at the gray prow of the *Homer C. Martin*, whoever he was and wherever he'd departed for, and who hadn't the slightest idea it was George Ballantyne, Sr., down below in the box. He had no real thought of how Homer C. Martin would have taken it, but it was a desperate shock to him, George Ballantyne, Jr.

The rain came slanting in. He moved up as far as he could and pressed against the rail, all alone.

"Come out of the rain, Mr. Ballantyne."

George turned and there was the undertaker, right behind him.

"No," he said in alarm, "I'll stay here."

His father had promised to live to the age of four hundred and twelve. "An arbritary figure but you've got to stop somewhere. Maybe four hundred and eleven is enough." And now, at seventy-three, he was down below in the box. "Just said oh," the lady at the rest home said. "We were playing a game of cribbage and he just said oh and died."

And now they were all gone but him and Haig, and what with the cost of higher education even Haig hadn't been able to come and share the voyage of the *Homer C. Martin*. In any case, though his cold and desolate reflections turned often and yearningly on

Haig, it was Hazel who kept swimming and brimming and dancing and prancing and preening and queening up to the top of them every time he'd let her.

You'll never come back, Hazel, will you, even to answer my questions? Has your fair white body been ravished, violated, usurped, sneaked, grabbed, taken in sin? In the name of God, Hazel, where are you? The last immediate memory of her came from the morning of her seventeenth birthday, when he was just past twelve and Haig was nearly seven and he'd crept across the hall after dawn to see if Hazel was awake, and of course she was. Hazel was always awake, her lovely green eyes crinkling and reaching for whatever might happen to happen along.

Her brother George drew toward her beneath the flannel sheet and touched her astonishing marble, freckled shoulder.

"Hazel," he said, "I'm going to start saving up my allowances, I'm going to go out trapping gophers and get a paper route. I'm going to buy you an emerald ring."

"I know."

"I'll get it set with rubies, Hazel."

"I know you will," she said drowsily. Everything was lost on her. There was no being rid of the Vile Intruder; there he was, the absurd, ungrateful little man, with no idea of his stupendous luck, with George's shining fragrant sister waiting for him.

There she was, squirming and sighing at the barest hint of this interloper while her manly brother's rubies and emeralds went unnoticed.

"Hazel," he implored her, "don't go away, don't ever go away."

But away she went, away at seventeen as firm and laughy and bridy as some virgin swallow blown up on a rising wind. The fellow's first name was Jason, which was bad enough. His second name was Malcolm. He had a ghastly little mustache. If Hazel had to desert them, if she absolutely had no choice, it should have been with a man who had a pirate beard and a name like Wotan von Golgotha. Jason Malcolm!

They had only one letter from Hazel, a bright and valiant one from Omaha, and that was the last they ever heard. George sold everything he owned, his bike, his paper route, his baseball glove, a case of his father's beer empties, and forty-three pop bottles he'd collected around town, and ran away from home to find his sister Hazel in Omaha and rescue her from Jason Malcolm. But they stopped him at the border and sent him home again.

Mr. Massinov's party was easily the best he'd ever held. It was in honor of the birthday of his newest girl friend, a plump and pleasing widow who enjoyed the distinction of owning three-eighths of the seventh largest trust company in the Western Hemisphere.

All the wrestlers were there, except the ones occupied in Duluth or Minneapolis—Rodin Gargantua, José, pronounced Hosay, Wilberforce, Snapper Walter Snelgrove, Fatso Cunningham. Each of the wrestlers had brought at least one girl, and José Wilberforce had brought three.

The table was full of stuffed cabbages, *latkes*, lox, chopped liver, meat balls in sour cream, squid in ink, red caviar, bratwurst, knockwurst, liverwurst, diced onion, sliced onion, grape leaves, rice, salami, bologna, shrimp, smoked eels, Polish ham, cabbage salad, potato salad, beet salad, six kinds of cheese, and three roast geese the size of Strangler Lewis.

They had had a good night last Tuesday, and whatever anybody said about Mr. Massinov nobody ever denied he was a sport. For the most part, the wrestlers stormed around the table, growling with delight, ignoring their women to concentrate on the provender; the depression was far from over and the box office wasn't always good.

One of the girls, one of the ones brought by José Wilberforce, sat alone eating *latkes* and staring longingly at George. She weighed a good hundred and eighty-five pounds. Wrestlers tended to get the big ones. But there was no denying that she had a stupendous beauty; her rounded, tulip-flowered dress set her off like a giant pistachio-ice-cream cone.

When her immediate appetite had been subdued, she moved across the room to George's side.

"You're a newspaper fellow, aren't you?" she asked him. "You look more like the intellectual type. These wrestlers give me an insidious pain."

"Insidious?"

"Maybe I mean invidious."

José Wilberforce was glaring at them. His dark Mexican eyes smoked and reeked of homicide. Living dangerously, the *latke*, ice-cream-cone woman whispered, "Down the hall there's a bed as big as a life raft from the *Queen Mary*."

"What about José?" George said back in consternation.

"You're scared, aren't you?"

"I wish I knew."

"Boris told me you're going to the war."

"Who knows if there's even going to *be* a war?"

"Oh, you'll march off to the war all right, bugles playing, flags flying, shrapnel bursting at your feet. But you won't even come down the hall with me."

He stole a nervous glance at José Wilberforce, who had him pinned down with a murderous stare. José weighed two hundred and sixty-four pounds, quite a bit of it muscle.

"I'll be back," he said.

He went to see young Haig and found him gloating as usual over his books. Sophocles, Virgil, Aristotle, Balzac, Shelley, Turner, Toulouse-Lautrec, the whole pounding stampede of them, and him with nothing to worry about except if the left winger of the Winnipeg Monarchs learned to cut to his opposite side or the right fielder of the Winnipeg Maroons could push one to left field or if poor old Joe Wilson was good for one more year with the Winnipeg Blue Bombers. Haig was in his room, a twelve-by-six-foot crypt, with his books scattered knee-deep.

"You didn't have to come, George," Haig said distantly. "You didn't have to go to the war. Go ahead, though, go ahead."

"I'll go if I feel like it. How did you know that's what I came to tell you?"

"You're very predictable, George."

"Haig, we're the only ones left."

"So then?"

"You never knew Hazel, did you?"

"No, I guess not. I was only about eight when she went away, why should I know her?"

"I was twelve. Hazel would be almost thirty now."

"George?"

George waited.

"Was it true that Hazel turned into a tramp? A real round-heeled tramp?"

"You could get into trouble saying that."

"What sort of trouble?"

"I don't want to fight with you, Haig. You never knew Hazel. When Hazel walked down the street, the lousiest street in all of Winnipeg, garlicky grocery stores that wrapped the gefüllte fish in last week's *Free Press*, a red beat-up fire hall and six known convicted cat-houses, when Hazel walked down the street the whole place spread and blossomed like the Champs Élysées. All right, Haig, if you have to say it, go ahead. I've never seen the Champs Élysées."

"And you're going to the war, aren't you, George?"

"If there's a war I'll be there."

"And then there'll only be one of us. Me."

"Oh Haig, your problem's not like mine at all."

"Perhaps it is, George. But I'll tell you one thing about your war. It's wild and idiotic and indecent and I'll never get in it."

George therefore had to attend the recruiting office unsupported and unadmired, or he would have had to except for a last-minute inspiration that took him to the overwhelming, generous ice-cream-cone woman.

"I'll write you," she promised. "It doesn't matter about the others. You can depend on me."

It was now August 28. Although there was still some doubt about there being a war, he thought he'd better not take a chance. He enlisted on the twenty-ninth.

The news was well and generously received. The city editor paid him the eight dollars and forty cents he owed him from the hearts game, and the sports editor promised to pay him another three. Boris Massinov drew on his mysterious sources of income and held another party. All the wrestlers, of course, turned up full of eager hunger and festooned with girls as bright and bouncy as fresh scattered daffodils.

In spite of the temptation, George stuck to Dorothea, the loving ice-cream amazon who'd promised to write to him. His new battle dress scratched and smelled of disinfectant, but she made no complaint.

He had a week's enlistment leave, and on the third day of it a new and appalling complication entered his life. He was still feeling hopeless and defeated about Haig; as head of the family and one of its three survivors, he had been badly disappointed by Haig's negative reaction to his decision to join the Army. It hadn't been a true act of patriotism, but he'd hoped that Haig would at least pretend to be deceived by it. Then, to make matters ineffably worse, he went for late supper again at the Parthenon Restaurant, formerly the Roma, ex the Balkan, earlier the Elite Cafe, before that the Biltmore, the Waldorf, the Olympic, the London, the Paris, the Washington, and the New York.

There were only three booths in the Parthenon, each seating, potentially, four people, but George had never seen another single customer there. This time, although the place was again empty, he received a much warmer greeting than usual.

"My, you look nice," the young waitress said as she brought his usual bacon and eggs. "Some men can wear a uniform and some can't." She had never said a single unnecessary word to him before; this compulsive little torrent was so sad with anxiety and desperation that for the first time he raised his head and looked her squarely in the face. She was not, he realized in sudden pity and alarm, a bit older than Hazel had been when Hazel went away.

"What's your name?" he asked her.

"Vera Rebchuk," she apologized. "I don't have to ask yours. One of the printers who comes in for coffee told me. He told me you were just about the best writer on the paper."

"What is it you want from me, Vera?" He said it anxiously, with a sense that he was summing up some yet unrealized tragedy, describing some geological fault in the uncertain bedrock of his existence. What is it you want from me, my glorious sister Hazel? Emeralds? Rubies? No, George, all I want is Jason Malcolm. What is it you want from me, my little brother Haig? Nothing. Just nothing. What is it you want from me, my father? Only a little ride across the straits on the *Homer C. Martin*, Son; that's all I'll ever want from you again. What can I give you, eager wife of my wicked boss? Just the loan of your strong young body. What do you want from me, O lavish ice-cream woman? Just a walk down the hall and your forwarding address. What is it you want from me, old friend Boris Massinov? A few lines in the paper, Geortchie, we got a sonnomavitch good card next week. And you, Joe Wilson? Just save the pisser for somebody else, George old boy; that's what you can do for me.

She was a remarkably pretty girl, much prettier than he'd realized. She moved cleanly on her clean young limbs. Her hands were red but graceful. He guessed she spent a lot of her time out in the kitchen washing dishes. Her green and beige smock was lightly spattered with odds and ends of grease, and there was a spot of grease on her straight and delicate nose, but he could tell, remembering the lights on Hazel's tumbled drying curls, that her soft brown hair had been washed no longer ago than last night.

"I mean." To his surprise he stammered a little, aware that his first question might have seemed rude. "Well, I didn't mean it that way."

81

"I wish you'd walk home with me tonight," she said gravely, not coquettishly, but putting it as a simple favor.

"Now that I'm in the Army," he said, fencing, "I can't do everything that I'd like to do."

"It's not far," she said, looking over her shoulder in the direction of the kitchen. "I'm through in twenty minutes. You could have another cup of coffee and I could keep it off the check."

"Never mind about the check. You're scared."

"Yes, I am. Please walk home with me."

Her pink fall coat was as hard and practical and cheap and sergy as his battle dress. Her rooming house was barely two blocks away. They talked about the weather.

"You'll come up to my room, won't you?" Her arm was tense on his. "It's on the fourth floor."

"No, I won't." No matter how attractive she was, no matter how melancholy and rejected he'd been feeling, this was just too cold-blooded and abrupt.

"A while ago you told me I was scared. You never asked me why." He stopped her under a street lamp. Small tears were falling down her grave young face, making track marks in the faint powder.

"The reason I asked you to come up," she said, "is that I'm turning pro and I wanted to start with somebody nearer my age, someone I could like."

"Now look here, Vera, that will be enough."

"Mr. Zenith fired me this afternoon. He thought if he fired me I'd have no choice but to go to bed with him. Mr. Rossinov, my landlord, gave me one day's notice yesterday, thinking I'd have no choice but to go to bed with *him*. Mr. Zenith was only paying me two dollars a week and Mr. Rossinov has been charging me two-fifty for my room."

"Now look, Vera, I know about the depression. I know that awful things are going on, but I also know you're making this up."

"How I wish I were."

"Where's your father? Where's your mother?"

"My father's in jail and my mother's disappeared. George, I don't want any money from you. I just want you to start me off so I won't feel so disgusted."

He took her by the shoulders. "Vera," he said, "you're really crying."

"I didn't intend to."

"Vera, where did you go to school? A minute ago you said I wish I were where ninety-nine per cent of the human race would have said I wish I was."

"I think I got habits like that from my father. He had the loveliest hopes for me. By the time I was twelve I could recite every one of the main speeches from *Hamlet*. But then he robbed this bank. He had the ideals of St. Francis but he just couldn't stand being poor."

"St. Francis. Are you a Mick?"

"Well, more or less."

"Hazel," George said.

"Vera," she corrected him.

"I'm sorry, Vera. But anyway you must abandon this notion."

"I answered three want ads this morning. Mr. Zenith, hoping to speed my financial destruction, wouldn't let me use the free phone and it cost my last three nickels. I went to see the relief people and was put off by a terrible woman who said I should come back in ten days and obviously wondered why I wasn't walking the streets like all the other self-respecting girls."

"Vera, how many men have you been with?"

"None," she said, and he saw that he must believe her. "That's why I'd like someone I like to start me off," she added. "I don't think Mr. Zenith ever takes a bath. Mr. Rossinov is huge and besides he's got a cruel streak."

She was still crying, not hysterically or ostentatiously but with gentle resignation.

"Vera, will you marry me?"

He turned and walked her back a block under the darkly fragile Manitoba maples. The slender muscles on her slender arm tugged her away beneath his own.

He didn't dare tell her exactly what was in his mind, because he'd recognized her for a proud and chancy girl, no matter how much fright she had. He'd been on the verge of saying, "I could assign you my dependent's pay. It would be around forty dollars a month. It wouldn't cost me anything."

They walked on under the maple trees, over the cracked and sagging pavement of Smith Street.

"Vera," he said, "there's no one I can write to." He made a silent apology to the lovely ice-cream amazon, but it was Hazel alias Vera Rebchuk who needed rescuing.

Under the next street lamp a girl much like Vera, much like

83

Hazel, stood in her short print dress and her imitation fur, drenched in perfume from the Rexall One-Cent Sale, overwhelmed with hope and terror for what the night would bring to her.

"George," Vera said. "You didn't mean it. You can still come up to my room."

"Vera, how could I ask you to marry me if I didn't mean it?"

"Right in front of a preacher or a magistrate? With a license and a ring?"

"Vera, I forgot to tell you one thing."

"Yes?" she asked, now guarded and aloof again.

"The thing I forgot to say is that I love you." He had heard that younger women put great store in such declarations.

They were married two months before he went away. Their marriage was a great success. Vera had the same instinctive good will as he and considerably more native wisdom. She had not, incredibly, either lied to him or stretched the truth in any degree or any particular. It was George who brought up the subject of her father; she had not mentioned it again, and at first George had been certain that she had, understandably, deceived him on this one point. But after two weeks in their rented bachelor apartment—in the first rush of enlistments George's battalion had been more than glad to have him sleep out—his faith in her had grown so deep that he could say, quite naturally, "Vera, I want to see your father before I go away."

"You're so good, George. Are you sure you want to see him?"

"Have you told him, Vera?"

"Yes, I always tell him any good news I have. I haven't heard back. He's not allowed his next letter until Tuesday."

"Well, I'd like to meet him before I go."

"Are you sure you wouldn't be embarrassed? I don't mind going there, because nobody knows me. But don't you think somebody might recognize you?"

"I've thought of that," George admitted. "If it wouldn't embarrass you or your father it wouldn't embarrass me."

"We can go out and see him on Sunday," she said happily.

In his dark prison clothes Stanley Rebchuk had some of the rueful, appealing spunkiness of the girl George Ballantyne had asked to marry him.

"Don't you worry about Vera, George," he said. "I didn't do much of a job of looking after her before, but I'll be able to do better soon. I still own the farm and when I get out I can sort of crown my career as a jailbird by making a fresh start as a war profiteer."

"Vera's going to be O.K.," George said reassuringly. "So are you, Mr. Rebchuk."

"Wheat will go to three dollars," Vera's father predicted with a hint of pleased remorse. "At that price even I ought to be able to make a living." He was a smallish, wiry man, life-worn though far from beaten. He had Vera's grave dark eyes and the same fleeting smile, a little tentative and wary, but still clinging at the corners to some essential shred of optimism. "Thanks for coming out here with Vera," he said when they were leaving. "Your coming out here tells me all I need to know about you."

"Everything's O.K., Mr. Rebchuk," George said.

He was able to help Vera get a new and reasonably good job taking classified ads at the paper. With the help of her dependent's allowance Vera estimated she'd be able to start buying furniture and saving for a house at the rate of fifty dollars a month. George insisted that as soon as her father was released—the exact time still lay within the province of the parole board—she must rent a larger place and take care of him until she was absolutely sure he was ready to go back to the farm. By the time he left for Halifax their marriage, launched in so slapdash and scatterbrained a way, had begun to build a foundation of memories, plans, and minor in-law problems. They were even talking about the number, sex, and names of their children. If he had the chance, George thought even amid the excitement of his impending departure for the war, he might just cancel his enlistment papers.

Haig came to dinner with them on George's last night at home. Haig, the student, had so low an opinion of his older brother's world and means of livelihood that George had been afraid he'd take an active dislike to Vera if only through force of habit and, more seriously, show it. This had been a bad guess. Haig seemed drawn to her as swiftly and inevitably as he had been drawn himself. In spite of Haig's shallow attempts to expel their departed sister Hazel from the fragile remnant of their family, George persisted in the feeling that he remembered Hazel better than he would admit. Perhaps Vera brought back echoes for him too.

"For the last time, George," Haig said, taking a swig of beer out of the neck of the bottle while Vera completed the six steps from the kitchen alcove to the living-dining-bedroom table, "Vera does not remind me of Hazel. She's much better looking for one thing. You hear that, Vera? You're twice as beautiful as Hazel ever was."

"Oh, *I* know that," George said.

"George is very sentimental," Haig said forgivingly. "Some people would call him an outright slob. Not me. But some people would. It's the company he keeps." He sat back, preparing to elaborate. "I saw that dressing-room story the other day about the last game of the baseball play-offs. The part where our pitcher was unable to speak through his pent-up tears kind of got me. I also liked the part where that guy from Fargo attributed his home run to divine aid."

"Now listen," George protested. "You know damned well I didn't write that bloody piece. It was the managing editor's nephew."

Haig went on bantering. There was sometimes an edge of meanness or superiority when he got on to George about his never-never world and the glossy, panting women and the sweaty, sobbing men who seemed to be its chief inhabitants. But it wasn't like that on this night. Haig let his affection for his brother show as plainly and unabashedly as though they were boys again trapping gophers or picking chokecherries in the valley outside their village in Saskatchewan. More surprisingly still, he permitted himself a brief display of esteem.

"George," he said quietly when Vera was cleaning up the dishes, "I hope you've forgotten the way I shot off my mouth that night."

"It didn't bother me," George said untruthfully. "Everything you said about the war is right. But I can't stay away and that's that."

"You always liked to be in the middle of things, didn't you?" Haig said wistfully. "Me, I guess I was meant to be a monk or a mad trapper or a section hand on the C.P.R."

"What *will* you be, Haig? A writer?"

"Maybe, if I'm lucky."

"Tried anything?"

"A little poetry. Nothing's turned out yet."

George hesitated. He was on the verge of letting it drop that he'd attempted some poetry himself. Maybe he'd even find a means of working in the verse he'd tried on Sylvia Logan, the wayward wife of his wicked boss.

Affinity shines stubborn from the most neglected shroud.

Sylvia hadn't seemed to get it, but perhaps Haig would. He hesitated a moment longer and the moment was lost.

"I guess I'll be drafted anyway in a year or two," Haig said. "I see they're talking in Ottawa about some kind of compulsory training."

"We'll never have conscription," George said. "In 1917 it had us on the verge of civil war, or at least a lot of people pretended it had."

"Yes," Haig said. "We're a queer, acrimonious, disputatious people, aren't we? Some of us actually object to getting killed in other people's wars. It's supposed to be the French in us. In my case it must be the Irish."

"Haig, I hope you're not going to explain yourself to me, are you? It's wholly unnecessary."

Haig made a halfhearted attempt to work up an argument. He saw by the papers, he said, that they were more concerned about him than George was. He saw by the papers that those irresponsible college kids in England and in Canada and elsewhere were still a little slow about withdrawing those irresponsible resolutions about refusing to die for King and Country. He saw by the papers that there was to be a big mass recruiting rally at the Amphitheatre Rink, and the speakers would include such burning but ineligible patriots as Alderman—no Alderwoman—Elizabeth Partridge, the Reverend Homer J. Witherspoon, Coach Monty Mayerling of the Deer Lodge Titans, E. Q. Winslow, president of the Board of Trade, B. G. Smathers, presi—

"Stow it, Haig," George said. "Let's have another beer."

Haig had classes the next day and didn't come to the train. Nobody was supposed to know where the train was going, but of course everybody did. It was an old and famous regiment and half the city was out to see it off, security or no security. George's own personal *bon voyage* party was a large and liquid one, a bee-loud glade in a forest of children in new suits, women in new hats, men in new uniforms, and bagpipers.

Sylvia Logan arrived early with a jeroboam of champagne under one arm and her husband, George's wicked boss, on the other.

"Good old Mount Rushmore thought it was just a grand idea to come and see you off in person," Sylvia shouted in George's ear.

"What's that, Sylvia?" George's wicked boss shouted. "Mrs. Logan has had quite a few drinks already," he bawled apologetically at George.

"Very good of you both to come down, sir," George shouted.

"Probably some whimsical association"—a corporal and his girl, singing, thrust in between them—"probably some whimsical association," George's boss bawled, "between Mount Rushmore and our own Mount Logan."

"He's really a dear," Sylvia shouted. "Here, dear, open the champagne so we can drink George's health."

Boris Massinov, Joe Wilson, Mr. Gundarson, and Mr. Malloy arrived in a group with a joint presentation. It was a steel engraving of the queen of spades inscribed on the back: To Adolf. With the compliments of George of Ballantyne and the Winnipeg Chronicle Hearts and Hootch Society. They also gave him, to be retained by himself, a silver flask and a silver cigarette lighter.

Dorothea, the ice-cream woman, swept down the platform with José Wilberforce. And just behind them, in from Duluth a day ahead of time, were Rodin Gargantua, Snapper Walter Snelgrove, and Fatso Cunningham, each accompanied by a friend. George introduced them severally and separately to Vera, who, though dwarfed, refused to be overwhelmed. She stuck close to George's side, and every time he was compelled to kiss one of the other women, Vera made sure that he kissed his wife right afterward.

"Now that I've lost you," Dorothea shouted, sneaking in an opulent hug, "I think I'm going to marry José." José gave George a let-bygones smile, not altogether sincere.

"José wants to join the Army too," Dorothea yelled in George's ear. "But he's still a Mexican citizen and they won't take him."

"Besides," Boris Massinov added, "I owe José twelve hundred dollars, and if he runs out on me now he doesn't get a cent. Good wrestlers are going to be scarce."

"I never did trust them Germans," José shouted, passing the champagne. "I wrestled that Bruno Schmidt fourteen times and every time he was supposed to be trying to gouge my eyes out. The fifteenth time the son-of-a-bitch turned ugly and really did try to gouge my eye out. They're a very untrustworthy race."

The bagpipers burst, with a reedy despair almost beyond enduring, into the air of "Auld Lang Syne" and posses of NCOs turned suddenly on the lesser ranks to cajole, threaten, and finally thrust them bodily into the waiting colonist cars. When the train pulled out, he missed Vera at first in the giant redwood forest of the wrestlers, but at the last moment José Wilberforce grasped her waist and bore her upward into his full and tender view. He found

88

it comforting that Vera was weeping too, the same as he was and everyone else except a few of the more calloused NCOs.

Like most of the Canadian Army, George Ballantyne spent the next two years in a state of non-war. Dunkirk came and went, depriving the land forces of Britain and the Dominions of their only ally and their chosen arena of combat. The Canadian Army Overseas deployed, redeployed, practiced, and dug in to defend the South of England against an invasion that never came. Its great crusade dissolved into a procession of redundancies: an eternity of pub crawls, an infinity of inspections, parades, and exercises, a bottomless cornucopia of sausage rolls, seed cakes, mashed potatoes, Spam and Brussels sprouts, an amplitude of smiling, warm-hearted women. It was not an unpleasant or a particularly dangerous life, but it was a desperately uncheckered one. During his first twenty-four months in England, the most memorable event of George Ballantyne's military career was being narrowly missed by an incendiary bomb while coming to grips in Green Park, London, with a lorry driver named Pamela.

He suffered about equally from the pains of continence and the pangs of remorse. In one of his darkest and guiltiest moods he wrote Vera releasing her from her marriage vows. She wrote back calmly that she intended to keep her marriage vows as long as she could, adding that if she found she couldn't she would not make it any worse by telling him, at least while he was still away. George marveled once more that of all the one billion seven hundred ninety-four million female humans in the world—he worked the figure out with the help of an encyclopedia in a Salvation Army hostel—he had found the only one with an unforgettable body, a pure, forgiving heart, and a boundless store of common sense.

He depended on Vera almost exclusively for news from home, and her news was almost always good and cheerful. Her father was released from the penitentiary in the spring, in time to get a new crop in. Haig thought he'd done pretty well with his exams, although the results wouldn't be out until midsummer. In the meantime Haig had found a job helping one of his professors do research for a new book on Paul Kane, the artist. He was going steady with a "really brilliant and beautiful" premedical student, the daughter of a well-to-do grain broker. Except for cards on his birthday and at Christmas, George had no direct communication from Haig; their try at parting in the easy intimacy of their boyhood had come unstuck. George still couldn't get over the idea that Haig needed him. But what, precisely was the need? How precisely could it be filled? The narrowest part of the gulf between them, George had to tell himself, was the geographical part. It was the same with the gulf between him and Hazel. It was less a matter of distance than of some impalpable, untraceable failure of communications. He had to admit it, but he still refused to be resigned to it. Every time Haig's name leaped up at him from Vera's letters, it was like the lament of the bagpipes at the station, poignant, elusive, and gently edged with accusation.

"Haig's been called up for his month's training," she wrote near the end of his second winter away. "He's been given a deferment until the end of the university year and he'll be able to go back to university again in the fall."

Then, almost immediately: "They've extended Haig's call-up period to four months." And soon after that: "It looks as if Haig's in for the duration. They've made the reserve permanent. He says he'll be posted to a coastal defense unit or a training camp on permanent fatigue. He's a little disappointed but seems to be taking it in stride. He says to tell you not to worry about him getting into trouble. He says all that campus talk about hiding out in the Northwest Territories or the Rockies or the Laurentians was never more than another college stunt, like signing petitions from the Oxford Group and swallowing live goldfish. Haig says he still has a very low opinion of the whole idiotic business and won't get into it any deeper than they make him. But he'll obey the law. He'll do what the law orders him to do, no more, no less. Barbara Ransome—I don't know whether I told you that's his girl's name—is with him a hundred per cent. I don't blame her, either. Haig's attitude wouldn't do for you, but for him I think it's absolutely right and absolutely sincere and absolutely decent. If you could feel the climate developing here you'd also see that it's taken some courage. Try to understand him, George. I think it's going to be very hard on him before it's over."

Vera gave him Haig's new army address and his new army number. But through some compulsion of delicacy or self-consciousness he continued to send his own short and infrequent letters to Haig's last civilian address.

Later in the summer, he had a brief note from the city editor, Mr. Gundarson. "We're doing a roundup on the reaction of the overseas army to the zombies. CP's carried a little stuff and our bureau man has taken a pass at it. But I'd like an honest opinion from somebody in the Army, somebody I know myself. We won't quote you by name and I'm not asking you to break any rules; just give me a slant on the zombies as they look from your corner."

George cabled Gundarson collect: "Who are the zombies query never heard of them."

Gundarson's air letter had more details. "I'd forgotten that the papers and radio aren't using the word yet but it's become an everyday part of the spoken language. A zombie is a reserve draftee who refuses to volunteer for overseas. The Government's discovered again that it can't maintain a big, autonomous Canadian Army without some form of draft. But Quebec, just as in 1917, won't stand still for overseas conscription. So we're drafting the young guys ostensibly for home defense. But once the Army gets them in uniform it starts working on them to 'volunteer' for service anywhere. Some genius thought of calling them zombies—the Army's walking dead. This cute little gimmick alone has shamed or bullied a lot of the reserves into going active. The whole deal is compromise, hypocrisy, and hokeypokey in the highest tradition of Mackenzie King. If it works we'll have all the military advantages of conscription with none of the political disadvantages. If it doesn't we could be heading for another God-awful mess, both military *and* political, the same kind as in 1917. What I'm interested in right now is how much talk there's been over there about the zombie issue. To put it briefly, how much bitching do you hear or do yourself about the reluctant dragons back home?"

It wasn't a difficult question to answer and George answered it promptly. "Of course we're conscious of the zombies over here, even though the name for them is new. (Very ingenious, also.) There's no strong feeling either for them or against them or in fact about them. After a year, two years over here—even longer for the first contingent—everybody thinks we've got too many troops already and too damned little action. Let the bloody reserves, or R-men, or zombies queue up and take their turn. We don't need them. And a lot of us, given another guess, would be zombies too. What the hell use have we been to anybody, sitting on our asses in Sussex anyway? We'd be just as well off at home too. I hear the whisky's holding out better there and they still light fires in the winter and turn on the street lamps at night and serve steaks in the restaurants.

"P.S.: I guess you didn't know I've got a younger brother in the

Army. I hear he's an R-man—excuse it, zombie. I don't know how I'd feel if a real tough shooting war happened to bust out again. But right now all I'd say to him is: More power to you, boy. Don't panic. Don't let them stampede you. Stick to your empty guns till hell freezes over."

George's third spring in England blossomed with the yearned-for scent of danger. America was in the war now, Russia was in the war now, the mighty aerial display called the Battle of Britain was over and won and many hundreds of millions of people—including many hundreds of thousands destined to die thereon—were demanding the Second Front.

George's division was rushed from the green downs of Sussex to the rhododendron roadways, rocky beaches, and tall cliffs of the Isle of Wight. It submerged its identity in a new being called Simmerforce and committed its future to a pending event called Operation Rutter. For two months Simmerforce and Rutter coiled and gathered. The rumors coiled and gathered, the frustrations coiled and gathered, the death hunger coiled and gathered, the life hunger coiled and gathered. The men of Simmerforce and Rutter obtained new Sten guns, new rifles, new rubber life belts, new shoes, new bullets, new hand grenades, and, for the extremely lucky ones, new girls. They raced across the stony beaches, clambered up the rocky cliffs, panted down the slender roadways, clawed through the clutching rhododendrons, ducked beneath the tracer fire of Bren guns manned by former friends. They never ceased their cursing, but this new thing by God at last was getting close to It.

On a June night they were loaded in their assault boats. George had acquired a new best friend, a small but muscular excontender for the professional lightweight boxing championship of Canada. His name was Slade O'Brien. Slade was a sardonic little man and just barely bearable. His favorite boast was that he had once fought ten rounds with Jimmy McLarnin, lost every round, and never got hit. "Well," Slade O'Brien said when they were jammed into their flat-bottomed Landing Craft Personnel on this June night, "Well. It looks as if they've finally carried this too far."

The assault boat went rolling out to sea, pitching and yawing and dipping and heaving. Excluding the two navy men in charge of the navigation, there were twenty men aboard and six of them were very seasick. Of the fourteen others, three got down low beneath the bulkheads to comfort the afflicted and the eleven others stood up with their guns pointed at whatever might come.

Just at dawn, beautifully timed, the boat jammed into the shale. "Cease fire!" someone bawled. They were back on the Isle of Wight. They dragged up past the rhododendrons to their huts.

This was exercise Yukon. Ten days later, armed once more, fed once more, briefed once more, they put forth upon the Channel again and returned once more to the Isle of Wight. This was Yukon Two. Then there was Klondike One. Then, and no one knew the difference until it was too late for making jokes, there was Operation Jubilee. The target of Jubilee was the small French city of Dieppe.

George Ballantyne reached Dieppe by many accidents. On the way across the channel the fragile, thin-skinned vessel he was riding in got lost, as so many of the others did. They were supposed to touch down on Green at H plus five minutes, but they floundered onto Blue at H plus thirty-five. The more prompt men were all lying at the edge of the water or up on the first edge of the beach. Most of them were perfectly still. They were dead, well and truly dead, and that was that. A few others kept reaching at the morning light, stretching their curved and stricken hands. Some crawled toward the gray breakwater where there was protection from the noisy demands of the machine guns on the cliffs above. Some quit and waited for the Germans in the shooting gallery at the top of the cliffs to do whatever they wanted to do. Some ran ahead, straight at the cliffs and their tiny crevices, straight at the wire, straight at the machine guns. Of this tiny some, an even tinier few broke through into the streets and fields behind the cliffs, and George was one of them. George was beyond the beach, with the plain ahead and the strewn red rocks and the blooded, wired sand behind, the pitched corpses in good array, the ruined little boats of the ruined little fleet caught between the hidden mines and the distant inland guns, the ruined boats lurching, wallowing, charging, fleeing, exploding, sinking—and now and then one of them breasting the choppy gun-metal waves as high and gallant as Nelson's *Victory*. His mind was white and swaying, his ears almost deaf, his eyes almost blind. He fell face down into a patch of brush just above the lip of the headland.

"Take it easy!" Slade O'Brien shouted right behind him. George swung around. He still had his Sten gun. The noise of the killing below them on the beach was partly shut out by the cliff, but O'Brien still had to raise his voice. "Take it easy, George," he shouted. The closest other sound came from a German pillbox less than a hundred yards to their right. The forward slit of the pillbox looked down on the beach, but there was no opening on the landward side. Hidden by the gorse and on its flank, George and Slade O'Brien crouched watching. The contest between the gun above and the men below had a curious fascination for them. In the hour since they had discovered each other there had been much learning on both sides. The Canadians pinned down on the sand had learned not to waste their movements or their risks. The Germans firing on them from above had learned not to waste their ammunition or their chances. Most of the Canadians pinned and ambushed on the beach were bent on getting from the medium-sized rock they were sheltering behind to a much better-sized rock thirty or forty feet away. Every now and then one of them, driven by claustrophobia or the crack of bullets against the smaller rock or by a mortar blast or by some wild vision of reviving the spent and wrecked attack, would sprint out into the clear, making a break for the larger rock. Each time the machine gun on the cliff above hit him and he fell and died.

"Where do you think we are?" Slade O'Brien shouted into George's ear as they crouched together in the gorse at the top of the cliff.

"I don't know."

"Those navy sonsabitches! They not only got us on the wrong beach, I bet they got us on the wrong God-damn' continent."

"I think those are the Royals down there! I got a look at some of them on the way up. They're not our guys and they're not the South Sasks. They must be either the Royals or the Hamiltons."

"Christ! If it's the Royals we're four miles from where we should be."

"Did the rest of our guys make it from the boat?"

"I don't think so. When I came up I only saw one other of our guys besides you. It was Cookie Wallace. He was floating and I made a grab for him but he was gone. When I saw you running up the path I went after you. You looked as if you knew some-thing."

"Listen, O'Brien." George had got his breath back now. Things were sorting out and he was under the merciless obligation to think. "We've got to get that gun."

"What gun?" O'Brien shouted, as if gun was a word he'd never heard before.

"The one right over there."

"The gun in the pillbox there?"

"Yes!" George shouted. "We'd better see if we can get it. I don't think those guys down there know what's coming at them."

"They'd be perfectly all right if they'd just stay still." Another man ran out from the shelter of the rock. The gun hammered at him and he fell down in the shadow of the rock. "See?" O'Brien cupped one hand around George's ear. "They're just stupid, that's all. Just plain God-damn' stupid."

"I've got two grenades left." George's hand now made an ear-trumpet for O'Brien. "One of us can go and roll a grenade through the slit. And the other one can be behind him with the Sten in case they come out."

"Look, George." Already they had devised a sort of expertise in communication. They traded ears and cupped hands as easily as radio broadcasters trading a microphone. "I think they've hit everybody down there anyway. I don't think there's anybody left."

"No, there are lots of them left. Come on, Slade. What do you want to do? Take the grenade or take the Sten."

"I haven't got either one. I lost everything when the boat went down."

"That's all right." George thrust the gun forward in one hand and one of his grenades in the other.

"Go and get yourself some stripes, George!" O'Brien yelled below the hollow of his palm. "Get yourself a pip or two. I don't take orders from *every* son-of-a-bitch that comes along."

O'Brien was weakening and they both knew it. "Jesus Christ, George," he implored, but he looked at the pillbox carefully and appraisingly. "Well, then," he yelled, "let's toss a coin."

George pulled out a penny. "You call it!"

"Heads. Heads you go in first. Tails I go in first."

"Here she goes." They were crouched so low that the penny turned only once before it lay in the grass, tails up.

"Two out of three." O'Brien and his voice already seemed to have receded a little. It was the same voice calling from the same improvised cave and yet it was not the same.

"Balls to that, O'Brien. Go on, I'll cover you."

It was a short distance. Everything on the headland was focused so intently on the beach and the killing that they made only the most perfunctory attempt to use the gorse as cover. Once he had accepted his fate, O'Brien took the grenade in his right hand and ran straight toward the back of the pillbox, like a boy racing into very cold water for the first swim of the year, bent on getting wet before he loses his nerve. George kept ten or twenty feet behind. Fifty feet away O'Brien pulled out the pin. Then in the last two or three strides he swung out in front of the open firing slit and rolled the grenade straight in. But his count had been too fast. It was a good two seconds before the grenade went off and in the last of the two seconds a startled German swung the Spandau down and chopped Slade O'Brien in two. George fired the Sten back across O'Brien's body, but the grenade beat him to it. From inside the pillbox there was a big quick flat metallic whang, like a Twenty-fourth of May firecracker exploding under a tin can.

George crawled around Slade O'Brien into the shallow, smoking fortress. The two Germans had been killed cleanly, much less messily than Slade O'Brien, and their Spandau seemed to be undamaged. When he got in behind it he saw that it was too big to carry and from here there was nothing to fire at except the Canadians pinned down between the waterline and the cliff below or at the broken little boats struggling aimlessly in the sea beyond. A pair of binoculars hung from the neck of one of the two dead Germans, his new and only companions. George took the binoculars off, spent a minute adjusting them and reflecting, from the size of the adjustment he had to make, that their former owner must have had great trouble with his eyes. The morning haze had lifted now. Someone from somewhere far off had thrown some smoke shells in and the smoke billowed up the cliffsides and drifted back toward the sea. Artillery and mortar bursts leaped up at the edge of the water, one at a time, two at a time, then a spray of twenty or more all falling far away into the waves.

There was a low white building below and far to the left. He'd been briefed on Dieppe twice, once in June when they hadn't come, and now in August when they had. He recognized the building as the Dieppe Casino. He recognized the curving, alabaster, tomb-colored sea wall and he recognized the black rectangles of the tanks stalled and shattered below its shadow. The glasses would not pick up anything more detailed. He knew, at last and at least, where he was. His own battalion was somewhere irreducibly distant. It was past the headland, past the casino, invisible and lost.

He was extremely tired. He wasn't frightened any longer, he was just tired. It seemed as if he hadn't slept for a year and he needed to sleep now. There were no more Germans that he could see up here, and if he wanted to get back into the fighting there didn't seem to be any way except to go back down the cliff. It occurred to him that it would be a good and decent thing to bring Slade O'Brien in, to bring him in from the ground and place him in the shelter of the pillbox, to give Slade, an honest and honestly cowardly man, some kind of honest burial in the place where he had come to die. But he didn't. He went to sleep.

He slept beside the two dead Germans for an hour or more. Then he got up and crawled through the hole in the pillbox and looked around the ground outside. The distant noises had not diminished, nor had the close-in silences. There were fewer boats and most of those that could be seen were trying to get away from the reaching shellbursts. On the beach straight below, the beach where he and Slade O'Brien had decided the Royals were, there was now no sign of life at all.

He decided to go inland. Maybe he'd find something else. Maybe he'd find another Canadian or a Limey. Maybe some kindly Kraut would tell him to put his hands up and press bread and cigarettes upon him and put him in a cage and let him sleep forever.

He came to a crossroad and a sign pointed to the landward side. Puits, it said; Dieppe, it said; Berneval, it said. While he was studying the sign, drunk with exhaustion and the first symptoms of a modern ailment he had not yet heard of under its modern name, an ailment called battle fatigue, he sank down in the ditch beside the road. A fight was going on overhead, a lot of Spitfires against a few Messerschmitts. Every now and then someone's plane threw back a trail of black smoke and went pounding down into the sea. George found this of small consequence. He had no way of knowing for certain, even with the help of the binoculars, whether the plane that went down was his or theirs and even if it was his the end was quick and soaring and cleansed with wind, a mile up in the air, far away from the spilled unseemly guts of Slade O'Brien. He envied all creatures of the air.

He walked down the road. He checked his Sten gun and reloaded it. His briefing on the sealed boat had been marvelously explicit. Cross the beach, delouse the mines, go up the path (clearly shown here in the appendix), seize and wreck the mortar battery, shoot the sonsabitches up, back to England by blackout time.

I've got sixpence,
Jolly jolly sixpence,
I've got sixpence
To last me all my life
I've got sixpence to lend
And sixpence to spend
And sixpence to send home to my wife.
My eyes are dim, I cannot see, I cannot place my trust in thee—
I've got sixpence to lend—

But his briefing had made no allowance for this especial predicament. His battalion was miles away, lost behind the smoke and the far-off headland. He could report to the Royals, but in spite of the deadly feat of Slade O'Brien, there did not appear to be any Royals left. Even with the Spandau stopped no one was moving from the small rock to the bigger rock, and the few boats left in sight had overcome their indecision and were fading back toward the shore of England. He walked on to the edge of a village and lay down again under the shoulder of a ditch. It was only then that he discovered he'd been wounded in the arm. It must have happened when he'd come across the beach. The flesh at the back of his upper arm was torn away and the bone had been hit. There wasn't much bleeding, though, and his field dressing stopped what there was.

When the dressing was in place and the bleeding had stopped he lay resting in the green ditch. He lay there for perhaps half an hour, and then he got up and went toward the village. At the first house, a house half hammered down and smoking from an artillery shell, a little girl stood and greeted him in the yard. She was small, fair-haired, not more than six, wearing a dress of the kind that, in Saskatchewan, would have been instantly recognized as a former flour sack.

The little girl was crying, but she stood with her feet apart in the middle of the yard. The house had stopped burning and the thick stone wall around it offered another place of refuge, but the little girl stood there where she was.

"*La mère est morte,*" she sobbed at him, desolate but not yielding her ground. George had some high-school French and some St. Boniface bootlegger's French and he thought he understood. "The sea is dead," he translated.

"*Vous êtes Allemand,*" the little girl said.

"No," George said. "*Pas Allemand. Canadien. Anglais.*"

"*La mère est morte. La mère était très belle. Très, très, belle. On a tué la mère.*" His ear responded to the child's slow and careful phrasing. Obviously she had been accustomed to speaking slowly to *les Allemands.* The mother is dead. The mother was very beautiful. Very, very beautiful. They have killed the mother.

"*Triste,*" George floundered. "*Très, très triste.*" He took her by the hand and led her back into the house. He found a root cellar, made sure it wasn't burning or about to burn, went upstairs and gathered an armful of blankets, and went back into the cellar and bundled the little girl into a corner. "*Restez,*" he said. "Stay here."

"*J'ai peur, monsieur.*" The little girl, buried in the blankets, fixed him with one brown, regretful eye. "*J'ai beaucoup de peur.*"

"*Aussi,*" George reassured her. "I have fear. I have much of fear. *Mais fait rien, fait rien,* young buttercup. It's nothing. *Restez.*"

"*Pourquoi restez? Pourquoi pas reste? Vous ne m'aimez pas.*" The little girl was crying with a deeper desolation than before. "I do like you," George said. "I like you more than anybody in the world. I'm just no good at French. *Je ne parle pas bien français.*" He'd committed a graceless sin, created an awful turbulence in the mind of the child who wanted so much to trust him. He'd been talking to her formally, like a distant formal adult.

He put his hand on the top of the blankets. Her one visible eye looked straight up at him. "*Il faut partir,*" he said. "*Je suis Georges Ballantyne. Dans le temps*"—her one brown eye was closed now and it didn't matter anyway—"in the times ahead you must remember that I was George Ballantyne, I came here and got everything bitched up, I got onto the wrong beach, I won a toss and killed my best friend, I lost my regiment, all the things I thought I'd do I didn't do; *j'ai peur,* buttercup, but I am, was and will be George Ballantyne and please don't think badly of me."

Both the little girl's eyes were open. "*J'ai entendu, Georges,*" she said. It had become very noisy again. Another battery of eighty-eights had begun searching for the beach, but there was no prospect of hitting it. The cliff was too steep and the shells either hit the headlands or dropped into the sea among the drifting little boats. Right above them, a Spitfire, caught from behind by an ME-109, dived for the earth and tried to pull out but tried too late.

The noise of the fight between the Spitfire and the 109 brought George into the middle of the yard. He had decided to go along the high ground and try to find his battalion. That was what his instructions said he must do in a situation like this, and although the instructions seemed totally and implacably insane, they were the last thing he had to lean on. The beach was gone, the boats were going, Slade O'Brien was chopped in two on his own, George Ballantyne's, advice and insistence, the only guns still shooting were the guns of a fat and faceless undescribable enemy hidden in caves and concrete, taking long, leisurely pulls on Turkish cigarettes, sipping Moselle out of gleaming stem glasses, throwing chicken bones over their shoulders, polishing their monocles like those phony German movie actors and every now and then decreeing, rather languidly, "Fire!" George decided to go down the top of the cliff toward the main part of the city.

First he went inside the house again, down the stairs into the root cellar where he had left the little girl. She was wide awake beneath the blankets. "*Allo, Georges,*" she said tremulously. "*Allo, Georges Ballantyne.*"

"That's good," George said. "That's perfect." He opened the deep pocket on the thigh of his battle dress and took out his pay book and the stub of a pencil. "*Le nom?* I'll write to you."

"*Marcelle,*" she said a little shyly. "*Marcelle Dansereau. L'adresse est Puits.*"

"That's a good name, Marcelle. See, I'm putting it down. I'll write to you when I get back home and then you can write to me." She understood him perfectly. "*Oui, Georges,*" she said. He pulled the blankets up and left her looking after him with one eye.

He moved down the headland as fast as he could. He tried to sustain himself in bitterness. Balls to Simmerforce, balls to Rutter, balls to Yukon One and Yukon Two and balls to Klondike, and balls, most mightily, to Jubilee. He came to another house and went in from the back. He had his second grenade left, but he remembered Marcelle Danserau. "*Allo!*" he shouted. The place was empty. Up here he could find neither foe nor friend. He decided that he might as well go back to the beach.

A new complication set in. Getting back to the beach was as hard as getting away from it. The daggerbush of wire that he'd struggled through once already was as quick to strike and grab on the way down as on the way up. It clutched at his battle dress and tore through to the flesh, and once it brought him sprawling on the warm body of a man so freshly dead that new blood was still trickling across his forehead and down his cheek. The heavy machine guns from behind chopped all around him, the mortars broke everywhere and the eighty-eights searched out to sea among the few remaining boats.

He got, nevertheless, to the edge of the water, amid the screams of the men calling for some final shred of comfort from their girls and mothers and priests and gods. All he had to do, now, was find a boat. There was, miraculously, a boat right there. The tide was going out and the little sledlike landing craft was jammed on the rocks and swaying against a three-cornered iron mine stake. A dozen or more soldiers were trying to push it free. They were up to their shoulders in the water, pushing desperately at the boat to get it back afloat but also holding on to it so that if it did start drifting off they'd be able to climb aboard before it escaped from them.

George ran into the sea and reached the boat just in time to help with the final sobbing heave. He tried to pull himself over the gunwale, but someone already there put a boat hook at his face. "Get away!" the man behind the boat hook screamed, holding the dark lance of wood and iron steady.

"Get away!" a man beside him in the water shouted. "This is our boat."

A ranging eighty-eight chopped into the water just to their left and another hit the water to the right. "Watch out!" George shouted, and fell over on his back and started kicking toward the beach. The third shot from the eighty-eight hit the boat square on. It was the last boat left.

George had a sudden surge of strength and confidence. He'd outguessed them all, the proprietors of the boat and the boat's destroyers. He remembered his father's fine and happy boast that he'd live to be four hundred and twelve. He, George Ballantyne the younger, mightn't get that far, but he would get beyond this day and absolutely no fooling.

When he reached the sand again, he sat down calmly and took off all his clothes. The shelling had begun to thin out; now that the final boat had gone from this part of the beach there were no economically sound targets left. George walked into the sea and started swimming. Behind the smoke screen out ahead there must be other, more hospitable boats. His wounded arm seemed to be all right, but he didn't want to risk opening the wound again and he swam on his back, using the other arm and his feet. Staying afloat was no problem in the heavy water, but he stopped a drifting body, removed its rubber life belt, wrapped it around his shoulders, and struck out once more. He had always been a durable swimmer, though not a fancy one, and now that this surge of adrenaline and angry determination had subdued his exhaustion and his fear he felt no need of making calculations. He'd just go on swimming. He was past the drowned and battered boats, past the great dangerous shoulder of the headland, past the immense white tombstone of the Dieppe Casino. Another body floated by, even though he was now far out. George swam over and took off its lifebelt too, so that he now had two of them. He felt no emotion about taking the life belt away, but when the dead man stayed afloat it was impossible not to feel good for him too.

He was not going as fast as he'd hoped to. The water was colder and more choppy. Even with the two life belts it kept lapping over his face. The sun was now far past noon. He'd sworn not to bother about this kind of arithmetic, but it was hard to avoid guessing how many hours might be left till dark. It was impossible to hold his head entirely clear of the cold caressing waves for more than a few seconds at a time, but swimming on his back all the time now he had developed a drill that served almost as well. Watch for wave; hold breath; breathe quick. Watch for wave; hold breath; breathe quick. Watch, breathe, watch, breathe, watch. It demanded immense concentration, for the waves had no set rhythm and each little cycle had to be judged and carried out separately. Once he closed his eyes and took the next breath from habit, just after the last wave had passed on across his face. Instantly another one darted in and filled his mouth and nose and half his stomach with a bitter, strangling douche of salt. Gasping, retching, and fighting for air, he floundered at the sea, beating the waves back with his fists while he lifted his head high enough to get four or five quick lungfuls before he sank back again, very weak but still conscious. He did not risk closing his eyes again.

His hurt arm was very sore. He was less certain. Maybe they've got me after all. Oh no they haven't. He summoned all the people he'd ever known to come now and bear witness to George Ballantyne's need for maintaining his vigil against the sea. Summoned his father riding away from Saltspring Island on the *Homer C. Martin*. Watch, breathe. Watch, my son. Breathe, my son. Summoned his young brother Haig. Watch, George. Breathe, George. I've never told you, but I'm in trouble. I need you. Summoned his lost sister Hazel. Watch, breathe, watch, breathe. Honest, George, I never really left you. Summoned old Boris Massinov. Vatch, Geortchie, for God's sake, Geortchie, vatch. Summoned the ice-cream woman and summoned the wife of his wicked boss. Watch, breathe, watch, breathe. And above them all he summoned young Vera Rebchuk. Watch, breathe, watch, breathe, watch, breathe, if you don't come back what will I ever do? watch, breathe, watch, breathe. In spite of his earlier resolve he tried to cheat again and close his eyes and another big wave hit him and he got a big lungful of water. He floundered over, face down, righted himself somehow, miraculously got a breath of air between the next two waves, stared in puzzled recognition at the pitching sky above him, rolled over again, got more water, fought back, and got his head up for more air, saw the sky racing and plunging and falling away, then another wave, and then he didn't much care what he saw next.

Then he heard a shout from very near. "Come on over here!"

"No." With a last effort he lifted his head again and croaked back resentfully, "You come over here."

A little rowboat, an incongruous survivor of the mighty fleet of the earlier morning, hovered in the upended space between the sea and the sky. "Come over here," a strained, blackened, and very ragged soldier yelled at him across the edge of the boat. "I'm over here," George mumbled through another wave. The boat drew up beside him.

"Give me your hand," the soldier shouted.

"I don't think you can lift me all that way," George mumbled. "It doesn't matter anyway."

"Give me your hand!" the soldier yelled. George put up his hand as far as he could and the soldier strained and groaned and dragged him in. George fell on the bottom of the rowboat and lay there feeling the waves still trying to get at him through the thin wooden hull.

They were very kind to him in England. He'd become some sort of an epic hero, which he knew he wasn't. Staff officers questioned him, standing respectfully beside his bed while he divulged what he remembered of their staff officers' experiment in Opposed Amphibious Landings on an Enemy-held Coast. Doctors poked at his hurt arm as reverently as though it were the new-found relic of an apostle. The nurses were infinitely tender and sometimes broke into tears. He asked them all how many had been killed at

Dieppe, but no one would tell him. Finally a man in the next bed said, "I was with the Royals. We got six hundred men across and sixty of us got back and thirty-some of them were wounded."

"Did you hear about the Camerons?"

"They got hit kind of hard, but not quite so hard."

He was in the hospital for two weeks. Then a captain came and sat down beside his bed. "I'm in charge of reassigning you, Son," he said. "You've got a category. We can't send you home, but we can't put you back in the infantry. If there's anyplace else you'd like to go I might be able to fix it."

"No, sir," George said. "If I can't go home I don't care where I go."

"That's not the right attitude," the captain said. "There's still a war on."

"I know there is, sir. I found that out."

"Please don't get smart with me, Son," the captain said. "I'm doing my job and you've done yours and I'm trying to help you."

"You're sure you can't send me home, sir?" George asked.

"No, I can't. Your arm's going to be fairly good. You can go to the Service Corps or to Ordinance or REME or almost any non-combat outfit you want to pick. I'm trying to help you, Son."

"Well, then, sir, get me to a place where there's no more shooting. If they start shooting again I won't be any use. Not for a while anyway."

"Don't be ashamed, Son. I've looked you up. You did very well. You're a good soldier and if I could send you home I would."

"Well, then, I'll leave it to you, sir."

"There's an outfit up in Scotland that would be exactly right for you. It's called the Canadian Forestry Corps. They chop down trees and make boards and railway ties and pit props. Bushwackers from up around Sudbury and Port Arthur and Noranda. Eat like horses. They've drunk all the beer north of Edinburgh, chased all the women clear to Stornoway and the Isle of Skye. I'll put you in the Forestry Corps. You're a good man, Son—I took the trouble to find it out—and these are good men too."

"Thank you, sir," George said. He really didn't care much one way or the other. He wasn't particularly frightened of going back to the war; he'd just lost his heart for it.

CHAPTER FOUR

It took Frankie Koerner a long time to realize there was anything wrong. He lived in a busy and generous world, a world bursting with places to play and shout, a world alive with reflections on good worlds past and just as good worlds to come. Every time he walked the three blocks down and around the corner from Eighty-seventh Street to Eighty-sixth and on to school, the bounties and enchantments of beng alive stormed at him from everywhere. The washing hung out from the red tenements as clean and valiant as flags. The other boys were spilling out into the cobbled streets hollering, "Frankie, you're a bat!" The girls were coming out more primly and pretending not to notice him, but he knew perfectly well they did. The little stores and shops and bars and delicatessens offered more of the day's abundance. The Burmeister Pork Butchers, Yorkville's Pride Since 1902; the Gilmaster Pork Butchers, Yorkville's Pride Since 1901; the Bavarian Bakery, the Vienna Bakery, the Berlin Hofbrau, the Black Forest Casino, the Student Prince Hofbrau, the Werner C. Schmidt Jewelery Co., the Mildred Flack Hairdressers and Couturiers, the Herman Schram Bookstore and Music Center. Almost always almost everybody opening up the stores said hello.

The finest adventure was arriving at school. It was unfashionable and unseemly to like school and even worse to like teachers, so Frankie had to be constantly on the watch. But the simple and degrading fact was that he loved P.S. 77 with all his heart.

It was a fine big school, slanting down crazily from Eighty-fifth to Eighty-sixth. At the top it was a five-story building and at the bottom it rose to six. It had immense iron fences around it, and the Stars and Stripes floated high above the roof, and there were two cement playgrounds, one marked Girls, one marked Boys. Every morning Frankie stood in the classroom with his face alert and his hand on his heart and said and meant it with every fiber and corpuscle: "I pledge allegiance to the flag of the United States of America and to the republic for which it stands, one nation indivisible, with liberty and justice for all."

Frankie never missed a meal, although when he was twelve and thirteen, in the first years of an accident called the depression, the meals sometimes came slow and thin. His mother was working at the Perfection Laundry down on Eighty-fourth and Second. His uncle Otto Koerner was getting ninety cents a day helping make out income tax returns for a notary on Lexington, and Franz himself after school hours was delivering from the Schumacher Drug and Pharmacy, which was right below their house. They ate, sometimes just on potatoes, but they ate. Later the jobs kept changing and sometimes running out altogether, but they continued to eat.

Frank Koerner's main friends and deities at that time were, of course, headed by his mother, Hattie Koerner. Hattie was a trifle plump, but she was so fair and sweet of face and she smiled so easily and her blue eyes lighted up so quickly that even when she was going on for fifty she was acknowledged to be one of York-ville's main attractions. It was well known, or often said, that every rich widower and bachelor from Sixty-third Street north had proposed to her at least once; mere propositions, of course, were unthinkable. Any fool could tell from the pride of Hattie Koerner's walk that she'd knock a man down at the barest hint of freshness. No night went by, no matter how late they were at the store or laundry or delicatessen where she was working, that Hattie didn't make him his good-night cup of cocoa and tell him some kind of joke and give him a kiss to go to sleep on.

His uncle Otto Koerner, his father's brother, was so different that it seemed unbelievable they should belong to the same family, even as in-laws. Uncle Otto was heavy where Hattie was plump, dark where she was blond, scowling where she smiled. But they got along well because Hattie refused to get along badly with anyone.

"Jumping Jesus, Hattie!" Otto said every time he tried and failed to start an argument. Frankie felt deeply for his uncle Otto, just the same, because Otto was all he had for a father and it was there-fore impossible to feel any other way.

Hattie was at the delicatessen that day and Uncle Otto again was out of work. "Would you like me to tell you about your father, Franz?"

"I'm not sure, Uncle Otto."

"Sometimes," Otto said, "I wonder if you understand he was my brother. Hattie was his wife and you're his son but I was his brother."

"He died the year I was born, didn't he?"

"I know your mother doesn't talk about him much because she thinks it would give you pain and add to hers. You should know about him, though."

"All right, Uncle Otto."

"I think I'll tell you about him, Franz."

"All right, then."

"Franz, I suppose you've never wondered that I never call you Frank."

"I've thought about it, Uncle Otto."

"Your father's name was Franz and no one ever called him Frank. We don't talk enough German in this house."

"There's some coffee on the back of the stove, Uncle Otto."

"Oh, sit down. He was my brother. For seven years we slept together in a bed at most a meter wide. At breakfast there was pumpernickel and porridge and not much of that and if either of us tried to take more than his share"—Otto laughed—"it would be neat and nice to pretend neither of us ever did, but I'd better say this honestly. Some nights he pushed me out of bed. Some nights I pushed him out. Some days, if I really needed it, he gave me a little of his bread or porridge. Some days I gave him some of mine. I'm damned if I know how we got it figured out which was the hungriest but we usually did."

"There's some coffee on the stove," Frank said. "Can I get you some, Uncle Otto?"

"Let's wait a minute. What I was coming to was how your father died. It took me more than five years to find out."

"How did it happen?"

"It took me more than five years to find out. When you lose a war it's not so easy to move around or ask the right questions or get the right answers."

"How did my father die?"

"It wasn't very special or very complicated. They just ran a tank over him."

"Really, Uncle Otto?"

"Yes," Otto said, "it was one of the first tanks. Your father had this Mauser."

Frank said nothing.

"It was one of the first tanks," Otto said. "Nobody expected them or knew what they were. Your father—it took me five years to find it out—came around a clump of trees, bewildered, I guess, but willing just the same. He had this Mauser. Not much good on tanks. But he stood there anyway, firing his Mauser at this queer and clanking machine he'd never heard of, firing away at this vast contraption.coming at him through the night as thick as a rhinoceros and as long as a city block. He stood there firing his rifle and then the tank ran over him. Well, that's what happened to your father."

"Do you think it would have hurt him much?"

"No, I guess not. He wouldn't have allowed it to."

"He must have been brave."

"Yes, he was."

"Then we came here."

"You were only a couple of years old and things back home were difficult. The mark went up a million times. You had to carry money around in suitcases. Anyway we came here. Your father had a feeling, an advance feeling or a hunch—what do they call it down at that fancy school?—a pre—"

"A premonition. Or maybe a presentiment."

"Yes, he had a premonition about the tank. On his last leave home—we'd arranged to get our leaves together—he asked me to look after Hattie. Look after her, for God's sake, I can't even catch her. No, I shouldn't have said that, Franz. There's never been anything between your mother and me except the fact we both loved the same man deeply and forever. I've heard references to Teutonic self-denial. Anyway we've both been faithful."

"What would my father have been? I mean if the tank had missed him."

"He might have been a teacher of natural history. He had a great feeling for everything that lived. His heart bled to know things. When he had to quit school he cried all night thinking of the things he'd never learn. And before morning he swore to me, 'Otto, I'll find a way somehow. Times won't always be this bad. I'll learn and I'll teach.' We were very poor, but if it hadn't been for the way the war went—if we'd won the war as we should have—your father would have got around it."

"What would you have been, Uncle Otto?"

"I'd have stayed in the Wehrmacht. *Ach*, that was the place for a man, Franz! The politicians sold us out in the end, but the

Army was never defeated. Don't let them tell you it was. I'd have been at least a major by now. Who knows, perhaps a colonel, perhaps a general."

Otto never did get himself rearranged or replanted. His choice of words, even in English, was usually sound enough, but he did have a thick accent and, coming in the wake of Weber and Fields and Kaiser Bill, a big stout German new from the other side was supposed to fall automatically into the role of a dialect comedian or a villain from the movies. It looked to a lot of people as though Otto was putting on airs. He was in constant trouble with his bosses and with the clients of his various and short-lived places of employment. In their first dozen years in New York—first in Queens and then among their own kind in Yorkville—Otto had and either was discharged from or stalked out of more than thirty jobs. One week he'd be tending bar down on First Avenue, another he'd be slicing smoked meat and dishing out *latkes* on Eighty-sixth, another, bursting with rage, he'd be crammed into an ill-fitting, comic-opera uniform and working as doorman at one of the big apartment buildings over toward Park and Fifth. But whatever he was doing Otto either got mad at the wrong person or the wrong person got mad at him. During the frequent periods when Otto was out of work, Hattie gave them the best breakfast she could manage, put the best lunch she could manage for them in the icebox, gave Frankie an affectionate pat on the bottom, gave Otto a chaste kiss on the top of his dark and scowling head, and went bouncing down the five wooden stairways of the walk-up tenement as happily as though she were parachuting in from Venus.

"You be a good boy, Frankie," she said.

"You bet I will."

At the school another universe was waiting. Sometimes on the way in Mr. Hoffman, the principal, who had no regular classes, was prowling around the lower corridor discharging, as he once said, the school principal's duty to make a general nuisance of himself. Mr. Hoffman knew every single girl and boy by name. He was a diligent reader of the morning *Times*, and if the mood was on him he'd be as likely as not to stand there in the hall and give a three- or four-minute discourse, in the time before assembly—you didn't have to listen, but you could—on the pitching career of Babe Ruth or on the melodies of Irving Berlin or on the League of Nations or on the falling price of wheat. Miss Margaret Kelly was Franz's first teacher, a dark and slender young woman who had the advantage of being slightly cross-eyed. Her being cross-eyed may not have seemed an advantage to Miss Kelly, but it prevented the girls from being jealous and the boys from being insecure. Miss Kelly was not likely to desert them on the arm of the first patent-leather-haired intruder. Miss Kelly's wisdom, though apparently boundless, was dispensed without any evidence of superiority, and she won almost the same unassailable unsulliable devotion from young Franz that his mother had had from the start.

Franz was a big, dark boy, bigger and darker and far handsomer than most. He got into only one fight in all his years at P.S. 77, and that was with a boy a little bigger still. Franz won the fight easily and went home swaggering.

That night Miss Kelly came and visited them. Visits were fairly rare. It was a long way up and there was no telephone. By the time she had passed the third floor Franz recognized her quick and able little step and began to wish it was someone else's.

"I'd like to talk to Frankie," Miss Kelly said.

"Why certainly, Miss Kelly," Franz's mother said. "There he is right there."

"I couldn't speak to him alone?"

"Well, sure. I guess if there's anything I need to know I'll hear about it anyway."

"There's not much room here, Miss Kelly," Franz said. "Mother sleeps in the bedroom and Uncle Otto sleeps on the day bed here and I use this couch. There's just no room for private conversation."

"Well, I would like to talk to you, Frankie. If you want me to say it in front of your mother and"—she tried a weak cross-eyed smile on Uncle Otto, who was already angry through force of habit —"and your uncle I'll do so."

"Now look," Uncle Otto said. "We've had about enough of this sneaky schoolma'am language. If Franz has done something, speak up and say it."

"May I, Frankie?"

"Well, if you really have to, Miss Kelly."

"I wouldn't be doing this, Frankie, except that you're an exceptional boy. May I go on, Mrs. Koerner?"

"If Frankie says so."

"It's not really all that bad."

"You might as well go on, Miss Kelly, now you've got this far."

"All that happened was that Frankie got into a fight with a larger boy. I was looking out the window to the playground and it was begun before I saw. I'm not going to tell you the larger boy's name. Anyway he's the school bully, or was, and Frankie gave him a bad beating."

"Good for you, Franz!" Uncle Otto sat forward.

"We can't have this, Frankie," Hattie said. "I won't have you doing this sort of thing."

Miss Kelly looked at Franz out of her green crossed eyes. "The thing wasn't just the fighting, Mrs. Koerner; it was that Frankie liked it. He enjoyed beating up this bigger boy. When he left the yard half the other boys were following him and the girls were staring. Frankie's not that sort of boy."

"I won't do it again, Miss Kelly."

"I wish you wouldn't, Frankie," his mother said.

"Now you're turning this boy into"—Uncle Otto got up and started for the stairs—"what are you turning him into? Well, I'm going out. Good night, Miss Kelly. Good night, Hattie. Good night, Franz. I'm going over to the park to contemplate the sins of courage. You go ahead and talk him out of them."

"I didn't mean it that way at all, Mr. Koerner," Miss Kelly said.

"Otto," Franz's mother said severely, "you shouldn't have said that."

"Well, I did." Otto stamped out.

"I suppose all I can do is go on crying," Miss Kelly said.

"No," Hattie corrected her, "we won't have any of that. Frankie and I always have our cup of cocoa at this time of night. You stay and have some. Otto's difficult. You're a friend of ours, Miss Kelly."

"I should never have come up."

"Sit down."

Otto's announcement that he had joined the Bund was no occasion for surprise. He'd been a member, almost since their arrival in Yorkville, of the Teutonia Society, and part of his dues went to the National Socialist Party back home. Later he joined the Friends of New Germany and still later the *Amerikadeutcscher Volksbund*. All these organizations were subjected to sporadic investigation or, as Otto put it, persecution by various arms and instruments of the U. S. Government. It was another of Otto's defeats that he never got to be any more than an ordinary member of the Bund. All he was allowed to wear was a swastika arm band

and a black cap and a white shirt. If he'd made the storm troops he'd have had a Sam Browne belt and a full green uniform. They kept telling him that he was forty pounds too heavy. Otto accepted this disappointment, but he was at Hattie almost incessantly to get young Franz into the *Jungvolk* or, later, into the *Jugendschaft*.

"It's like the Boy Scouts," he kept saying to Hattie. "Jumping Jesus, what's wrong with that? This boy could get into the O.D. He's strong and smart and his life is wafting past."

"I don't know, Otto. If Frankie really wants to join I won't stop him. But I'll never encourage anybody into a uniform."

"Hattie, I suppose you know this country is going to hell. You don't want your son to do anything about it."

"I don't see much that's troubling me, Otto. Nothing that's troubling me as much as when everybody was getting into uniforms."

"That God-damned cross-eyed schoolteacher. She's chopped you down, Hattie, and she's making you chop down your boy."

"Hey," Frankie said, "can I get a word in?"

"Yes," his mother answered.

"Uncle Otto," he said, "for now I'm doing what my mother says."

"You could go to Camp Siegfried out on Long Island and see a lot of your friends there."

Hattie walked out to the kitchen. "I can't understand all this Bund talk, Otto. I wish I could but I can't."

"Then let me tell you what's official. The Bund is a militant organization of patriotic Americans. That's what our disgraceful propaganda says. Awful, isn't it?"

"No, Otto."

"The Bund intends to combat all atheistic teachings and all abuses of the pulpit designed to undermine the morals, ethics or patriotism of Americans! Jumping Jesus, Hattie, it's a wonder we haven't all been shot for treason."

Otto was pacing around the tiny living room. "Now this is another of our awful heresies, Hattie. We say it so it can be understood. We're against all racial intermixture between Aryans and Asiatics, Africans or other non-Aryans. Have you any comment on that?"

"You mean I shouldn't let those big black wrestlers chase me around the block?"

"Mother, what's come into you?" Frankie said sternly.

"Oh, when anybody tries to lecture me I get a little giddy."

"I vas merely attempting," Otto said, "I vas attempting"—
Otto was usually good about his *w*'s and *v*'s, but when put under
sudden duress he occasionally was overcome by Prussian dignity
—"I vas attempting to offer some thoughts of consequence. May
I proceed?"

"Please do, Otto," Hattie said, beaten down temporarily.

"I insist that you listen to this and listen to it exactly and precisely. 'The Bund exists so that dictatorship of a small, racially
and ethnically alien Jewish minority, to which the mind of the
entire nation is being rapidly subjected, may be broken.'"

"Good heavens, Otto, come and have some cocoa."

Otto was a stubborn man. "This is true, Hattie."

"Well, if you'd sit down."

"This country," Otto said, carrying on his pacing, "is being
taken over by the Jews and communists. The papers are controlled
by Jews and communists. The political parties are controlled by
Jews and communists. The schools are controlled by Jews and
communists."

"Surely, Otto, this is one charge you won't make against Miss
Kelly."

"Hattie, you're putting words in my mouth. That's a favorite
trick of all the paid spies and half-baked editorial writers."

"Otto, I still don't think Miss Kelly is a Jew. And likely not a
communist."

"Oh, jumping Jesus, Hattie!" Otto flung his thick hands across
his eyes. "I believe you're trying to drive me crazy. Miss Kelly is
not a Jew. But that boss of hers, that principal, that Hoffman or
Hoffmeister is a Jew, he's never tried to deny it. And he's also a
communist, everybody knows it just from what they're trying to
teach the kids down there."

"Mother," Frankie said, "may I go out for a while?"

"Yes, but be back by nine."

As he left he heard his uncle Otto demanding, "When did you
get your last new dress, Hattie? When did Franz get his last new
shoes?"

Most of the families were on relief, but even with Uncle Otto
in such a ceaseless riot of disturbances with employers, past employers, and potential employers and their past and potential customers, the Koerners avoided this indignity. Frankie was graduated
from P.S. 77 and went on for two years to another school, up north,

but he never had the same feeling for it and when he got a chance delivering part days for one of the nearby meat stores his formal education ended.

His best friend, Hans Boeselager, joined the *Jugendschaft* and spent his summer holidays singing and marching and doing push-ups and heiling Hitler at Camp Siegfried. Hans kept urging Frankie to join too.

"Your mother has this weird idea that we're somehow in favor of war."

In the middle of a cribbage game at Hans's house Hans took out his *Jugendschaft* dagger and held it up so Franz could read the inscription. *Blut und Ehre.* "Blood and honor, Frankie, these are the things we all live by. But I'll kiss this dagger, Frankie, right in front of you, right this second and vow on the blood and the honor that I'll never use it unless somebody tries to use a longer, sharper one on me first."

"You're getting het up, Hans, just like my uncle Otto. Whoever said us Germans are stolid and phlegmatic should have had another think coming."

"Frank, I'll kiss this dagger right now and make the vow and all I'll ask is that you come down to Siegfried and look around and decide for yourself if there's anything wrong."

"Hey, Hans, they haven't made you a recruiting officer, have they?"

"I won't lie to you, Frankie. Everybody in the Bund wonders why you're not with us. Everybody knows your uncle Otto's in and you're not and I've been asked to talk to you."

"To tell the brief and simple truth, Hans, I don't much give a damn. Otto's at me all the time, just the way you're at me now. My mother doesn't want me to join but she doesn't press it. Gracie thinks the whole notion is pretty close to criminal, but her father's an importer and he's got to keep people satisfied in Berlin as well as here and so he's now an assistant group leader. Incidentally, who decides, and on what basis, when and how that knife gets used?"

"I do. It won't be used wrongly."

"Oh hell, Hans, I don't want to fight with you, because I'm not even sure I'm right. The division between us is really fairly tiny. You have to weigh these things and let your conscience decide."

"You're seventeen, aren't you, Frank? You talk as pompously as old Herbert Hoover himself."

"I didn't mean to, Hans, and anyway I don't know enough. Seventeen or not, I have an awful feeling that my education started tapering off when I left P.S. Seventy-seven and Mr. Hoffman and Miss Kelly—they all keep cropping up in our conversations at home."

"Fifteen two, fifteen four, fifteen six and a pair is eight. Want a Coke?"

"Yes, please."

"So you won't do anything?"

"There are some difficult ingredients, Hans. First my mother loves every single member of the human race. Second my uncle hates them all except one and this one's name is Schicklgruber. I can see myself storming the gates of history but it is hard to imagine doing so behind a man named Schicklgruber. I guess I just want to hide out on the side of the angels."

"Hey, you got a real fat crib there. Looks like fourteen and one for the jack. Now look here, Frankie my dearest friend, knife or no knife, smart remarks or no smart remarks about Adolf Hitler, I've been given the job of getting you into the Bund. Will you at least do us both the favor of listening?"

"Yes, Hans."

Hans walked across the room. The living room of the Boeselagers was a little bigger than the living room of the Koerners, and there was an extra plush easy chair in the corner. Hans went behind it to the china cabinet and came back with a paper pamphlet. He put the pamphlet on the dining-room table between them, and then, on a theatrical impulse, he took the dagger out and put it there alongside.

"This is what the *Bundesführer* said. It's right here, Frank, in his first main speech as leader of the Bund. There was nothing in it that the Jew papers couldn't have reported if they'd wanted to. The cops and spies were there, they plant cops and spies at all our rallies but the *Bundesführer* spoke up openly, as he always does."

Frankie said, "I've got a hunch I've already heard all this from Uncle Otto."

"No, this has just been printed. I won't read it all to you. Just a few paragraphs. *America is not benefited by the dissolution of the honest, forthright, race-conscious German element into a mongrel horde of citizens infected with the lure of Hollywood, with a tabloid intelligence, impractical ideals and Sunday bigotry. The time will come in America when materialism and idealism shall fight it out to the death and when that time comes the element among the citizenry which has remained strong in the conscious-ness of its individuality, like the Germans will become most dire-fully needed."*

"Come on, Hans, it's your deal."

"I am dealing. *The Bund is American in its inception and in its field of endeavor, German in its idealism and character. The German American Volksbund is inspired with the National Social-ist world concept. We have no intention of Germanizing members of other nations, but merely of closing the ranks of German Ameri-can citizens in order to forestall their complete extinction.*"

"Oh, for God's sake, Hans, I've had so much of this it's coming out my ears."

"*Let us take,*" Hans went on, "*the leader of all Germans, Adolf Hitler, as our illustrious example.*"

"I still say Schicklgruber."

"*He too endeavors under all circumstances to preserve peace with all his neighbors. Arise and fight, not with guns and pistols, but with the weapons of the intellect, against Communism and its leaders of an alien race in this country under the Constitution and for the United States, forming a bulwark against the would-be destroyers of our race-consciousness. A bulwark must be erected against Marxist, Communist and Jewish arrogance.*"

"Yes, Uncle Hans," Franz said.

"This is where we come to you," Hans said. "*Our special task, the Bundesführer said, is to look after our youths. Unless we pro-ceed seriously and diligently to organize them*—I guess this is where we've come to me—*our movement will not endure beyond a generation. Our movement is not a pilgrimage, it is a dynamic war, a last call for you to rally to the rescue. We certainly have not much time to dally; the opposition has even now succeeded to an ominous extent in poisoning public opinion.*"

"Then let's not dally. Your deal."

"You won't listen. You've closed your mind."

"Hans, I'm afraid of getting mad. I only got mad once in my life and I sure arrived that time. Right now if I got really mad at you I'd throw that measly little dagger out of the window and—Oh, Hans, I apologize for even thinking of it."

Hans inspected him with some alarm. "You're bigger than I am, Frank."

"I know. Let's get on with the cribbage game."

"You're quite a bit bigger."

"I know, Hans."

"Well, all right, then." Hans was an intelligent boy too, and now that this contretemps was over he grinned with good nature and resignation. "Will you at least talk to Gracie again?"

"I talk to Gracie all the time. About all kinds of things. Why should we talk again about this?"

"Ask her, Frank. That's all I say. Just ask her."

Gracie's true name was Gretchen Waldeck. Her father was a dealer in smoked meats, a thin, aesthetic man who was always going to concerts or reading about concerts or taking long bird walks over into Central Park. Gretchen was almost inhumanly beautiful, blond hair piled up on a sculptured head, a clean young figure, and a clean young stride very close to terrifying. There was never any suspicion or any hint, not since the first years at P.S. 77, that she was anybody's girl but Frankie's.

"I've promised to ask you again about this Bund stuff, Gracie," Franz said.

They were walking hand in hand down toward the East River.

"You've known that dad's got into it."

"Yes, I have."

"Frankie, stay out. There's something about it that scares me. It scares your mother and it scares my mother and it scares me. It's hard to say what's wrong but there is something wrong. Stay out."

"I will."

She tightened her grip on his hand. The moon was overhead, the original, Yorkville moon, and they walked on down toward the river. A few taxis hooted and a few bars of Viennese music called at them from one of the music halls. "Oh, Frankie!"

"Why did Hans want me to talk to you again?"

"You know. They've been after my father the same as they've been after your Uncle Otto and after Hans Boeselager. They want you more than you realize. Give my hand a squeeze, Frank. I need it."

"I need yours too, Gracie. Hey," he added hesitantly, scared already of her answer. "Do you think we're too young to get engaged?"

117

"We've always been engaged, Frankie." She stopped right there beneath a white street lamp with the red neon light of the Bavaria Grill and Delicatessen going on and off a door away and mixing with the moon and the street lamp and lighting up her own natural radiance in a way that baffled definition. Somehow in those changing lights Gretchen looked like Joan Crawford, Sophie Tucker, and Shirley Temple all at once. Frankie would have been pleased enough to be engaged to any one of these, but to be engaged to all three of them, plus Gretchen Waldeck, was a bounty and a mercy that his uncertain gods had never even hinted at.

"Hey, do you think it would be all right to kiss you, Gretchen? I mean right here in front of all the people?"

"I think it would be all right, Frankie," Gretchen said, and then added cautiously, "As long as you don't make it too long."

Frankie's luck was in that week. He got a three-day job pushing a barrow for a wrecking firm. It didn't pay much, but it paid enough to give his mother two dollars and still buy his new fiancée a banana split approximately a block and a half long—so she said —and covered with so much lovely junk it should have been put on display over at the Museum of Modern Art.

Uncle Otto even got a job, or really three jobs. He was selling subscriptions to the *Weckruf und Beobachter*, selling the *Weckruf*'s pamphlets, and enlisting merchants in the German Business League. The last job was the easiest because any storekeeper or professional man who refused to join the league came under an official business boycott; unfortunately Otto lost this job through the error of making excessive threats against a prominent bookseller who had been ordered by a higher authority, and for apparently strategic reasons, not to join the league. It was one of the few defeats that Otto took philosophically. He held the *Weckruf* jobs and was temporarily full of optimism. "This is a great paper I'm associated with," Otto said. "Would you consider it out of line if I read your son a simple little item from the issue of even date?"

"As long as it's clean," Hattie laughed, "read him anything you like."

"Well, now, this is a pretty good summary, Frankie, the best new summary I've read in some time. It's very easy to follow. Even Hattie might follow it if she'd let her reason and common sense and powers of observation have a chance against this blindness people are disguising under the name of tolerance."

"Oh, go on, Otto, and get it over."

"Very well. This is what it says and this is all it says. *He is a minority of the people but a majority of the rulers.*

"*Believe it or not, he controls the Republican Party, he controls the Democratic Party and he is the Communist Party.*

"*He holds sixty percent of America's high political offices. He controls or owns the majority of America's great industrial firms.*

"*Like a parasite he invades Gentile culture, education, fraternal societies and clubs. He believes his race superior to any other race of people. For 4,000 years he has tried to gain control of the world. He caused the Great World War, he started the Russian Revolution, he founded Communism and at present he is undermining the American government. Who is this fiend who controls your life, looks upon you as an inferior, weak race of people and he as a superior race of people? He is the JEW.*" Otto's voice magnified the italics. "*The unholy JEW, who for 4,000 years has kept the world in bitter turmoil.*"

When Otto had finished, Frankie sat silent for a few moments. Then he said, "All I've got to say, Uncle Otto, is you sure believe it."

"I sure do, Franz, and there's far far more."

A night or two later Otto produced a pamphlet he was selling on Adolf Hitler. "*In what light,*" he asked, beginning with the questions part of the questions and answers, "*should Hitler be regarded by Americans?*"

Otto was up, pacing the tiny floor again. "This is how Hitler would be regarded by Americans and I say it to you, Hattie, and even more importantly to your son. *Certainly not in the light cast upon him by those whose interest it is to make him appear odious and detestable, but as a patriot in his own country, who has performed miracles in snatching his people from the brink of ruin and despair, putting them back on their feet in a few short years. Few men are judged fairly by their enemies or the victims of ignorance. In the eyes of their opponents, George Washington was a Hun and Lincoln deserving of an assassin's bullet.* I guess you never knew, Hattie, I guess you never knew, Franz, that Washington was called a Hun long long before there was any Kaiser Bill, any Hitler, any Bund, any me or any one of you."

"Next speech," Hattie said. "Supper's almost ready."

"*How,*" Otto demanded, quoting again, "*do you explain Hitler's rise from the position of an obscure house painter to that of Ger-*

many's dictator? Like so many fairy tales concerning the German leader, this is just another fiction of the same complexion. Hitler is an artist of considerable ability. Granting this, his career may well remind us that Abraham Lincoln was a rail-splitter, President Garfield a tow-boy on a canal and that Shakespeare was not prevented by humble home surroundings from becoming the world's greatest dramatist. And the term Dictator is misapplied to Hitler. He has on three different occasions polled an unprecedented plurality and actual majority of the German vote."

"Ach, Otto!" Hattie's blue eyes flashed. This was the first time Franz had ever seen her angry, much less angry to the point of scorn. Even Otto was taken aback, as though his ordinarily placid sister-in-law had turned into a raging Valkyrie. Otto put the booklet down and went to the icebox muttering something about seeing whether there was any beer, which he knew perfectly well there wasn't.

It was months before Otto mentioned Hitler directly again and a week or more before he even mentioned the Bund. He turned for support to other oracles. "I see," he'd say with a—for him—remarkable lack of passion, "where even this Catholic priest Father Coughlin is admitting the depression wasn't an accident, it was deliberately created. Says in the new issue of *Social Justice:* 'The depression robbed you of your bank savings accounts, then of your jobs and in many cases, of your homes—and nobody in America shot a banker. We continue without jobs, 12 million of us; 22 million subsist on dole rations—and we do not revolt! How much will we stand?' I wonder how much," Otto would sum up reflectively.

"Are you asking my opinion?" Hattie would ask.

"No, no, just making conversation. I see where that man Arcand up in Canada has at last produced complete documentary proof that Roosevelt is a Jew. Of course everybody knew it anyway."

"I didn't, Otto."

"You know it's not just the patriotic German-Americans who see what is wrong with this country. The America First Committee, the Christian Front, the American Destiny Party, the American Patriots, the Gray Shirts, the American Women Against Communism, the National Gentile League, the Anglo-Saxon Federation of America, the No Foreign War Committee, the National Workers League, the Union for Social Justice—I could name at least a hundred, all headed by the finest Americans of all kinds."

"Many Negro or Jewish organizations in there?" Hattie asked with just a trace of malice.

"Jumping Jesus, Hattie!" Otto said. "You make me sick."

Otto further modified his approach. At supper a few nights later he said, "I've been over in the public library this afternoon reading some of the news magazines and respectable papers—nothing subversive like our own *Weckruf*. No, just magazines like *Time* and *Newsweek* and papers like the New York *Times*."

Hattie glanced a little nervously toward Franz, but contented herself with passing the mashed potatoes.

"I see even Roosevelt's top hirelings and bureaucrats and, yes, some of his inner cabinet have had to admit just what a God-awful mess we're in."

"Otto, I never said we weren't in a mess. Not lately anyway. This depression. I just can't agree that you've hit on the way of getting out of it."

"Well, anyway, Hattie and Franz," Otto said equably, "J. Edgar Hoover—that's the man that spends so much time investigating constructive and law-abiding and peace-loving groups of Americans—"

"Like the Bund, Uncle Otto?" Franz, who hated to see his mother in any kind of difficulty, made one of his rare interventions.

"Yes, like the Bund," Otto said, unperturbed. "Especially the Bund. Anyway J. Edgar Hoover has had to admit that while the FBI is carrying on all this political persecution, there was a major crime in America every twenty-two seconds last year. And he admits this was a big increase, a very big increase over the year before."

It was plain that Otto was wondering why he hadn't embarked on this simple line of discourse long ago. He was fairly beaming. "And then, in the very same issue of the very same magazine the President of the American Council of Education had to confess that the schools of America are often poorly administered and inadequately financed. The teachers are often below intelligence and ill-prepared. By the way, Franz, have you seen that Miss Kelly lately and—who was that principal, Hoffmeister?"

It had been a mistake, after all, to try exchanging ad libs with Otto. Franz could only mutter, "Aw, lay off Miss Kelly, Uncle Otto."

Otto did lay off for that evening, but next evening he had a fresh set of statistics. "I see the Treasury Board has just reported our national debt has increased to thirty-seven billion. And Mr.

Roosevelt's precious Madame Perkins has just admitted another one million three hundred thousand workers lost their jobs between December fifteen and January fifteen."

"Honestly, Otto, do you think this is getting us anywhere?" His mother looked at Franz in the same queer, nervous way he'd noticed the night before, as though she were half fearful that the arguments might just *be* getting them somewhere.

"Just let me give you one more news item. I read this in *Newsweek*. The National Industrial Conference Board has reported another drop in production for the United States, Canada, Great Britain, France and Belgium and increases for Germany and Holland."

By now Gretchen Waldeck was going to Columbia. Although his business had fallen off, Mr. Waldeck was still immensely prosperous by almost any basis of comparison, particularly by any comparison available in Yorkville. One night when Franz was waiting to take Gretchen for a walk Mr. Waldeck observed carelessly and with more than a trace of unconscious self-satisfaction that he didn't really care what Gracie learned at Columbia; he just didn't want her growing up as a waitress.

When they were strolling aimlessly along the springtime streets a little later Franz quoted the remark and said with a touch of vengefulness, "I'm glad you don't have to be a waitress too, Gracie. But how about telling your father if he can get me a job as a waiter, or even a dishwasher, I'll sure be glad to have it."

She grabbed his arm more tightly. "Frankie, please don't talk like that."

"I'm sorry," he said. "But I can't help it. We just don't live in the same world any more."

"Now don't you be foolish. If the truth were known Columbia is kind of a creepy place. Kids parading all the time, professors, with huge glasses and stupid unlighted pipes, very boring classes."

"But you're doing something, Gracie. You're being something. I'm not doing anything, I'm not being anything. It's been that way for a long time."

"You mustn't get discouraged, Frankie."

"Oh, I'm not discouraged. Why should I be discouraged? My mother's got this swell job in the laundry. Uncle Otto brings in a dollar every now and then. I even had three days' work myself less than four months ago. That was the time I bought you the banana split, remember? Stick with me and you'll work up to a *double* banana split some year."

"Please, Frankie." They were on one of the dark back streets, where he had hoped to be able to find the shelter of somebody's brownstone steps and sneak a kiss or two. In the dark he couldn't tell from her voice whether she was laughing at his mordant wit or crying.

"We've never drawn a relief check anyway, and that's something, I suppose. Hans Boeselager's family has been on relief for eight months. You know what they get for the four of them every week? Two dollars and fifty-nine cents. And they nearly lost that the other day when Hans's old man got half a day on a construction gang at fifteen cents an hour and that old bitch Miss Schultz found out about it and squealed to the relief inspector. No, I've got no reason to be discouraged."

She drew him down the stairway leading into a little basement shoe-repair shop and for a long sweet minute she held him in a close embrace. Their kisses had always had, though not always through Franz's doing, a wait-until-we're-married chasteness; she had always been affectionate but careful, every inch the pure and proper *Mädchen* from the pure and proper *Deutscher* home.

"Hey, Gracie," he whispered shakily and anything but reprovingly, "are you making a pass at me?"

She drew back in alarm. "Oh, Frankie, you mustn't think that. I was just—"

"Just what?"

"Just—"

"Just showing me how sorry for me you are. Just comforting me. Come on, I'll walk you home. It's getting late."

They were silent for a good three blocks. It was not so much that they had lost their affinity as that they had discovered their despair.

When Franz decided to speak, he said almost matter-of-factly, "Gracie, I've decided to join the Bund after all."

He had expected some protest or at least some expression of surprise. But she spoke as though she had read his thoughts.

"Perhaps that would be for the best, after all," she said brightly. "I know Daddy's a lot more enthusiastic than he was at first."

"At least I'd have something to do, something to think about besides thinking that I'm doing nothing at all." He added quickly and earnestly, "And there *are* things in this country that need fixing and the people running it now are either letting slide or deliberately making worse and worse."

"I hope your mother won't mind too much."

"I hope not either. But you know I think in the last few months she's been starting to see a lot of the sense in what Uncle Otto says. Oh, there's a lot of wind and blather in it all right. Even if he was arguing in their favor, Otto would make the Sermon on the Mount or the multiplication tables sound at least a little like wind and blather."

By the time they reached her door, he was feeling elated as he hadn't felt since the days of his only other true adventures—the days of swinging around the corner to start another week at P.S. 77 and wondering in the thrill of seeing the vast red building what the new week would bring; deliciously uncertain but absolutely sure it would be exciting and fresh and that when the week was done he, Frankie Koerner, would be a much different person from the Frankie Koerner of that moment. Nothing ever stayed still then; nothing would ever stay still for him again. Suddenly he was so happy that he almost forgot to kiss his girl good night.

He made his announcement at home next morning. Otto rumbled around the table and clasped him in a giant, flabby bear hug. In the excitement of the moment Otto even called him Frankie, and his accent grew noticeably thicker. "Frankie! Frankie! Vot vonderful news!"

His mother looked down at her plate. There was nothing but oatmeal and powdered milk that morning, but she might have been some temple goddess consulting an omen. At any rate when she raised her lovely oval face to her son there was nothing in it but acceptance, understanding, and love. She too went around to him and kissed him quietly.

"Perhaps it's for the best, Frankie. I know how hard everything has been for you."

"You're sure you don't mind too much, Mother?" Franz said gratefully.

"No, I don't mind."

"And," Otto asked hopefully, "you're not even mad at me, Hattie?"

"No, Otto. You didn't fight very fair, but I know you thought it was for Frankie's good. Now it's done I intend to assume it is for his good. There's only one thing I'm going to ask you, Frankie."

"What's that, Mother?"

"Don't forget this is your country."

"Of course it is!" Otto burst in heartily. "Nothing is changed about that. We're all good German-Americans. All that's changed is that Frangkie has decided to be a better American and a better German. I tell you, Hattie, the best Germans and the best Americans stand for exactly the same things. Frangkie's found it out and he'll help you find it out too."

Like new converts to many other faiths, Franz threatened to surpass his preceptors in diligence and zeal. Within a month both his uncle Otto and Hans Boeselager were astounded at his mastery, not only of the fundamental writ, but of the minor and subsidiary canons. Gracie's father, who was now a full district leader, even seemed impressed in a half-appalled sort of way.

Franz had no personal hatred of any Jew, but soon he was explaining earnestly to his mother that it was only a fact, "a simple undeniable fact," that 60 per cent of the public officials listed in Who's Who were Jews. "There's nothing wrong with that in itself, Mother," he explained one suppertime, deliberately pretending to a reasonableness he didn't feel. "But Jews are at the root of communism and it stands to reason that this gives communists a strangle hold on the Government."

Soon he was bringing home the Bund youth paper, *Junges Volk*, and showing his mother how much in common the National Socialist martyr, Horst Wessel, had with the American martyr Abraham Lincoln. "They were both great patriots, murdered by enemies of their country."

Soon he was quoting learnedly from *The Protocols of Zion*. He read *Mein Kampf*; he read everything else Uncle Otto could give him on Adolf Hitler, drank in pamphlets, books, and newspaper clippings as thirstily as an alcoholic coming off the wagon and making up for lost time as fast and fully as he can. It made him weep for shame to think he had ever been so presumptuous and callow as to doubt this giant among men.

Far from thinking of Hitler now as Schiklgruber, he scarcely dared think of him as Hitler; he was the Führer.

Franz could hardly wait for summer. Though much of the opposition was frightened and surreptitious, Yorkville was anything but unanimous about the Bund. In Brooklyn, New Jersey, and the other main German-American communities of the East many of the community leaders spoke openly against it, spoke openly against the Führer, spoke openly against the whole rising phalanx of Silver Shirts and America Firsters and Knights of the White Camellia; fascists, some called them all, not intending a compliment. And so, although the Bund's membership was growing steadily, it was not growing fast enough and it still included too few young men as strong, tall, handsome, intelligent, and devoted as the new recruit from Eighty-seventh Street, Franz Koerner. For the rest of the winter his duties consisted of attending one meeting a week, listening to lectures, and learning to drill. The drills were usually conducted in the drafty ballroom of the Black Forest Casino or in whatever school basement was available for social gatherings. The drill wasn't at first very complicated, mainly learning to raise the right arm properly and, for ceremonial uses, to do the goose step. One night in March, Franz's group leader called him aside and asked him if he'd like to be a leader that summer at the youth camp at Camp Siegfried. "You mean all summer, Herr Kahr?"

"All summer. And by the way, Koerner, your German's not all it should be. The instruction there is entirely in German, as it is here."

Uncle Otto was delighted at Franz's suggestion that they talk German at home. His mother shrugged and said only, "If it will help you, Frankie."

"And Mother—will you start calling me Franz?"

"All right, Franz," she agreed quietly.

"This boy"—Otto had switched to German already—"this boy is going a long way, Hattie. Someday you'll be so proud of him you'll bust. I'll bet you within a year, well, a year and a half at the most, they'll take him in the storm troops. I happen to know— I've got good connections at headquarters, you know—that the *Bundesführer* himself was asking about Franz by name only the other day."

One spring afternoon he ran into his old friend Miss Kelly. He watched to see if her face would fall or her green cross-eyes would turn away when he told her of his plans. "I'm sure you'll enjoy it, Frank," she said gravely.

"It's really a lot like being a senior Scout." He answered the unmade accusation quickly. "Or counselor at a summer camp."

She shook hands when they parted. It was a strangely formal thing to do, and when Franz turned and watched her trim little figure disappearing down the familiar street, he had an impulse to hurry after her and assure her that they'd be running into each other lots of times again. But he kept on, over toward the subway where he'd promised to meet Gracie and walk her home.

Camp Siegfried was the loveliest place Franz had ever seen. He had of course often wandered off his native heath of asphalt, cobblestones, and tenements to sample the rustic greenery of Central Park. But Camp Siegfried was his first contact with what, in his first excited postcard to Gretchen, he described as "the real outdoors." The camp sprawled out under native trees and around a little lake, and for the first time, he bragged to Gretchen, he understood what poets meant when they spoke of the scent of pines and the whisper of the wind among the birches and the lapping of clear, pellucid waters. "And hey! Get this, Gracie—I'm sleeping in a tent!"

The *Jugendlager* was set a little apart from the storm troopers' area, but there was a good deal of coming and going. It was, for all the air of sylvan relaxation, a purposeful and orderly place. You could almost say that it held the best of both worlds, the worlds of untrammeled nature and of disciplined man. The swastika and the Stars and Stripes flew together above the administration building. The boys of the *Jugendschaft* in addition had their own flag, a jagged symbol of lightning on a field of black, and the girls of the *Mädchenschaft* had a separate blue and white flag with a swastika. Except during the recreation periods everybody dressed correctly: brown shorts or skirts, white shirts or blouses, and brown scarves for the cute little *Jungvolk*; blue skirts and white blouses for the older girls; riding trousers and military boots and Sam Browne belts for the older boys. Everybody behaved correctly, down to the smallest five-year-old. When the command "*Achtung!*" rang out over the loud-speaker system, everyone sprang to attention, even the oldest and most splendid storm trooper. When any boy or girl was addressed by a junior leader or by a storm trooper in uniform, it was required that the heels be brought smartly together and the right arm be thrust out in salute. Any girl or boy caught speaking any language but German lost the right to wear the uniform for two Saturdays, a particularly humiliating penalty, since Saturday was the day for visitors.

Far from considering the rules difficult or oppressive, almost all the campers found a deep security and sense of unity in them. Everything bolstered the conviction that everyone there was committed to everyone else there; they were all committed bravely and unflinchingly to a better future. The signs scattered around the camp all gave Franz a surge of warmth and jubilation—from the homey, hospitable *Herzlich willkommen* at the gate to the simple *Ein Volk, Ein Reich, Ein Führer* inside.

Around the evening bonfires the songs rang out no less reassuringly in the evergreen-laden air: *"Horst Wessel"* always, of course, and *"Deutschland über alles."* One he hadn't heard before was as rousing as either of the old favorites: *"Heute Hoert Uns Deutschland—Morgen Die Ganze Welt"* (Today Germany Hears Us—Tomorrow the Whole World).

Several nights, after he'd seen the two tentfuls of boys in his charge safely into bed, he wandered over to the storm troopers' part of the camp, attracted by the lusty choruses swelling through the woods like golden thunder. Almost every night the O.D. men sang the old original song of the original Brown Shirts of the Fatherland, the tragically misled originals of the S.A., the martyrs who had been betrayed into betraying the very cause for which they had given so much blood. He found the song so moving that, after hearing it several times, he made a crude translation and wrote it down, meaning it for Gretchen and perhaps his mother.

> *Up, up for battle, we are born to battle,*
> *Up, up for battle for the German Fatherland,*
> *We are sworn to Adolf Hitler*
> *And to Adolf Hitler we extend our hand.*
>
> *Firm stands each man, as firm as an oak*
> *Braving every storm as well as he can,*
> *Maybe on the morrow we will be all corpses,*
> *As happens indeed to many a Hitler man.*
>
> *Up, then, for battle, all you brown battalions,*
> *The Third Reich our goal shall ever be;*
> *The world war's departed, all of those two millions*
> *Are forcing us to battle and gain a victory.*

One night as he heard the last strains of the song he found himself fondling his *Jugendschaft* dagger and thinking of the words inscribed on it. It took a conscious effort of will to hold back the tears. *Blut und Ehre. Blut und Ehre.* How could he ever have been so cynical toward his friend Hans Boeselager?

Franz's duties as a youth leader consisted largely of supervising games and hikes and seeing that the dozen young men in his group attended their lectures. He was not allowed to give them formal talks himself. "Indoctrination," the camp director explained at the outset to all the new leaders, "calls for experience. And also for care. Monstrous as it will seem to your clean young minds, we know that there have been police spies in this very camp. There are very powerful forces—you can guess from what class they come and what their reasons are—who would like to close Camp Siegfried down altogether and, yes, throw its officers into prison. One false word might easily be seized on by our enemies, and as you know most of our courts are controlled by Jews and communists."

Only the senior officers, in short, were allowed to give lectures or even lead discussion groups. "Of course," the camp director added, "you young leaders may read to your groups from published works or direct their attention to approved publications. I especially recommend our own official magazine, *Junges Volk.*"

At eighteen Franz was a remote giant to his nine- and ten-year-olds. But he felt the same special and intimate obligation toward them that he now realized Uncle Otto must have felt toward him during his own years of stubborn darkness. Of course these boys were all good Bundsmen in heart and spirit already, but Franz hastened to make what tiny contribution he was permitted to make toward the advancement of their education. At the pole nearest the entrance of one of the two tents he posted one quotation from *Junges Volk.*

The slumbering embers Adolf Hitler has fanned into fire in the hearts of Aryan men will break out in a blaze that will consume the enemy when he raises his red flags. The world quivers with the convulsions of an approaching earthquake that will shake each nation to its bedrock and clear the way to leave a world of virile, progressive, race-conscious nations.

In the other tent he tacked up a poem.

Youth, youth—we are the future soldiers
Youth, youth—we are the ones who carry out future deeds.
Yes! Through our fists will be smashed all who stand in our way.
Youth, youth—we are the future soldiers,
Youth, youth—we are the ones who carry out future deeds.
Führer—we belong to you; yes! we comrades belong to you.

But the days of fireside song and iron catechism and Spartan verse were rushing to their close. Events—immediate, concrete, and occasionally ugly—began impinging on the domain of words. Soon after Franz's return to the city there was a mass rally at the Black Forest in honor of Adolf Hitler. It was a happy occasion—or began as one—for there was much to be happy about. Through strength of character, strength of arms, statesmanship, and the rightness of his cause, the Führer had just completed his great and peaceful victory over Chamberlain and Daladier at Munich. Now the Sudetenland, like Austria before it, was restored to the Reich. The iniquities of Versailles were at last being corrected, one by one; now the gaze of the Fatherland, so long rooted in the dust, had risen to the stars. "*Sieg Heil!*" Franz shouted with three thousand men around him. "*Sieg Heil!*" Now, as never before, Franz's heart ached for his unknown father, the unknown man with the tiny Mauser, defying the unknown tank and dying before his son was born. If only his father could have seen this night. A procession of speakers marched across the platform, under the gleaming single beam of light, beside the flag of America, beside the flag of Adolf Hitler's Germany, the Germany too of Franz Koerner's unknown dead father.

". . . the beer-hall *Putsch!*" *Sieg Heil!*
". . . the Weimar Republic." *Boo!*
". . . the birth of National Socialism." *Sieg Heil!*
". . . the destruction of the Reichstag!" *Boo!*
". . . the Jews." *Boo! Boo! Boo!*
". . . the Rhineland!" *Sieg Heil!*
". . . Schuschnigg." *Boo!*
". . . Austria." *Sieg Heil!*
". . . Barney Baruch." *Boo!*
". . . the Sudetenland." *Sieg Heil!*
". . . President Rosenfeldt." *Boos and laughter.*
". . . Danzig." *Sieg Heil!*
". . . the communists." *Boo. Boo. BOO!*
". . . the Führer, Adolf Hitler." *SIEG HEIL! SIEG HEIL! SIEG HEIL!*

For all its intensity the air was cushioned by a comfortable, confident feeling of great triumphs achieved and greater ones to come. Even the booing, though it was loud, fulsome, and apparently unanimous, had a good-natured quality; in the reassuringly crowded hall, crowded as much with certainty as with humanity, even the Jews and communists seemed an object of scorn rather than alarm. President Rosenfeldt and his lackeys were contemptible and laughable, but it was paying them an undeserved compliment to treat them as a full-fledged menace.

But then, at its peak, the spell was broken. One of the editors of the *Weckruf und Beobachter* was speaking when, suddenly, two rows directly ahead of Franz, a tall, angry-looking white-haired man jumped to his feet, whipped an American Legion cap out of his shirt front, thrust it on his head, and shouted, "Will there be any speeches in English tonight? Is this an American meeting or a German meeting?"

The speaker on the podium froze for a moment. "Is this," the tall, white-haired man began to repeat, "an American meeting—"

More than a hundred storm troopers of the O.D., the only Bundists in uniform, had been posted around the walls. Now, their momentary paralysis broken, they rushed as one toward the loud intruder. Two outraged men in business suits grabbed at him first, but then he was surrounded by a little forest of accomplices, all of whom had suddenly brought out American Legion hats too and closed in around him trying to form a protective ring.

"Go on back to Germany!" the intruders were shouting. "Get the hell back to your fascist heaven."

The crowd directly around them began to surge forward, then fall back, then push forward again in a rain of fists and ineffectual kicks. A confused roar went up and the speaker was drowned out altogether. "Dirty Jews! Get the Jews!" On some wildly hopeful impulse the big brass band grouped around the podium struck up *"Deutschland über alles."* Trying desperately to get through the crowd to the little pocket of invaders, the storm troopers of the O.D. were shouting, "Make way! *Achtung!* Make way!"

Franz found himself face to face with one of the invaders, a dark-visaged man who had thrust his Legion cap on so quickly it covered one eye completely. The other eye had a wild, malicious, clever gleam, and for the second time in his life Franz surrendered completely and utterly to the joy of complete and utter rage. He lashed out at the man's face and felt his fist skid off. The other man's blow hit him squarely in the mouth. He tasted his own blood, then lunged forward and grabbed the other man around the throat with one big strong hand. He drew back the other arm, but before he could strike, a leather blackjack swung over his shoulder and caught his adversary across the temple. The man fell away from him into an underbrush of overturned chairs, flailing legs, and threshing arms. The storm trooper who had swung the black-jack bulled on through into the melee like a charging fullback. Another one came right behind him, swinging his hard Sam Browne belt like a leather machete. Another of the visitors went down and then another, and Franz had one final glimpse of the tall, white-haired man, his face now streaming blood, before the truncheon of a storm trooper caught him squarely across the bridge of the nose and he dissolved from view. The band continued its lunatic brassy invocation, but the shouting gradually died. One of the uniformed O.D. men jumped to a chair in the middle of the hall and bawled authoritatively, "Everybody return to their seats! Return to your seats at once!" The band stopped playing. Everybody returned to their seats. "The disturbance is over," the storm trooper shouted. "The meeting will continue in a few moments." A police whistle sounded in the street and a dozen blue-uniformed officers of the New York police force burst in. Eight of the visitors, including their ringleader, had to be carried out. The rest, a dozen perhaps, were able to walk.

Franz, nursing a thick lip, walked home with his uncle Otto. They were both still excited. "*Himmel!*" Otto said. "*Himmel und* jumping Jesus! Did you see the way the O.D. moved in? Didn't it make you proud, Franz?"

"Even with surprise on the other side and all the God-awful confusion," Franz acknowledged admiringly, "it must have been all over in a minute."

"Ah, those O.D. boys know what they're doing. Soon you'll be one of them."

Franz savored the thought while he ran his tongue under his thickening lip; the break had healed already. "Otto"—it was the first time he'd dropped the Uncle, but the time seemed somehow appropriate—"why do they hate us? I got a good look at that guy who landed on me—a lucky punch and how I'd like to see *him* again—and you know, Otto, he did hate me. Maybe that particular one was a Jew. But the tall one who started it wasn't and somehow he didn't sound like a communist."

"Well, of course there are nuts and fanatics who don't classify as anything *but* nuts and fanatics."

"But why nutty and fanatical about us and us alone? My God, on St. Patrick's Day they clear all Fifth Avenue for the Irish and everybody turns out to cheer. Once I had the radio on on Bastille Day and here was this Wop mayor La Guardia right on the city hall steps trying to talk French to the French consul. Did anybody get up and yell, 'Why don't you go back to Italy, you bloody Wop?' or 'Why don't you go back to France, you lousy Frog?'"

"It's persecution and you know it, Franz. The Wops and Frogs and Micks get along O.K. because they're not bothering the Jews and commies. Not bothering this lousy government, not bothering anybody at all. And with all respect to Mussolini they haven't produced an Adolf Hitler and had the guts to stand behind him. You don't see the Dies Committee messing into their affairs and planting spies on them the way they're doing to the Bund. You know why? Their affairs aren't important enough to be worth messing into."

The next day's papers carried gory pictures of the white-haired Legionnaire and several of his companions.

"We may be closer to *der Tag* than anybody realized," Otto remarked with dark satisfaction.

The following Sunday two thousand pickets invaded a meeting in New Jersey at which the *Bundesführer* himself was to have spoken. He went unheard above the crude catcalls of his enemies, and when the truncheons and brickbats came out it took all the O.D.'s valor and strength to get him out of town unharmed. The Dies Committee on un-American activities was listening, entranced, while the whole country eavesdropped through the Judo-capitalist press, to the alleged revelations of a buxom young renegade from the Mädchenschaft and a newspaper reporter who'd joined the O.D. under a false name and and—as Otto put it—"by his own barefaced admission, just to see how much dirt he could dig up." Otto's summary of the young woman's testimony was that what she was complaining about was not the prevalence of sedition in the Bund but the lack of seduction. As for the reporter, "You can't take his word for anything unless you first take his word that he's a liar." Another fifth columnist went into court and testified that when he enlisted in the O.D. he was made to swear allegiance, unlawfully, not to the United States or any of its insignia or officers, but to the instrument of a foreign power, Adolf Hitler. The papers created a one-day sensation over a miserable, half-crippled little lawyer over on the West Side who made it his hobby to turn out mimeographed propaganda sheets against the National Socialists in Germany and the Bund in America. One night, according to his story, four young men surprised him in his miserable little office while he was working on one of his poisonous little broadsides. They tied him to his chair, produced the flag of the Third Reich, and demanded that he kiss the swastika. When he refused they carved a swastika on his naked chest.

"Do you think it could be true?" Franz could not conceal a note of shock.

"If it isn't it should be," Otto rumbled.

Franz was prepared for any test except the test of cynicism. "No, Otto," he insisted. "No joking. Could it be true?"

Otto, gazing into the younger man's troubled eyes, became more serious. "No, no, Franz," he said quickly. "If it happened at all it was a plant, another put-up job."

"That's what I thought," Franz said, relieved.

Although Uncle Otto's unfortunate inability to take off weight, together with his chronic incompetence in other practical affairs, had impeded, perhaps fatally and totally, his official promotion with the Bund, he had acquired a certain ex-officio influence at the fringes of power. The *Bundesführer* himself was reported to have remarked indulgently that if Otto Koerner was a fool all the movement needed was three or four million more fools like him. Through his indirect connections at the walk-up headquarters at Third and Eighty-fifth, Otto heard of a job that might be just right for Franz, and toward the end of September, Franz went to work delivering for and occasionally filling in as clerk at the Nathan Hale Bookstore.

His new employer came directly to the point. To several points, in fact. She was a tall blond woman, not more three inches shorter than Franz, who was now past six feet. She was remarkably handsome in a mellowed ivory sort of way. Franz guessed that her age must be away up in the forties, but she had no wrinkles and her gray eyes were as clear and alert as his own Gretchen's, though not nearly so soft. Franz had been told only to ask for Mrs. Lucas, and it was only by degrees that he learned that her full name was Mrs. Rodman R. Lucas, Jr., that she was divorced from Mr. Lucas, that she had been divorced from a Walter J. Endor before that, and that even before she married either Mr. Endor or Mr. Lucas she had been a wealthy woman.

She came to her several points one at a time, not overlapping, as his mother or Otto always did when there was more than one matter to be discussed or disposed of. She took each one alone, got it out of the way, and went on to the next.

"So you're the young man from the Bund," she said. "The Bund is doing some good work," she pronounced. "Some very clumsy work, too. Just understand one thing. I won't have any of your hooligan friends hanging around here or coming in here at all."

Franz didn't have time to do anything except blush. There was no opportunity to protest or even to work up a feeling of resentment. "Surely you have a better tie." Her white hands, firm but kindly and smelling of gardenias, made a swift adjustment to the knot of his existing, discredited tie; fortunately it wasn't either the one from Gretchen or one of the ones from his mother or he'd likely have left right then and there. "This is a nonprofit bookstore, Franz," Mrs. Lucas said. "I own it, but I don't try to make money from it. We have only one purpose: to sell books, magazines, and pamphlets that will help keep America American. Perhaps I should have said make America American. Do you understand?"

"More or less, Mrs. Lucas."

"If anybody comes in here while I'm out and asks for the new Edna Ferber or the latest Marquand or the sonnets of Shakespeare tell them to go to Macy's."

"Yes, Mrs. Lucas," Franz found himself saying.

"We try to carry a good stock of everything that has to do with the new leadership in Europe. Essentially, as they have told you in the Bund, their goals are similar to the proper goals of America. Look around the shelves. In addition to what you see there we'll fill subscriptions to almost any paper or magazine in Germany, Italy, or Spain. If you want the job come back tomorrow at ten. Our hours of business are eleven to four."

Of the few clients who came into the store in person fully half called Mrs. Lucas either Hilda or My Dear. The women were as prosperous and elegant as she, although none was nearly so beautiful. The men ran to tight-fitting, striped tab collars, graying sideburns, and stitched pigskin gloves. Between the customers and the authors, editors, and subjects of the books, magazines, and pamphlets he was encouraged to inspect during his frequent periods of idleness, Franz came in contact with a whole new world. It was not nearly so forthright, abrupt, and earthy a world as the world of Yorkville and the Bund, and that made it all the more fascinating. This new world introduced him, if only peripherally—often through their butlers or chauffeurs, or their own distant voices on the telephone or their own distant names in print—to the famous Colonel Sanctuary, to Mrs. Lois de Lafayette Washburn, to Dudley Pierrepont Gilbert, to George E. Deatherage, Pequita Shishmarova, Dr. Ignatz T. Greibe, and General George van Horne Moseley. It brought him in direct or vicarious touch with Kurtzurhippe Bernhard Weissengeld, with Manfred Zapp, John B. Snow, George W. Christians, and James True. Franz still had the vestigial remnant of his sense of humor, and many of these new names sounded like some boisterous, half-drunk collaboration between John Bunyan and Sinclair Lewis, but he looked them up in Who's Who and there they were as real as—he nearly thought as real as Adolf Schicklgruber.

At the Nathan Hale Bookstore, under the benevolent and sometimes alarmingly proximate tutelage of the handsome Mrs. Lucas, Franz made the acquaintance of many publications that had nothing to do with Germany. *The Christian Mobilizer, Social Justice, The American Gentile, The Vigilante Bulletin.* One difficult request came up. Mrs. Lucas was at the back of the store. "I know we haven't got it in," he said to her, "but this gentleman wants *The Protocols of Zion.*"

"Tell him to try Brentano's. Better still Gimbels." It was impossible to think of anyone striding in that tiny store but Mrs. Lucas strode. Franz stood up but she still stood over him, five feet ten *versus* six feet one. The measurements had lost their point. No matter how tall he got, she got taller.

"I'm sorry, sir," Franz said into the telephone. "Perhaps the public library."

Mrs. Lucas guided him to the striped settee. "Franz, *The Protocols* are a fake. They're lies. Manufactured lies, pointed-head lies, nothing to do with us. They're clumsy, they're stupid, they do more harm than good. I hate to think of them."

Franz sat in gloom. Her white hand stole over to his knee. He pretended not to notice, pretending to be oblivious, impervious, unassailable, undefilable, imperturbable, unruffled, knowing, and sophisticated. It was unreasonable, just the same, that anyone so firm and fair and tender should be crowding him off a striped settee.

"I'd better be getting home, Mrs. Lucas," Franz said.

"This is your home." She got up and locked the door and pulled down the shade.

"Put your arms around me, Franz. Franz, can I capitalize things? I know you're an Innocent Boy. I'm an Awful Woman, perhaps even an Abandoned Woman. But right now I love you."

In a while he reeled off the settee and sat down in the Louis Quinze dining chair. He felt shocked and half murdered. Mrs. Lucas extended a hand. "What have you done?" she asked.

"I don't know." He'd had wild ecstasies in his sleep and sometimes invented them by himself, but never with a real woman, much less a woman who had the flesh of Arab houris and the scent of dancing girls from Kashmir and blond hair spilling down.

"Help me with my hair," she said.

"I'll try. I won't be much good at it."

"Franz, you've got a girl. You've got a girl—let me bring out the capital letters again—you've got a Girl and you were a former Innocent Boy and I'm an Abandoned Woman and what you're suffering from now is Pangs of Conscience. Help me with my hair."

Franz closed his eyes, tried to close his ears, tried to close all his other senses to the sweet and terrible fragrances of her body. "Put your arms around me again," she said.

A long time later, it might have been two o'clock in the morning or it might have been four o'clock or six o'clock, she pressed his shoulder and said, "Franz?"

"Yes?"

"How old do you think I am?"

"I don't care."

"I'm forty-nine. In all those forty-nine years I've never done a single decent thing. Now I want to do one. Will you help me?"

"I'll do anything I can."

"Well, then, Franz, put on your clothes. Put them on slowly. Put them on carefully. Put them on so I can see you. Put on your shorts and your shirt. Put on your socks and your shoes one at a time. Put them all on and then don't ever come back."

"I don't think I could do it that way." He still didn't know—it had begun only a few hours ago—whether she was Mrs. Lucas or Hilda or Her or She or Madame Is Not Here at the Moment, or Nathan Hale Bookstore, Koerner Speaking. All he knew for certain was that there had been, clean beyond describing, breasts against his breast, thighs against his thighs, lips against his lips, his hard hand softened and his lean cheek sweetened in the soft flowing of her soft and flowing hair.

"Franz," she whispered, "do be a good boy and go."

A good boy. The universe was unseated and rearranged, he personally had been assassinated and restored, everything that was ever light had grown much lighter, everything that was dark was darker than the darkest midnight, the onyx gleam of life was right there, right within his grasp, and she told him to be a good boy.

"I'm putting my socks on," he said.

"What's the name of the girl you're going to marry?"

"Gretchen. Sometimes I call her Gracie."

"Love her as well and deeply as you've loved me."

"Yes, I'll try. Good night. Or"—he attempted to be casual and knowing, as befitted the Nathan Hale Bookstore—"on the other hand good morning."

She reached through the darkness for his arm. "Franz, there's no end to the places where you'll go."

"I guess not." His heart was breaking, but he kept his voice firm and level.

He tried to tell Gretchen about it. Now that he was out of a job again he had to tell her something, anyway, but he didn't want to tell her everything because, in spite of all the time they'd known each other, they still had and required their own little hoards of privacy. For instance everybody knew that the hot water came on only twice a week even in the Waldecks' big brownstone flat on the Lexington Avenue side, but just the same Gretchen always smelled as if she'd had a bath. Everybody knew that Uncle Otto had false teeth, but no one mentioned it.

This was a far more important matter. Franz did not describe it well.

"Frankie," Gretchen said, "if you'd just tell me a little more simply."

"Well," he said, "Mrs. Lucas and I—well. Mrs. Lucas."

She looked at him with sudden sorrow. "Frankie!" she said.

"I didn't want to tell you, Gretchen. But if I can't tell you who can I tell?"

They were walking toward the East River, hand in hand, and Gretchen, incredibly, did not take her hand away. "She must be rather older," Gretchen said wistfully.

"Yes," Franz answered, "she's rather older."

"Lots of the kids up at Columbia don't—well, don't wait."

"No, I guess not."

"There's a lot of talk about companionate marriage—there's a judge out in Denver that says it's perfectly all right. At least two members of our own English faculty are living with women they're not married to."

"What are you trying to say to me, Gretchen? I've tried to apologize. I've tried to tell you I'm sorry and ashamed."

They were back under one of the neon lights of Eighty-sixth Street and Gretchen's face glistened with tears. Not Sophie Tucker tears, not Shirley Temple tears, not big, dramatic, or considered tears, just the small tears that Gracie Waldeck was trying to keep away.

"What I'm saying is that if you want a woman I'm the woman you want. If you need a woman I'm the woman you need. I'm not afraid, Frankie."

"Hey, Gretchen, look—"

"You heard me."

"Oh, Gretchen, look at you standing there. Gretchen, if you knew how beautiful you are—beautiful right now, beautiful in all the time past and all the time ahead—"

"Poet!" she said. "Did you talk like that to her?"

"Gretchen, Gracie, darling. I'll never marry you on a striped settee."

"Where will you marry me?"

"Honest to God, Gretchen, I'll tell you. There'll be silk sheets, the finest sheets you ever saw, so fine and soft you won't even know they're there. I'll carry you over the doorway, Gretchen, and put you down there so easily you won't notice it and then if you love me I'll love you."

"I love you."

"That's the way I'll marry you. You'll be the most married girl in the history of the human race."

"I know that."

"Now I've told you nearly all I've got to say. There's one other thing. I'm sure hitting the jackpot."

"You're going into the storm troops."

"Yes, Gretchen, I am. I know you don't like it any more than my mother will."

"Has it got anything to do with the Dragon Lady?"

"Gracie, dearest, don't call her that. You're too big to be vindictive."

"I'm not as big as you think."

"Gretchen, we mustn't quarrel. We mustn't ever quarrel."

"Whatever you decide, Frankie, whatever you do—with the sole exception that from now on you stay away from old blondes and in fact young blondes and all the blondes but me—we won't quarrel."

Franz's induction was a silent one, all the more moving for its silence. The post *Führer* explained that there could be no spoken oath; half a dozen officers of the Bund were under sentence for allegedly—he said allegedly and Franz had no reason to doubt him—demanding that new recruits to the storm troops swear their first allegiance to a foreign power.

"Your oath rests in your hearts," the post *Führer* said. "If it's not there, speaking won't put it there."

Two hundred storm troopers, uniformed and spic and span and rigid, were drawn up in the drill hall to make a V. At the back of the V, Franz and the five other new men stood stiffly under their gaze. At one side of them the American flag was near; at the other the German flag. Behind them there were three heavy drums.

"Koerner!" the post *Führer* summoned. The drums rolled in fearful majesty. Franz stepped forward and, as he'd been instructed to do, gave the National Socialist salute. The post *Führer* grasped his left hand and put the edges of the two flags there while the drums went on rolling. Then he looked Franz squarely in the eyes, held his eyes for several seconds, and nodded in approval. That was all there was, but it was far more stirring than any bugle call.

In spite of all her doubts his mother couldn't help blushing—actually blushing—when she saw him in his uniform.

"Good heavens, Frankie, even if I say it, you're the handsomest man this side of New Jersey."

He walked across the little room and kissed her. "What's so good about New Jersey?"

"Frank, this is the last time I'll ever nag you. But please think one thing out and help me think it out. Suppose there's another war and America and Germany are on opposite sides."

"That's ridiculous, Mother. The Jews and the English and the French and the Czechs and the Poles and all the profiteers right here at home are trying to drag us into a war. But we won't get there. We're just not that dumb."

"But suppose we do? I'm serious, Frankie."

"We won't."

"Suppose we do?"

"Mother, you said you weren't going to nag me."

"This is the last time."

"I can't answer, then. Everything about this country exalts me and appalls me. Hey! That's not so bad. Gracie exalts me and appalls me. Otto exalts me and appalls me. So do you. The entire U.S.A. exalts me and appalls me. I really wonder what I'd do."

The decision wasn't his anyway. It was made for him at the George Washington birthday rally of February 1939. Every inch of Madison Square Garden was jammed. The streets outside were alive and shouting with ten thousand pickets and nearly two thousand policemen moved among them. Big signs waved everywhere, homemade signs mostly: "Down with fascism!" "Down with tyranny!" "Death to Hitler!" Franz's assignment, like that of the other storm troopers, was to help keep order inside. He stood erect in the main aisle before the platform, proud and square in his Sam Browne belt, and until the meeting was nearly over there was not the slightest trouble at all.

A portrait of George Washington, at least twenty-five feet high, towered behind the stage, and on each side of it columns of stars and stripes and swastikas reached as high. Before the portrait a massed band played "The Star-Spangled Banner" while a young woman sang the verses, ineffably sweet and glowing.

Then the speeches began. There were half a dozen of them and they all ended with the thrilling cry "FREE AMERICA!"

"We are living at a time when every crackpot and bankrupt lawyer thinks he must save our country from an imagined, terrible menace of nazism. FREE AMERICA!" The waves of cheering mounted. A forest of arms reached out in the diagonal, open-palm salute.

"The Gentile American is being sold down the river by Mr. Hull and his Jewish consorts—the Jew Barney Baruch, the Jews Henry Morgenthau, Walter Lippmann, Madame Perkins, Léon Blum and Georges Mandel-Rothschild. FREE AMERICA!"

"*Mein Bundesführer*, American compatriots, Bund members and friends . . . A patriotic American nationalism . . . The Oriental cunning of the Jew Karl Marx . . . Mordecai! . . . Jewish-International moneyed interests. FREE AMERICA!"

"These United States are the product of a particular racial group, the Aryan. Not the ever-homeless parasite, the Jew . . . We must develop the race legislation of the United States to the point where those who may rule us, judge us or in any way direct our minds and souls may be only white men. FREE AMERICA!"

A famous woman journalist burst out in peals of mocking laughter. Two storm troopers, standing alertly nearby, escorted her from the building, but she was allowed to return amid a chorus of angry boos.

The *Bundesführer* himself was speaking, when a little man, obviously a little Jewish man, flung himself from the floor, vaulted onto the stage, and shouted, "Down with nazism!" The storm trooper next to Franz was the first to move. He had the little man by the ankle and started hauling him out. Franz grabbed a wrist and twisted it hard. They had him out in no time.

Franz had foolishly arranged to meet Gracie afterward and walk her home. It was against the rules. Storm troopers in uniform were never supposed to go anywhere without at least one more storm trooper with them, but it was a rule that everybody broke and Franz broke it now because he wanted desperately to walk Gracie up through Central Park and maybe grab a kiss from her and tell her how the exciting happenings of the night had seemed to him.

But when they got out on Eighth Avenue, there were still ten thousand people milling there. The police were trying to hold them back, some on plunging horses, some waving their night sticks.

"You go home, Gracie," Franz said quickly. "You go on up Eighth Avenue and cut on over to Madison. Now get moving right away. Take a bus if you want to or go over to Lexington and get the subway."

A man bumped into Franz. "You weren't pushing, were you?"

"Maybe I was."

"Grace, will you get moving?"

"Franz, I won't leave you."

"Look, Grace, you get out of here."

"I could take off my shoe." They were pinioned in a crush of shoving, shouting people. Franz's uniform stood out like a red flag.

"This is the last time. For once you do what I say."

She walked up Eighth Avenue. The crowd parted for her but then closed in again on Franz. A man rushed at him and struck him hard on the mouth. Franz swung back joyfully. But then an officer came riding up on his horse and knocked him down. He fell beneath the horse and the horse placed a delicate, well-trained foot on his chest and moved away. He got up and lashed out with his fists. Then a man from the other side of the street raced across and hit him very hard with a policeman's billy and he went down and stayed down.

It was very late when he got back to Yorkville. The blood had dried but he still ached all over. He went to Gretchen's. His splendid uniform was drenched and soiled with the dirt of the street, and for the first time in his life he felt hurt and beaten.

"Oh, Frankie, what have they done to you?"

"Never mind. Just give me a towel."

"Frank, I should never have left you."

"Don't worry about that, Grace. How about some coffee?"

Her father came out of the main bedroom. "Well?" he said.

"Yes, Mr. Waldeck. Well." He put the wet towel to his face and let it rest there. "You saw those lunatics outside, all those cossack policemen treating them as gently as a Sunday-school choir."

"Frank, how did it happen?"

"Well, they just came at me. I didn't care about the Jews and commies and marchers. The thing I cared about was the police coming at me with their sticks and horses. I'm getting out of here, Mr. Waldeck."

"I couldn't blame you much."

"Frankie." Grace was pale and she went across the room and touched his bruised face.

"I'm getting out of here, Grace. I'd been thinking about it before, anyway, but tonight was the last straw. I have a chance to go to Germany. I can work my way on the Hamburg line and when I get there there'll be some kind of a job. What's more I won't get beaten up by cops."

She was silent for a while. "Frank," she said, full of timidity, "are you leaving me?"

"No, I'm not. I'll go over there and when I get your passage money saved I'll send for you."

"Suppose I won't come?"

"You'll come, Grace. You'll come because as long as I live I'll never live without you."

"I guess I'll come all right, Frankie."

"Yes, Gracie, you will. This country will come to its senses sooner or later and then we'll come back again right here to Yorkville."

Germany did not fully meet his expectations. The Bund had given him the name of a man to report to, but he could not find him; moreover in all Berlin, a teeming, hungry, angry city filled with dread, he could find no single person who would acknowledge that the man he sought had ever lived.

He moved into a small pension on one of the side streets near the Wilhelmstrasse. He had no ration card and it looked for a few days as though he would just quietly and undramatically starve to death. But his landlady, a kindly, daring woman who'd lost a son in the purge of the original German storm troops, kept him alive on boiled potatoes, boiled beets, and pumpernickel. He made a daring, desperate attempt to enlist in the Wehrmacht. The recruiting officer turned as white as a sheet. He was an elderly and fussy man, not at home with trouble.

"My God, Son," he said, "you must be insane. Because you seem like an honest young chap I'll tell you in strictest confidence what seems to be going on. We're getting ready to fight the English, the French, the Russians and especially the bloody Poles. But we are *not* getting ready to fight the Americans. We don't want to fight the Americans. Surely if we take on two-thirds of the world that's enough."

"But I believe in your cause," Franz said. "That's why I'm here."

"I haven't made myself understood," the old recruiting officer said. "We just aren't taking Americans. It would be bad advertising."

"If I thought you were ever going to fight against my country I wouldn't be trying to enlist."

"Of course not. Now look, Son, I'm going to have to report you to the Gestapo. I'm sixty-three years old and every year left to me is about eight times more rare and precious than every one of yours. I wish you good luck with all my heart."

The Gestapo came in a most unspectacular way. "Mr. Koerner?"

"Yes, I'm Mr. Koerner."

"Oh, my God!" His landlady put a hand on the Gestapo man's shoulder. "I had nothing to do with him. He just came in looking for a room."

At the headquarters on Prinz Albrechtstrasse he was put to sit in a small cubicle. He sat there alone for perhaps half an hour, and then a big and pleasant man came in and sat across the wooden table.

"Mr. Koerner," he said, beaming pleasantly. "You're the American spy."

"I don't know who you are," Franz replied, "but I'm not an American spy or any other kind of spy."

144

"We have means of finding out. Would you care for a cigarette?"

"No, thanks."

"You're quite an independent young man."

"Yes, I am."

"We can cure that. Rather quickly. Indeed quite quickly."

"You go ahead and cure it, then."

"Did you really and honestly come here the way you said?"

"Yes."

"Mr. Koerner, I'm going to release you. Thank God, you'll never know what else might have happened. You're a young man of great folly or great courage. Be very careful what you do from now on. Your actions will be observed. Don't do anything else that could be misunderstood."

In time he found a job as a translator at the Foreign Office. It was dull and routine work, mainly making abstracts from the press and sending them to the embassies abroad. His mail was carefully and capriciously watched. He wrote Gretchen twice a week and his mother once a week, but in all his first two years in Germany only two feeble little notes got back to him. One said that his mother was sending him some socks—which never arrived —and the other said that Gretchen would wait for him forever, which he never doubted for an instant.

In spite of the chilling air of suspicion and fear, he found Berlin an exciting city to live in during the jubilant days of 1939, 1940, and 1941. The war began, as all the papers and the radio said and clearly proved, when the perfidious and arrogant Poles tried to invade the Fatherland. It continued with France, Belgium, and Holland magnificently crushed and England at bay in the west and Russia at bay in the east. Right until Pearl Harbor it seemed inconceivable that, for all the ravings of the Wall Street imperialists, the United States would dare join in the conspiracy to encircle the Reich.

Every two or three months Franz repeated his first attempt to join the Army, but the complication of his citizenship was still an impossible one. He had moments of black despair when it seemed that his life was fated to wither away in an interminable anticlimax. He had come to Germany offering the *Blut und Ehre*, the blood and honor of a devoted warrior, and there seemed no way of escaping the life of a very junior clerk. But the day after Pearl Harbor he was ordered to report for induction.

The enlistment officer had several special questions.

"I have your file here," he said. "You may or may not know that the Gestapo had been keeping an eye on you for a long time."

"As it should have done," Franz said tactfully. "After all I'm a foreigner here."

"Technically you've just become an enemy alien. Does the prospect of carrying arms against the United States not trouble you?"

Franz was so anxious to get into uniform, where he belonged, that he lied a little and a little too sanctimoniously.

"Not really, sir. I love the good things about my country, but the bad things have been taking it over. If I can help root the bad out I'll be happy."

The officer's regard was tinged with cynicism. "Well, that's the right answer to that, Koerner. Now I see you've attempted to write —let's see, well over two hundred letters to two different people in New York and they've attempted to write as many back to you. Do you think that was wise?"

"They're my mother and my girl," Franz said. "And I still don't know what conceivable harm could have been done to anyone."

"I'd advise you not to go around questioning regulations. Fortunately—very fortunately, I might add—there was nothing harmful, as such, in any of the letters. Of course you'll stop the whole futile attempt now."

"I suppose there's no choice."

"No, there's no choice. As one man to another I'd strongly advise you to forget them both."

"That won't be easy," Franz said bleakly.

"No, these aren't easy times. Well, Koerner, you've had some semimilitary training back in America. If the doctor finds your physical condition as good as it looks I'm going to recommend you for training in the SS. There's talk of forming a new unit from the Hitler Jugend. They'll be mostly boys, some of the best boys in Germany. They'll need older men for their officers and non-commissioned officers and it's just possible that you can qualify."

But it was still more than two years more before Franz had a chance to realize his dream of becoming a front-line soldier. Immediately after he finished his training he was posted to the Afrika Korps to interrogate prisoners of war, and when the southern front folded back to Italy, he was transferred to a parachute division. It was far from glamorous work and it struck him as the very opposite of heroic, much more suitable for the fat civilians of the Gestapo. He was nearly always within the sound of artillery fire, and through the long retreat the engineers were constantly exploding bridges or blasting out new holes to defend for a few hours, a few days, or a few weeks; beyond an occasional small air raid by the RAF or the American fighter bombers those were the only authentic sounds of war he heard.

In a considerable degree the Afrika Korps and the division he joined in Italy conducted themselves with absolute Teutonic "correctness." They fought as well as they could—from El Alamein onward against heavy odds—and treated their few prisoners according to the requirements of the Geneva Convention. A prisoner could be compelled to state his name, rank, and serial number and nothing more, but the intelligence officers on both sides constantly tried to cajole, trick, or threaten their prisoners into supplying information on troop movements, pending orders, casualties, morale, and any other details that might help to fill in the "broad picture," which practically all intelligence officers practically always misjudged anyway.

Franz was not good at this part of his duties. His unmistakably native American accent made him uneasy both in the presence of American and of Canadian and British prisoners. If he had been fighting them in the line, he might have felt different, but hounding and bullying exhausted and sometimes terrified men who'd been conquered in fair combat troubled him, a noncombatant, more, he knew, than it should have. Once, behind Monte Cassino, a wounded and half-shell-shocked GI cost him a whole night's sleep by blurting, "My God, you're a Yank!" "Shut up, you swine!" Franz barked, and then added menacingly, "*Warum haben sie nicht geantwortet?* In your language, my brave American friend, that means 'Why don't you answer me?' and if you know what's good for you you'd better answer and save your insults for someone else." The GI, terrified, told Franz not only the name of his division, regiment, battalion, and company but their precise whereabouts and the number and location of their supporting tanks. It was one of Franz's few wholly successful interviews. But except for that one shocked explosion his vague sense of guilt acted as a check on him rather than a goad. In his other interviews he seldom elicited any more information than the bare and meaningless parrot words required by the articles of war. "Sanders, Joseph. Sergeant. B-18789." "Smathers, Reginald, Corporal. 1756982."

His superior officer, a tough and eager captain, almost invariably had better luck and he constantly hinted—though he never put it as an order—that Franz might show a little more zeal. The physical torture of prisoners was specifically and firmly forbidden. That didn't mean, however, as the captain kept telling Franz, that an insolent or unduly defiant prisoner couldn't be punished with a few well-aimed punches or even a blow or two with a pistol butt. But the best methods were psychological; tell a man, for instance, that his company or platoon commander had already been captured and had told everything, and all the Wehrmacht asked now was confirmation of what it already knew. If there was reason to suspect that the PW had really useful information to give, it often helped to put a pistol unobtrusively on the table before the questioning began. Three or four times, the captain admitted, he had marched a prisoner out behind a tank, a building, or a wall and made him dig his own "grave" while the questioning continued. The captain was quick to say that he'd never sent a man into the grave and never would, but the possibility that he might sometimes brought quite agreeable results when everything else had failed. Some intelligence officers, the captain hinted, had actually gone all the way with one or two prisoners when there were one or two others on hand to watch and be questioned later. That method, too, could bring agreeable results, but only the SS units had the stomach to use it often.

"*Ja, Herr Hauptmann,*" Franz would say, pretending respectfully that he was waiting for a direct order. The captain never gave it. Franz concealed his horror and his tiny sense of superior virtue as diplomatically as he could. The fact was, perhaps because he'd seen so little of it at the intimate level where men die or are torn open to live a while screaming out their lungs in naked pain and terror and where other men lose their nerve and grope back blindly toward their amoebal jelly—the fact was that Franz still had a vision of war not dissimilar to the vision of Camp Siegfried and the soaring speeches of the Führer. It was essentially a chivalrous affair, with a cleanly medieval cast to it; a great if dangerous adventure in which the best and noblest men and armies and nations always won and even the losers died suddenly and with a certain, though lesser, honesty and dignity. The idea that in this environment any good soldier of any race would murder a defeated and disarmed opponent was not only vastly and sickeningly repugnant to him; it was almost totally unthinkable.

His education in these niceties and abstractions remained static and severely limited until at last he was assigned to an infantry unit in the west. His corps was withdrawn from the lost Italian campaign in the winter of 1943, and Franz was transferred to the new Hitler Jugend division in the early spring. This was the SS Panzer division he'd first heard of on the day of his induction. Now, much later, it was completing its training in Belgium and had already been tentatively assigned to the role of mobile reserve for the soon expected advent of the second front.

Franz loved everything about his new surroundings. The accepted adjective for the teen-age youngsters of the Hitler Jugend was "fanatical," and they wore it proudly while they awaited their first battle, certain that they would earn it when the time came. It was the Hitler Jugend after whom the Bund's *Jugendschaft* had been patterned. Although he had now outgrown the young men in age, he still felt as one with them spiritually; he was back home at last. Beverloo, Belgium, was a long way from Yapahank, Long Island, and Camp Siegfried, and the countryside here was softer and much older. But the air was full of the same excitement and lofty purpose. Here he could begin fulfilling the mission of *Blut und Ehre* beside consecrated young men to whom the ideal behind the words was as sacred as the ideal of their personal god and patron, the Führer.

The young privates and corporals willingly paid him the iron respect due to a sergeant and an older comrade, and willingly yielded to an iron discipline. Yet he knew by instinct that when the fighting started these younger men would all be at least as brave as he himself. He felt the responsibility of leading them and living up to them as he would have felt the fine heft of a golden sword. He took a particular liking to one seventeen-year-old private, SS Mann Dietrich Wulff, a blue-eyed boy from Cologne who held himself like a ramrod on parade but laughed like a merry child in the canteen or on the way to the Sunday-morning movie. Another special member of his platoon was an eighteen-year-old corporal, SS Rottenführer Gerhard Siegel, a dark, intense boy who was bent, in time, on becoming an opera singer and had the fine warm voice to go with his ambition but was happy to forgo all personal ambitions until the enemies of the Reich had been destroyed or forced to sue for mercy. When Gerhard Siegel sang *"Lili Marlene"* or, in a different mood, the Horst Wessel Lied, it took a strong man indeed to keep his eyes wholly free of moisture.

The troop lieutenant, SS Obersturmführer Willi Seldte, was a much older man who had actually competed for Germany in the 1936 Olympic Games and fought for two years on the Russian front. He was a stern, aloof, demanding man, but he exuded an immense confidence and an unassailable loyalty to his men. It was from the regimental commander, next only to their special relationship to the Führer, that the Hitler Jugend drew their surest, strongest sense of unity. Standartenführer Paul Raubal was already a legend, not only in the SS, but in cafés and meeting halls and newspapers all over Germany. Standartenführer Raubal was not so remote or exalted as the generals and field marshals; his rank was high enough to make him an important leader, an important factor in important battles, and still low enough to allow him to ride right into the teeth of the Russian armies, leading his own columns in person on his own motorcycle. On one famous occasion, already known to every German who could read, he had ridden into a village near Kharkov with his famous long rubber jacket flaming like a giant torch. The war correspondents called him *Schnell* Raubal for his speed at long-range penetrations and sometimes Panzer Raubal for his skill and daring in handling tanks. By the time he returned from the East with the famous Liebstandarte Adolf Hitler to take his new command in the Hitler Jugend, he had been twice wounded and had been awarded the Iron Cross first class, the Infantry Assault Badge, the Knight's Cross of the Iron Cross, the German Cross in gold, the Oak Leaves to the Knight's Cross and the Swords to the Oak Leaves. The Reich had only one higher decoration for bravery in its gift. Besides his German medals he had two others, from Bulgaria, and three from Romania. When he put on his full-dress uniform, as he usually did for his Sunday-morning talks to the assembled regiment, his hard, proud chest shone and gleamed like a sunrise on the Rhine.

No officer ever worked harder at perfecting both the physical training and the indoctrination of his men.

"You are young," he said, addressing the massed regiment for the first time. "Your membership in the Hitler Jugend is the only guarantee I need of your faithfulness, your loyalty and your understanding of the political causes involved in this hard and bitter struggle on which you are about to stake your lives. But because you are young, it is my duty and the duty of your officers to see that nothing is overlooked in your military orientation, your military philosophy, your military understanding."

He imposed Spartan rules, which no one complained of except

in the willing, jesting spirit of an irrepressible youngster like Dietrich Wulff. For all men in the regiment there was to be an absolute prohibition against alcohol and tobacco. For soldiers under eighteen an absolute prohibition against relations with women. "Too bad they liquidated Ernst Röhm and the S.A.," young Dietrich grinned in mock consternation.

The Standartenführer spoke to them at least once a week. "Your discipline must stem from the ideas of the family," he told them. "You have had good family upbringings, otherwise at your ages you could not have become good National Socialists and members of the Schutzstaffel. You are among brothers here, whether you are among your officers or among yourselves in the privacy of your billets.

"Now," he said surprisingly, "I must say a word about God. God cannot be proved but He is to be believed. Man only becomes man when, through his conscience, he feels himself responsible to his God. Your fighting motto must express the true soul of the true soldier: 'I am nothing, we are everything.'" Coming from Paul Raubal, everything was right, everything was exactly true.

In April they moved into France and on across the Seine and took up positions about seventy kilometers from the English Channel. The gentle countryside was radiant with springtime and electric with anticipation. Amid the rolling fields the first green shoots of wheat appeared, the fat cattle grazed placidly outside the stone farmyards, and the bells rang forth softly from the slender spires of the churches. A soldier of ordinary tact—"It is astonishing how many of us have just passed our eighteenth birthdays," young Dietrich Wulff remarked—had little trouble finding a friendly young peasant girl, for many of the young Frenchmen were still away, some in labor camps, some in prisoner-of-war camps, some, alas, dead, some across the seas in Algeria or England making foolish sounds and foolish faces at the side of the foolish General de Gaulle. Everyone knew these soft and fragrant days were about to end. The big bombers went over constantly, the silver American Forts flying very high by day, the English Lancasters much lower and much louder by night. It was common knowledge that there were more Amis now in London than in New York. Soon the Amis and the Tommies would bring forth their own *der Tag*.

"Well," the platoon commander, Obersturmführer Seldte reminded them, waving theatrically in the general direction of the

English Channel, "they've come this way twice already. In 1940 the end was Dunkirk. In 1942 it was a pitiful little escapade called Dieppe. I wouldn't have realized how long ago all that was. But I was talking to the landlord of the hotel this afternoon; Dunkirk was four years ago, Dieppe two years ago. They've come twice, why not, after all, again?"

Yes, they must come again and soon. The poor wretches had no choice but to come this spring or stay and wallow forever in the suffocating *Wunderscheisse* of the fat Mr. Churchill and the crippled Mr. Roosevelt.

Standartenführer Raubal, the regimental commander, quite obviously agreed, although he would not have defiled the ears of his young crusaders with so coarse a word as the word that Seldte used.

"We hear too much talk about the weapons of the German people," Raubal shouted one morning after another massive wave of daylight bombers had gone across to rain death on Berlin, Cologne, or perhaps some other city of the Fatherland. "We hear too much about exacting revenge through the U-boats, the new V-weapons, the flying bomb and the rocket. I tell you, my brave young comrades, the weapons of revenge are right here, in our fists. The Allies will come and then our reprisals and revenge will not be achieved by science or black magic; it will be achieved through our personal action, through our blood, through our spirit of attack and thus through the annihilation of the enemy."

And the next day, his voice mounting higher, his dark, strong face set in invincible determination, his black, burning eyes looking directly at every individual soldier and at that individual soldier alone, he added another part of his credo. "After the end of each war, every prisoner should be in a position to prove that he fell into captivity guiltlessly. I myself have sworn to myself, to my wife and to my family that I would never be captured while I was conscious. Do not forget, soldiers of the Twelfth Panzer Division, that you have a dual privilege such as has never been granted in the history of the human race. You are boys of the Hitler Jugend; you are at the same time men of the SS. It is not for idle reasons that, even before you have entered your first battle, you are known and famous throughout the Fatherland as an elite division. Your status in the elite is twofold and you have twice the ordinary need to live up to it. No matter how bravely you fight, you may find yourselves in grave difficulties. If that should happen I solemnly

152

charge you to remember this: the last bullet belongs to you."

Walking away from the little football stadium in which this last assembly had been held, Franz, without intending to, overheard a conversation between his platoon and company commanders, strolling just ahead. "You fought with him in the East, didn't you, Seldte?" the company commander asked.

"For more than eight months," the platoon commander said proudly.

"Is it true he took no prisoners himself?"

"Long enough for questioning. Then—"

"Did it never trouble you?"

"Why should it have?" Seldte asked, whether in surprise or mild braggadocio it was not easy to determine. "For one thing, the Russians aren't men. They're cattle. For another thing we were usually at least three-quarters surrounded, with guerrillas behind us and those bestial muzhiks they call soldiers on our flanks. What should we have done with our prisoners? Suspended the battle to build steam-heated villas for them and prepare their meals? Naturally"—out of his broader experience the lieutenant felt entitled, in this off-parade interlude, to patronize the captain—"naturally, Hauptsturmführer Oberg, we executed our prisoners."

"Is it your impression, Seldte, that that is what the *Standartenführer* intends us to do here in France?" Franz deliberately slowed his pace. He already wished he had not heard this much.

Before he went to the sergeants' billet to clean up for the noontime meal, he dropped into the school basement in which the corporals and privates had been quartered. One of the men had an accordion going and Rottenführer Siegel was already leading a chorus of the song that had filtered back from Italy. When his pure, lyrical voice hit the word *"Mama!"* he deliberately allowed it to break; it was almost as poignant as *"Lili Marlene."* Franz stood in the doorway only for a minute or so, watching the earnest young faces, sixteen-year-old faces, seventeen-year-old faces, eighteen-year-old faces, while they changed expression one by one and by degrees. Because they had to look like men and feel like men, the whole regiment—with a few exceptions like the merry young Dietrich Wulff—had developed a look as characteristic as its insignia—stern, concentrated, stoical, intent, unconsciously patterned on the military scowl of Panzer Paul Raubal. Under the spell of the music and the thoughts it evoked the stern young faces gradually softened and turned away from each other in the embarrassment of their simple boyish yearning. Franz hurried away, hoping none of the younger men had been watching him.

The division began moving the next day. There was no sign of panic, merely a businesslike haste. The order had been half expected since early morning, when the coastal divisions reported an Allied parachute drop east of the Orne and landings in force from the sea farther to the west. Long before noon Obersturmführer Seldte ordered Franz to have the platoon ready to mount its trucks in battle order on two minutes' notice. "The best guess up there," he confided, waving vaguely in the direction of regimental and divisional headquarters, "is that there's some sort of feint going on to draw our reserves away from the real invasion. Or maybe it's just another suicide raid, like Dieppe."

Seldte came over from company headquarters around noon. "All right, *Hauptscharführer*," he said unhurriedly. "Get the men mounted. We're moving off. For your information we're going to Caen."

For all their careful training the young panzer grenadiers almost fell over each other in their eagerness to get aboard the trucks. And for all their carefully cultivated adulthood they chattered like happy schoolboys on the way to a big football match. "Anybody happen to bring a spare pair of swimming trunks?" Dietrich Wulff shouted. "I intend to have an evening dip in the Channel."

"Sure, Wulff," someone jeered good-naturedly, "maybe you can swim all the way to England."

For the first hour their only problems were the domestic traffic problems of any sizable military formation on the march. They moved in routine convoy along a single hard-surfaced road. There was a little singing, a little cursing, a little grousing, a little noisy speculation from the people in the rear as to whether the bastards up in front knew where they were going and, if so, why the hell they didn't go faster.

Then, far more abruptly than lightning—for lightning never comes out of a clear and sunny sky—the 12th SS Panzer Hitler Jugend Division felt the chaotic lash of war. With a sudden swish and roar of motors a dozen Mosquito fighter-bombers raced in very low and very fast from the west and fled down the backbone of the column, belaboring it with thumping truncheon blows and leaving it as battered and confused as a blind giant set upon by invisible pygmies.

The men who could floundered to the ditches in time to escape the next raking assault by the machine guns and light cannon of a squadron of Hurricanes. On the whole the 12th SS Panzer Division behaved admirably during this first ten minutes of its business life. Many of the wounded, of course, screamed in pain and terror, and, looking on the wounded and the dead, a few of the others became so sick and fearful that only the threat of instant execution restored them to their senses.

Franz made a quick check of his platoon. One of its trucks was burning out of control and the engine of another had been demolished by a direct rocket hit. Three men, including Rottenführer Gerhard Siegel, the platoon troubadour, had been killed. Two others were badly enough wounded that the stretcher-bearers took them back at once. Only one man showed any sign of undue nervous disturbance. After he fell into the ditch, the platoon jester, Dietrich Wulff, lay trembling, face down, with his arms up over his ears, whimpering dismally while the companions nearest him pretended with growing uneasiness that Dietrich was only pretending again. It had all happened in such brief tumult that Franz was still acting half on instinct. He ran into the ditch where young Dietrich lay moaning. He grabbed Dietrich hard by the shoulder and tugged him over. "*Achtung*, SS Mann Wulff!" he shouted in the boy's ear. "Come to attention in the presence of"—it sounded absurdly stilted, but it was all he could think of—"come to attention at once in the presence of Standartenführer Raubal." Afterward he was never fully certain whether it had been a command or a plea, but at the name of his regimental commander, SS Mann Wulff did in fact remember that he was an SS man and did in fact spring unsteadily to his feet just as Raubal came striding down the column past the burning tanks and trucks, past the flung corpses, past the stretcher-bearers, looking to each side as coolly and casually as though he were inspecting a dress parade. Raubal was wearing his motorcyclists' jacket over his green and brown camouflage uniform and he'd lost his visored hat—it was said he'd never worn a helmet in his life—but no king in steel mail and silver casque ever carried himself more regally. His dark eyes were oddly calm and rested, the eyes of a lover who has waited long and been well sated. The battalion commander, the company commander, and Obersturmführer Seldte followed him in that order. He paused when he saw the still-quivering Dietrich Wulff, standing with his scared eyes ahead, his hands at his sides, his Mauser clutched tightly by the barrel.

"*Wind sein?*" Raubal laughed sympathetically. "Don't worry, young comrade. The Führer himself once told me that he had once known fear."

He stopped at the roadside and signaled the other officers closer. But when he spoke it was loud enough so that the men in the ditches could hear as well. "It could have been much worse," he said calmly. "Your battalion has done well, Oberst Wagner. I have just had some gratifying news from the beaches. They have come ashore in some strength. Now we shall resume our journey and tomorrow we throw these little fishes back into the sea."

The regimental commander strode on down the column. Seldte dropped off to confer with Franz. "They've bombed the main crossroad ahead and in any case our orders are to disperse to the side roads. The grenadiers will go ahead on foot. The trucks will be behind and will pick them up again after dark. The tanks will follow right behind the infantry. We'll rendezvous near Caen and attack at first light."

There had been half a summer, a whole autumn, and the beginning of a winter in which to remember, ponder, and forget the brave disaster of Normandy. In spite of constant attacks by the unopposed *Jabos*—the word covered all the makes and marks of Allied fighter-bombers—they did indeed reach Caen before the long night was over. Unfortunately the division's other infantry regiment and its panzer regiment were either not so lucky or not so well led. When the counterattack went in, it was a regimental attack instead of a divisional attack. Paul Raubal, of course, led the regiment in person. Franz Koerner led his platoon in person, for his immediate superior, Obersturmführer Willi Seldte, an excellent officer in every respect, had been killed by one of the *Jabo* raids just before dusk.

The counterattack on the beachhead on D-Day Plus One neither succeeded wholly nor failed wholly. It stopped the Canadians well short of Caen, long enough for other reinforcements to come up and stabilize the front for a full month. But it never reached the sea; the little fishes remained ashore and multiplied and grew and in another month they swirled in voraciously from three directions and tore the division to shreds and finally picked its bones as cleanly as a school of piranhas falling on a wounded ox. The strength of the 12th SS Panzer Division on June 6—when it regrouped much later, Franz was given a temporary office job and thus had access to the precise figures—had been 520 officers, 20,020 enlisted men, and 150 tanks. On August 23, at the end of the violent attrition of Normandy and the final catastrophe of the Falaise gap, its official strength was 300 men, all ranks, and 10 tanks.

In the long months since, the things that had at first made the greatest impact on him had been the first to run together and flatten out and lose their separate shapes and colors. One little attack or one little last-man defense was so much like the last one; one field of wheat and poppies repeated the field adjoining; the sweetly terrible smell of one quarter section of strewn, unburied, week-old corpses became indistinguishable from the smell of its neighbor; one artillery barrage, one mortar screen, one sobbing little dash across the ground was an almost exact copy of the one that had gone before and of the other one that, for the survivors of this one, would follow after. The things Franz Koerner remembered now, waiting on this other, much colder but more promising roadside in Belgium, were all intimate and special. As stubbornly and repeatedly as he kept reminding himself that he must, at all costs, think not in the past but in the future, there were three events from Normandy that demanded his further contemplation at least once a day, sometimes at least once a night as well. There was no discernible pattern to them, except that they all insisted on being recalled, surveyed, and reflected on.

It had been either on the sixth or seventh day after the invasion that he found himself sharing a *Hochloch* with SS Mann Dietrich Wulff. Bloody though they were, those were still relatively opulent days. Reinforcements still sometimes came forward, and Franz had been relieved as acting platoon commander by a genuine officer fresh back from the East. The platoon was still at nearly half its strength, and the new officer had ordered Franz to direct the defense of its left flank in person. He hadn't had a chance to talk to SS Mann Wulff since that morning in the roadside, but he knew young Wulff had been fighting well, because twice—once when tanks got in among them—Wulff's section had clung to a tiny corner of a tiny orchard whose loss might have left the whole company cut off and surrounded. Dietrich was pale, ragged, and dirty, but who wasn't? He no longer looked merry and mischievous, but who did?

They crouched together in the little trench. They had been there for three hours without having exchanged more than a word or two. But now the artillery barrage was over, or rather the two barrages were over, and they were waiting for the Canadian infantry to come. That an infantry attack would come was absolutely certain and that it would come between ten and twenty minutes from now was almost certain. They were still crammed into a narrow bridgehead, barely ten kilos from the sea and less than that from Caen, and the little set-piece attacks, battalion against battalion, company against company, occasionally platoon against platoon, had developed a ritual as settled as the ritual of a folk dance. The attacking side would open with a very heavy creeping barrage, twenty-five-pounders mostly for the Canadians and British, eighty-eight millimeters for the Germans. The defending side would put its own slowly receding barrage just behind the slowly advancing barrage of the attackers. This was to stop the attacking infantry from coming in right behind their own artillery and storming the slit trenches while the men defending them still had their heads down or still were dazed by the danger, noise and concussion.

When the barrage or rather the two barrages ended, Franz and Dietrich Wulff began watching the break in the stone wall ahead and just to their left. They knew as well as they had ever known anything that Canadian soldiers with rifles, grenades, and possibly bayonets would begin coming through the break in the stone fence in a very short while, but not so short a while that there wasn't an opportunity, if they so wished, to talk between themselves.

It was young Dietrich Wulff who began talking. "Hauptscharführer Koerner?" he said softly.

"Yes, Wulff."

"Did you ever hear Standartenführer Raubal tell the story about Napoleon and being young?"

"No, I don't think so, Wulff."

"Well, Raubal—you don't mind if I call him Raubal—"

"Not if you feel as I do about Raubal."

"Well, I do and I know how that is. Raubal dropped into our billet just before we left Belgium. He told us to sit down and he took off his cap and sat down himself and chatted almost as if he was one of us."

"And this was when he told about Napoleon?"

"Yes. I don't think we understood it then."

"Just a minute." Franz touched the younger man's arm. "Did you see a movement over toward the far corner?"

"It was a calf. How it's stayed alive this long out there—"

"All right. But lower your voice. Go on."

"Well, when Napoleon was about twenty-four or twenty-five and still an obscure captain he went to the marshals of France and outlined a plan for a campaign in Austria and asked to be allowed to lead it. The marshals were impressed by the plan but finally called Napoleon in and said, 'You are too young to lead this campaign.' 'Gentlemen,' Napoleon said, 'by the time I return from Austria I shall be either old or dead.'"

"Not *wind sein* again, Wulff?"

"No. Not *wind sein*. Never again, I hope."

"So?"

"So I'm just remarking that Paul Raubal is not only a great soldier but a great prophet. By the time we get out of here we'll all be either old or dead. Or both."

There were two light crumps directly in front of the fence they were watching and two balls of smoke burst and began dispersing and drifting across the intervening ground. "Here they are," Franz said. "Good luck, Wulff."

"Good luck, Scharf."

There was a little breeze, just enough to part the smoke by the time the first dark forms appeared. Wulff picked off one with his Mauser and Franz stopped one more with his Schmeisser. Then two others were right on top of them, shouting familiar North American obscenities, rendered all the more obscene because of the induced, threshed-up and weirdly hopeful rage that attends the voices of all men who shout in battle. Franz and Wulff were shouting now too, though what it was Franz never remembered. Wulff had fixed his bayonet. One of the Canadians tried to jump into the *Hochloch* with them. Wulff impaled him in the chest but then could not wrench the bayonet free. Just as Franz's Schmeisser hit the second Canuck an unpinned grenade dropped to the floor of the trench. Without a sound young Dietrich Wulff dropped belly first, gathering the bomb into his chest with both hands. As it exploded a splinter of steel caught Franz in the thigh along with a geyser of Dietrich Wulff's blood and a huge gob of flesh from beneath Wulff's right rib cage. Franz was back on his feet at once, firing into the disappearing smoke, but there was no one else there.

The other episode he could not forget from the first week had antedated the death of Dietrich Wulff by several days. By the second day of the campaign, Raubal had established his regimental command post in a monastery just behind the vortex of the small but murderous attacks and counterattacks. On the morning of D Plus Two, exasperated by the inability of his company or battalion to supply him with information on the enemy dispositions, Franz's new platoon commander sent him back to see if the regiment had set up a map room as yet and, if so, what was showing there. A headquarters of sorts had been established in the courtyard, a small field kitchen exuded promising scents from a small stable nearby, there were a few motorcycles scattered here and there, and an antitank gun and a heavy Spandau commanded the main road from the direction of the sea. From the ground Franz could see Raubal himself, surrounded by a handful of his staff officers, standing in the main tower of the monastery, with his binoculars on the temporarily quiet fields to the north and west.

He recognized one of the others as the regimental intelligence officer and decided to wait a few minutes in the hope that he would descend. He walked over to a nearby drinking trough and sloshed water over his dusty face and then emptied his canteen and filled it with fresh water from the pump beside the trough. It was only then that he noticed a dozen prisoners sitting against a stone granary under the cradled machine gun of a field policeman. They were the first prisoners he'd seen in Normandy. The first feeling he had for them was one of triumphant hostility, but their mere presence there forced him to admit something to himself that he had been trying to keep away since the afternoon before. In the waning hours of daylight seven of the best soldiers of his own platoon had been still out of contact, pinned down by a Canadian machine gun, a mortar, and at least two sections of riflemen. When they were still missing at dawn, he had pretended to believe that they had died to the last man, as the Hitler Jugend and the SS were meant to do. But in his heart he knew this was not so. Through the nearby orchard he had heard the cry of *"Kamerad!"* with his own ears, heard the sound of men marching off at the double to angry, swift commands.

So, disappointingly though they might have behaved, he could not resist the hope that those unfortunate—weak, perhaps, but still unfortunate—members of his own division were being treated as well as these unfortunate Canadians were being treated here.

Most of the Canadians had taken their helmets off and lay back exhausted against the wall of the granary, but a few were talking among themselves in very subdued, low voices. One had a bandage on his head. It was a clean and expert bandage, not the improvised wad of field dressing an unskilled comrade might have helped him fumble into place right after he was hit. No, this was a new, professional bandage; it could have been applied only by a stretcher-bearer or perhaps even a field doctor after the man had been captured.

For a moment Franz permitted himself the unsoldierly luxury of being grateful to the wounded Canadian prisoner for making it possible for the 12th SS Hitler Jugend to display its humanity and chivalry. He had a wild impulse to walk over and talk to these beaten men from the far-off, ill-fated, and betrayed continent where, for all its stupidity and greed and tragic knuckling under to the Jews and communists, there still dwelt the grimy shrine of P.S. 77, the worn, warm cobblestones of Second Avenue, the beckoning windows of the friendly little stores all going bravely broke, the fresh washing hanging unabashed from the fire escapes, where dwelt his fat uncle Otto, where dwelt his comely mother, Hattie Koerner, where dwelt his lovely and bereaved young Gretchen Waldeck. What would he talk to them about? Not baseball—Canadians weren't a baseball people. Hockey, then. Who was that big roughneck he used to read about in the newspaper stories about the Rangers? Ching Johnson? Bill Cook? It was an impossible notion anyway. At best it would seem like gloating. At worst it would seem like something close to treachery.

He started to walk back toward the tower. Raubal and his group of officers had already descended and emerged into the courtyard. Raubal went over to the pump and took a drink from the tin cup hanging to its spout. His eyes fell, apparently for the first time, on the row of prisoners. He looked at them for a long ten seconds, frowning distastefully. Then he said loudly, to no one in particular, "What shall we do with these heroes? The only good they're for is to eat up our rations." Then he turned abruptly and strode back toward the tower.

Franz hurried after the intelligence officer. He saluted, introduced himself, and explained his mission. The officer was about to dismiss him and had, indeed, begun to reprimand him for daring to interrupt an important operations group, but Raubal overheard. "Tell the young man what you can, Müller, if anything," Raubal ordered. "And ask him to give my compliments to his platoon commander. If all my officers and underofficers showed as much interest in what's going on and as much initiative in finding out we might be at the Channel by now."

It took Franz only a few minutes to mark up the map he had brought with him. Then he walked back across the courtyard toward his motorcycle. At first he could not comprehend what had begun to happen beside the granary. Eleven of the twelve Canadian soldiers were on their feet, looking around them in bewilderment. The twelfth, the man with the bandage, was being helped up by the man beside him. They looked around them and looked at each other like puzzled children caught up suddenly and helplessly lost in a world beyond their comprehension. And then, one by one, their faces achieved an expression of understanding—first understanding and then disbelief. Then belief, dismay, and a gray, slack emptiness.

A junior officer stood nearby with a drawn Luger and a sergeant at the officer's side held a Schmeisser.

"All right, first man," the officer said in English. Without a word the soldier at the end of the line turned and walked stiffly, weaving just a little on his stiff legs, toward a small open doorway leading into an inner courtyard. Franz could see partly through the doorway. Three steps led downward toward a patch of green grass. To one side of the steps another sergeant stood with another Schmeisser. As the soldier put his first foot on the grass the sergeant took a half step forward, lifted the Schmeisser, and put a single shot through the back of his head. The soldier pitched forward on the grass.

"Next man!" the officer commanded.

The second man made a half turn, reaching out to shake the hand of the man behind him. But his movement was uncertain and jerky, almost spastic, and the other man did not at first grasp what was intended. Their hands missed contact, as in these foolish, low-comedy greetings of old acquaintances welcoming each other to bars, and the second man walked on through the doorway alone, unfarewelled and unsped. The next three went in the same way, spastically and unprotestingly. One was weeping softly, but it was hard to detect fear behind the tears; they seemed to be tears mainly of regret and swiftly flowing memories; this weeping man held his head higher than any of the others. Only the sixth man cried out and he only in physical pain when the waiting sergeant beyond the doorway bungled the first shot and had to use a second. Only the last man, a thin sad boy young enough to be in the Hitler Jugend, attempted a speech. When he began his little walk he could see the bodies of his eleven former friends sprawled across each other below the steps. He stopped and faced the German officer and said in a reproachful, schoolmasterish tone, the tone he might have used to lecture a little sister, "You know, this is against the rules."

"Yes, I know," the officer said. "Get moving."

"*We* don't do this, you know."

"Well, you will. You will. Get moving now."

The young soldier started to obey.

"I didn't mean *you* will, yourself," the officer called out in clumsy haste. "I wasn't trying to be funny. I mean your people will."

The young soldier had no real will to resist; the will to resist and the means to resist, like the will and means of his companions, had already drained away in the irrevocable shock of what had happened already. He was hurrying now. He had reached the bottom step and the officer's further, anxious shout of explanation came too late to be heard. "Everybody does sooner or later. These things can't be helped."

In spite of the clutching horror with which Franz had watched this orderly little massacre, he clung against every rebuff to the tattered remnant of his innocence. He could not, of course, have done anything to stop the officer at the monastery, but he could and did revile him as a butcher and a traitor to their vision. Raubal could not have heard the shots; Raubal could not certainly have given the order; to have been capable of either would have been to desert his conscience and sully his oath as a soldier of the Reich. In these first few days there were shootings of prisoners by all the armies everywhere—or so it was sometimes charged and sometimes boasted. But in the heat of battle all trigger fingers were heavy and in the instant of surrender every man took his own chance. This cold-blooded execution of men disarmed hours earlier, far back from the front at a senior headquarters—there was a darker kind of blood in this and no honor. Franz could not and would not believe that a warrior such as Paul Raubal would ever, knowingly, allow such a grisly offense to go unpunished.

And so amid all the filth and agony and bitter weariness he guarded the shreds of his innocence as a ravished virgin will guard her final secret. A war, however painful and tragic, could in some circumstances be good and necessary. However hideous and unsightly the surface of it might be, there was still room within for an immaculate, knightly flame. This was the flame the Bund had shown him first, the Führer had shown more clearly, and Paul Raubal and the true leaders of the true Schutzstaffel would guard strong and undefiled in victory or defeat.

At the end of the retreat from Falaise, Franz saw Raubal again. There were no platoons now, no companies now, no battalions or regiments, but there was still, according to Raubal's stubborn calculation, a 12th SS Hitler Jugend Division. By some freak of chance, some prim thread of order in the almost total breakdown of communications, the report of the original divisional commander's death had somehow got back to the High Command, which had promoted Standartenführer Raubal to Brigadeführer and sent the order forward through the proper channels.

It was true that by the time he had finished herding, hounding, coaxing, bullying, and smuggling the sad remains of the 12th SS through the gap and lurched on with it toward the Seine it was down to less than one fiftieth of its original strength in men and a fifteenth of its strength in tanks and it had no artillery at all. There were only four officers left besides the new Brigadeführer. On the second day of the attack one of them had found Franz leading the only two survivors of his own platoon down a broken side road and ordered him to go up another road and report for duty to divisional HQ. Raubal recognized him at first only for his underofficer's badges, which in the prevailing circumstances would have been a strong recommendation in themselves. Then he remembered him from their brief meeting at the monastery. "You're the man my intelligence officer reprimanded for thinking," he said, smiling through his weariness. "Stay here and act as my adjutant."

The dwindling remnant of the division contracted on itself like a jumble of men and metal flung at random into some vast centrifugal machine. By day they hid against the relentless Jabos, sweeping down still unopposed at the level of the black and splintered treetops. There was no hiding against the artillery, which by now had closed in to within four kilometers of the main axis of retreat on either side and fired night and day, and sometimes, when the heavy, relentless guns caught one of the fleeing columns in between, piled the dead men and dead horses almost as high as the turrets of the shattered tanks, the roofs of the burning trucks, and the barrels of the broken eighty-eights. But the new *Brigade-führer* made it an inflexible order that no one must move by day, not even to forage in the blackened fields for turnips, which were now their only rations, or to search the ruined farmyards for water, which had become almost as desperate a problem as food. And thus, floundering in darkness amid the smoking waste of machinery and heavy weapons and the corpses of men who had passed that way before, Franz got out of the Falaise gap at the side of Paul Raubal. It took almost a week, but they did get out.

They crossed the River Dives just before the pincers closed completely. They took refuge together for the last part of the last afternoon in the cellar of a bombed-out café on the outskirts of a crossroads village.

Poking around the rubble, Franz, incredibly, turned up a liter of good hard Normandy cider and three rounds of slightly green but perfectly edible Camembert. When he had eaten and drunk his fill, Raubal scooped up a mound of powdered brick and folded his field jacket over it to make a pillow. Then he stretched out luxuriously under the warm August sun, with the clear sky overhead and the sheltering walls around. Franz sat on a wooden box, munching the last of his share of the cheese.

In the six days of their desperate animal race for existence, Raubal had never for an instant relaxed from the role of major general. But now he unbent.

"You have been a good comrade, Koerner," he said. "A good comrade and a good soldier."

Franz flushed with pride. "Thank you, *Mein Brigadeführer*," he said.

"Now tell me a little about yourself."

Franz found himself talking freely and eagerly. Not of course about his early doubts, not about the memorabilia of his family life, and only a little and then in a gently patronizing way about the meager but haunting attractions of Yorkville. He talked chiefly about the matters that he knew would win Raubal's warmest approval, the virtues of the Bund, the mass American iniquities that the Bund had tried to combat, about the millions of genuine Americans whose voices had been smothered in their country's carefully manipulated stampede into a war it neither wanted nor understood.

"Ah well," Raubal said consolingly, "even in Germany it took the people a long time to know the Führer. I was one of the fortunate ones who could see from the beginning. I joined the Party in 1930 and soon after that the Brown Shirts and the SS. Up to then I was a coal miner and an ordinary country policeman. Your fate only comes to meet you once, *Hauptscharführer*. Turn it away and it may not come again."

"That's more or less what I decided when I decided to come to Germany." Franz glowed with modest virtue.

"And you did well. You'll never regret it."

Franz had fallen silent. "Will you?" Raubal asked quickly. And then he added, more quickly, "Have you?

"I'm sorry, *Mein Brigadeführer*," Franz said. "I guess I'm more tired than I realized. I wasn't paying attention."

"*Have* you ever regretted it?" Raubal asked again. "I mean the need to go into battle against men who were born in the same country?" Franz could not be certain whether Raubal was asking through clinical curiosity or a shrewd desire to test his dependability. He still hesitated.

"Well?" Raubal asked. "Don't be afraid to talk to me. Be careful what you say to me tomorrow, but today we are comrades. I would like to know."

"Only once," Franz said slowly. "And even then I wasn't sure."

"And that was when?"

"One day at your headquarters in the monastery," Franz said slowly "—I was surprised that you remembered seeing me there that day when I came to look at the maps—well that day at your headquarters I saw a dozen Allied prisoners shot down one by one."

"Yes?" Raubal raised his head a little. He spoke without inflection.

"I've always wondered," Franz said, almost dreading to go on, but unable now to stop, "whether the officer who gave the order was ever punished for it."

Raubal lay back, laughing aloud. In a moment the laugh subsided to a chuckle and he sat up and clapped Franz on the shoulder. "Forgive me, *Hauptscharführer*, I wasn't laughing at you. I was laughing at—well, I guess myself—at everything, I guess. In case you end up there when the division reassembles, I might as well explain one rather essential thing about my headquarters. The important orders are given by one person only. And that's me."

"I see," Franz said.

Raubal touched his shoulder consolingly again. "*Ach*, you're still just a big Yankee. A good Yankee, but still a Yankee. Never mind. You'll learn."

"Yes," Franz had said slowly. "I guess I'll learn."

An officer wearing the uniform of an American major came down the snow-covered roadside to where Franz sat in the front seat of his American jeep. "About thirty minutes from now," he said in English. "Everything O.K. here?"

"Everything O.K., sir," Franz said.

They hadn't used their *Hochlocks* after all. He stirred Erich Tannenbaum back to wakefulness in the other front seat. "Better have a stretch," he said.

A U.S. Sherman tank, its lighter silhouette clearly distinguishable from the Panthers and the giant Tigers, lumbered through a ditch and swiveled into the roadway. As it completed its turn its near track grazed a fender of their jeep.

"Hey!" Franz yelled indignantly.

A dark head turned from the tank's open turret and a guttural voice shouted gaily down, "Balls to you, buddy boy!" And then, chuckling with self-approval, "How you like dot agzcent for right from Brooklyn, buddy boy?"

"You got a real winner there!" Tannenbaum shouted back at him. "Stick with it!" Then to Franz, "There's one guy that doesn't need to worry about the PW cages. If they nail *him* they'll ship him back to the—what's the name of that outfit that supplies the Amis with dancing girls and crooners?"

"The USO?"

"Yes. If they nail that bird they'll send him back to the USO to do imitations of Charlie Chaplin doing imitations of the Führer."

Franz reached across and fingered the American divisional flash on the other man's GI jacket. "None of us have to worry about the PW cages," he reminded him. He put his map board across his knees and turned his small hand light on it again.

CHAPTER FIVE

"I've heard on good authority," Henry Whelan said, "that the sergeant is going for rank."

The sergeant laughed. Usually his laugh was either aloof to a fault or hearty to a fault. With some men a noncommissioned officer had to be careful not to be too friendly and with others he had to be careful not to be too distant. For this occasion the sergeant went down the middle.

"Maybe. Oh, maybe."

Another bottle came in from the edge of the circle. David Kyle, having learned many lessons in military prudence, took a long drink while it was there. Then he passed the bottle on.

"Aaah," the sergeant sighed. "Aaah, that's great."

"That's an officer talking," Henry Whelan said. "A loo-tenant. I always figured Jack Kennebec was loo-tenant material. I could give you a dissertation."

"Henry," Carmen Ruiz asked anxiously. "You not getting drunk, are you?"

"Do you want this dissertation on loo-tenants or not?"

"We could get along without it, Henry," Dave Kyle said. "Most of us have heard it."

"Another time won't hurt. This word loo-tenant fascinates me. Loo-tenants fascinate me. I used to have a Limey broad who used to say frank and open, 'I have to go to the loo.' Most Limey broads think it's more ladylike to say, 'Excuse me a moment, I've got to spend a penny.' But this broad came right out and said she was going to the loo. Well, once you know what a loo is it's no trick to figure out the tenant of a loo. And congratulations to you, Loo-tenant Kennebec."

"Henry, you lay off now," Carmen Ruiz said.

"Oh, let him have his fun," Sergeant Kennebec said wearily. "If it wasn't Henry it would be somebody else."

Henry hadn't heard. "Just for a handful of silver he left us," he recited. "Just for a ribbon to put on his coat."

Colhurst, the new sentry, now thawed out and made giddy by considerably more than his fair share of the booze, submitted a correction.

"Riband."

"Riband?" Henry Whelan demanded. "Who said that?"

"I did," Colhurst said.

"Well, well, we got two loo-tenants. What was your remark again?"

"Riband," Colhurst said doggedly.

"Riband. I say ribbon. How would you like a good praying punch right between your praying prayerful eyes?"

"Take it easy, Henry." Carmen Ruiz pressed Henry Whelan's shoulder and the ring of dark hunched figures settled back.

"Just for a ribbon to put on his coat. Riband!" Henry said, lifting Carmen's arm away. "Pray that!"

"Henry," Carmen asked, "why can't you swear in a straightforward stand-up way like everybody else?"

"I've got standards."

"Ever since we—well, had that trouble around St. Lô you've been hipped on this word pray. I think you're making fun of the rest of us for using the other word so much."

"No. The only word I object to is riband."

"Honest to God, Henry," Sergeant Kennebec said. "Why do you get so much pleasure out of being ugly?"

"Don't you know there's a war on?"

"Honest to God, Henry, it wasn't my idea. I could have been an officer a hundred times. I could have been a thousand of your praying loo-tenants. But this is my last chance and I'm taking it."

"And you'll go home a loo-tenant, O Sir, O Riband. I never did ask you, Jack: are you in the insurance game?"

"That will do, Henry. That will do," Carmen Ruiz said. "If it wasn't for Jack Kennebec you'd be eight feet deep. So would I. So would Dave."

"Jesus," Henry said. "Some gangster you turned out to be!"

"You better slow down, Henry."

"Carmen, you talk like a Unitarian preacher." Henry chuckled in appreciation of his cleverness. "No wonder Al Capone got in so much trouble."

"Henry," David Kyle sat up on his haunches. He was feeling the booze as much as anybody else. "You've used up your quota of brilliant sayings for one night. You open your mouth just once more just one eighth of an inch and you are going to get a handful of fist rammed down your throat and right down to the inside of your belly button." Dave levered his lean shadow upright against the small orange glow of the fire. He had never in his life used such coarse language; the experience was exhilarating.

"I'm talking to Jack Kennebec, Dave."

"Talk to him better."

"All right. When do you go, Jack?"

"Today."

"Today?" Henry felt it like a deadening hammer blow and didn't care who knew it.

"I have to go back to Luxembourg and draw some equipment and get remustered. There's a jeep picking me up and a guy from Baker."

"Today?"

"I thought I'd keep it quiet and save all this yakking."

"Well if you're going today, that's the day you're going. I heard about it but I didn't know it would be so soon."

"The only reason I didn't say anything was to stop this yakking."

"If I'd known it was going to be so soon I wouldn't have been so smart-ass."

"That's O.K., Henry. I'm glad it was you and not somebody else."

"Well, I hope it turns out all right for you, Jack."

"Thanks. I hope it turns out all right for everybody."

"I'm hitting the sack," Carmen said. "Well, in case I don't see you, Jack."

"In case I don't see you, Carmen."

The sergeant stretched his hand across the fire and touched the hand of each of them, like a pope.

CHAPTER SIX

The wound that got George Ballantyne, the eager warrior, out of the war was in part responsible for getting Haig Ballantyne, the stolid pacifist, into it.

Haig was completing his basic training at Camp Salute when the radio brought the first news of Dieppe. He lived in a state of deep anxiety for two days, remembering better than he'd remembered in a very long time how kind and strong and generous a brother George had really been to him. Even through the haze of censorship it was not hard to deduce that Dieppe had been a great disaster and that, as a combat soldier of the Second Division, George had almost certainly been among the victims. It was impossible to shut out the image of his kind, strong, generous—and yes, in his own way, proud—brother George lying dead and perhaps still unburied on the far-off foreign shore or being marched off, broken, hungry, and humiliated into some even farther and more foreign abyss of barbed wire and dungeon keeps. When Vera telephoned the news from the Defense Department that George was safely wounded back in England Haig blurted aloud, "Oh, thank God!" a blasphemous, incongruous, and wholly shameful observation, considering its source, for Haig did not have a God, and if he had had one He'd have wished anything but thanks for such seedy little enterprises as Dieppe and, for that matter, Tours, Agincourt, Crécy, the Plains of Abraham, Gettysburg, Passchendaele, and the whole God-damned—damned well and truly and eternally by any God worthy of the name—lot of them.

But Haig's relief for George was so warm and genuine that he sat right down and wrote him a long letter. At first he tried not to put too much sentiment into it, but then, because he knew this would please George more than anything else he could possibly say, he inserted a tender thought about their sister Hazel and even cooked up a couple of recollections to support it.

Toward the end of the following week, George's old paper, the Winnipeg *Chronicle*, carried a three-column story on Page One announcing boastfully that George had been awarded the Military Medal. The announcement was date-lined London. It was hard to tell exactly what George had done at Dieppe, but there was a description of his wound, a lurid account of his having taken out a German pillbox somewhere beyond the beach at Puits, and a summary of his escape by swimming undaunted and alone out into the lonely blood-streaked Channel. It sounded very much as though George had truly earned his medal. Haig had no desire to belittle his brother's glory, but he had no desire to share in it, either, and it was with a feeling of profound dismay that he read, near the end of the *Chronicle*'s own bragging biographical sketch of its ex-employee, that "a brother of Private Ballantyne, Private Haig Ballantyne, is a member of the Canadian Army Reserve."

As he had known it would, the news of George's exploit caused two basic kinds of reaction in Haig's own cranny of the Army. His fellow reservists—the handful of men who, like Haig, were still resisting the Army's dogged efforts to nag, coax, or frighten them into volunteering for duty overseas—were uneasy, sympathetic, and just faintly reproachful. They were tactful but they withdrew a little from Haig, as though some blemish had just been discovered in his blood. But the men who had already volunteered reacted more directly.

Two of them, standing behind Haig at the next meal parade, staged a highly audible colloquy for his particular benefit and for the general benefit of the whole training platoon.

"I guess the little bastard will be ashamed to stay out now," one said.

"Yeah, he'll go active now for sure. Christ, if *my* brother went through a thing like that—"

Haig had built up a partial immunity. He'd been subjected to endless such taunts and insults but had always been sustained by the certainty of his present fortitude and wisdom and of his ultimate vindication by history. It was a hard, mean game the politicians and the generals were playing in the hope of raising a conscript army without making conscription legal and official. But Haig kept reassuring himself that he could be as hard and mean as anybody else; they might think they were getting to him, but they weren't. They had got to most of the others, one by one and by various methods, but they weren't getting to him. If they wanted him in the trenches, let them pass a law and take every man in his lawful turn. Why should he, Haig Ballantyne, make a public display of his guts and then, most likely, yield them up on some remote and stinking battlefield merely in order that the Prime Minister and the other members of the Government might be spared the inconvenience of standing up in the House of Commons or on the hustings and displaying theirs? If any.

But it was a hard, mean game that all of them were playing. At Camp Salute—which of course was only a nickname to express the distaste of newly-ex civilians for the simpler absurdities of the military life—there was at first no hostility between the R-men and the A-men, or even anything that could be called coolness. Since most R-, or reserve, men, went A, or active, within a week or two anyway there was, in most cases, no occasion for it.

But later the climate of their ninety-man hut came to be as carefully and expertly managed as though it were controlled by a thermostat. The visible differences between the R-men and the A-men began to achieve some importance, not only within the hut and within the camp but on the civvy streets outside. An active soldier wore the cap badge of the corps to which he would soon be posted: the infantry, the artillery, the engineers, ordinance, or the Service Corps. A reserve soldier wore a noncommittal maple leaf. An active soldier had badges saying Canada on his shoulders and the ribbon of the Canadian Volunteer Service Medal on his chest. A reserve soldier had nothing on his shoulders and nothing on his chest.

And then, by degrees, less palpable differences began to make themselves apparent. The daily Part One orders began, with some regularity, to order the R-men in the hut to report for special parades, while the A-men carried on with their foot and rifle drill and the kitchen and hut fatigues. One rainy day there were, by an actual count that escaped no one's attention, eight A-men washing dishes and handling garbage, two more working on the coal pile, two in the latrines, two on the rations truck, and one on hut orderly. All twenty-seven R-men meanwhile sat snugly in the lecture hut, listening to another exhortation on the evils of fascism and the splendors of democracy.

They were making everything as nice as they could for the R-men, one of the recent converts to the active ranks complained, on the assumption that they would all go active just to oblige the NCOs and officers. That was the way these camps were judged in Ottawa, almost everyone was now agreed—not on how much the graduate privates and gunners knew when they went on to their advanced training centers, but on how many of them had volunteered to go overseas. In the meantime the brave and honest volunteers did fatigues for the maple-leaf wonders and the Mother's Boys. And then, without warning, the R-men would for a while draw all the fatigues. And for a while the little coterie of officers and NCOs who took the daily parade inspections would walk past the A-men without remark, glancing in silent approval only at their Canada badges and their Volunteer Service ribbons. During these climatic changes the company commander would almost invariably stop before at least one R-man and point his swagger stick at an exposed gaiter buckle or a protruding shoelace and say, "Mr.

173

Johnson, this man has spoiled your whole platoon. What's his name?" The company commander would say, "Rossosky, sir," or "Robertson, sir." The company commander would stare hard, as though trying to forget some distasteful secret and say, "Yes, I know that name." Once he commented on the imperfectly shined shoes of one R-man, the not quite immaculate gaiters of another, and the only moderately polished cap badge of a third, and as he returned the subaltern's parting salute, he said loudly, so that the whole platoon could hear, "Mr. Johnson, most of the men in your platoon are playing ball. But I won't put up with this sloppiness by a few. You will confine the entire platoon to barracks for the next two days."

Almost every day two or three of the R-men were fallen out of the squad and told to report to the company commander's office. Sometimes they returned looking virtuous and a little sheepish, avoiding the anxious glances of the other R-men. Sometimes they were sullen and defiant. It was never hard to tell whether they'd changed their minds. By midsummer there were only nine R-men left in the platoon of ninety.

Even before Dieppe and the long new thoughts about his brother George, Haig had begun to wonder a trifle defensively about the total motives of his eight colleagues and with growing belligerency about his own. No two of them, he had been forced to concede, saw the issues exactly the same. Forsee, a spectacularly stupid farm boy from Northern Manitoba, was not qualified to spell Hitler, much less to fight him. Rossosky and Robertson were cowards plain and simple; the only principle they were capable of standing on was that they didn't want to get hurt. Two other men, there was almost incontrovertible evidence to show, were not lacking in courage but they were homosexuals: they loved the Army, loved it for its environment and its opportunities, which could not possibly be improved on and might be seriously impaired by their transfer to a theater of combat.

One other man clung to an uncluttered pragmatism. "It's all right for those other bastards," he confided to Haig one day on the way to the canteen. "They never had it so good. Half the bastards were on relief. But this has cost me a lot already. I was making forty-five a week." Still another was so mad with passion for his new wife and the new delights of marriage that the mere thought of putting an ocean between them drove him, almost literally, to the verge of a nervous breakdown.

Marcel Benoit, a voluble little truck driver from St. Boniface, was the only one of the last holdouts who had been affected, even obliquely, by the intimations of history.

"Balls to de bloody h'English," he squalled, not caring in the least who heard. "Las' time, nineteen seventeen, dey crucify de bes' Canadian who ever live', Sir Wilfrid Laurier. Dey lie. Dey say no conscription. Den, *vite*, dey got it. My h'uncle, he get kill'. For who? For de h'English an' he hate deir guts h'all de time and so do I. Now dis Mackenzie King, he say no conscription again and what's de sonofabitch tryin' to do? He's tryin' to conscrip' me just like Borden conscrip' my h'uncle. If dat king and dose h'English want me to fight anudder of deir wars, dey can bring it over here. Den I'll fight it good."

After a final private interview with the company commander, Benoit was transferred, mysteriously but speedily, to a Quebec battalion that had been assigned to the defense of the west coast of Vancouver Island. The day he left, he gave Haig a private, triumphant wink. "Stick wit' it," he said. "If 'e gets you alone, wit'out witnesses, jus' look dat major right in de h'eye and tell him to go screw himself. W'en 'e see you really mean business, 'e'll do what 'e did wit' me—get rid of you. 'E don't want you spoilin' de camp record."

But Haig was still determined, in spite of the growing isolation, not only to have his victory, but to have it on his own lofty and uncompromising terms. Almost every day the objective became more murky and the task of holding to it more complicated. A week before their sixty days of basic training ended the two fairies went active after all. If they didn't, the camp commandant had warned them, one of them would be posted to Halifax and the other to British Columbia; if they did he'd arrange for them both to go to Barrie in the same draft. One of the two clearly identifiable cowards, Rossosky, signed up for the Service Corps after the platoon lance corporal took him out behind the drill shed and cut him quietly to ribbons in what everyone except Rossosky, who was not consulted, agreed was a fair, clean, stand-up fist fight. The forty-five-dollar-a-week pragmatist, when invited to a similar test of his patriotism, declined and enlisted in the engineers. The last word for the last two recalcitrants came down from the major himself at a special company commander's parade for the whole platoon.

The major walked with a permanent list. He stood with a permanent list, his whole left side adroop under the weight of his old campaign ribbons. His sharp, sallow face listed beneath the scraggly gray counterbalances of a mustache that he allowed to grow too long because it would not grow thick enough. His speech listed; he began his longer sentences strongly and confidently, but they trailed off and fell away in threshing shadows. Some of the individual words listed. He pronounced "ing" like "een."

The major was smiling and his yellowing teeth listed humorlessly beneath the smile. "Well, men," he said, "I have good news for you. At least I think it will be good news for you. You've been traineen hard and workeen hard and I know you've found companionship and a new sense of purpose and I know you've profited by the experience of the ah experience."

The major paused. "And now," he said, "you will soon be goeen away. I shouldn't tell you when you will be goeen, but you have been such good soldiers here that I was just sayeen to Mr. Johnson I don't believe there has been a finer platoon in camp than Number Nine and I have been watcheen men come and go ever since."

One of the two fairies, lounging at the stand-easy in the rear file just behind Haig, whispered to the other fairy, "Good old Wylie! A prince among men."

"You said *prince?*" Rossosky, one of the rehabilitated cowards, interjected.

"You will be goeen on to your advanced traineen centers in five days from today." The major deliberately underplayed the drama and waited for the ragged cheer to subside.

"Some of us"—the major made a stalwart adjustment to the list of his shoulders—"some of us will have to stay behind. But our thoughts go with you. I think all of you know a bit about my own small record and when I think of the humble part I have been able to play as a soldier of the British Empire I can't help thinkeen of the humble part and envyeen, yes, envyeen."

"A heart as big as all outdoors," one of the fairies whispered.

"But you don't want to hear a speech," the major protested. "There's just one thing I want to say. You will be goeen on to other camps where you will find that they are not as generous in giveen you leaves as we have tried to be here. And before you go, as a reward for your fine performance here, I want you all to have a leave with your families because you may not for a long time. I have put it up to the colonel."

Under cover of another, much louder cheer, one of the fairies said aloud, "When they made old Wylie, they threw the mold away."

"And not a damn' bit too soon," the other added.

"The colonel consented," the major went on, "on one simple little condition. It's a fair condition. It applies to all the other platoons in the camp and they will be getteen special leaves too if they meet . . ."

The major's voice positively staggered under its burden of sentiment. "We are proud of the record of this camp. Oh, I know you call it Camp Salute and I know exactly why." He listed forward companionably and confidentially, gathering them into the embrace of his yellow, listing smile. "I was a private once, you see, just as some of you will be majors someday and yes, even colonels and brigadiers."

He waited for the nobility of his admission to sink in. "Yes, we're proud of the record of Camp Salute. When we can send out a draft that is one hundred per cent active we are proud and we know that you are proud too because in the final analysis. Today is let's see Wednesday. The drafts to your new traineen centers go out on Monday. So that leaves nearly two days. If good old Number Nine platoon can show a one-hundred-per-cent-active roster by Thursday night the whole platoon will go out on seventy-two-hour passes on Friday morning and I'm confident. It just means all pulleen together and talkeen it over among yourselves. I know that some of you, perhaps for what seem to you to be good personal reasons, haven't been as fast as the rest to decide about goeen active, but I know that no man in Number Nine would want to deprive his whole platoon of the last leave they'll be getteen for a long time and I know even if he did. So talk it over among yourselves and pull together among yourselves, this is your own decision and it's none of the business of your officers and NCOs. And after all that's the British way, the way that means so much to all of us."

The major smiled affably and listed to attention. "That's all, Mr. Johnson."

Before the subaltern gave the order for dismissal, Haig glanced down the length of the middle rank. The men closest to them were glancing speculatively in his direction and, four places away, in the direction of Jerry Needham, the only other R-man left, the man who was mad for the love of his wife and the love of his marriage.

"See you two guys in North Africa," one of the fairies giggled, more in sympathy than in malice.

Everything went into suspended animation for the rest of the day. No one said anything in particular to Haig or to Jerry Needham during the remaining drill and small-weapons periods, or, so far as it could be ascertained, avoided saying anything in particular either. Supper was no quieter or noisier than usual. None of the A-men spoke directly to Haig except to say, "Pass the ketchup" and "Pass the bread," but that was all they'd been saying to him anyway during the last week or two. Haig decided he would play it by ear, doing whatever he had to do as its necessity made itself apparent.

Nearly all the A-men asked for and received midnight passes. Haig saw an early movie in the drill hall and then went to bed. Jerry Needham was already asleep, or pretending to be asleep, in a lower five bunks away. Three or four soldiers were doing laundry in the washroom, three or four others were lying in their bunks reading or writing letters, and a handful more were playing or kibitzing a desultory game of hearts.

At midnight the hut was dark and quiet and still nearly empty. The beds were silhouetted flat and naked in the sludgy bath of starlight from the windows. There was no sound but the occasional heaving of a restless body against the creak of bedsprings and now and then a quiet cough. The room smelled empty; it was warm, but much fresher than usual. The washroom door had been closed, but a slab of yellow light fell through its crack across the middle of the floor.

Haig looked at the luminous dial of his watch. Ten past. There was a sound of scuffling feet in the gravel outside the open, screened front doorway. They wouldn't all come in together. Two or three or half a dozen at a time. The screen door squeaked open and then slammed noisily shut. "Not so much noise!" somebody complained from one of the bunks near the end of the room.

Two tearful voices were singing from one of the dark corner bunks.

> "If I had my way dear,
> You'd never grow old—
> A garden—"

178

The far end of the hut had filled now with aimless milling figures. One of them detached itself, threw the double doors to the washroom open, and propped them apart by jamming two bayonet scabbards between their lower edges and the floor. The middle of the hut between the two rows of two-tiered bunks was a flood of pale light. A Babel of excited whispers broke out at the far end, and a bottle rang a hollow high C against the iron of a bedstead. The whispering quieted and a swaying file of shadows moved down the hut through the slab of light from the washroom door and merged in a knot in the corridor between the beds. Haig propped himself on one elbow and watched, dry-mouthed, tense, and wary. The only form recognizable from its shape was the tall and bulky one of a soldier named Lister. He broke away from the clump of other shapes and led the way to Jerry Needham's bunk. Jerry Needham was still shamming sleep beneath his blankets. Lister looked down for a few moments. Six men sat down on the bunk, three on each side. The covers stirred blackly and then were still again.

The glaring beam of a flashlight stabbed through the darkness, played on the white corner of the pillow and focused on Jerry Needham's face. His face was white and slack and his eyes were two startled slashes of copper, like the eyes of a cat caught in automobile headlights.

"Wake up, Needham!" The words broke the silence permanently.

"Shut up. I'll handle this."

Haig could make out Lister's heavy features now, thrust close behind the flashlight, close to the white face on the pillow.

"It's me, Jerry. Al Lister."

"Hello, Al." Jerry Needham's eyes were squeezed tightly shut against the light. His voice tried to duplicate the casual warmth of the other. It failed; it was a scared voice.

"Good old Jerry." Lister leaned forward with the torch. The six soldiers seated on the edges of the bed leaned forward and down, pinioning Jerry Needham beneath the blankets. Lister's free hand reached down and patted the right cheek of the face on the pillow. And then, not exactly heavily but sharply, it slapped each cheek three times. There was no sound of protest.

"Like a drink, Jerry?"

"No thanks, Al."

"Sure he does. Give him a drink. Where's the jug of goof?"

Another hand thrust the neck of a bottle into the beam of the torch. It glinted purple in the light as it probed for the lips of the man imprisoned under the blankets and the wine spilled over the lips and rolled down Jerry Needham's flabby chin in a red smear. Needham tried to rub it off by squirming one shoulder beneath the blankets, but the six men who held him in the vise of their bodies leaned forward again, pinioning him closer than before. Lister curled a fringe of the top blanket in his free hand and swabbed the chin dry with delicate, oversolicitous dabs.

"All right, Jerry?"

"All right, Al."

"That's not the first drink we've had together, Jerry." Lister turned his head away from Needham, but he still held the flashlight close to his face. "Me and Jerry used to kick around a lot when we first come here," he said to their assembled comrades. "Me and Jerry are pals. Ain't we, Jerry?—Ain't we Jerry?" he repeated.

"Ain't we what?" For the first time Jerry Needham spoke with a hint of spirit.

"Pals." Lister moved his free hand an inch or two.

"Sure," Needham said, fully co-operative again.

"Sure what, Jerry?"

"Pals."

"Pals, who?"

"What do you mean, Al?" Needham asked anxiously.

"That's what I mean, Jerry. Al. Just Al. You remember my name, Jerry. You just said it. It's Al. Tell them what we are, Jerry. Tell the boys right."

"We're pals, Al."

Lister patted one of the cheeks and then slapped the two cheeks again, three times on each side as he had done before, but this time harder.

"Well, Jerry," Lister said. "I guess you know what the boys have been saying." He moved the flashlight closer, so close it was almost touching Needham's nose.

"The boys have been saying you're yellow, Jerry," Lister said. "That hurt. The boys say you're not only yellow, but you're terribly, terribly selfish. The boys say you don't care if we get our leave tomorrow or not. The boys say you'd do us out of it.

"I don't like that kind of talk, Jerry," Lister went on staunchly. "And the talk isn't the worst part of it, Jerry. The boys were real mad at you. Some of the things they talked about doing—well, they're just sickening, Jerry. Just sickening, that's all."

Lister took the flashlight away for a moment. "Since we're pals and everything, Jerry, I've been doing my best to talk the boys out of it. I said a little innocent horseplay was O.K. between friends, but roughstuff just don't go. I said it was all right to do like this."

Lister's foot scraped against the floor as he bent forward across the bed. He drew his free hand back to the level of his shoulder and slapped Needham hard across the mouth, twenty times or more. Each slap made a sick crash in the silent room.

"That's all right, Jerry," Lister said when he was done. "That's between pals. I told the boys you wouldn't mind that."

Needham tried to twist his face toward the pillow. He ran his dry tongue across the blood on his swollen, broken lips.

"I told the boys you'd go active in a minute, Jerry," Lister said. "I told the boys if we'd put it up to you man to man there wouldn't be any argument. And there wouldn't, either. Would there, Jerry?"

Needham began to open his eyes, but the harsh light from the torch ground them shut again.

"Would there, Jerry?"

"I don't know, Al. I just don't know."

"You don't know! You mean you're *still* not ready to go active?" Lister turned around, stunned and solicitous, appealing for help. "Gee, fellahs, whatever old Jerry's got, he's got it bad."

"Oh Christ, Al." One of the men near the back snorted in disgust. "His only trouble is he likes his quiff."

"Is that so?" Lister said, as though marveling over some miracle of science. "Well, well, now, isn't that remarkable?"

"That's all that's wrong with him," the man at the back said through the darkness. "He just doesn't want to lose his quiff."

"Well, well," Lister repeated. "Really most remarkable." He returned his attention to Needham. "Why didn't you tell us in the first place, Jerry?" He sounded as though his feelings had been hurt but also as though, whatever offense he had suffered, he was determined to rise above it. "That fact is, Jerry, that *most* of us like our quiff. And that's one of the beauties about going active. You'll get more of it, not less. You must have heard about the way it is in England. Why, for God's sake, Jerry, over there they put it out every night just like the milk bottles. It comes as regular as the BBC news. If *that's* all you're worrying about—"

"It's special quiff he's worrying about," the man at the back said. "He just got married."

"Oh. Is that right, Jerry?"

Needham kept his eyes tightly closed. He lay perfectly still, seeking refuge in some other world, trying to seal off his senses.

"Maybe we should know more about this special quiff of Jerry's," Lister said. "How we gonna help him if we don't have more details?"

"He hides his mail under the mattress," the man at the back reported.

"Well, then," Lister said, "we better just have a look at it. When it comes to helping my pal Jerry here I say we better leave no stone unturned."

One of the other men groped beneath the mattress and handed a sheaf of papers to Lister. A photograph fell to the floor. Lister picked it up and held it to the flashlight while the others pressed around.

"Man oh man!" someone shouted. "Man oh man! That Jerry!"

"Hey, lemme out of here!" Another man pretended suffocation.

"That's her wedding dress."

"Take it off!" someone squealed excitedly.

"I already have. I can see right through it. I can feel right through it. Boy *is* that special quiff?"

"Now I wonder," Lister speculated judicially, "what a dish like that could see in a miserable little zombie bastard like my old pal, Jerry Needham. Let's see." He put the photograph aside and held a letter up in its place. "Maybe we can find a clue here."

"Nice handwriting," a man leaning across Lister's shoulder announced.

"Very nice handwriting," Lister agreed. "Young. Schoolgirly. That's the best kind of quiff there is. Jerry's got taste."

"What's it say?" someone demanded.

"Well, it begins all right. If it ends any better I don't know if I'll be able to stand it."

"Read, God damn it, Lister!"

"O.K. O.K. Keep your shirt on. We got all night and there's lots more. It starts like this. It starts"—Lister dropped his voice in a husky parody of Charles Boyer—"'My wild and lovely darling lover—'"

In a desperate writhing convulsion Needham threw himself momentarily free of the men holding him down and clutched at the letter. Lister stepped back as Needham's captors grabbed him and pinned him down again.

"Shall I go on, Jerry?" Lister asked levelly. "Shall I continue, wild and darling lover?"

"No. For God's sake, no," Needham sobbed. "Put the picture back. Put the letters back and let go of me."

"And you'll go active, Jerry?" Lister asked, not without sympathy. "First thing in the morning?"

"First thing in the morning," Needham said dully.

"Leave him alone," Lister commanded. He led the dark clump of men down the corridor. "This won't take long," someone giggled.

Haig jumped off his bunk and stood in the middle of the floor, his bare feet wide apart. Lister stopped directly in front of him.

"How about you, Ballantyne?"

Haig had had a whole afternoon and a whole long evening to rehearse the scene. It was not going exactly as he'd expected it would, but some of the lines were still usable.

"You know how about me," Haig said. "It's the same as it is with at least thirty of you before you started caving in. The difference is I'm not caving."

"No?" Lister temporized. "You sure?"

"Let me tell you one thing before you start," Haig said. "I'm going to say it in front of all your ninety witnesses and I'll say it loud enough so they can still be witnesses when I'm tried for murder."

"Well, then say it."

"I'll fight any one of you man to man. Even you, Lister. But if you try to do anything to me like you just did to Needham I'll kill you. I'll blow your brains out while you're asleep right in this camp. And if you get away from this camp before I do, I'll get away from it too. I'll find out where you've gone and I'll catch up with you and I'll blow your brains out and that and nothing else will be my sacred lifetime mission."

"The bastard's crazy," someone said uneasily. "He's gone right off. We better get the M.O."

"No. Wait a minute." Lister waved the others back and he and Haig were standing alone in the pool of light from the washroom door, Lister already much thicker and broader and half a head taller and now swelling with a manufactured outrage. The floor had grown unaccountably cold under Haig's bare feet, but he pressed his feet down more firmly, locking his knees against the trembling of excitement and some other feeling that refused to be dismissed.

Wouldn't it be great, he found himself thinking, if at this dramatic juncture I proceeded to piss myself.

"Your talk about killing me is just funny," Lister orated down at him. "What I don't like is this crap about caving in."

"You know what it means." Haig's voice was wavering with excitement. It had shot up half an octave since his venomous announcement of a moment before. "Six weeks ago, Lister, you were talking the same way yourself. No, by God, you were talking even worse. You were talking like a God-damned commie. I heard you. They all heard. Half of them were cheering you, just as they're cheering you now. Sure you'd go—in your turn. Just so they made everybody else take *his* turn. And if they wanted conscription of manpower, how about conscription of wealth? If they wanted to raise their God-damned army like they were running a tag day or a frat rush, let them go ahead, but they better include you out."

"Shut up!" Lister's bellow fed and reinforced his rage. Then his voice dropped into a virtuous harangue. "Sure I bought that crap about the principle of the thing for a while. Until like anybody with eyes or an ounce of brains, I found out how stupid and senseless it was. Principle of the thing—Jesus! Everybody's got principles, when they make him feel better about doing whatever he wants to do anyway or not doing what he doesn't want to do. Hitler's got principles. Mussolini's got principles. Stalin's got principles. You've got principles. Well, I've got bad news for you, Ballantyne. I've got principles too. And right now the principle I'm working on is that no lily-livered, holier-than-thou sniveling, welshing zombie is going to cheat ninety men out of a seventy-two-hour pass."

The mention of passes set off an eager, urgent volley of reasoning from the circle of onlookers.

"My God, Haig, I just figured it out in my head. Ninety men times three days is two hundred and seventy days. Almost a whole year's leave that just you, just one man, would be costing this one platoon."

"It's worse than that, Ballantyne. Everybody's got so worked up about this leave that if we don't get it, everybody will go on the loose anyway."

"That's right, by God. And that's twenty-eight days each in the glass house. Ninety times twenty-eight—Holy God, it's a life-time!"

"If you won't think of the guys right here in your own hut, Ballantyne, at least you can think of your brother."

"Yeah, how about that, Ballantyne? When he hears what a hero you turned out to be that poor bastard of a brother of yours will take his medal out and bury it."

Haig remembered that he'd never been in a fist fight before. George had always intervened, either as the gentle and sagacious peacemaker or, once or twice when Haig had been on the verge of combat with a much larger or stronger boy, as a stand-in. George never lost a fight; the undefined corollary seemed to have been that Haig would never have won one. He'd never even learned how to hold his hands. Now the most dismaying prospect of all was not that he'd be outweighed and overmatched, but that he'd be ridiculous. Not ridiculous by comparison, but innately and independently ridiculous, ridiculous per se.

"You're all wasting your breath." His voice still wavered a little, but it carried through the hut. "Come on, Lister, let's get it over with."

Lister threw off his battle-dress jacket. The men in the circle closed in and pushed them together through the doorway into the big washroom. Then they parted and made a square around the walls.

Haig put his feet apart again. Then, prompted by some theatri-cal stirring toward knight-errantry, he removed the top of his pajamas, folded it, and dropped it into a tin washbasin on one of the wooden tables that ran around three sides of the room.

Lister stepped forward and inspected his firm and lean but hardly formidable chest. Lister had come in with his hands held high in the classic John L. Sullivan stance. But now he lowered them until they reached the level of his knees. He opened the palms and came slowly across the room, swinging them from side to side. "Look, Ballantyne," he said contemptuously, "no fists!"

Haig rushed toward him and his first punch actually grazed Lister's cheek. As he stumbled on past, the heel of Lister's right hand caught him deafeningly in the left ear. Lister turned and knocked him upright with the other open hand and then sent him sprawling to the floor with another fearful backhanded slap against the mouth.

The room was silent except for the hard crash of Lister's hands, the lurching pad of Haig's bare feet and the two men's breathing. Lister was breathing evenly and calmly, though a little more loudly than normal; Haig was already panting and gasping. He put his head down and rushed straight ahead. This time his own wild blow missed completely and all he felt was Lister's vast hard hand again. He thrust himself off the floor a second time. Lister let him get closer and then sent him spinning past a wall of pale, expressionless faces all the way through a second open doorway into the latrine area. Lister followed him and knocked him down still again. Haig reached up and hauled himself half erect by using the upper part of one of the urinals. At first he could not see where Lister was. He wiped a wet splash of blood away from his eyes and half fell across the room. This time he went to his knees without being hit. He pulled himself up once more and once more looked around for Lister.

Instead, the platoon lance-jack was in the center of the room now. He had one arm up, up good and high so his single stripe was clearly visible and clearly designated as being in use. The lance-jack looked alarmed and so, Haig noticed to his shame and infinite regret, did the faces of the other spectators.

"That's all," the lance-jack said hurriedly. "Jesus, Lister! You might have killed him."

"It was his idea." Haig still could not find Lister, but Lister's voice reflected the same alarm that showed on all the faces.

"Somebody wash him up and see if he needs stitches. If he does I'll take him to the M.O. The rest of you get to bed."

"What the hell, Corporal?" someone broke in. "What the hell? You said you were taking an overnight pass tonight."

"Well, it's a good thing I didn't. Get to bed."

"Yeah, but what the hell. What about our leaves?"

"Maybe you'll get them anyway," the lance-jack said consolingly. "I guess you did your best anyway. I'll try and talk to the major about it."

Haig needed, as it turned out, seven stitches. The camp medical officer, half full of whisky and the other half full of resentment at being called away from a snooker game in the officers' mess, did the job quickly.

"What happened, boy? Fall outa bed? I gotta put something down on the report. Fall outa bed O.K.?"

"Yes, sir," Haig mumbled. "Fall outa bed's all right."

"You're one of the R-men in Nine Platoon, aren't you? What happen' to the other one tonight? He fall outa bed too?"

"He's decided to go active."

"In'restin'. Mos' in'restin'. There now, you'll be O.K. Just watch that fallin' outa bed now. Make sure it doesn't get chronic." The major laughed appreciatively and hurried back to the mess to share the witticism.

Haig got to sleep, aching inside and out, just before dawn. No one gave any sign of noting his lonely return to the hut from the medical office. He lay awake trying to consolidate his sense of stoicism and triumph, seeking exultation in the knowledge that he'd stood up to them all, mocked and demeaned and crushed them as utterly as they had set out to mock and demean and crush him. But desperately though he bade them, the feelings he had so painfully earned and dearly paid for would not answer his summons. Lying in the dark and fingering his stitches and his bruises, he carried on a dozen imaginary conversations, made a score of caborundum-hard debating points, won the wonder of a hundred admirers, and routed a thousand blind, inane, or willfully malevolent detractors. But they were all, he realized with growing desolation, the creatures and creations of a shadow world. In real life, the right circumstances and the right people to test and ratify his own rightness had ceased to exist. He was alone and totally alone, the last survivor of a cause that for most of those who had dropped away had never been a cause at all, but only a convenience and an excuse. Still more agonizingly, he began to ask whether, if there was any real way to get to the root of it, even he might be in the grip of some subtle and therefore more insidious form of self-deception. Reason had vanished into a limbo of *non sequiturs*. "Say, waiter, I think there's a fly in my soup." "Well, don't you know there's a war on?" . . . "Hitler's got principles. Right now the principle I'm working on is that nobody's going to cheat ninety men out of a seventy-two-hour pass." With a sudden chill of panic he discovered that he, himself, the only audience left to applaud or argue, was showing signs of deafness too.

In all the world only one person had anything like perfect comprehension. That was his bountiful, bouncy young sister-in-law Vera Rebchuk Ballantyne. Right now, for the first time, in the middle of the long, tormented night, he remembered something about Vera that he hadn't even noticed at the time. After her father came to live with her and she moved into the apartment, Vera had designated the chesterfield in the living-dining room as Haig's bed and insisted that he use it rather than the Y.M.C.A. anytime an overnight brought him into Winnipeg. He'd visited her three times since he'd been drafted. The free lodging had been helpful, but Vera herself had been indispensable. She was the most sympathetic and uncritical listener he had ever known or even dreamed of. When, as he had a great need to do, he explained to her, as he did again and again, the moral niceties—not just the niceties either, but the fundamental unassailability—of his military attitude and status, she had understood perfectly and assented both warmly and with a touch of comradely wrath. But now he did remember the little cloud of last Sunday, remembered it only because it fitted the context of this Wednesday night; fitted it in bleak retrospect, as last year's small and then unnoticed wound suddenly begins to fit the corpse of this year's love.

Vera, naturally, had been still full of George and Dieppe and his medal, and her own overwhelming devotion. Haig was on a day pass and had to catch an early bus, and there had only been a short time to redefine and reaffirm his own position and wait for her eager re-endorsement and her wrathful redismissal of the forces that were arrayed against him. But Vera's father came in just then and they were talking about George all over again. Just before he left, when Vera followed him to the outer stairway, he had tried to reopen the more complicated subject, but Vera still babbled on about George, urging Haig, now that he'd written his first long letter to George, to continue writing regularly. "I know you have some kind of complex about him," she said fondly. "And he's got some kind of complex about you. But you *do* mean so much to him, Haig. He *is* so proud of you—so proud of you and so much a worrywart about you, too. Oh Haig, George had such an awful time in that awful place, he's so brave and generous—Haig, please! Write to him again. Write him every week." It was not unnatural for Vera to be dabbing her eyes from happiness and longing and general female weepiness, and it was only now, in the dark debris of his afterthoughts, that the black suspicion came to him: maybe she was changing the subject deliberately; maybe she doesn't want to discuss *my* army any more; maybe my hidden hole-in-the-corner of a hell has begun to look small and sordid beside George's great big, glorious hell, with its headlines and its medals. Maybe—God, not maybe, certainly—I have no right to expect more of Vera than of Barbara. Vera's only related to me by marriage; Barbara was going to be part of me by marriage.

Losing Barbara Ransome had not really been an undue hardship. They had never been deeply involved. Barbara said that she loved him for his pure white mind and Haig said he loved her for her pure white body, and they sometimes exchanged these sacred sentiments in public, making bright conversation on double dates. With the war almost two years old and the traffic from the campus to the services growing steadily it was the fashionable thing to be engaged. It was also still moderately fashionable—although this fashion was going out—for earnest young women to beseech their chosen ones to stay away from the battlefields and for pseudo-cynical young men to promise, with highly contradictory gleams in their eyes and strong, alluring smells in their nostrils and ancient lusts churning in their bowels, that staying away from the battlefields would remain their firmest and if need be final end in life. The young men continued to go to the war and the young women continued to wave good-by.

Haig soon perceived how difficult it was becoming for Barbara. Even though controls, the wheat pools, and government interference had left the Grain Exchange in ruins, Barbara's father was still one of the biggest men in Winnipeg. He was head of the current war savings drive, and Barbara's mother, "one of the most popular matrons in River Heights," was head of the current drive for salvaging tin, cigarette foil, and paper. Right up to the time Haig came back from camp on his first leave, Barbara nevertheless continued to assure him that he must on no account even consider wavering. But she was a terrible actress; she was so unnecessarily vehement that it had become perfectly clear she was wavering herself. It was a relief to them both to get it over with in a single evening.

He'd come in to Winnipeg to attend a June dance sponsored by Barbara's sorority. Bundles for Britain. Half the men were in uniform. To his annoyance and faint discomfort, he discovered himself looking around to see how many others were without Canada badges and the red, blue, and green ribbon of the Volunteer Service Medal. He saw only two. It was a well-bred gathering and there were no incidents, overt or incipient. Most of the girls he danced with were already acquainted with the field marks of the A-man and the R-man, the non-zombie and the zombie. After a swift, sidewise glance at the unadorned chest and shoulders of his uniform his dancing partners politely avoided the military aspects of the war and concentrated on the awfulness of rationing, of university food, and of the public transit service to and from Fort Garry. For Barbara it was not so easy. She chatted gaily during their dances together, but once, when she rumbaed past with another man, he heard her say distinctly, "He's not sure when he'll be going. He's trying to get posted to the Little Black Devils." He didn't know the man she was dancing with, nor, he felt fairly sure, did she. This only increased his certainty that they must be talking about him; only to a stranger could she have pretended that her fiancé was already enlisted for overseas.

Going to Child's afterward for bacon and eggs was as much a part of any big college dance as the music of Frank Wright's Orchestra or the mickey of Silver Fizz gin. Barbara hadn't wanted to go to Child's at all, and when he persuaded her to change her mind she had insisted that they go alone. "Oh, I just feel accident-prone," she said rather ill-naturedly as they drove to the restaurant in her father's Lincoln. "And I'm really not very sociable or very hungry. Don't ask me why. I don't know."

By now Haig didn't have to ask and he was feeling accident-prone too, and that made it all the more imperative to hurry on and meet the accident and get it over with.

It was really quite unspectacular. Three men in new ground-crew uniforms of the RCAF with their three girls at the next table. One of the RCAF men making a few of the tired, overstandardized, overfamiliar, overstale, and overstupid remarks. Haig listening carefully for bad language, the point of no return. Hearing none and searching across the table for Barbara's eyes, trying to catch her with the amused superior smile they'd exchanged in similar situations before. Barbara studying the menu. The loudest of the airmen underlining his next observation with the word "sonofabitch." Haig walking over and saying with careless hauteur, an inspired mixture of Cyrano and Silver Fizz, "Look, it's not so much what you say, which is a matter of indifference to me. It's the way you say it, which is offensive to the lady I'm with, if not to the ones you're with."

The airman's two friends pulling him back to his chair. The headwaiter pulling Haig toward the doorway. Barbara Ransome fleeing alone down Portage Avenue. Haig overtaking her. Their silent ride back to River Heights.

Barbara saying at last, while the big darkened car sat before the big darkened house, "Haig, I've been thinking a lot lately."

Haig saying, "Yes, Barbara, I can see you have."

"Haig, if you want to change your mind, it's all right with me."

"I can see that. But I don't want to change my mind."

Barbara saying, "Haig, it's not only now we have to think of. It's five years from now, ten years from now, twenty years from now."

Haig saying, "Sure, Barbara, we must think of the children. What did *you* do in the war, Daddy? No, Mr. Ballantyne, I won't buy your pretty barley futures, I won't buy your oats or wheat. Because you refused to fight for King and Country."

"It's hardly a matter for flippancy any more, is it? Trying to make me feel cheap won't help either of us."

"No. And what's more it won't work on either of us, will it, Barbara? Sad but true. True but sad." He was attempting to recover the lofty mood of Child's, but both Cyrano and the Silver Fizz had exhausted their kick.

"It won't work on *me*, Haig," she said. "I see nothing cheap about trying to use my intelligence."

"A chip off the old block," he said irrationally. "Old Pater been reasoning with you? Old Mater helping you see the light?"

"Oh, the hell with it," she said abruptly, and handed him back his ring.

"That's what I say," he agreed, opening the door of the Lincoln and preparing to depart from River Heights on foot. "The hell with it."

In some ways his desertion by Barbara had been a relief. Now that it was ended he thought mainly of the Carrara-marble coolness she had brought even to their brief, strained split minutes of passion. He thought of the hearty pomposity of her father and the plump, wheezy and vaguely sweaty rich-bitchiness of her mother. All right, then, sour grapes; the fact was they *had* been sour. But it was not the same at all with Vera. If Vera hadn't been married to his brother George, he'd have tried with all his heart to marry her himself. In the meantime, while the world simultaneously closed in on him and turned away from him, she was its one steady source of light, the one mirror in which he could find his true reflection, his reflection unflawed, unsullied, and unchallenged.

No, it couldn't be! Vera would never make the mean little mistake of thinking that she had to choose between him and George.

She could never be enticed into the flat gray faceless barren land where every turning was the same and whoever sought a new one must be damned and forsaken forever.

And yet, remembering again in the new setting of this new, bitter night, he could not deny that Vera *had* denied him. Consciously or not she *had* changed the subject.

At last he slept for a while. Vera's face raced across his dream, her eyes wide, a hand across her mouth holding back some cry. George was there, pointing a stern, Jehovah-like finger to some cringing hybrid figure that looked now like Lister and now like Barbara Ransome's opulent, faintly smelly mother. And then a dream he'd had before, because it had really happened and he'd been told about its happening.

"Yes, dear, your name was chosen long before you were born. When your father came back—it wasn't actually until the spring of 1919—he said, if we have boys they'll be named George for the king and then Haig for the greatest British soldier and then Arthur for Sir Arthur Currie, the greatest Canadian soldier. These days it seems old-fashioned and more British than the British, but when your father came home in 1919, it didn't seem that way at all. And anyway, they *are* all good, sturdy, good-sounding names, aren't they, dear?"

When he was old enough, Haig, a studious boy by nature anyway, had begun reading whatever he could find about his famous namesake. He started these researches eagerly and continued them in a state of growing shock. The Great Disillusionment was at its height by the time he reached high school in the early 1930s. It had produced no more naked a victim than the late Sir Douglas Haig, the briefly revered commander in chief of the British armies in the war of 1914.

The younger Ballantyne boy learned about the prototype Haig, not with any feeling so dignified as horror, but rather with a sense that he had been plundered and defrauded of his birthright. It was the prototype Haig, the butcher of the Somme and Passchendaele, the ineffable forerunner of the ineffable Colonel Blimp, who had began five years of suicide and slaughter with the forecasts that "artillery seems only likely to be effective against raw troops," and "cavalry will have a larger sphere of action in future wars." It was Field Marshal Haig-Blimp whom a cravenly acquiescent British Prime Minister had accused of "an inexhaustible vanity that will never admit a mistake"; of being "one of the individuals who would rather that ten millions perish than that they should own—even to themselves—that they were blunderers"; of "a narrow and stubborn egotism unsurpassed among the records of disaster achieved by human complacency."

The fiercely fatuous old field marshal was somewhere in his dream too. But where and how Haig couldn't be certain, for he was awake again, staring not into the past and its visions but into the present and its reality. The first gray light had appeared in the row of windows across the room. Without thinking why, he prized up on an elbow and looked out from his upper to Jerry Needham's lower just down and across the corridor. Needham appeared to be sleeping. If there was any pity anywhere, Needham deserved to sleep forever.

As much sorrow and regret as he felt for Jerry Needham, it was mixed with a sense of superiority. But then—to be fair, this had to be admitted—Needham had been much more vulnerable than he. Suppose, well, just suppose, to get some fair basis of comparison, he'd had a picture like that of, well, suppose, of Vera and a letter like that from her supposing she hadn't been married first to George. Supposing this, supposing himself helpless to fight back with his fists, helpless even to hurl himself against some vastly stronger and cleverer set of fists, supposing all this as well, what would he, Haig-but-not-Blimp Ballantyne have done? He couldn't be positive what he'd have done, and the swift revelation that this was so frightened him far more than everything that had gone before.

He had said again and again that they'd never wear him down. But they'd been at it only two months and look at what they'd accomplished already. Look at the furious husbanding of will he'd needed, the thick shield of scar tissue he'd had to build. The really sad and shameful thing about Needham was not that he'd quit and not that he'd lost, but that he'd quit while he was losing. Haig hadn't quit and he hadn't lost. He'd licked Camp Salute, licked its permanent establishment and its transient hostages and vassals. But there would be other camps, other establishments, other forms of logic and persuasion, other challenges to his stamina. Suppose this long two months of attrition stretched out to two years, five years, even ten? And then beyond that still no cessation and no silence. All right, then, Daddy, since you brought it up: what *did* you do in the war? Where were you when Uncle George was getting full of bullets and Auntie Vera was crying herself to sleep and only the zombies held to and hid behind their rights?

And now he knew he'd quit sooner or later. He lacked the size to be a martyr. He wasn't, after all, as he'd told George once, heroic enough to be a coward. The next best choice was being cowardly enough to be a hero. All right then if quit you must, quit then while you're winning. All right, old Haig-Blimp—quit young Haig-Ballantyne, leave him for dead, and up with the bugles.

After breakfast he asked the platoon sergeant to parade him before the company commander. He had his Canada badges on his shoulder and his Volunteer Service Medal on his chest when he left next morning with the rest of the platoon for the bright long-weekend's freedom.

George was not far from their ancestral home when Vera's letter informed him that still another Ballantyne had heard the pipes and grasped the claymore. "The stupid little bastard," he said. "Oh, the poor stupid bastard."

He knew at once that he must bring Haig here too. It was true that they were three generations removed from these Perthshire Highlands, but their father had kept the memory fresh for them almost to the day of his last lonely voyage on the *Homer C. Martin*. George Ballantyne, Sr., had spent all his leaves from the Princess Pats amid these very hills. In the farmhouse in Saskatchewan and later in the four-room suite in Winnipeg there had been a whole album of penny postcards. This very Mount Ben-y-Gloe, then almost thirty years younger, rested serene and mysterious beneath its lace mantilla of mist. Below lay this very pass of Killiecrankie and these moors of heather and pink gorse.

There was less romance in their work than in their abode. But it was hard, clean, satisfying, belly-emptying, lung-filling work. In official deference to it they were given extra rations, excused from wearing uniforms except on their very rare parades, and fitted out with the standard garments of the Canadian Bushwhacker, corduroy pants, high, heavy boots, flannel shirts, brimmed felt hats, leather jackets, blue Mackinaws, yellow horsehide mitts, and for heavy rain sou'westers and high-topped rubbers. They left their rifles in their billets and sallied forth each morning with the cant hook, the lumberjack's ax, and the crosscut saw to reap the larch, Scotch pine, and Douglas fir, the beech and oak that were as essential a part of the armies' muscle as their metal and their powder. In their mills they shaped and planed the harvest logs into railway ties, mine props, navy timbers and boards, slabs, planks, and scantlings for a hundred other uses.

Their full name was Number 38 Company, Number One Forestry Group, Canadian Forestry Corps. They called themselves the Sawdust Fusiliers. Most of them were robust bushmen from the Lakehead; some, like George, were category men, medically unfit for combat duty. George's job was driving a jeep for the company adjutant, or occasionally one of the light trucks. At first, still half comatose from the long, dark hangover of his morning at Dieppe, he had taken little interest in or inspiration from his surroundings. But Ben-y-Gloe and Killiecrankie would not be denied indefinitely, and in a few weeks life looked as good as ever, he was as confident of himself as ever, and he began wondering whether, pleasant as he found it here, there wasn't some way to get back a little closer to the shooting, which, after all, Dieppe or no Dieppe, was what he'd come for. His arm was a little stiff, but he was certain that he could handle a rifle if that was the only way to return to the heart and eye of this greatest of all man-made adventures.

The news of Haig confronted him with an obsession to replace what was still only a tentative urge. Vera's first stark sentence told him everything. "Haig's gone active!" She needn't have used the exclamation point, much less the anxious words that followed. Nevertheless George marveled once more at her quick, sure understanding. She knew Haig as well as he did.

"He won't tell me exactly why he changed his mind," Vera wrote. "But it's pretty obvious that everything about it has been a nightmare for him. All I know for certain is that he's broken his engagement with Barbara Ransome, or more likely it was she who broke it. Haig's so hurt and defensive about it that all he's given me is a hint that Barbara still refused to let him go active. I'm pretty sure it was just the opposite. She couldn't stand him staying in the reserve as long as he did. It's got to the stage where they're passing out white feathers in the streetcars, you know. There's been some talk in the papers and a few inquiries in Parliament about coercion and moral press gangs in the training camps. Haig won't talk to me about anything like that. All he'll say is that he suddenly decided the war is going to go on and on and on, perhaps go on forever, and since we're all going to die in it anyway he's chosen to die all at once instead of a day at a time peeling potatoes and sloping arms. He's always leaping from one mood to another, sometimes dramatizing himself and full of some kind of queer bright excitement and then full of despair and self-despisal.

"The really terrible thought is that he has no faith in what he's done, that they forced him to surrender in a moment of weakness and now there's nothing he can do but blame himself. What worries me most is that he doesn't try to justify himself any longer, at least not to me. He used to spend hours explaining it all when he was still in the reserve. But now he acts as though it isn't really worth while talking about reasons or motives or hopes or doubts. The other afternoon mainly to see if I could get through this shatterproof windshield I asked him if he had any idea when he might be going overseas. 'Oh, I haven't the faintest,' he said. 'Those things aren't my business any more. Nothing I do is any of my business any more.' He cut me off as if I were some prattling little half-wit child. Then he insisted that we go to a Wheeler and Woolsey movie and, God help us, we did!

"Looking at the above," Vera's letter went on, "I wonder if perhaps I *have* been prattling like a half-wit child. I haven't put down what I think is the most serious danger of all: It's not either that Haig has knuckled under or even that he's knuckled under when he believed doing so was wrong. He knuckled under to them when he still had at least some chance left of standing up to them, at least for a while longer, and now most of the hate he was starting to feel has been transferred to himself. How I wish you were here, George, to talk to him. I know he always pretended not to take you or your work or your ideas very seriously, but in fact he did and does. I think you'd find some means somehow of helping him get sorted out. As it is I'm desperately frightened: even if he never gets past Halifax this hideous business might cripple him for life."

"The stupid little bastard!" George said. "Oh, the poor stupid little bastard."

He recognized all the dangers that Vera had recognized and was filled with tender admiration for her perceptiveness. But he also knew that Haig stood in another danger whose dimensions neither she nor Haig could guess. Haig wasn't built for war. If Haig got into the spilled-guts, Slade O'Brien part of the war, if he got into anything half so shattering as Dieppe, it wouldn't matter whether a bullet or a bomb or a piece of shrapnel found him or not. He would still be completely and finally destroyed and where the explanation lay would be of no more consequence or consolation than the postscript on a tombstone. It wouldn't have mattered at Dieppe, nor would it matter at any future Dieppe, whether Haig's chief trouble was being too sensitive or too brittle or too aloof or too what. What became of his body would be equally irrelevant. His body might come back intact and unimpaired, but his soul would come back in a basket or a shovel. Some men recovered from battle crack-ups but Haig's crack-up, George was dismally sure, would be total and permanent.

That afternoon he was driving the adjutant along the narrow roadway that wound across the foot of Ben-y-Gloe. The adjutant was a moody little man, often jovial and easy to talk to but inclined to sink into long silences on the days when the mess was out of whisky and his private ration was exhausted. This day had begun badly for them both, but, divining that the captain's distress, while more transitory, was nearly as deep as his own, George suggested that they detour a few miles past the Dirk and Sporran. "They'll be dry too," the captain prophesied gloomily. "But sure, let's try." The captain's glad astonishment had been so great when they found the roadside pub newly replenished that he invited George in. That hadn't been George's object. He'd been stirred by no impulse more devious than Christian sympathy. But it would have been uncivil to remind the captain that he wasn't allowed to drink on duty, because the captain was on duty too. They had two doubles each.

As they turned back on the road to Ben-y-Gloe the captain interrupted himself in the middle of a verse of "The Road to the Isles."

> *"Braggart in me step—*
> *Ye'll never hear the—"*

"Pardon me, Private Ballantyne, but I can't help noticing. Something's bothering you."

"Sir?" George fenced, keeping his eyes on the road, which needed careful watching just now.

"It must be serious if two double Dewar's can't at least get the cure started. Anything I might be able to help with?"

"I don't think so, sir. Well, maybe." At least it wouldn't hurt to talk. He sketched the barest outlines of Haig's military career.

"Hmm," the adjutant said. He drifted away for a moment, gazing into the high timbered mountainside where the cutters were at work on the new scars and slashes in a green stand of larch and pine.

> "I belong to Glasgy,
> Dear old Glasgy toon—
> But what's the matter wi' Glasgy,
> For it's goin' roon' an' roon.

"Frankly, Ballantyne, I wouldn't have expected any brother of yours to be a zombie, even a converted one.

> "I'm only a common old workin' chap,
> As anyone here can see,
> But when I get a couple of drinks of a Saturday—
> Glasgy belongs—"

The adjutant broke in on his song as abruptly as before. "Anyway he isn't any more."

"Isn't what?" The Dewar's was speaking now, cresting in the late-afternoon sun with the unfathomable radiance of Ben-y-Gloe itself.

> "Glasgy belonn-nngs to me.

"Who isn't what?"

"My brother. You said he was a zombie."

"Well, isn't he? Or wasn't he? Isn't that what you said?"

"I didn't say it. But he was, all right. I wish he still was."

"No offense meant anyway." The adjutant sat up stiffly, putting his thoughts in order. "No offense meant. No skin off my ass. None off yours either, Ballantyne. You may not know it but there's not a single man in this whole company—no, and not an officer either except the O.C., who got a Military Cross at Ypres and a D.S.O. at Vimy—there's not a man or an officer who wouldn't give his right leg to have your record to take home with him. You've got nothing to be ashamed of."

"I'm not ashamed. I'm just worried."

"Yes, but it's no worse for your brother than for you or any of us. If his name's on a bullet or a piece of gunk, he'll take delivery no matter how or where."

"Horse-shit," George said boldly. "Anyway you've missed the point. If you take delivery or I take delivery it was our own idea. This kid had other ideas."

"I'd just say the hell with him." The adjutant giggled and his voice imitated the accusing tone of any bored and lazy waitress or any shopkeeper sparring for a gray-market price on the goods he kept under the counter. "Doesn't he know there's a war on?"

"With all respect, sir," George said severely, "may I make a remark?"

"Certainly, Ballantyne."

"If you're too God-damned thickheaded to understand what I'm talking about I'd rather talk about something else."

"Well spoken, Ballantyne. Very well spoken. Turn left at the next corner. Let us investigate the situation at the Rose and Pibroch."

They played a game of darts at the Rose and Pibroch and had two more drinks each, singles this time, for it was getting late and they both were deeper into the stuff than they had intended. They played three more games of darts and talked mainly about the woman situation in Dundee as compared with the woman situation in London.

They drove back to the camp almost sober, and it was the captain who reopened the earlier subject. "I seem to remember looking at your papers," he said. "Your next of kin is your wife. But who's listed as your brother's next of kin?"

"I guess I am. Both our parents are dead. There's an older sister somewhere in the States but we've sort of lost touch with her."

"I can see you *are* worried about your brother. I'm sorry I tried to brush it off."

"That's all right. It's not an army affair anyway. It's a family affair and I guess there's nothing to do but take what comes."

"Look, Ballantyne, if I'd been thinking I'd have suggested this before. Why don't you claim your brother?"

"Claim him?"

"If you're his next of kin that gives you a right to claim him into your unit. All you need is his consent and you can get him posted right to this company. You can keep an eye on him, talk to him, be around, make it easier on you both. And if you're concerned about how he'd stand up to a dose of blood and guts there's no better place in the world for not finding out than right here. Next to the Special Pessary Platoon of the Canadian Women's Army Corps I can't think of any outfit that's less likely to hear those ol' debil shots-in-anger."

George put on the brakes. "You're not kidding?" he asked.

"No. This is absolutely on the level. Oh, the Army's thick-skinned, Private Ballantyne, and as you were kind enough to point out to your superior officer a while ago, it's also thickheaded. But beneath that rough exterior there beats a heart of top-grain leather. You know that the book allows for compassionate leaves. Well, these claiming regulations came out of the same book. Normally your brother would be posted to some unit close to home and come over with it or after it as a reinforcement. But if you claim him and he consents and the claim's allowed Thirty-eight Company gets itself another Ballantyne."

"Even so," George objected gloomily, determined not to let his hopes rise too high, "he'll get lost in red tape and still end up in the infantry."

"You forget, Private Ballantyne, that your company has one of the most alert, efficient, aggressive, determined and abstemious adjutants in recent military annals. Come into the orderly room after breakfast tomorrow and we'll start it moving."

To George's surprise and relief, Haig signed the necessary papers promptly and with only a token show of reluctance.

"Don't kid yourself, George," he wrote, "that you're kidding me. I'd bet tomorrow's buck-thirty that Vera's told you I'm a psycho and you'd better start looking after me again or I'll go all the way around the bend. You were always good at looking after me, George. Now and then it got pretty damned tiresome and humiliating but I won't deny there were times when it helped. Oddly enough, George—and maybe this is just the apprentice psycho talking—I don't think I need your help now. But I'm still glad to be going to your outfit. Number One: because as you so touchingly and awkwardly tried to avoid saying the Forestry Corps is probably safe enough even for a natural and incorrigible chicken like me. Number Two: because the more I think of it, the more I feel I've allowed myself to be had and if through this dodge you offer I can have the Army in return, it will give me naught but evil, cackling glee. To put it more sententiously, I have deserted the only ethic I ever had in this great colloquy and the only other ethic I plan to recognize until further notice is the ethic of self-defense. Number Three: that incomparably magnificent person, your wife, you lucky bastard, tells me to do what you say I should. Number Four: you are a stalwart and a noble man. I would rather chop down trees at the side of George Ballantyne than sail the roiling seas with Odysseus."

It was a good winter and a good spring. Haig worked hard on the end of a crosscut saw and started, in his own pleased phrase, building new muscles in his arms to go with the ones in his head. He played a little poker, drank a little Scottish ale, and chased a woman or two. It was Haig, not George, who suggested that they try to get their fourteen-day leaves at the same time. They stayed in a Salvation Army hostel off Portland Street and spent more of their time together than they had intended, working on a loose system of alternating priorities. Haig led George to the British Museum and the National Gallery and to two concerts at the Albert Hall. George led Haig to the horse races, to the dog races at Wembley, a cricket match at Lord's and one spectacularly bad welterweight boxing match.

On their last day, a combined eleven shillings and eightpence short of being stone broke, they inspected the free attractions listed at the reception desk in Canada House. They agreed it would have to be the Lord Mayor's reception for Commonwealth other ranks. George said there might be free beer. Haig said he'd like to see the Mansion House's portrait collection.

Milling toward the exit—the portraits were disappointing and there was no beer; nothing but fish-paste sandwiches, seed cake, and lukewarm tea—they stepped into a small anteroom. There, on full display in open cases, lay the Mansion House gold plate; one souvenir of every Lord Mayor since Dick Whittington. They stood awed and silent, straightening up their battle dress like two grubby conquistadors gaping at the entrance to an Inca treasure house.

An aircraft man from Australia crept in behind them. "Lor'," he whispered. "Lor' a' mighty Jesus! Look at all that bloody gold."

Besides George and Haig and the Australian the only person in the room was a seedy, uncomfortable little civilian in a suit of molting Harris tweed.

The Australian rubbed his eyes and stared at the glittering Golconda again. Then he looked around furtively. "Lor' a' mighty, old cobber," he said in a voice of wonder and endearment. "There doesn't seem to be anything to stop a bloke from having a bit of that, now does there? A bloke could just put a tiny saucer and a cup or two under his jacket and just toddle off and flog it at the nearest grogshop. Couldn't he?"

"*You* could, sir," the man in the Harris tweed said sadly. "But I couldn't. You see I'm from Scotland Yard."

"Cor!" the Australian groaned, and fled. George and Haig fled after him into the streets of the City, laughing like schoolboys.

On D-Day Plus Forty they completed their move into Normandy. The front was far ahead and they set about their peaceable task of reaping a forest of beech, birch, and maple a few miles inland from Arromanches. George's arm was improving steadily. He'd lost his job of chauffering the adjutant and was sharing a crosscut saw with Haig. Then, as the front kept moving, they moved to a royal forest near Brussels. And now they were in the forest of Arden—God damn it, Haig, why do you always have to be such a smart aleck? *Ardennes.*

The night was half gone. Someone stumbled through the doorway. George sat up. "Bugger off!"

"This is Captain Earnshaw."

The adjutant. George laughed happily, saluting a friend. "Like a drink, sir? I've got some armagnac hidden in my extra shirt."

"Is that you, Ballantyne?"

"Yes, sir."

"Knew your voice, know it anywhere. Of course I'd like a drink. As a conscientious adjutant I am personally checking these new billets to see if any of my men lack anything I can provide or can provide anything I lack."

"Slan-ze-va, Captain Earnshaw."

"Up your kilt, Private Ballantyne."

The captain lowered his voice. "He O.K.?"

George looked down at Haig, sleeping on the floor. "Fine."

The adjutant tugged at the neck of the bottle.

"That's good armagnac, Ballantyne. I heard a broadcast last night that said counting line-of-communications troops and odds and sods like us there are eleven million people employed in one way or another on this front."

"I wouldn't doubt it."

"Let me finish. Of the whole eleven million I'll bet not more than two officers and five other ranks know the difference between armagnac and cognac."

"No, I guess not. A Russian wrestling promoter taught me."

"It's a very useful piece of knowledge." The captain sat down on the edge of the bed. "That's *damn'* good armagnac! Makes a man almost sorry to be going home."

"Almost," George agreed. "But not quite."

CHAPTER SEVEN

It hit them in various ways and in various parts of the anatomy. In those primitive days, limited by primitive weapons, it was impossible to hit an army as an army. An army was too big, amorphous, and scattered to offer an inclusive aiming point. The army had to be hit as a corps (not too easy either), a division, or, on a scale of rising promise, a brigade or regiment or a battalion or company or platoon or section or squad. Or a man. Anatomy was still a major part of military science.

"Go for the balls," Carmen Ruiz said once. "It's kind of mean, but it works."

At first twenty divisions came through the forest with six divisions opposing them. The odds were really greater than twenty to six, for of the six, two were green and inexperienced and two others, one going into the line and one going out, were in each other's way, fighting for roads that in turn fought them. The roads fought the trucks with ice and frozen snow, fought the tanks with barely melting mud, and always and everywhere and impartially fought the men on foot.

The divisions, regiments, battalions, companies, and platoons called to each other through the high white forest in a strange and desperately hopeful jargon.

LOG

0010: Index has patrols out. Impressive Blue goes thru area in morning.

0635: What is the shoot about.

0641: Cant get capt haines. All fwd lines out.

0647: Repeat. what is shoot about.

0659: White is moving as of 0659.

0702: Can't get Maj McIntyre as all fwd lines out.

0715: One line is in to Div.

0716: What does Div say about shoot.

0717: Contact lost with div.

0723: It is probable that white will move today. it is possible that red and blue will move. told red they have a chaplain.

LOG

0726: Red did not request chaplain. has chaplain.

0727: Red definitely requested chaplain 0643.

0729: Thirty repeat thirty trucks available for White at 1300.

JOURNAL

0812: S-2 told Capt Cairns to instruct all motro officers impress on all drivers they must keep 75yd interval all times.

LOG

0817: Line is out to red.

0843: For period 160600A to 180600A Dec you are auth to expend 350 rds 105 ME M-3 HE plus all unexpended balances for period 130600A to 160600A Dec 44.

JOURNAL

0844: Line out to div.

0846: Password armor knight. Alternate sunset rain. All units advised.

JOURNAL

0917: S-3 told Maj. Tanes to keep a record of where they are committed also send us an overlay of their positions and what happened while they were there.

1011: Div 3 informs that Inspire Minus Blue passes to Corps or Army reserve prepared to move motorized as directed by Corps or Army Vortex Baker. Vitamin D will be attached on move. Impede may move.

1048: Trucks not arrived.

1052: Password armor knight. Alternate sunset rain.

1057: Line from Ivanhoe is out.

1058: Password armor knight repeat armor knight alternate sunset rain.

1059: Line is in to Danger Two.

1126: Seven stragglers from 970 FA BN reported to Ivanhoe.

JOURNAL

1212: Ger troops and our troops badly mixed. Impossible for Arty to fire.

LOG

1219: Heavy shelling. SP 88 on loose.

JOURNAL

1235: S-3 inquired for G-3 whether Inspire Blue should send a billeting detail to Dauntless if not who will arrange for billeting of Inspire Blue.

1241: Talked to Capt. Wallace about supply of Blue. We to supply until they are committed at which time Dauntless will supply and Lt. Collins will let us know when.

1311: Water point at 982044 opens at 1200.

1311: Victor 3 called and said they sent 66 trucks in last bunch instead of 60 and they want 6 returned.

1322: G3 reports 7 tks broke through at 9704 heading for 9504 and 9205.

1327: Runner not reported.

1329: Capt Nelles has 50 men at 9603.

Tanks broken through.

1352: Maj Hirschfield reports TD's and bazookas in position. Requests bazooka amm. CO instructed Maj Hirschfield to get positions set up and rds blocked. Recon rds to Elsenborn.

LOG

1359: Send bazooka amm at once. Tigers pt blank.

1417: Maj Hirschfield can not carry out recon as ordered. Can not get vehs over due to snow drifts. Might get troops over on foot but bazooka amm still needed.

1432: Tec 5 Barnes on fwd obs with CO Q 986 FA reports CO M 894 Inf in retreat. Had only radio Comm and it out most of time. Most of 894 pulling out.

1453: Index reports 38PWs. PW statement says 3 Bns moved into area yesterday.

1457: Co Z reached AT ditch. Needs bazooka amm. Asks permission withdraw.

1502: All units instructed terms retreat and withdraw not admissible. Correction of line or consolidation permitted when needed for info of adjoining units. Retrograde action is term wh may be permitted in extreme cases.

1509: Maj Hirschfield asks authority take retrograde action. Asks info best direction.

1512: To Maj Hirschfield hold position.

1514: To S-2 Inspire. Maj. Hirschfield holding pos heavy cas.

1519: Inspire to Maj Hirschfield. Continue hold pos. Contact L CO Index re bazooka amm.

1523: L CO Index not in contact. Only contact Inspire.

1529: Maj Hirschfield reports some men his unit and adjoining units taking retrograde action on own initiative.

1534: Maj Hirschfield ordered to halt all retrograde actions.

1538: To Inspire for info and transmission to Index if poss. Maj Hirschfield became fatal casualty 1537. Capt Kane in command. Can I send in clear statement my strength and position.

1543: Message in clear admissible if wire out.

1543: Capt Kane to Inspire for Index. Effective strength one officer four men. Pls ack.

1544: Repeat prev msg.

1545: Effective strength one officer four men.

1546: If retrograde action authorized what route contemplated?

1547: Is route to 9205 open?

1548: No recent info re 9205. Believed in Ger hands.

1549: Can you suggest alternate route re retrograde action?

1550: Regret no useful info.

1551: Capt. Kane to Inspire. Request permission surrender. Men extremely cold. One has slight wound one other serious wound.

1552: Regret surrender cannot be authorized.

1554: Red to Inspire. What is the shoot about?

1603: Inspire to Red. PW info clarifies. Code name Gers using for overall operation is Watch on the Rhine. Indicates heavy local attacks to slow our final assault on Ger.

1620: To Inspire for info and transmission to Index if poss. Capt. Kane became fatal casualty 1639. Cpl. Phillips in command.

1628: Inspire to Cpl. Phillips. What is present strength your pos?

1629: Cpl Phillips to Inspire. Present strength this pos is PFC Rogers who is operating signals. Also me his commander.

JOURNAL

1634: Permission granted Cpl. Phillips to surrender. Cpl. Phillips reported not desirous of doing same.

1637: Contact lost with Cpl. Phillips.

It hit them just when Sergeant Kennebec was getting his gear together and preparing to go out to wait for the jeep. He was moving around the room almost stealthily, trying not to wake anybody up. The first bursts came in very fat and big, not with the flat and murderously swift crash of the eighty-eight and not like the big mortars and rockets with their soaring, longing cries, floating above and calling for companionship as though they themselves were lost and helpless. These were much fatter and bigger than the eighty-eight or the Screaming Meemie or the Moaning Minnie. They had scant individuality, nothing of the selective mating call of the smaller, more intimate weapons. They weren't looking for any chosen and waiting person; they weren't looking for Anybody, they were looking for Everybody.

These were great big ones, one-fifties at least and maybe a lot bigger. When the first one hit, Jack Kennebec knew something very serious was about to happen. An instant before he had been anxious not to disturb them, but now, as the second burst came in, this time a little closer, he was raging and clutching and hauling and poking at them with stark and deadly fury.

"Out!" he shouted. He grabbed Dave by the shoulder. "Get out to the big hole, Dave!" he shouted.

"I just got to sleep."

The third shell hit over by the barn and a big chunk of it knocked off a corner of the living room above them. Pulverized brick floated down, mingling its plastery abrasive smell with the hot medicinal smell of powder.

The sergeant had Henry Whelan by the hair.

"Out!" he shouted.

He kicked Carmen Ruiz between the shoulders. "Out! Out!"

Colhurst sat upright and stared around. "This place is burning down. I smell fire."

"You'll smell more. Out, God damn it!"

"You're pulling my hair, Jack," Henry Whelan complained. "That's a pretty damned uncivilized thing."

"Come on now, Henry, they've got us zeroed in. This is real bad."

"Look, Jack, I need my sleep. I thought you were on the way to that officers' course by now."

Another shell grazed the corner of the house. A cascade of heavy stone and splintered wood came down the cellarway.

"I'll go with Dave!" Carmen shouted.

"O.K., riband!" Henry Whelan shouted at the sergeant. "I'm going too."

"Wait for me!" Colhurst shouted.

They were all crowding up the cellarway.

Kennebec just made it. The fourth shell was another direct hit. But they were all out by then, scrambling into the wet and cold dark foxholes and looking out from them to see what was coming next.

The shells reached in past them now. The barn behind was burning mightily, and the stone house was smoking and sizzling like a damp, expiring cinder. The individual shells could not be counted any longer, but rolled continuously beyond and back.

Dave was in the big trench. "They just got lucky," Colhurst whispered, getting up close to Henry Whelan's ear. "They have no idea where we are."

"That makes us even," Henry Whelan said.

"You don't think they're coming, do you?"

"Oh no, they're not coming. They think on account of this heat wave it's the Fourth of July. They ran out of firecrackers so they're using this other stuff instead."

Kennebec crawled in from the trees. "I just checked our mine field. The bastards finally blew it up. If we have to attack just ignore the mines."

"Did you say attack?" Henry Whelan shouted above the steady obbligato of the big fat breaking shells. "You must be out of your mind. Who we going to attack and what with?"

"I said if we attack," Kennebec shouted back. "I've had enough of your lip for one night, Henry."

"Jesus, you are going for rank, Jack. They'll never stop you at loo-tenant. You'll make it all the praying way to those praying eagles."

"That's bad, Henry," Carmen Ruiz said. "I had an uncle who was in the other one. He had this song. 'Would you rather be a colonel with an eagle on your shoulder—'"

"'Or a private with a chicken on your knee,'" Henry Whelan finished.

One of the big shells fell much shorter, perhaps a true short or a change of plan or the forerunner of a new pattern; in any case a legitimate source of anxiety. It shook the sides of the big trench and threw up a spray of snow and frozen earth.

"Shut up, Henry," the sergeant shouted. "Did everybody make it?"

"I think one guy got hit," Carmen Ruiz shouted. "He was just behind me but I don't know who it was. He went down and I didn't know if he was hit or ducking."

"That was me," Dave Kyle yelled. "I went down for a minute but I'm O.K."

"All right. Start spreading out. Whelan, you and Colhurst stay here. Dave, you and Carmen take the two holes over to the right. I'm going looking for the other squads and then for platoon HQ and if I miss it I'll try and find company. That God-damn' corporal had to go and get the clap and now you got no squad leader. Kyle, you're in charge."

"Jack," Henry Whelan said with honest feeling, "why can't we forget the praying book and just keep our heads down?"

The guns stopped. "They called it off," Colhurst said in the sudden stillness. "They're licked and they know it."

"Kyle, you're in charge," the sergeant repeated. "This is going to be a real hairy one. Real real hairy."

"How far away are they, Jack?" Dave lifted his head and gazed at the trees, high and white with snow, menacing and accusing and condemning them but at the same time protecting and hiding them, white pointing fingers and white sheltering arms.

"There's no hurry," the sergeant said. "Half an hour."

"Half an hour smaff an hour," Colhurst said with sudden spirit. "They're licked and they know it."

"Well I don't know they know it."

"If I were you, Colhurst," Henry Whelan said, "I would sort of fade out of this discussion."

David checked his rifle and fumbled at his ammunition pouches. "I left my grenades back in the house," he said.

"Who didn't?" Henry Whelan asked.

"I didn't. That's who didn't. I didn't." Carmen Ruiz was excited and angry. "I got more grenades than Rockefeller's got dimes. So who gets the credit? Jack's the boss. Dave's the second boss. Henry does most of the talking. When he shuts up we hear from Colhurst. Everybody's got rank or talking privileges but who's got the God-damn' grenades? Poor old Carmen."

"How many grenades have you got, Carmen?" The sergeant was sprawled at the lip of the big trench, half up on an elbow and getting ready to move away. Ruiz stood up below him. He was fat with his paunch of drooping metal; his three-day beard was rimed with the new frost and his helmet had drifted down askew. He looked like a furious badger.

"How many grenades you got?" the sergeant asked.

"I got eight," Carmen Ruiz snapped.

"Holy God, Carmen," Henry Whelan said. "If they ever score a direct hit on you it will be worse than the bombing of the Ruhr."

"How did you get eight grenades, Carmen?" the sergeant asked with great deference. "I only got three myself."

"I saved them."

"You're a marvel, Carmen," Henry Whelan said. "If I ever seemed to knock you I tender my apologies. Eisenhower hasn't got eight grenades. Roosevelt hasn't got eight grenades."

"I'm going to find platoon or company." The sergeant stood up. "We'll spread those grenades around."

"So long, Jack."

"Give two of your grenades to Dave. Give two to Henry. Give one to Colhurst."

"I don't think I'll do that, Jack."

"What do you mean?"

"I mean no. These are my grenades. I'm not sure I want to give them away."

"I may have heard you wrong. There's something going to start here and I want to see our fire power spread around."

"Jesus, Jack," Henry Whelan said. "You really talk like an officer."

"You've heard your orders."

Ruiz shook his dark, frosted head. "If you insist, Jack, I may place these grenades where they will do you an absolute minimum of good."

"Are you refusing to obey an order, Private First Class Ruiz?"

Henry Whelan offered an amendment.

"Not only refusing to obey an order but refusing to obey an order in the face or presence or however they say it of the enemy. They shoot you for that, Carmen."

Carmen's indignation was still growing. "Who shoots me, Henry? Them or you?"

"Well, not me, Carmen. Me and you have achieved a sort of indestructible friendship that survives all these small vicissitudes and dangers."

"We're wasting time," the sergeant said. "I never had a high-priced lawyer or a high-priced English teacher. But you start spreading those grenades around."

"Yeah," Colhurst said. "What about those high-priced teachers? Vicissitudes, indestructible, all in one sentence."

"Look, Colhurst," Carmen said, "you haven't been here long enough. Henry makes the jokes here. The sergeant makes the jokes."

"No," the sergeant said, "I just give the orders."

"The Commands," Carmen said. "All right, Commander. I guess that's what we came for. You have Commanded me to give two of my grenades to Private Kyle. Here are two grenades for Private Kyle."

"That's all right," the sergeant said.

"You Command me to give two grenades to Private Whelan. All right, Private Whelan?"

"Well, thanks," Henry Whelan said. "Just what I wanted."

"I got nothing against you, Colhurst," Carmen said. "But are you sure you know how to handle this grenade?"

"They're not coming," Colhurst said. "There hasn't been a sound in the last five minutes."

"Take it. Make sure you use it."

"You're in charge, Kyle, until I get back." Sergeant Kennebec levered himself upright and stood in the darkness, as lonely as one of the slender trees plucked away and set apart.

"There hasn't been a sound," Colhurst said. "Not one sound."

"No, and not a sight but that barn." Carmen's voice had grown sour. "It will burn itself out."

"No sounds, no sights," Colhurst said. "They're just not coming."

"In case they do, Colhurst, what are your plans?" Henry Whelan was tossing one of his grenades up and down from one mittened hand to the other, extracting what feeble warmth he could from the tiny friction.

"There hasn't been a sound."

"Sergeant Kennebec. Jack old friend," Henry Whelan asked, "why are you still here? You keep saying you're going somewhere, to look for platoon or company or the other squads. But all the time here you are."

"Well, it's dark."

"The barn's still burning. There's a little light."

Kennebec sat down on the hard, cold ground. "I think I'll wait till the barn's stopped."

"Jack," Carmen Ruiz said, "how about I go with you?"

"No, I don't think so. I'll be going in a minute."

"Jack," Henry Whelan asked, "you not planning to take a walk? I mean a long long walk?"

"Why would you say a thing like that? Now just why?"

"Well, that stuff about the hairy stuff and getting Carmen's grenades spread around and leaving Dave in charge—I don't know, Jack, you just started to sound like a man planning a walk."

"I never took a walk yet, did I? I been here since Normandy. Have you seen me taking a walk? Even *seeming* to take a walk?"

"Well, not till they made you a loo-tenant."

David Kyle grabbed Whelan by the shoulders and lifted him halfway up the trench. "You've got a dirty streak, Henry, an extremely dirty streak. Get it under control or I'll do it for you."

The sergeant was still hesitating at the edge of the trench.

"They're not coming," Colhurst said. "There's not a sound of any kind."

"The reason," the sergeant said, "that I've been standing here and kneeling here and pondering here and wondering here and debating here and groping here dismayed by all those big words Henry's fat-assed prep-school teachers taught him—more likely his narrow-assed prep-school teachers—the reason I am standing here is that I am trying to make an appraisal of the immediate military situation and the probable consequences thereof."

"Thereof!" Colhurst cried. "That's the one that did it. Thereof. Jack, this is your finest hour."

"Jesus, Jack," Whelan said in admiration. "This officers' crap has really got power. It's got you talking English."

"They'll come with tanks," Kennebec said. He said it as solemnly as an announcement in a church and they fell quiet before it, like the communicants of a Mass silenced by the bell. The quiet went on until Carmen Ruiz broke it.

"The hell with that!" Ruiz jumped erect in the bottom of the trench.

"Tanks?" Colhurst burst out.

"I've got to find platoon," the sergeant said, "but I'll be back."

"Tanks!" Carmen Ruiz said.

"Tanks, for Christ's sake," Whelan echoed in disgust. "What's he up to now?"

"They're not *his* tanks," Dave pointed out, trying to be reasonable but feeling a great dark chill in the bottom of his heart.

"There'll be tanks. Now listen. They'll have infantry around them. Or behind them or ahead of them. Don't waste your ammo by shooting at the tanks."

"Holy uttermost saintly Jesus." Colhurst was on his feet too. "You inventing these tanks and now you tell us we got no right to have a belt at them."

All at once the quiet broke apart with the desperately close whap-whap-whapping of a pin-point barrage of eighty-eights. Kennebec dived into the big trench just before a piece of shrapnel hit its ridiculous tin roof and threw it up and off into the trees behind. And then behind the eighty-eights there was a good two minutes of Meemies, higher in the air and at their closer range more dangerous.

No one spoke through this or tried to speak except Sergeant Kennebec. Dave Kyle and Carmen Ruiz were flattened out at one

213

end of the trench and Whelan and Colhurst at the other. Kennebec was in between. Two or three times he yelled at them, "Listen for the tanks!" But no one paid attention. Carmen Ruiz grabbed Dave's arm in a quick convulsion, clutching comfort and giving it back. Then the shooting stopped and not far off the tanks were grinding in, foraging among the trees like half-blind dragons, groaning and belching and panting and salivating at each new eager twist and turn. Now and then one stalled against the trees and emitted a fiercer roar as it backed away and came on again with its appetite further taunted and inflamed.

"Get out of here!" Kennebec yelled. "They'll run right over us!" He took Henry Whelan by the arm and half threw him out. "Over to the right," he yelled. "There's room for three of you in there. Dave, you and Carmen and Henry get over there."

One of the tanks had made the clearing, searching and sticking out faint tongues of flame.

"Come on, Colhurst," Kennebec said more quickly. "Over here to the other hole."

"I don't think I'll bother," Colhurst said. "I think I'll stay here."

Kennebec slithered across the snow as flat and lean and careful as a Texas rattlesnake. The tank had come across the vanished mine field. It was a Panther, a medium-speed tank, but it was having a little trouble in the frozen mud. Now that it was in the clearing its turret, with the big main gun projecting, turned slowly around and around, sniffing.

It saw the big trench and went right for it. It slid in and with astonishing quickness got through to the other side, leaving the remnant of Private Colhurst behind. Colhurst didn't even have a chance to scream, or if he had it was lost in the now much fiercer and urgent growling of the tank. Then the tank backed across the clearing, went to the right and then went to the left. It found the hole where Dave Kyle and Whelan and Ruiz were sprawled down together. It stood off a little way and tried one shot with its big cannon. But the cannon would not depress enough to do more than hit the lip of the hole, and after one more round the tank moved in closer and tried to get into the trench with its machine guns. It chopped a hard spray of frozen earth down on the huddled men below, but the bullets themselves were still too high. The tank backed away and came in from the side but the same thing happened.

"Oh, God," Carmen said. "Isn't there something?"

"Keep down," Dave said.

The tank backed off and came at them a third time. It still could not get its guns low enough. Again the hard chunks of earth sprayed in, but the bullets missed them.

"I'm all done!" Carmen shouted. "If they want me that bad they can have me. I'm going to get up off my ass and throw just one of my grenades at them."

"That's a praying good idea," Henry Whelan yelled. "I'll go with you. It might spoil their paint job."

"No, you won't," Dave yelled.

The machine-gun bullets were coming in now in short bursts, almost playfully. It was clear that the tank had become certain of the position and was basically pleased with it but still frustrated in a good-natured, indulgent way.

"Listen, Commander," Carmen shouted at Dave. "If it wasn't so cold—"

"That's what I say," Henry Whelan shouted. "Come on, Commander, let's all stand up and unpin and heave one of the precious praying grenades of our great and good friend Carmen Ruiz."

Another burst of machine-gun fire jabbed at them from above.

"If it wasn't so cold. I got Spanish blood and holy Jesus."

David had no idea what to say. If he hadn't been put in charge he'd have done exactly what they suggested. But Kennebec had put him in a difficult position and for an instant all he could think of was a snatch of verse from his school days.

> *Three corpses lay out on the shining sands*
> *In the morning gleam as the tide went down*
> *And the women were weeping and wringing their hands*
> *For those who will never come home to the town.*

He almost called the rest to Henry Whelan, who was sure to know it anyway.

> *For men must work and women must weep,*
> *And the sooner it's over the sooner to sleep*
> *And good-bye to the bar and its moaning.*

Mary had always protested when he recited that one to her. She said it was morbid.

"Hang on," David said. The tank was now silent, pondering its own smaller problem.

"Why? I'm getting up and throwing this grenade."

"No, you're not, Carmen. It will only bounce off."

"Carmen's right, you know," Henry Whelan said. "There's nothing that can happen. We've had it."

"No, we haven't."

"Name one thing that's going to happen." Carmen wasn't crying, not even complaining particularly, he was only persisting in the logic of doom.

David had an inspiration born of his own despair.

"They'll open the hatch."

For some reason this forlorn prediction shattered Carmen's calm as abruptly as a new burst of gunfire and threw him into a wild and bitter rage.

"So they'll open the Jesus Christly hatch," he screamed, not caring who heard. "And then some bastard will stand up and let us have it while we're squirming here like a God-damn' bowl of goldfish."

Carmen thrust himself to one knee. Dave grabbed him by the neck. "Keep down, Carmen!" he yelled. "That's an order."

David was now in a state of abjectness as deep and dismal as the other two. But he had this larger burden. Kennebec had robbed him of the option of escape, of dying in his own way and in his own time. The cold had become a greater and more incurable imminence than the fretting tank at the edge of their little grave, but some thrust of conscience grabbed him as hard as he had grabbed Carmen Ruiz, and forbade him as sternly and piously to find his rest and solace in the arms of either enemy.

Piety! That's what it is! he thought with a sudden gust of tenderness for himself. Deep down he was still as much a Christian as the Crusaders. He had as much respect and reverence as ever for the lake of fire; he would never enter it of his own volition.

Carmen Ruiz was struggling in his grasp. But though Carmen was hard and wiry, Dave was much bigger. "Carmen!" Dave shouted. "There's a lake of fire up there!"

Carmen subsided, panting. "I'll be back, Dave," he panted. "Nobody ever beat me yet."

"Carmen, I'm not trying to beat you." Dave felt he was talking in a mixture of Rotarian platitudes and his boyhood theology, but

216

he went on just the same. "I'm not trying to beat you, Carmen, I'm trying to save you."

Carmen relaxed under his grip. "Don't get overconfident, Dave," he said. "I'm just gathering my strength. There was this fellow in Buffalo and this other fellow in Chicago that both thought they had me beat. There was a smaller one in New York City that thought he had me beat too. It turned out they were mistaken."

Henry Whelan had been trying to massage some life into his hands by working over one of his grenades. The tank's motor idled just above them, waiting.

"I always was tempted to ask you this, Carmen," Henry Whelan said. "But I didn't want to hurt your feelings. Are you trying out to be a gangster with a heart of gold? Or are you just on the lam? You must be—what?—forty?"

"Well, forty-one."

"One of those Chicago blondes got to be too much for you. I went to Chicago once for Easter vacation—I'm not trying to up-stage anybody, but I did go to a prep school—and of course I stayed at the Sherman—that's where all the college kids stayed, and I went over to State Street and I met this Chicago blonde and honest to God, she would drive you not just into the war but into all the wars back to ancient Sparta." They all knew Henry was trying to make his peace.

There was another bored burst of four or five machine-gun bullets from the tank above.

"You're getting warm, Henry." They all knew Carmen was accepting the well-meant invitation to leave something behind in the form of an epitaph. "I don't mind telling you now. I just got plastered. I never learned to handle it. But I think I mentioned once about this sister of mine—well, what the hell, she's my sister—she got engaged to this young Spanish boy, every bit as good a family as ours, well, my sister was engaged to him and all of a sudden out of the blue, no warning whatsoever, this dirty little spik goes and enters the priesthood."

"This disrupted your sense of values?"

"You're a good talker, Henry. I enjoy listening to you. I think you've put it right. Anyway for some reason I took it so big I went out and got stoned and I was walking across the square down there by the Statler and there was this recruiting office with a God-damn' phonograph and a broad outside that smelled of Lifebuoy soap—in my game the broads don't use Lifebuoy and this only added to my confusion—anyway I joined the Army. I just got carried away."

Carmen started to get to his feet again. Dave held him down.

"Dave," Carmen said, "you better get out of the way. I know a very bad method whereby an awful little man like me can take care of a splendid big man like you. I wasn't brought up fighting clean. And whether you like it or not, Dave, I'm going to give those pricks up there just one little bang."

"You said nobody ever beat you, Carmen," Dave said.

"I mean not while I was off my feet. Plenty got me down but I always tried to get up. I'm getting up now and quit trying to stop me."

The tank roared into gear again just then and ran back toward the edge of the trench. Then it stopped. There was a pause of nearly a minute. Then a new noise, a more careful one, a sound of scraping metal.

"Come out!" An accented but perfectly intelligible voice cried across the ten feet of ground. They'd opened the hatch after all.

"What do you mean, come out?" Dave shouted back, still keeping down and holding Carmen down with him.

The call that returned was laden with heavy, confident playfulness.

"Well, just come out."

"And what then?"

"Well, come out and see." There was a long chuckle from above. "How is the weather down there by the way?"

"Don't try it, Carmen," Dave said. "He's got his guns right on us."

"Are you coming out? I can't wait forever. I'm due in Antwerp."

"How about you come in?" Henry Whelan shouted. "There's lots of room here."

"Very well. I'm coming in. My driver has just told me something I should have remembered for myself. Although our guns cannot reach you we can put our tank across your hole and the exhaust will asphyxiate you. Or is smother a less offensive word? If you would come out you would spare yourselves some needless pain and save me some petrol and some time."

"If we come out," David shouted, "What will you do with us?"

"I am an officer of the Wehrmacht." The German voice had grown less jubilant. "My honor as a German officer will not allow me to make promises that I cannot fulfill. I have lost touch with my infantry and have no way of dealing with prisoners. But I must press on."

"Well, Dave?" Carmen said.

"Yes," Dave agreed, accepting it at last. "You were right all along. All right, let's all come out with a grenade ready and see if we can get it off."

He started to get up and as he did so he took Carmen's arm again, this time in an almost tender and courtly way.

"I don't need any help," Carmen said.

Then, as unexpectedly as a summer storm driving in with summer warmth and healing into this arctic stricken wilderness, there came a new series of sounds. There were two closer and smaller explosions, barely harder than the patter of big raindrops, and then there were a few muffled cries of hurt and terror and wild disbelief. For another moment there was nothing further, no elaboration or explanation but the shuffling sighs of quick burning in air dead with cold. There was one more cry and then the little burning sound grew larger, and then there was a long, thunderous roll of explosions right on top of them. They listened in wonder. It was Henry Whelan who at last broke in. "Holy praying Jesus praying Christ! He got them!"

The burning sound increased, but nothing human mixed with it any longer.

"Jack! Jack Kennebec!" Henry Whelan shouted.

For the second time Kennebec's tall body fell in on top of them.

"How in the name of God—" Carmen started to ask.

"It was easy," Kennebec panted. "This Kraut was standing up there with his head half out, making this speech like he was running for mayor. I just climbed up and dropped these two grenades down his ass. He slithered out of sight and I closed the hatch again. It was like dropping firecrackers down the grate in a sidewalk."

"They had us in trouble, Jack." Carmen raised his cold and frosted head and spoke in stupid appreciation.

"They've still got us in trouble."

"What do we do now?" Dave asked. He stood up and looked over the lip of the trench. The tank was not five yards away. A few rounds of ammunition were splattering off inside it and the evil scent of burning flesh was already coming across the cold ground with the smell of overheated metal.

"Well, let's take a breather." Kennebec's voice was now quite unsteady. So were those of two of the others.

"I be go to hell!" Carmen was muttering weakly.

"We all just about did." Henry's laugh was high and giddy.

"It looks like a real big attack," Kennebec said shakily. "Before I came back I found one of the other squads over on the other side of the farm, dug in by the creek. It's a better spot than this. So far they haven't been hit. So I guess we'll go over there and put in with them."

"Praying Jesus, Jack." Henry was petulant now. "You mean after all this we're not pulling right out?"

"That wouldn't be a good thing for us to do." Kennebec was heavy with regret. "Anyway it doesn't seem there's any place to pull out to. I figure there were at least four tanks in that one little mob. The three others just went around. They're likely a good mile behind us already."

For the first time there was no bickering, no forced humor, no comment of any kind from anybody. They pulled themselves out of the trench and began shuffling on once more through the frozen trees in the direction from which they had come.

CHAPTER EIGHT

When at last the attack began, two hours before dawn, Franz's first sensation was of being hurled personally from a gigantic cannon into a bottomless sea. On the way down he plunged gasping through layers of water that changed swiftly from geyser heat to the iciest cold. He had been prepared for something big, but for nothing half so big as this. The battles in Normandy, vast and in the end at Falaise terrible almost beyond enduring, offered no true basis of comparison. For him their beginning had been the small convoy raids of the Jaybos on the march to the beaches. The true battles had gone on and on endlessly and in growing terror and cruelty for almost eleven weeks, but their growth had been gradual. Here, although he could not know the precise number, almost two thousand heavy tanks and a quarter of a million men were launched into or committed to battle in a matter of seconds.

Franz's column had been in place for some time, a gnarled and inert vertebra of tanks, self-propelled guns, tracked machine-gun carriers, command cars, ammunition trucks, other trucks heavy with infantry. Just before the barrage started Franz's immediate superior, a Wehrmacht officer named Ziegler, whom Franz had been drilled to acknowledge only as Major Joseph McNair of Omaha, Nebraska, appeared from the head of the column. Ziegler-McNair picked up Franz's face in a pencil flashlight.

"Ah, you're the captain from Manhattan." He chuckled gaily. "Almost rhymes, doesn't it?"

He handed Franz a little bundle of cloth. "Here's the last of your cloak-and-dagger kits," he said.

"What is it?"

"Scarves. Blue parachute silk. Be sure to put them on. If you run into any other Yankees wearing them treat them as friends, at least until they start shooting." The major guffawed. "Oh yes, and wear your jackets with the second button undone. Another recognition signal is to rap twice on your helmet."

"Rap twice on my helmet?"

The other man guffawed again. "On the theory, I guess, that you'll be mistaken for a woodpecker." He grew serious. "Well, damn it, that's what the order says. I suppose if one of our squads ran into another of our squads in the dark and nobody knew who anybody else was—oh, the hell with it. But remember the scarves and the buttons."

The officer seemed to want to linger over the talk, not an unusual tendency just before an operation.

"Little old New York. What a town! Captain, you'll be home by the Fourth of July."

The thought brought such a rushing storm of other thoughts— Gretchen, his mother, even Uncle Otto and P.S. 77 and, quite unpredictably, the Burmeister Pork Butcher, Yorkville's Pride Since 1902—that he sat alone with them in a sort of dumb vacuum.

"You don't believe me," the major said, a little offended at the lack of a reply. Franz came to abruptly.

"My God, Major," he said. "Don't scare me like that."

"Well, remember I was the first to tell you." The other had recovered his joviality. "When you get there I can give you a couple of addresses. From 1934 to 1938 I worked out of New

York and Washington as chief correspondent of the *Frankfurter Zeitung.*"

"It's a pretty staggering notion," Franz said wistfully.

"This is going to be a staggering operation. I don't pretend to know the whole plan or the whole size of the build-up but mark my words, as they'd say back there, we're going for broke on this one. And we'll make it. No question of it. I'll see you in Antwerp at the very latest tomorrow morning."

"I'll be there," Franz answered, and meant it and almost believed it.

"And that, my dear Captain from Manhattan," Ziegler-McNair continued, "will be the end of the war, at least in the West. The East will follow soon enough after. You'll be right up there at the head of the German-American Friendship parade, rolling down Fifth Avenue right behind the mayor and the German Ambassador."

The image somehow had turned to a disturbing, even a distasteful one. Franz couldn't bring himself to hope it was utterly crazy; he couldn't bring himself to hope it ever would come true. He was glad when his superior officer, with a wave for good luck, walked off down the column.

Perhaps the strangely unsettling conversation had something to do with his strangely unsettling reaction to the attack—more likely not. The attack itself was enough to shake any man. Sitting under the barrage, there was no way of knowing what was precisely what. The gigantic railway guns, the heavy field guns, the workhorse eighty-eights, the mortars, and the rockets merged their thousands of individual sounds into three corporate, organic sounds: first the tumultuous crash from their platforms and launching pads to the rear and in the neighboring woods, then the softer, weirder sound of the shells passing overhead, fluttering and crying like some vast, tormented flock of birds; then the thunderous roar and rending that signaled their arrival in the American gun pits, foxholes, roadways, supply dumps, vehicle parks, and command posts far ahead. Every half minute the labored awk-awk-awk of the new V-1 flying bomb beat the deeper sky like a dying raven, and once a V-2 rocket howled and reached far out of sight and raced on to shred and trample God knew what and God knew whom and God knew where. Only now and then could the muzzle flashes or brighter shellbursts of the ordinary guns be seen through the stricken forest, but the forest itself seemed to be moving, lumbering agonizingly free of the trembling earth.

It was fully a minute before anyone in the jeep spoke. The first to do so was Erich Tannenbaum.

"Birnam Wood to Dunsinane!" he cried.

"You'll still be showing off at the gates of hell!" Franz shouted back. "That's public school stuff. Even I know it."

Nevertheless he was reassured to discover that so far Erich's habitual pose of the well-educated, slightly snobbish clown was still holding up. So far there was no reason to believe that Erich would be a failure. His own first sensation of being catapulted violently into some hitherto unimaginable other world had passed away completely. He was fully concentrated now on the job that lay ahead, waiting for the signal to begin. He personally was going to be all right; so, conceivably, was Erich.

He glanced toward the two men in the back seat. Lemmering, his fellow member of the SS, was leaning forward, expectant but not unduly tense, like a well-trained hunting dog. Occasionally he permitted himself an approving "Ah!" and nodded his head like the pleased conductor of a symphony. Lemmering never spoke unless spoken to, but Franz, as leader of the squad, had been shown his papers. He knew that Lemmering had spent thirteen months in Russia and had been twice wounded there before his third wound sent him back for eventual remustering. The legend in the SS was that those who returned from the Eastern Front returned either hopelessly broken or so firmly tempered that they were forever immune to suffering or fear. Franz had never doubted that the taciturn Lemmering was among the latter group. Now he was more certain of it than ever. He had already been half decided, simply because they of the SS were tougher men by definition, that when it came to a really tight spot it was Lemmering, rather than Erich, on whom he would rely most heavily. He reached across and put his hand on Lemmering's shoulder in what he intended as a reminder of their special comradeship. Perhaps mistaking the gesture for one of unneeded reassurance, the other man drew away.

Franz now focused his last-minute inspection on the fourth member of his squad. Gotthold Preysing, alias PFC Henri Lachaise, he of the Cunard Line English, of the stomach division, of the buck-toothed children, he of the visions of Iron Crosses and special parades and speeches by the burgomaster in honor of his coming home, had shrunk during the few minutes since Franz had observed him last. His shoulders had shrunk a little farther into his already too large U. S. Army helmet. Under the growing self-doubts incurred during the last weeks of training his gaze had already shrunk from the stars to the horizon. Now it had shrunk from the horizon, too. Gotthold Preysing had eyes neither for the marching forest nor for the dark tanks now beginning to move with and through the forest, nor for the muzzle flashes behind and around them, nor for the flickering orange bursts ahead. If his eyes were open at all, they were fixed on the floor of the jeep.

Franz grasped him by the jacket and snapped him roughly forward. "Private Lachaise!" he yelled. "What's wrong with you?"

"*Was?*" Preysing mumbled. "*Was? Was? Warum—*"

"Sit up!" Franz commanded harshly. "And speak English!"

"*Jawohl, Mein Hauptscharführer,*" Gotthold Preysing muttered.

The column had begun to move. Franz released his grip on Preysing. "Corporal Christianson!" he shouted to Lemmering.

"Yes, sir?"

"I'm putting Private Lachaise in your charge. Try to see that he comes to no harm. Above all, see that he does not bring our mission to harm."

"Yes, sir."

"You have full authority to use your own judgment in any situation that may arise. You understand me perfectly?"

"Yes, sir. I understand you perfectly."

Ziegler-McNair hurried down the side of the road again, past the U. S. Sherman tank ahead. "I've had a look at that first side road," he shouted. "You know the one I mean?"

"According to my map it's about eight or nine hundred meters ahead," Franz shouted back. "I've been thinking about it."

"That's the one. I walked down it a little way. It's a little soft—too soft for the tanks and very narrow. You should be able to use it. You'll have to do some pushing but with luck you'll have it to yourself. I'll be peeling the other jeeps off later."

The other man waved good luck again. Franz started up his motor. The column's motion had at last been transmitted to the tank ahead. Franz put the jeep in gear and crept forward, grateful for the faint heat of the tank's exhaust.

It took nearly half an hour to reach their side road. When he turned away from the column and pointed the jeep into its own private tunnel in the forest, he felt a momentary pang of abandonment and loss. But the shells still roared behind and crashed ahead and fluttered and cried above and there was something deeply comforting about them now. It was as though the jeep had acquired, not only its private tunnel, but its private canopy and its private shield. As they drew farther distant from the noises of the tank and infantry column, it became possible to converse again without undue strain.

"The map case and flashlight are beside the seat," Franz told Tannenbaum. "You'd better take a look."

In the almost total darkness and on the uncertain road it was impossible to do more than a few kilos an hour. As they crawled along the slender corridor in the trees Franz outlined his tentative plan.

"We'll keep going away from the column until we hit that village called Freiheit. See it?"

"Just a minute. Yes."

"Then, if another of our columns hasn't beat us to it we'll turn down the road that goes west again. We'll keep going until it's light. By then we should be well ahead of the tanks."

"A veritable Clausewitz!" Tannenbaum applauded.

Franz jammed on the brake too late to stop one wheel from slithering into a broken shoulder of the narrow roadway.

"Get out and push, Sergeant Foster," he commanded.

"Yes, Captain."

They were heaving the jeep out for the fifth time when the barrage stopped. A little dogfight had broken out between a lonely German Stuka and three Messerschmitts on one side and on the other a flight of Mustangs defying the thick clouds, but it had nothing to do with them. They were so preoccupied with their own minute but difficult enterprise that no one noticed the silence until they were under way again.

They had already passed their crossroad and had been crawling west for half an hour. A little gray light was showing through the treetops. A little sleet and snow were coming down; an excellent portent, for this meant there could be no air observation or air attack. In these minutes after dawn Franz was deliberately not hurrying. He was looking for spoor. His first task—perhaps the most crucial task he would face all day—was to disengage his squad from the Sixth Panzer Army of the German Reich and lose and dissolve it in the First Army of the United States of America. So far since their departure from the column they had seen no sign of either army. What he was searching for now was some sign of the front, the front as it had been two hours ago, the front as it was now or the front as it might be two hours hence.

As they crept farther to the west the trees showed signs of damage, a few broken in two, a few uprooted, many more shorn of their upper branches. But old snow lay on the wounds like penicillin dust. They still had not reached the area of the barrage. But then the wounds began growing black and heavier, and suddenly they passed a copse of smoldering pine. A moment later they had to manhandle the jeep around a shell hole so fresh that it bore only the very faintest dust of the very newest snow. The shells that had landed here were probably all shorts, but if there had ever been a firm and settled front in this neglected backwood Franz guessed they were already across it. He accelerated a little, still watching carefully.

"Still no sign of the God-damn' Amis." Tannenbaum might have been reading his mind. "What the hell's wrong with them?"

"Well, they're very thin on the ground." Franz had said it before he realized how he was saying it. The note of quick defensiveness was not lost on Tannenbaum.

"Franz," Tannenbaum said, with one of his rare bursts of understanding, "I wasn't drawing any conclusions. I was just wondering."

"According to our intelligence," Franz said, coldly military, "They've got at the most four divisions holding eighty-five miles of front. There might be a road block or a standing patrol this far forward. It's been so quiet on both sides there can't have been anything more."

The road took a turn and they came on another small village. The village had received half a dozen shellbursts at least and it had not, unfortunately, been a large enough village to accommodate so many. A big hole had been torn in the steeple of the church. A bigger hole had been torn in the stone wall of the big house on the corner and a wide wooden bed, its feather mattress still serenely in place, hung halfway out above the cobbled street. Another fresh-minted pile of rubble had been the *boulangerie*; although it was charred and splintered at one end its sign had come to rest face up in front of the neighboring and miraculously undamaged Café Coeur d'Ardennes. Two adventurous dogs were sniffing for food; otherwise the streets were empty.

Franz had seen and passed through a dozen such villages during that far-off Norman summer. His experience told him that it would be a waste of time to stop. The only reason to do so would be to find shelter or food or to obtain information about the enemy. But they did not require shelter or food and at this early stage of this vast crisis in its tiny municipal affairs, the village would be too bewildered and demoralized to offer reliable information about anything outside its own borders. Most, if not all, of the population would still be in their cellars, recovering from the initial shock. If they were forcibly brought out, or forcibly visited in their cellars, they would be too terror-stricken or distraught to offer useful testimony. If you sought to enhance their terror or make use of it they would try to placate you by babbling denunciations of the enemy—whom they had recently been, as any fool must know, succoring and befriending; they would try to quiet your anger and impatience by exaggerating the enemy's weakness, or quite as likely, they would appeal to your ego by exaggerating his strength. They would, in any case, almost surely lie whether they meant to lie or not.

If, on the other hand, you sought to quiet the fears of the villagers and win their confidence they would become overfriendly or overdemanding of your sympathy. An old man would begin shouting about the loss of his pig, a woman about the loss of her house, a child about the loss of its mother. They would try to give you wine and eggs and home-baked bread. They would ask you when you thought the war would end. They would ask if you had chanced to see or hear of a young man, believed taken prisoner near Sedan, named Gaston Pellideaux—a most unusual name, there couldn't be so many with that name, a rather fair young chap with blue eyes and a small mustache, of medium height, twenty-one years of age to be precise, no twenty-two, it was in 'forty that he was taken and his birthday was in June. They would ask if it was true that conditions in the labor camps back in Germany were actually much better for the French than for the others, particularly for those dirty Russians.

It did occur to Franz that it would be instructive to discover how a newly bombarded village would receive the Amis. His instinct told him that although there might be something to learn about human nature there was probably nothing to learn about the immediate military situation.

"Not stopping?" Tannenbaum asked in surprise.

"No. We'll wait until we find a village that hasn't been hit."

A kilo farther down the road they came upon the spoor. The jeep descended from a little rise and there, not twenty feet from the roadway, lay a dead American soldier. A small corner of the soldier's head had been sheared off, apparently by a piece of shrapnel, and the soldier had fallen on his back, decently concealing the unsightly pulp of his brain and leaving a surprisingly clean red scalpel line along the base of his skull. It seldom went so neatly with the freshly dead. This man might almost have been laid out by a mortician. His eyes were wide open. His expression was intent and determined, not a particularly pleasant expression, but not an unpleasant one, either. His long, thin legs were stretched out as straight as two cedar rails. One arm was flung across the snow and the other had fallen over the soldier's chest. His rifle lay near the far hand. The only disorderly thing in sight was the dead man's helmet, crushed and mangled and red at the edge of the roadway.

A small carrier of some kind had brought the soldier here and then suddenly turned in the roadway and sped back in the direction from which it had come. The track marks were as fresh in the snow as the little patch of crimson blood. There were two heavy footprints at the place where the carrier had swiveled on its axis to begin its flight and where the soldier had bailed out to begin his own vain race for the sheltering trees.

"We'd better see if he has any documents," Franz said. He knelt beside the body and began searching the pockets. This was the first dead American soldier he'd ever seen up close. In Africa and Italy he had encountered only live prisoners; the enemy dead he'd seen in Normandy were British or Canadian and an occasional Pole. He had no reason to feel anything new, he told himself as his hands touched the still warm body; no reason to feel anything and no desire to feel anything. He laid a crushed, half-empty package of Lucky Strikes and a Zippo lighter on the snow, then a handkerchief, then a pocket comb and nail file set in an imitation-leather case, then a money clip with a small wad of occupation money and Belgian francs, and then a little pile of coins.

There was nothing else. Franz went over the body again, looking for secret pockets, but there was nothing else at all. No documents, no photograph of the girl back home, not even a wallet to hold it in. No letters. There was something wrong, someone had been cheated. But who? This other soldier so far from home or he, Franz Koerner, also far from home, and suddenly so eager, so unreasonably and sadly eager, to share the memories of this other wayfarer on the ground? "He must have had letters," Franz said out loud. "He must have had pictures."

"I guess he left them on the carrier with his gear," Tannenbaum speculated.

Franz started to get up.

"What about the dog tags?" Tannenbaum asked.

"No, leave them."

"They might be useful."

"Leave them, I said," Franz repeated. And then, wanting to explain. "They can't bury him right without them." And then wanting to explain still further. "If they stop us extra dog tags would just cause more questions. Come on, we're wasting time."

They had not gone a hundred kilometers on their way before he was grappling with a suffocating urge to turn the jeep around and go back and retrieve the dog tags after all. If Tannenbaum hadn't been there he'd have done it, but Tannenbaum was too knowing. The dead man's concealment of his letters and his pictures had struck out at Franz, kneeling eagerly in the snow, as harshly as a curse. He had not dared risk another by looking for the little identification plates that should have hung around the dead man's neck. Suppose they should turn out not to be there either . . .

The one easeful thing would have been to discover that this man for whom he had felt such pity and who, not understanding, had rejected and denied him was the possessor of some outlandish name like Murgatroyd or Montmorency or Czyzyk. But now he would never know that the name was not one of the familiar ones, Smith or Schmidt or Kelly or Klein or even Waldeck or Boeselager, a name belonging by inference and perhaps real kinship to the place he'd started from.

Erich Tannenbaum was regarding him with careful interest. Franz was mooning like some God-damned girl and apparently it showed.

"Private Lachaise!" he called abruptly over his shoulder.

"Yes, sir." Gotthold Preysing responded uncertainly, but he did respond in English.

"You all right now?" He had been on the verge of lashing out against the shrunken little grenadier, but suddenly he wanted to protect him. How much brutality lay ahead there was no guessing; it would be good to leave a blaze mark of kindness behind. He broke the rule and spoke a few words in German.

"That was some racket, wasn't it, Gotthold? My God, I thought my ears would burst."

"*Ja*," Gotthold Preysing laughed gratefully. "Some racket. It had me scared for a while."

"It had us all scared. Didn't it, Lemmering?"

Lemmering hesitated. He replied with a trace of distaste. "Yes, Captain."

"Just remember to keep your head, Gotthold, and you'll be all right and so will everybody. Now that's absolutely the last German we'll speak."

It had grown noticeably lighter and the silence was now absolute. Franz changed places with Tannenbaum and concentrated on the map and the road ahead.

"Another village coming up," he said. "Hohzbach. If it missed the bombardment we'll stop."

The village was a little larger than the last one had been. Unlike the last one, it was undamaged, and where the last one had gone, en masse, underground, this one was alive with all the excitement of a country fair. Apple-cheeked children, reactivated to the war games abandoned since autumn, raced back and forth across the icy square pointing their broomstick guns and yelling, "*Kamerad!*" "Hands Up!" and "Bang! Bang! Bang!" and "Boom! Boom! Boom!"

Housewives gathered in their heaviest shawls before their doorways, two or three to a doorway, exchanging gossip of the early morning, pointing to the east to where they had heard the first sounds, to the west to where they had heard the next sounds, overhead to where the mighty shells had miraculously passed without harm, joking and marveling and breaking into long heated arguments about who had been first to awake and first to wake her children and first to guess whose guns they were and first to drive her stubborn husband to the cellar and first to say a special prayer not only for herself and her family but for the whole village; who had been first to perceive her prayers answered and bid her husband go and see that the fool cow had not run away, and first to embrace her children and first to divine that perhaps it was all a blessing in disguise and at this rate someone must finally lose and someone must finally win and even that must be growing plain to those high and mighty idiots who started it in the first place and why God only knew.

The men of the village had gravitated to the Perle des Ardennes to toast the miracle in red wine and *mark* and fit the stupendous events of the morning into their past forecasts and future expectations. In spite of the cold the door was open. The impromptu assembly of electors had spilled out into the street.

The first man to spot the jeep shouted a single word. "Yankees!" and the whole square fell still. The shawled women parted nervously and disappeared sidewise through their doorways. The playing children raced down the side streets. Three men from the doorway of the Perle des Ardennes gulped down their drinks, handed their empty glasses inside, and started walking with unnamed apprehensions across the square.

Franz spoke quickly. "Sergeant Foster and I are going into the café to see what we can discover," he said over his shoulder. "Corporal Christianson, you and Private Lachaise will remain in the jeep. Don't talk to anybody about anything. I don't need to tell you, Christianson, if you absolutely have to, you can say, 'Ne parle pas.' No more. You won't accept any wine. Private Lachaise, you'll say nothing. Not one word. Understood?"

Lemmering answered his part of the question at once. "Yes, sir."

"Lachaise?" Franz asked.

"Eh?" Gotthold Preysing, sensing something new in the shape of crisis, was receding again.

"Watch him, Foster," Franz commanded sharply.

"Yes, sir. I will."

One of the men from the tavern, still halfway across the square, half waved and half saluted. "*Bienvenue!*" he shouted tentatively.

"*Merci!*" Franz shouted back. He spoke hurriedly to Tannenbaum, recapitulating instructions they'd gone over in the barracks.

"Now, for God's sake remember. Your language is English. You have no German at all. You're my interpreter. I don't know how good your French really is, but don't make it too good."

"O.K."

"These people should be friendly but in this sector they're mainly of German stock. They may not really like the Yanks at all."

"Jesus!" Tannenbaum said. "We're their enemies but we're really their friends. So we pretend to be their friends and it turns out we're really their enemies. How do you say *that* in pidgin French?"

"Come on. And stow the bright sayings, will you?"

On the way across the square Tannenbaum gave Franz a running translation of his conversation with the most voluble of the three Belgians. The Belgian paused every few steps to make his gestures more explicit.

"The last German they saw here," Tannenbaum recapitulated, "was away back last summer, just after the Germans lost Brussels and Liège. The word he uses is 'lost,' by the way—*perdu*. Sounds a little melancholy, God bless his stout old heart."

"Never mind the asides," Franz said. "Just tell me what he's saying."

"The Americans never did occupy this village. They've been ahead of it and around it, but no Americans have been billeted here. All they've seen of the Yankees is a few patrols and an occasional stray looking for booze or for Mademoiselle."

"But we're definitely inside the Yankee lines. Ask him how far inside."

Tannenbaum and the Belgian exchanged more words and gestures.

"Seven kilometers. That was as of yesterday afternoon. He started to tell me he's been selling the Germans eggs and that's why he can be so exact. But then he remembered I'm a Yankee—"

"Never mind the asides," Franz commanded again.

They were at the doorway of the Perle des Ardennes. The men clustered there parted, and when they moved through to the low, dark, beamed room they were greeted with a ragged cheer. "*Vive les Americains! Vive les Yanks!*" Franz pushed his way as politely as possible to the unfinished-pine bar, Erich close behind. The proprietor, a short bald man with the narrow, flesh-set, crafty eyes of a rich peasant, proffered a sidewise grin.

Franz reached across and shook hands.

"Cognac?" the proprietor asked, holding a bottle aloft. "On the house," he added in thick English.

"*Café?*" Franz asked.

The landlord shrugged. "*Très mal,*" he warned them, but drew two cups of black liquid from a battered aluminum contraption of tanks and tubes, valves and spigots.

"*Santé.*" Erich took charge now and bowed around the room.

"*Vôtre.*" "*Santé.*" The other guests were crowding close, bombarding them with excited questions.

Franz held up his hand. "Tell them we're sorry, but we haven't much time. Say we'll tell them everything we can but first we'd be grateful if they'd tell us everything *they* can."

"They can't figure us out," Tannenbaum said. "They thought the Yanks were all on the run and they think we should be running too."

"Watch it," Franz said softly. "Some of them must speak English."

"I'm watching it. While the bombardment was still on several farmers who live west of the town came into the village. They say the Americans have been moving out since dawn."

"Moving out how?"

Erich put the question to the assembly at large. It set off another general explosion.

Erich pretended to fall into a state of deep emotion. He paused dramatically, waited until the room was silent and took a sip of coffee, permitting his hand to tremble a little. Then he regarded Franz gloomily and croaked, "Captain, it looks like a rout."

Franz shook his head soberly. Tannenbaum was hamming outrageously, but his hamminess sometimes had its uses. It could also be infectious.

"Tell them," Franz instructed, "that we are bound to admit the situation, for the time being, is bad."

If the ejaculations that followed were heavy with sympathy and concern, there was also an undercurrent of pleasure and controlled malice. From the back of the room one voice leaped singly forth, the purest essence of weariness and disgust. "*Vive la libération!*"

The landlord shouted for silence and started to apologize.

"*Monsieur le patron* assumes," Tannenbaum translated, "that it is no doubt only a matter of days before the American armies recover from this morning's sneak attack and return to hurl the Boche back into the Rhine."

"Don't answer that for now. Get them to come forward and show us on the map everything they know about American formations in this area. The ones that pulled out. The ones that haven't pulled out, if any. How many men and guns and where their headquarters are, or were. Tell them we're on a special liaison mission from the army commander."

However mixed their original sympathies might have been— however those sympathies might have been readjusted by the events of the early morning—few of the guests of the Perle des

Ardennes were able to resist the invitation to assist in the recording and direction of the Second World War. When Tannenbaum put the map board on the bar they clustered around, shoving and elbowing and stabbing with their thick leathery fingers, shouting and arguing, pleading for Tannenbaum's attention, appealing over Tannenbaum's head to Franz, appealing over Franz to the very saints in heaven. No two could agree on anything.

"It's no use," Tannenbaum muttered after ten minutes. "It looks as though there is, or was, something between four and thirty American tanks on the far side of this hill over here"—he struggled for and won possession of the map from the village notary and the livestock agent—"and I guess there was a battalion headquarters or at least a company headquarters in this village over here. There was a road block straight ahead of us about four kilometers."

"See if you can find out some more about the road block."

In response to Erich's next question two hitherto neglected farmers fought their way forward and contested over the map.

"Yes, it's there all right," Erich announced. Under the strain, which was partly nervous and partly physical, he had broken into a heavy sweat. "At this intersection here." Franz managed to get another look.

"Probably a tank," Erich panted, clinging to the map board. "Or there was a tank when the barrage started. Likely a heavy machine gun. A detachment of six or eight spread around the woods."

"Are you sure they're not holding out on us?" It no longer seemed of great importance whether their private conversation was intercepted or not.

"I don't think so. It really does look as though the U. S. Army is in the father and mother of all flaps."

"All right. We might as well get moving. Tell them I want to make an announcement."

"I suppose you know," Tannenbaum said, "that half these people don't speak much more French than you do?"

"Never mind. Speak to them in French."

Tannenbaum shouted dramatically for silence. In a moment the room was still.

"Tell them," Franz said, "that much as he has regretted doing so, the commander of the American armies has ordered a general retreat throughout Belgium and Luxembourg."

Several members of the assembly caught the essence of Franz's words before Tannenbaum had time to translate. This time the result was no mere commotion, but outright pandemonium. There were shouts of dismay, shouts of disbelief, shouts of triumph, shouts of exultation, shouts of anger, shouts of joy, shouts of pity, shouts of vituperation, shouts in French, in German, in Flemish, and—whether in commiseration or in scorn, there was no way of being certain—even shouts in English. A florid man in heavy farm clothing seized a smaller, relatively dapper neighbor by his threadbare topcoat, hurled him to the plank floor, and began pummeling his head, crying, alternately and methodically, "*Abzugskanal! Schweinhund! Abzugskanal! Schweinhund!*" In a moment two or three others pulled him off; they did it almost absent-mindedly, keeping their eyes on Erich all the time.

"*Achtung!*" the landlord bawled. Then he flushed. "*Pardon, monsieur,*" he apologized in Franz's general direction, stricken with embarrassment by his lapse into German. "*Attention!* Shut up, everybody!" he bawled again.

"Tell them," Franz said, "that the Germans will be coming at any hour. Tell them, although the American commander appreciates their bravery and loyalty, he advises them not to resist the Germans. To do so would be useless and very dangerous to their families."

The room erupted again. There were several fist fights. The landlord essayed an ingratiating smile. "You will doubtless be back, nevertheless?" He ignored the Brueghel-like turmoil around them.

"Who knows?" Franz said stonily. He did not offer to shake hands a second time but led Tannenbaum out and across the square. "Don't hurry too much."

"That was a nice balance you struck." Tannenbaum's tone was respectful.

As the jeep turned out of the square toward the countryside, a solitary rifle bullet clapped through a front fender, just missing the tire.

"A very nice balance indeed," Tannenbaum amended.

It *had* been a nice balance, Franz told himself. "You did O.K., Sergeant Foster," he complimented Tannenbaum.

He stopped the jeep and changed places with Tannenbaum again. "If nothing better shows up, we'll see if that headquarters is still there and try and find their wire. Take it slow through here."

The road turned into a small clearing. They were almost past before he noticed the carrier, badly smashed, overturned, and half hidden behind a snow-covered hummock, the carrier itself, half hiding the bodies of two more American soldiers. These two new bodies, unlike the first one farther back, set no moral or philosophical thoughts in train. The only question they raised was a tactical one. He stuck his foot out and put the brake on softly, held up his hand for quiet, and waved Tannenbaum and Gotthold Preysing into the ditch on the far side of the carrier. Then he signaled Lemmering to reconnoiter from the right. He himself grabbed his Tommy gun, slipped into the ditch, hurried forward bent double, then slithered across to the other side and began crawling through the trees. In less than a minute he and Lemmering had the clearing covered from above and below. There were no footprints leading away from the wrecked vehicle. Franz stood up and waved to Lemmering to do the same.

These two corpses were much messier than that of their late companion. The carrier evidently had received a direct hit from a heavy. One of the bodies had lost all its shape and definition. There was nothing clean, orderly, or professional about it, as with the earlier one. The second body was intact from the waist up. "Take off his dog tags," Franz instructed Lemmering. He turned and walked back toward the jeep. He had no desire to know what this man's name had been, no interest in his letters from home, no curiosity about the photographs he carried. With his sense of detachment there came a wave of relief. He had been away from the real war too long. The vaccination against shock and useless pity and foolish qualms had almost worn off, but now he had had his booster shot and it had taken hold. He felt better, more easy and relaxed, than he had felt in weeks.

Preysing, he saw, had been vomiting in the snow. "Get into the jeep, Lachaise," he said coldly.

Another kilometer down the road he ordered Tannenbaum to stop once more.

"If the road block's still there, we'll probably have to identify ourselves. They may be too excited to bother but they may be pretty edgy and suspicious. Unless it's absolutely unavoidable nobody but me will open his mouth."

They turned another corner and braked once more. Franz swept the road ahead with his binoculars. A thousand meters away a soldier in a white helmet—this, he knew, would be the helmet of an MP—was leaning against a double barricade of heavy logs. The logs were so arranged that any vehicle passing through would have to come to a dead stop and tack past from the side. At first the MP seemed to be alone, but after another minute's inspection Franz picked out two more soldiers sitting a few meters down and just off the road behind what appeared to be a carelessly camouflaged Browning automatic rifle. He continued his scrutiny until he was satisfied there were no other soldiers or weapons. He reached under his seat and pulled out a square of white parachute silk, then walked around and tied it over the radiator of the jeep. He climbed back in and nodded to Tannenbaum. Tannenbaum had grown pale, but he still looked all right. It wasn't necessary to look at Lemmering, but he turned a final time to Gotthold Preysing.

"What's your name, soldier?" he asked.

"Eh?"

"What's your name, God damn it!" He put it this time with quiet menace. Preysing had heard the question in just that way at least twenty times in his private English classes with Tannenbaum. "Your name, soldier, and hurry up!"

"*Jawohl,*" Gotthold Preysing muttered stupidly. Then, with a great effort, "Chust a minnude blease, Herr Captain. Mein name?"

Then, in an instant, he became a man transfigured. He shook himself erect. For the first time in a month he seemed to have recovered his full stature. His eyes were remote but they were also alight as they had not been since the shrinking of his body first set in. His voice shook with wild jubilation, pouring out his native language in a torrent.

"My name is Gotthold Preysing!" he sobbed happily. "*That* is my name. My name is Gotthold Preysing! You thought you would make me some stupid *Englischer* fool called Lajass but I am not the *Englischer* Lajass. I am the German, Gotthold Preysing!"

Gotthold was attempting to poke the startled Franz in the chest for emphasis, but Lemmering gripped his arm. "All you smart bastards make fun of Gotthold Preysing because he is not a good enough *Englischer,* not a good enough Yankee. You make fun of Gotthold Preysing because you think he's scared. You think Gotthold Preysing's scared of being killed, being butchered and ground up like those dirty Yankees back there."

"Shut up!" Franz barked, but without any real hope of getting through.

Preysing's voice had broken completely, but there was no sorrow in it, only a wild flood of release. "I was never anything but Gotthold Preysing. I don't *want* to be an *Englischer* or an *Amerikaner*. I want to be a German. It was not Gotthold Preysing who was scared. It was that miserable fool Lajass."

Fearful that Preysing might have been heard at the road block, Franz turned for another hasty look ahead.

From behind, the chant continued, "I am Gotthold Preysing! I am Gott—*Aaah!*"

It ended not so much on a cry or another sob as on a little shout of greeting and surprise. There was no protest, no pain, just the long, astonished ejaculation and the clatter of a rifle falling against the floor. Franz stiffened but did not turn around.

"Private Lachaise has fallen on his bayonet." Lemmering's voice was without inflection.

It was a moment before Franz spoke. He still did not turn around.

"Is he badly hurt?"

"He is dead." This time Lemmering spoke with a hint of reproof, objecting to the implied slur on his competence.

Erich Tannenbaum put his arms across the steering wheel and cradled his head. His whole body was shaking. "Oh Jesus, Jesus. Oh God, Oh Mother of Mary," he whispered.

"Sit up!"

Tannenbaum grasped the wheel as rigidly as an epileptic and drew his head erect. Franz groped in the khaki haversack at his feet and produced a small flask of cognac. "Take a good pull," he said.

Tannenbaum coughed on it. "Oh hell! Oh Jesus hell!"

"You did what you could for him," Franz said. "Now forget it."

Tannenbaum looked at his wrist. He laughed shakily. "Do you know what this bloody Yankee watch says? It says it's still only ten o'clock in the morning."

He'd have liked to console Tannenbaum by telling how long his own first day of war had been. He'd also have liked a drink of the cognac.

"Shall I put him out?" Lemmering was asking from the back seat.

"No." Franz thought he'd seen the MP raise a pair of glasses in their direction.

"Shall I start, Captain?" The cognac had worked quickly on

238

Tannenbaum and he was almost like a child, contrite and pleased and anxious to show that he was being good again.

"Yes. Go slowly but don't stop unless they shoot. Corporal Christianson, put a field dressing on Private Lachaise. Fast."

The MP ahead watched them steadily as they drove down the road. Franz picked out two corporal's stripes on his arm, and when he put the glasses down a four-day stubble of beard covering a gray, gaunt, weary face. The corporal raised a carbine and knelt on one knee behind the barricade. The two men on the Browning took aim too.

"Keep going," Franz ordered Tannenbaum.

When they were thirty or forty yards away the corporal shouted "Halt!" just as though he were reading from a manual.

"Stop." Franz said. Then he stepped out in the roadway. He deliberately refrained from holding his hands up, but he stretched them out toward his sides to show that they were empty.

"Daddy Warbucks!" the corporal shouted.

"Just a minute, Corporal," Franz shouted back. "Can I come in?"

"Daddy Warbucks!"

"Let me come in alone, Corporal."

The MP hesitated.

"Tell your men to get out of the jeep and hold up their hands."

"One of them is hurt. I'll get the other two out."

He nodded to Tannenbaum and Lemmering. Lemmering propped the sagging body of Gotthold Preysing against the steel supports of the jeep's canvas top. He followed Tannenbaum to the far side of the roadway.

"All right, come in alone," the MP said.

When he was ten feet away, the corporal stood up, still pointing his carbine. "That's far enough. Daddy Warbucks!"

Franz was pretty sure he'd hit a piece of remarkable luck, but he didn't want to press it too hard.

"Look, Corporal, I just haven't got the countersign. We've been out on an artillery recon for a week. It's been so quiet up there until they bust loose this morning that everybody's been getting sloppy. Including me, I guess. We've been on our own and I just haven't had a chance to pick up the passwords."

The corporal still kept his carbine to the front. "Well, Captain, you could have guessed, couldn't you? Any GI I know would have got it right away."

Now, Franz decided, was the time to cash his luck. "Sure, Corporal." He spoke easily, man to man. "I could have guessed Little Orphan Annie. But suppose your counter had been Orphan Annie or just Annie, or Sandy the God-damn' dog. So I get a near miss and a hole in the head."

The corporal grinned through his weary beard and relaxed a little, but still did not lower the muzzle.

"Well, I got orders not to let nobody through here unless they got both the countersign and the right documents. Not nobody. Let's see your card."

"God, Corporal, I don't know who you're working for, but I'll make a blind bet he's fresh out of West Point. This isn't one of those neat little Stateside exercises. There are Krauts up there. Real live Krauts. God knows you heard 'em a while ago. Well, when we went up to do this long artillery recon the colonel made us leave our cards behind. Even our personal mail. I guess he thought we might end up in the bag."

"Maybe you will, maybe you have. You got nothing to show? Nothing at all?"

"We've got our dog tags."

"I'll see them later."

"Well, damn it all, doesn't the uniform mean anything to you? The jeep? Our weapons?"

"Don't try to rush me, Captain. All I know for sure is some paratroops landed near here this morning and our division picked up quite a few Krauts in GI clothes with GI transport and GI guns. That's one of the things I know. The other thing I know is I got my orders."

"Look, I've got a man bleeding to death back in that jeep. He caught a piece of shrapnel and I've got to get him to the medics." Franz paused. "You think we're O.K. You know damn' well you do."

"I know I got my orders."

"I can see it from your point of view. Well, then, how about calling back to your headquarters and explaining the situation. I know they'll give you permission to let us through."

"Call back! Friggin' call-back friggin' how? To friggin' headquarters? What friggin' headquarters?"

"Haven't you got a line in?"

"Line? Jesus, Captain, I haven't even got a radio. I haven't got a carrier pigeon."

"Look, Corporal," Franz said. "Why don't you place yourself and your men in my command? I'll take the full responsibility of relieving you of your assignment here. We'll go back and find your outfit and then I'll find mine."

The corporal fondled the idea for a moment. "No," he said uneasily, "I couldn't do that."

"Corporal," Franz said. "You're a credit to your uniform. But I know personally, I know absolutely, because that's one of the reasons I'm in a hurry, that there's at least one squadron of Panthers straight down that road not more than two and a half miles. They're coming this way and there's not one God-damn' thing to stop them but the snow and mud and trees and a few shell holes in the road."

"I—oh hell, I can't. I guess me and my boys will take off when we see them. But not till we see them."

"Are you going to let us through or not? Are you going to stand here—going to make me stand here—and watch that poor kid bleed to death?"

"Who was the Georgia Peach?" the MP asked suddenly.

"Ty Cobb. And the Sultan of Swat was Babe Ruth. And the Rajah was Rogers Hornsby. And Lou Gehrig was the Iron Horse."

"Oh hell. All right. If you see anybody from Nine Seven Three Regiment back there tell them for Christ's sake to get regimental headquarters and ask them to give me some kind of contact. Tell your men to get aboard and come on through."

Franz nodded without expression and waved back to Tannenbaum and Lemmering. When the jeep drove up he climbed in.

"Just a minute," the corporal said. "One of my BAR men used to be in the medics. Maybe he can help your man."

"No. Thanks just the same. We'd better try to get him back to a dressing station or an ambulance."

"Hell, Captain," the corporal insisted hospitably, "the way everybody was moving out two or three hours ago you won't see another friendly face before next Tuesday. Hey, Buster! Come on up here and take a look at this guy."

One of the men behind the BAR got up and plodded around the road block. "Nice day," he said to Franz. Then to the corporal, in a tired voice that indicated the topic was not new, "We pulling out *now*, Ryan?"

"Later. Look at the guy in the back, will you? He got a piece of shrapnel."

"You ever see a Congressional Medal winner, Captain?" the

BAR man asked sarcastically. "Well, you're looking at one now. Corporal Thomas Gerald Ryan, known to his former friends as Horatio at the Bridge."

"Take a look at him," the corporal said.

"Couldn't you *order* us to pull out, Captain?" the BAR man asked. "I mean everybody else high-assed it down the road like they'd never stop this side of St. Louis, Missouri. But not Thomas Gerald Ryan and his indomitable little band of broth—"

"*Look at this man,* I said! You want him to die while you stand here bitching?"

"I don't want nobody to die. Me included. Where's he hurt?"

Lemmering moved the body of Gotthold Preysing forward a little and indicated a place between the shoulder blades. The BAR man put his hand through the neat long hole in the combat jacket, felt at the wet wadded dressing Lemmering had jammed inside, and then took Preysing's wrist.

"Hey, what the hell's going on *now?*" he demanded, a man perpetually hoodwinked and at last driven to the edge of fury. "This son-of-a-bitch *is* dead."

"No!" Not for the first time Franz wished he had Tannenbaum's talent for acting.

"At least half an hour," the BAR man said.

"You can't tell that close, can you?" The corporal's interest seemed to extend beyond the routine matter of another life and another death. "How can you tell he didn't go just this minute?"

"Because, for Christ's sake, he's half stiff already. In this weather they get stiff fast, but not that fast."

"How come you didn't know, Captain?" The corporal spoke slowly, as though pondering the import of his question while he was still phrasing it.

"What difference does it make now? The poor son-of-a-bitch is gone and that's that. I guess we'll get moving."

"There's not quite so much hurry now, is there, Captain? I'd still like to know why you lied to me."

"But I didn't know, Corporal. I was sitting in the front seat."

"Well, what about the corporal here? Wasn't he sitting right beside him? Wasn't he holding him up? How come he didn't tell you? Do you always carry a dead man on these special artillery recons?"

"This is no time to be funny, Corporal. He was a damn' good man."

"I'm not sure it's funny. You back there!" The MP looked at Lemmering. "What's your name?"

Lemmering glanced toward Franz and Franz carefully looked away. "Peter Christianson." Lemmering said it well, perhaps a trace too well.

"Say it again."

"Peter Christianson." Lemmering was trying still harder.

"Where you from, Christianson?"

"Cincinnati."

"One of the Cincinnati Dutch." The MP had grown nervously affable.

"Actually," Franz interrupted, trying to re-form the conversation on himself, "his parents are from Denmark."

"Suppose you let your men talk for themselves," the corporal suggested. He had grown definitely excited. Without making a gesture of it, he had brought his carbine up again. "Buster," he said to the BAR man, but keeping his eyes on the three men in the jeep, "I guess we don't need you any more. Go on back to your gun. Get behind it. Point it this way."

"Jesus, more games!" The BAR man kicked a tire of the jeep, possibly to get some blood stirring, possibly to express a new dimension of disgust. He trudged back past the road block, taking his own time.

"What's *your* name, Sergeant?" The corporal spoke toward Erich. "Roger Foster; Philadelphia, Pennsylvania; English-American. Blame the English accent on Oxford."

"Never mind the speeches, Foster," Franz said. "The corporal hasn't got all day."

"Oh, I've got lots of time. Who's Popeye's girl, Sergeant?"

"Popeye?" Erich hesitated. "He's the comic-strip bloke."

"Yes, he's the comic-strip bloke. Who's his girl?"

"I wouldn't know. Why not try me on American presidents? I'm good on authors, too."

"What about Dagwood? Who's his wife?"

"Is that comic-strip too? If it is I plead the Fifth Amendment."

"I've got a hunch that's very clever. Suppose you just tell me who Blondie's married to?"

"Honest to God, Corporal." Franz tried to get control again. "Just because my sergeant is a long-hair, smart-ass, half-Limey jerk, you've got no right to—"

"Put your hands up again, all of you!" the corporal commanded suddenly. "Get out one at a time and walk down the road and then turn around. *Now!*"

"*Lemmering! Erich! Fire!*" Franz yelled as he lunged. His first kick against the gearshift sent him flying clear. He hit the roadway on one knee, right at the MP's feet, and slammed his helmet into the crotch, getting his head just under the muzzle of the carbine as the MP swung it down and fired. The MP doubled up. Franz sprang upward and grabbed the carbine away from him and began firing. Under the hard, thudding punches the MP spun away and down in a grotesque shuffling motion like a dancing bear going backward, flopped into the ditch, raised his head, opened his mouth as if to shout or perhaps only to plead, and then fell back wholly out of sight.

Tannenbaum had slipped and fallen on the roadway, but Lemmering had moved as fast and surely as Franz himself. He was down on one knee behind the hood of the jeep. He had Franz's Tommy gun balanced there. He took a long two seconds to make sure of his aim, and while the man who'd just left them was still scrambling to get behind the Browning and put it into action, Lemmering cut him and the other BAR man down as neatly and with as little trouble as though they were cardboard dummies on a practice range. Between them Franz and Lemmering had spent fewer than a dozen shots. The MP had got off one, the BAR none at all.

Franz looked into the ditch to make sure of the MP corporal. Lemmering walked over to the BAR.

"All finished there?" Franz had only to raise his voice a little.

"All finished here, Captain," Lemmering said.

Tannenbaum picked himself up and lurched across the road. "Is there any cognac left?" he begged.

"Yes. One drink for Lemmering and one for me. What does your Yankee watch say now?"

"Eleven thirty-two. Are you sure you can't spare a drink for me?"

Franz handed the flask to Lemmering and then took it back. It was the first drink of hard stuff he'd had in three months. Instead of reinforcing the vaccine it watered it down. With the warmth of the liquor he felt again the accusing nudge of softness or sentimentality or whatever it was that had made him wonder about the first of the dead GI's. He shook his head and drew in a deep lungful of the thin, evergreen air. He had no reason to be troubled, he had no right to be troubled, but he walked over and down into the ditch to the side of the GI corporal, the first American he had killed with his own hands, and straightened out his head. He took the khaki woolen scarf from around the corporal's neck and laid it across his tired stubbled face.

The dirty Jew vultures. The lousy commies. Look what they did to him.

"We might as well leave Gotthold here with them," he said as he turned away. "They were all in the same army anyway. They just never found it out."

He led the other two back to the jeep and got behind the wheel himself. He eased diagonally across the road and then back through the road block and went on again through the forest to the west.

CHAPTER NINE

The attack came as a total surprise to the brothers George and Haig Ballantyne and to all other members of Number 38 Company, Number One Forestry Group, Canadian Forestry Corps.

Number 38 Company spent most of that Saturday in a state of innocence and isolation.

Around noon a liaison officer from the U. S. First Army, into whose command the company had been transferred two days before, checked into the town hall, now the orderly room. "Hear any shooting this morning, Major?" he asked the officer commanding over a cup of fortified tea.

"Well, more than we used to hear in Scotland. Sounded reassuringly far away."

"Yes, I guess so. I dropped into the map room at advance corps around eleven hundred hours. The G-2 was playing all sorts of queer games with his colored pencils. But he obviously didn't have a clue. The Krauts have been taking such a quiet steady beating everywhere else it's my guess they just decided to see if their batteries still work."

"Where *is* the front, by the way? I mean how far away?"

"Who knows? They call this the ghost front. How far are you from Malmédy?"

"Maybe ten miles."

"Ten and twenty. Well, if the front is still where it was last night—if it *was* there last night—oh, say thirty miles. But it's my duty to warn you the boy with the pencils had it a lot closer this morning."

"Any new orders for us?"

"No, just get set up and start cutting. There'll be a man from supply along in a day or two to go into details. I just came to make sure you're here and happy."

"One thing you might do."

"I can try."

"My boys were like kids when I told them we were moving from British to U.S. command. No more M and V! No more beef and kidney pudding! No more Woodbine cigarettes! They crave your pork and cheese and chocolate and Luckies, but they're still on Limey rations. It's like Santa Claus not showing up."

"I'll get a truckload of K rations up this afternoon. Hell, two truckloads, ten truckloads if you can use 'em. Our men hate the stuff."

They spent most of the day setting up the mill, taking inventory of the trucks and tractors, overhauling the Diesel plant, sharpening the huge main rotary, the edger, the trimmer, the crosscuts, the bucksaws and the hand power saws and the axes. "We'll be in business by tomorrow," the O.C. told the adjutant over lunch, having forgiven him for his liquid conduct of the night before.

They had found a big monastery outside town, a cheerless but large and sturdy building left in charge of four or five old monks when the Germans had requisitioned and then abandoned it in the early autumn. The big basement common room became a general mess and writing and reading room for the other ranks, and a small chapel adjoining it became the company orderly room. The door of the chapel had disappeared, possibly into the high stone fireplace at the end of the main room. No attempt was made to replace the door; there were seldom any military secrets within the Forestry Corps anyway.

Around two o'clock the adjutant drove up in the company of a small, round, melancholy Belgian. The visitor wore a cap of blanket cloth, a very good green tweed suit, leather gaiters and heavy boots, and a sweeping black mustache gleaming with frost rime.

As he entered the orderly-chapel he was relying for balance partly on his low center of gravity and partly on a heavy blackthorn walking stick.

The adjutant, who appeared to be relying in turn and in a somewhat lesser degree on the shoulder of the visitor, shoved him hastily into the spare chair. He saluted gravely.

"Monsieur Pierre Gladu, sir!" The adjutant rolled it out like a train announcer fighting off a bad cold.

"Yes," the O.C. said coldly.

"Monsieur Gladu was—well actually *is*"—the adjutant paused long enough to subdue his voice—"Monsieur Gladu is the head government forester for this whole district. One of the three leading foresters in France."

"We happen to be in Belgium, Captain Earnshaw."

"That's what I meant, sir. Belgium. We've been in Belgium quite a while," he added understandingly, as though gentling a retarded child.

The O.C. turned red and got up and strode over to the window, turning his back and counting under his breath.

"The Germans put Monsieur Gladu to work on the end of a bucksaw." The adjutant's voice was heavy with accusation, so heavy it seemed doubtful the Germans could bear the whole weight of it themselves. Some of it, the O.C. divined, was somehow meant for him.

"Pigs!" Monsieur Gladu shouted. "Pigs!"

"Monsieur Gladu's got degrees from three universities. Monsieur Gladu studied in Oregon and B.C. and Norway and he knows every tree between here and Luxembourg by its first name."

"You met him in a bar no doubt," the major said.

"No, sir." The adjutant spoke gently again, forgivingly. "The town major introduced us."

"And then you went to the bar?"

"Well, briefly, sir."

The O.C. turned around.

"You *sure* about this bird?"

"Absolutely, sir. The town major checked him all the way back to Brussels."

"Well"—the O.C. had begun to thaw, but he still wasn't quite ready to give up his doubts—"if he really does know these limits he can save us a hell of a lot of wasted cruising."

"*H'if! H'if! H'IF!* 'E say h'if?" Monsieur Gladu rolled to his feet, thumped the floor angrily with his blackthorn stick and bayed the question straight at the adjutant, disdaining to address the officer commanding in person.

The adjutant uttered soothing words and pressed him back into his chair. "Monsieur Gladu is very sensitive, sir," he said reproachfully. "He's put up with a hell of a lot. Imagine! A man like this on a bucksaw! It's like using Luther Burbank as a rigger."

"God damn it, Earnshaw," the major said, "don't forget I'm a forester too." He walked over and thrust his hand out to the simmering little visitor. Monsieur Gladu burst into tears and a flood of vindictive French.

"What's he say?" The major, thoroughly startled, retreated two paces and appealed to the adjutant.

"*Lentement*," the adjutant begged.

Monsieur Gladu slowed down a little but went on with the same indignant fervor.

"Well, Earnshaw," the O.C. demanded, "are you going to tell me or not? Just what the hell's he saying?"

"I don't think it's you he's mad at." The adjutant might have been announcing some piece of great good news. "It's still the Boche."

"Pigs! Pigs!" Monsieur Gladu interrupted the main thread of his discourse but picked it up again immediately.

"Captain Earnshaw, either get this lunatic out of here or get an interpreter."

"Yes, sir. Right away, sir." The adjutant stepped to the doorway. Haig Ballantyne, who had drawn kitchen fatigue that morning, was wiping down the nearest table, wearing the virtuous, faraway mask of a caught eavesdropper.

"Do you hear any of that, Ballantyne?" the adjutant asked him.
"What, sir?"
"You know bloody well what."
"Well, sir, it isn't exactly University of Manitoba French."
"Did you get it?"
"Some of it, sir."
"Well, come on in and pretend you're getting all of it."

Monsieur Gladu had not permitted himself a second interruption. The O.C. had backed away a further two paces.

The O.C. nodded hopefully at Haig. "For God's sake tell me what this man is saying. If he really does know these limits he may have something to communicate."

Monsieur Gladu had paused for breath.

"What's he *saying?*" the O.C. appealed.

"Shall I summarize, sir?"

"Yes, for God's sake! Give it to me any way you like. Give it to me in précis and triplicate and blank verse if you like. But for God's sake, give it to me."

Monsieur Gladu mopped his streaming eyes with a blue polka-dot handkerchief and accepted a cigarette.

"Most of what he's been saying, sir," Haig reported, "is untranslatable. Untranslatable by me, anyway."

"He's been cursing like a God-damn' navvy," the major said impatiently. "Any damn fool can see that. But what's he getting at?"

"Well, sir, he says the Boche made him work like a common coolie. They would not listen to him about the forest. They tried to murder the forest. It will take fifteen years, twenty years for the forest to recover. The Germans fell on the forest like madmen. Their axes went Chunk! Chunk! Chunk! Their saws went Bzzz! Bzzz! Bzzz! Night and day! Day and night!" Haig's voice had begun to rise too; he had caught some of the little Belgian's fervor; it swept him along, slowly but surely inflaming him, as though he were a one-man mob falling into hypnosis. "Day and night! Night and day! Chop! Chop! Chop! Cut! Cut! Cut! Madmen! Assassins! O pigs and fiends of hell!"

"Yes, yes. We all know that. But he seemed to be asking something of *me*. Or was he just swearing at me too?"

"No, sir. He's been saying that there must be no cutting in this part of the forest for at least another ten years. Not one stick, not one branch. Otherwise the forest will be dead forever."

"Nonsense," the major said uneasily.

"He said you must take your saws and axes away and leave the forest to its sickbed. Then he said he knew you were sure to be too—pardon me, sir—too stupid and unfeeling to have any pity or respect for the beautiful violated forest, you would pounce on it, sir, with all the lust of the second man in line for a ravished virgin, your base appetite only whetted and your conscience chloroformed by the sight of what has already been done."

"Say," the major asked suspiciously, "you're not helping this bird out, are you? I just want a translation."

"No, sir." It *had* been a somewhat free translation. It was Haig's first opportunity for anything in the nature of a literary exercise since his arrival in Scotland, and he was not displeased with it.

"Well, tell him I'm sorry. Tell him I was a forester too, back on civvy street, and a good one, too. Tell him I've got orders to log these stands off at full mill capacity and our capacity is thirty thousand feet a day. Tell him I know this may be a little over the normal allowable cut, but ask him if he'll help us keep the damage to a minimum."

Haig's French was less eloquent. There was little time for eloquence. As soon as the O.C.'s figures of mill capacity were out, Monsieur Gladu was in full flight again, his face redder than ever, his blackthorn hammering the floor like a midget pile driver, his shrill voice swooping and beating at the chapel walls like the cries of a caged eagle. But in Haig he seemed to have detected an ally, for when Haig held up a timid hand he paused long enough to refresh his anger and allow the translation to catch up. He had begun to weep again.

"He says he knew it. He knew you—uh, sir—for an unprincipled vandal the moment he set eyes on you."

"Go on," the O.C. commanded stonily.

"Barbarians are barbarians anywhere. Whatever his nationality an assassin is an assassin. Why, he wants to know, do you assassins of the forests all, in spite of everything, cling to the same pretended God. The false God of dead stones and dead bricks, dead spires and turrets, dead churchyards and cemeteries guarding dead bones and rotted flesh. It is to all of you a special crime, a special sacrilege, to destroy or even to disturb a lifeless cathedral, a barren miserable country church, a ruined graveyard or the dead manure below it; this, your dead souls proclaim, is the unforgivable sin. But to kill the living forest, the source of life—the end of life, the highest essence of life—to kill the forest is necessary, is good, is practical, is virtuous. To kill the living forest does not require so much as a passing thought."

"Tell him this is not a choice between trees and churches," the O.C. broke in unhappily. "It's a choice between trees and living —not dead—human beings. Our armies need timber. They need lumber. If they don't get it the war will go on and on. Thousands more people will be killed. Ask him if he thinks trees are more important than human beings."

"He says of course they are." Haig had difficulty in restraining a gleeful smile. "Any fool knows that, he says."

"Oh hell, then." The O.C. shrugged. "What can you do?"

Monsieur Gladu spoke a little more quickly. "He says," Haig reported, "that he does know one stand not far from here where there is excellent spruce and pine. It could, he thinks, survive a few weeks cutting at eight or ten thousand feet a day. If you will deal with it humanely, according to good practice, it will replenish itself and endure."

"That's great!" the O.C. said heartily. "That's exactly the kind of thing Monsieur here can help us with. Hell! I don't care what he says. I've got as much respect as anybody."

"He says, sir, that if he helps you must restrict the cut to ten thousand feet at the most."

"God damn it!" The O.C. advanced a step or two. "I can't. I've got to deliver mill capacity and that's thirty thousand and that's what I'm delivering."

The round little Belgian waited only long enough to be sure that he had been turned down. Then he was off the chair like a ball of bouncing putty. He raised his blackthorn stick above his head and advanced, not directly on the O.C., but on the imagined body of a creature so beloved and so grievously hurt that he was compelled to end its suffering.

"Cut! Cut! Cut!" he shouted, lowering his low, round rump almost to the floor and sawing the air with the blackthorn like a golf club and whirling it wildly before the adjutant in a series of vertical circles. "Saw! Saw! Saw!" he cried. "Bzzz! Bzzz! Bzzz!"

"Shall I translate, sir?" Haig shouted.

"Don't be a God-damn' fool!" the major shouted back.

Monsieur Gladu knelt and turned the walking stick into a cannon. "Boom! Boom! Boom!" he cried. "Crash! Crash! Crash!"

"Monsieur Gladu." The adjutant, though stricken, was still deferential. "Don't you think—"

"SSSS! SSSS! SSSS! Burn! Burn! Burn!" The blackthorn was a flame-thrower hurling tongues of fire.

The little Belgian's cloth cap had slipped over one dark glaring eye. The rime on his mustache had melted and merged with his tears. His round face was as red and flooded as a ripe, dew-drenched tomato. The blackthorn was now an ax. He raised it high and stalked across the room to the chapel's small wooden altar and the plaster statue of the Virgin behind it.

"Chop! Chop! Chop!" The soft wood altar splintered. The Virgin's head flew off into a corner. "Chunk! Chunk! Chunk!" As abruptly as he had exploded, the Belgian composed himself. He lowered the stick, looked disdainfully at the wrecked altar and the murdered statue, squared himself away, straightened his cap, saluted the officer commanding, nodded distantly to the adjutant, smiled forgivingly at Haig, uttered a final "Pah!" and lurched from the room alone.

The O.C. sat down heavily. "Drunk," he muttered, seeking reassurance. "Drunk as a bloody goat."

His hurt and weary eyes settled on the adjutant.

"Earnshaw," he asked, "why don't you just go back to drinking alone?"

"Sir?"

"Drink in secret," he pleaded. "Don't drink with strangers. Look what it can lead to. By the way is there anything left in the mess stores? After last night?"

"Why, certainly, sir. Would you like—"

"Yes, I'd like. I'd like a big—Wait a minute, Ballantyne. I think you've earned a drink too."

The adjutant was back in a moment with a full bottle of Red Label and three tin cups.

"Well, what the hell," the O.C. said. "Up your kilts." He sat brooding over his whisky. Haig and the adjutant brooded with him.

"You know," the O.C. said, "drunk or not that crazy Frog had no right talking to me like that."

"I'm sorry, sir," the adjutant said.

The O.C. ignored him. "I'll say one thing for the old pisspot, he didn't *sound* old. Reminded me a little of the way I was twenty-five years ago."

"Aah!" The O.C. emptied his cup and held it out again. "Christ! Just after I got out of school I spent two years as a skinner on redwoods in B.C. Redwoods! Holy God! Starting on redwoods is like starting on Marlene Dietrich. I mean . . . I mean I guess you don't know *what* I mean."

"I—uh—was mostly in the accounting end," the adjutant confessed uncomfortably.

"Then I had a long spell on hard maple in Quebec. Well, Holy God! You ever feel a good piece of maple just after it comes away from the big saw? It's cool and starting to get smooth, but not too smooth, not phony smooth the way it gets when they plane it and plaster it with lacquer, but woman smooth. Not phony-woman smooth, real-woman smooth. With the smoothness and coolness there's also a little heat left from the friction of the saw. I'm no queer, Earnshaw, but I've often got a hard-on just touching new-cut maple."

The adjutant spilled more whisky into Haig's cup and his own.

"Then I was in a mill for a summer, resawing birch. As lumber birch isn't much, but as a tree on a Laurentian hillside—" The O.C. lowered his eyes, suddenly ashamed because he was growing maudlin and doubly ashamed because he was not articulate enough to express precisely what he meant. "Then," he finished lamely, "I went to work for Abitibi. There's nothing wrong with pulpwood but after twenty years on pulpwood, you forget some things. You can't, you just can't—"

Earnshaw took a deep breath. "Can't see the trees for the forest, sir?" he suggested sympathetically.

"You make that up?" the O.C. asked.

"I—I guess so, sir."

"You're not as dumb as I thought you were," the O.C. said generously. "Look, Earnshaw, I want to talk to that crazy Frog again tomorrow. See if you can get him in here sober. I mean *him* sober. You too, if that's not asking too much."

"Yes, sir."

"And Earnshaw."

"Sir."

"We won't start cutting tomorrow after all. Find some extra maintenance to do. I'm going back to army to find out for myself if they really do need thirty thousand feet a day from us."

Another domestic event of considerable magnitude occurred later in the day. The work parties were dismissed early and began drifting into the monks' assembly room to wait for supper, some talking beside the big fireplace, a few playing darts, others reading or writing letters. Just as the mess sergeant was laying out a boiler-ful of tea and hot Scottish scones, made from a recipe "direct and by popular request from the slopes of Ben-y-Gloe," the orderly arrived with a month of mail.

For some it was late Thanksgiving mail and for some it was early Christmas mail. There were of course three or four men who got no mail at all, but they were used to it and the others were used to them; they simply disappeared when mail was called, muttering sad Chaplinesque explanations about going to the can or changing their wet socks. But everybody else got a month's mail and there was half a truckload of duty-free gift Sweet Caporals waiting in the sorting room upstairs.

George got twenty-two letters, seventeen of them from Vera. The blue air-mail forms were numbered, as all the letters from the first had been. These were Numbers 417 to 433 inclusive. An appalling reminder of the gulf of time they sought to stitch together. Vera was an extraordinarily inventive letter writer. She had had to be, for when they parted they had no mutual friends except her father and his brother, no natural topics of discourse except the weather, the Winnipeg streetcar service, and the increasingly uninteresting activities of various athletes, politicians, radio announcers, band leaders, movie stars, and police-court celebrities, local, national, and international.

Her letters frankly set out to be cheerful and entertaining, but they revealed some of the same grave spunkiness and little-girl perceptiveness that had made him abandon his senses and surrender to his intuition on that first night at and beyond the Parthenon Restaurant. During the first year and a half she changed jobs three times, each time to a slightly better one, from a want-ad taker to a junior stenographer to a receptionist-switchboard girl to a semiprivate secretary in an insurance firm. Then, without George's advance knowledge or help, she got a job as a cub reporter on the rival paper. She did not say, and some indecipherable mixture of gratitude and reticence forbade him to ask, whether she had done so for his sake mainly, but the result was as good as though she had. She could send him the news of his world and its other inhabitants, not as a wife, not as a dutiful but baffled camp follower, but as one who lived there in her own right. Her English was good, her powers of observation were good, her energy was boundless, and her judgment cool and steady, and since nearly all the good male reporters under thirty-five were either at the war or in its environs, Vera was rapidly promoted from Obits through Suburbs, Women's Sports, Police, City Hall, and Legislature to General Features. She was getting by-lines within a year, and although her by-line was neither so famous nor regular nor well regarded as George's had been, the stories that appeared beneath it were as clean, crisp, and ungushy as Vera Rebchuk herself. If his corner of the civilian universe needed keeping warm, no one could have done it better.

As warily as she had accepted their mass descent on the station platform, she seemed to be keeping up some sort of running inventory for him of the people who had come to see George off for overseas. They had all of course wanted to be kind to her because of George. George guessed cynically but with undiminished fondness for them all that since they were all, in one way or another, creatures or dependents of the printing press, they'd have found a means of cultivating her and her fresh young by-line even if she hadn't been Mrs. George Ballantyne.

No. 419: "Had tea at Moore's today with Dorothea. I don't know whether I remembered to tell you, but she and José Wilberforce actually *did* get married. José is extremely busy because as a Mexican citizen he can't be conscripted by the U. S. Army and he's one of the four or five ablest-bodied wrestlers left on the whole circuit. My, Dorothea is nice! I'd never dreamed a girl so big could be so *handsome*. She talks about you a good deal. You must have been very good friends!"

George didn't attempt to guess whether she was fishing or merely hinting that she *could* have been reproaching him if she hadn't been above that sort of thing. But the suggestion of retroactive jealousy, the unspoken pledge of an honest trace of honest female bitchiness, made him feel closer to her than ever.

No. 422: "Had lunch today (Sunday) with your wicked boss Sidney Logan, and Sylvia. They've both been very sweet to me. Mr. Logan pretends to be mortally offended that I went to work for the other paper and he's actually paid me the good practical compliment of offering me ten dollars a week more to come over to the *Chronicle*. I pointed out greedily that salaries were frozen, but he said there were legal or at least semilegal methods of handling *that*. I don't think I'll move though. If you don't mind I'd like to keep working—it's really exciting for me—at least until we start our family, and much as I'd like to think you would, you won't want me under your feet all the time. The Logans' apartment is really lovely, isn't it? Sylvia let something drop while we were in the powder room that suggested you're quite familiar with it. She's really gorgeous and so sort of knowing and, well—un-naïve. I wonder why she calls Mr. Logan Mount Rushmore? He doesn't seem to know why either, but I gather he takes it as some sort of a special compliment that Sylvia prefers to keep a secret even from him."

Mount Rushmore. Great yacking faces with their balls invisible in uncut stone. George laughed out loud. Sylvia was, indeed, gorgeous and she was, indeed, as Vera had noticed, un-naïve. He decided he wouldn't bother mentioning Sylvia when he wrote to Vera next.

No. 423: "Disgraceful scenes at your home—and castle—last night. Mr. Massinov insisted on taking me personally to the wrestling matches. He was introducing a new Masked Marvel and said he wanted my objective opinion whether he was hateful enough to catch on with the hatpin girls. Afterward I asked him in for a game of chess and a drink. (I thought Dad had taught me a reasonable game, but a simple Polack girl should never try to play chess with the Russians.) Anyway this wretched woman across the hall saw us coming in. She made the janitor call the morality squad and I guess they wanted to get in out of the cold because three of these big hulking brutes burst in on us just as Mr. Massinov played P X R ch, and they as good as accused me of running a cat-house. Luckily Bill Hetherington—you remember him of course; he always asks for you when I see him at the station, says you practically *made* the police amateur bouts—he was duty sergeant and I was able to get him on the phone. The upshot was the morality squad settled in and drank all my whisky. Mr. Massinov said he was tremendously flattered and pretended to be trying to bribe the cops to take the cat-house charge to court. He said at sixty-three his reputation with the ladies had suddenly gone all to hell and he needed the advertising even if I didn't."

No. 425: "Very sad news yesterday about Joe Wilson. Everything seemed to be breaking at last for poor Joe. He made that wonderful comeback with the Blue Bombers last fall. He was everybody's all-Canadian tackle (not my phrase, your stand-in's). And he was even starting to sell policies, enough to start thinking about getting married to that girl in Eaton's he'd been going with so long. They came over one night for supper and I've never seen two people happier. Joe was just full of bounce and confidence, you wouldn't have believed the change in him, and Sally was radiant. Then Joe's number came up. I don't think he wanted to go overseas even as much as Haig did, but he went active right away. He was killed late in October on one of those canals around the Scheldt and his name came through on the last casualty list. I called Sally when I heard. She already knew, from the official telegram, and was still terribly broken up. And I honestly don't think a bit of it was for herself, it was all for Joe. Before he went Joe asked for his ring back. He knew he was going to be killed. He knew it, Sally says, as an absolute certainty, just as certainly he knew the sun came up and went down. 'It's no use,' he said to her. 'My luck's come back to normal again. That string of breaks last year was just a freak. Just a lousy cock-teasing freak.' Joe had never even said damn to her before, and I've never even said damn to you but it's too tragic to be dirty."

Dake it, Choe. Dake it now ze pisser. You.

No. 431: "José Wilberforce has just won the world's championship of St. Louis. He beat Snapper Walter Snelgrove two falls out of three last Thursday. Dorothea is furious. The syndicate wanted a change in St. Louis. Some snoopy reporter saw Walter Snelgrove on a bird walk with the Audubon Society and that finished poor Walter as a villain in St. Louis at least. Dorothea hates St. Louis, but now they're world champions there, they'll have to live there except of course when José's on the road. Dorothea wanted José to tell them he'd take the world championship of Toronto or nothing. But José never could stand up to Mr. Massinov and Mr. Massinov ordered José to quit arguing and get the hell down there to St. Louis and win the third fall with his Aztec Head Shrinker in not more than three minutes before the curfew. When they broke it to Walter Snelgrove, *he* threatened to turn rebellious too. But Toots calmed him down. Walter's going to get the world championship of Los Angeles early in the New Year and Fatso Cunningham is going from Los Angeles to Toronto. Dorothea still isn't speaking to Mr. Massinov and she's barely speaking to José."

No. 432: "George, when do you think it will be over?"

It was a good run of mail, gay enough to cheer him up, sad enough to reassure him that everybody still missed him. There were several letters from people around the office and one from Boris Massinov. They all spoke affectionately of this and that and, without coming right out and putting it that way, with pleased incredulity that George's little waitress, his little embarkation wife, had turned out to be a three-dimensional *person*. George leaned back on the wooden bench, resting against the long oak table and stretching his feet toward the fire. He had been reading for more than an hour.

For the first time he turned to Haig, sitting beside him before his own, smaller pile of mail.

"Make out O.K.?"

"Not bad. Not bad at all. Two or three old college chums. A

girl I've had apprenticed to replace the one I had to shoot. A couple from a girl named Vera. Does *that* one pine!"

"I bet," George smiled.

"You'll have to give her up, George. You're just not worthy. She deserves better. She deserves—well, for instance, me."

George smiled again. "Sorry. This one's a keeper." He paused a minute and added almost humbly, "I hope to God."

"Oh well—if you ever change your mind. How long till supper?"

George looked at his watch. "Still an hour. Want some more tea?"

When he came back a man on the far side of the table threw him a batch of newspaper clippings. "Like to catch up on the conscription crisis?"

Since the transfer into a U.S. command, they had been getting the *Maple Leaf* only occasionally and always late. The zombie question, exacerbated by a known and acknowledged shortage of reinforcements in the Canadian infantry, had blown up some mysterious new cloud formations above the far-off Oz called Ottawa, but, lacking hard and detailed news and not being personally involved, Number 38 Company had remained largely indifferent. The soldier who had received the clippings—a Finn from the Lakehead named Yuri Wuorio—was one of the few men in the company who "wasted his time on politics." The men who had known him back home dismissed him, in a not unkindly or intolerant but rather a bored way, as "one of those Red Finns." Hard-driven by one of Wuorio's frequent revolts against compulsory church parades, the padre had once, back in Scotland, preached a whole sermon against Godless Communists. The sergeant major, once forced to withdraw a minor disciplinary charge by Wuorio's superior knowledge of the King's Orders and Regulations, often referred to him, rather admiringly but with a hint of vengeful waiting, as the best little barracks-room lawyer this side of the glass house.

George leafed through the clippings, most of them from the Port Arthur *News-Chronicle*, the Fort William *Times-Journal*, the Winnipeg *Chronicle*, the *Free Press*, the Toronto *Globe and Mail*, and a Finnish-language weekly. Some were dated as recently as the first week of December.

"Hell, Yuri," George said. "I'm so far behind it would take me all night to digest all there is here. How about giving me one of your famous, unbiased précis on national and world affairs?"

"Gladly." Wuorio's blue eyes had a certain permanent glare to them, but they were not devoid of humor.

"You start, naturally, with the axiom that all politicians above the rank of village reeve are scoundrels and all soldiers above the rank of lance corporal are idiots."

A sergeant sitting beside the slender Finn looked up mildly, grinned, and returned to his mail.

"Naturally," George said. "But what's *new*, Yuri?"

"There's really been guts to clean this time." The Finn made no attempt to conceal his pleasure. "You know Ralston quit as defense minister six weeks ago because he couldn't get enough reinforcements without conscription."

George nodded. Haig had joined Wuorio's audience, as had several other men sitting along the table and lounging by the fireplace.

"Well, after pushing Ralston out because Ralston was honest enough to say we needed conscription and shoving General Mc-Naughton in because McNaughton was willing to pretend we didn't, old finger-in-the-ass Willie King has finally conscripted sixteen thousand zombies. Boy *is* there guts to clean!"

"Who the hell cares?" One of the men by the fire returned pointedly to his comic book.

"The papers are so full of lies all the time you can't be sure. But reading between the lines it looks as if the cabinet's in revolt, Quebec's close to revolt, the army brass are in revolt, the zombies are in revolt—Jesus, what a lovely balls-up!"

"You said it, Hunky!" someone else chipped in. "They should take all the God-damned zombies *and* Willie King *and* Andy McNaughton *and* all the generals and put them in a friggin' troopship and ship them C.O.D. to friggin' Hamburg!"

"You're just jealous," the Finn objected treacherously. "The only difference between you and a zombie is the zombie is smart."

"What about you?"

"Me?" The Finn shrugged. "I never claimed to be smart. But I'm eating regular and that's more than I could say in 1939. And nobody's shot at me yet."

"You know"—the man who had been trying to agree a moment before was now spluttering in anger—"I don't think you're a commie after all, Wuorio. I think you're a God-damn' peace-mongering fascist."

The Finn threw back his head and laughed. It was a forced laugh and therefore a deliberately insulting one.

Trapped, the other soldier had no defense left but to bank the fire of his rage still higher.

"You yellow son-of-a-bitch, you're *worse* than the stinking zombies!" He started to come around the table.

Ordinarily they'd have let him go, if only for the entertainment. But this was a soft day, a mail day, a day only nine days before Christmas, the fireplace was bright and benevolent, and the smell of what obviously was going to be one of the mess sergeant's best stews was already drifting in from the direction of the kitchen. Two or three men grabbed the Finn and two or three more grabbed the other soldier. George stole a look at Haig. If Haig considered himself a party to the dispute, directly or indirectly, his face gave no sign of it. His expression was solely that of a spectator.

Wuorio's would-be assailant subsided after enough curses and sufficient threshing around to satisfy his honor. The conversation broke into islands for a while. The adjutant appeared in the open doorway to the chapel-orderly office and called across the room, "Is Swanson here?"

"Sir!"

A short, bald soldier leaped from his chair by the fire and fairly ran to the doorway. In a moment a glorious bellow erupted from within and in another moment the bald man burst back into view, shrieking with delight and deliberate craziness. "Gold! Gold!" he shrieked, imitating a mad prospector. "I got it! I got it!"

"He got it!" someone else shouted with him and for him. "Swanson got his ticket home!"

Everybody stood up, hollering Swanson in, strewing his path back across the room with hosannahs.

"Well, how the bloody hell *about* that?"

"Long live Sigurd Swanson!"

Someone began to sing:

> *"Poor old Siggy Swanson's got an aching in his balls,*
> *Poor old Siggy Swanson's got an aching in his balls,*
> *Poor old Siggy Swanson's got an aching in his balls*
> *But his soul goes marching on . . ."*

There were envy and regret in the tumult, but there was a dazed happiness in it, too, a note of glad wonder, as at the passing of a miracle. It was less than six weeks since the *Maple Leaf* had carried the first announcement of the first Canada-leave plan. Only officers and men with "five years satisfactory continuous service overseas" were eligible. Sigurd Swanson, who'd come over with the First Division in December 1939 and had been retreaded from infantry to forestry a year later, was the only member of Number 38 Company who came within six months of qualifying. He became, particularly for the scores of other men in the company who'd been away from home more than four years but not yet five, a kind of sacred vessel, a symbol of their own lonely hopes of seeing Canada and their families again before the memories faded out and the dreams retreated forever and it was all better written off and forgotten. The round, bald figure of Sigurd Swanson held the proxies of their hearts' desire. If round, bald Siggy Swanson could somehow attain the unattainable, if Siggy could take wings from the handle of a bucksaw and soar away to the earthly paradise of home, so could anybody, so could everybody.

Siggy's application for Canada leave, warmly endorsed by the O.C. and carrying the silent prayers of two hundred officers and other ranks, had gone forward on the very day the scheme was made official. In the intervening weeks, barracks humor being the close kin it is to gallows humor, his well-wishers tortured him by wondering frequently, audibly, and with the profoundest sympathy whether Swanson was really eligible after all. It was true his five years would nominally be up on December 10, the fifth anniversary of the day when the *Empress of Britain* sailed out of Halifax Harbor. (*Of course, Siggy, if They want to, They can rule you weren't overseas until you landed, and for the sake of a few days They might just tear your application up or shuffle it down to the bottom of the pile.*) Everybody was deeply and apprehensively concerned, and lost no opportunity of telling Swanson so, about the interpretation They might place on the word "satisfactory." (*How about that time you got back a day late from your furlough in Glasgow, Siggy? But the O.C. let me off with a reprimand. It's the only charge that was laid against me in five years. But the charge sheet will be there with all your other papers. They have to send in the full record, Siggy. I don't believe it. I don't believe the major would send it in. Even if the major wanted to I'll bet the adjutant would lose the charge sheet. Gosh, Siggy, I sure hope you're right, that's all. I sure hope you do make it.*)

But now the suspense and the torture were ended and they

hailed Sigurd Swanson as a hero. The adjutant himself reappeared in the doorway of the chapel when the sounds of wonder had subsided to a sort of communion murmur. He shouted across to Swanson a second time, so all of them could hear.

"Come back in, Swanson, the major and I would like to drink a toast to you."

As Swanson, no longer seeming so bald, so round, or so diminutive, strode off to accept the invitation, someone sighed—the hundredth time those words had been sighed in the last ten minutes—"By God, I'd never have believed it could really happen!" and someone else wondered wistfully, "I wonder who's next?"

The sergeant sitting beside the Red Finn looked up. "I can tell you. George Ballantyne."

George didn't know whether anything was expected of him or not. He did know, now that They had proved They were really going to grant Canada leaves and not just go on talking about them, that he might conceivably be home in time for Vera's birthday. She'd be twenty-four and he'd be nearly thirty, an appalling, steadying thought. He'd stopped counting in days away back in 1943 but had started again when the new leave scheme came down.

"Don't hold your breath, Sarge," he smiled. "I won't be five years overseas for another six months, four days and"—he looked at his watch—"eleven hours and fourteen minutes."

The Red Finn broke in with a caveat. "Did you allow for the time zones?"

"Oh sure, Yuri. It'd be a hell of a note to wait that long and then miss the boat."

"I don't want to spoil anything for you, George, but you *have* missed it."

"I guess so. I guess the war will be over by then and I'll get back in the regular queue."

"The hell you will!" The Finn's thin dark face glinted like a gypsy fortuneteller's. "Swanson was just lucky. He just happened to hit a rock fault in the Army's rock head. The minute Germany caves in They'll fold the whole leave scheme and send us all to Japan."

The sergeant pondered the prediction. "Even the Sawdust Fusiliers?"

"Especially the Sawdust Fusiliers. How are they going to rebuild those wooden Jap houses the Fortresses have been burning up?

Where will they get the new wood? Who will get it for them? Who? Who will chop it down? Who will mill it? Who?"

"Not us."

"Why *not* us? Listen, Sarge. Put yourself in the shoes of those rock-head generals and those rock-head politicians. You've got Germany finally squashed but the God-damn' Japs still won't quit. So you see the only thing you can do is go on burning the whole God-damn' island down one shack at a time. But you know the Japs are cunning, evil, treacherous little bastards. They won't stay in their God-damn' burning shacks and get burned up with them. So the idea gets through even your rock head that when the last shack is burned down there'll still be seventy or eighty million more or less live Japs roaring around and bellyaching about inadequate housing conditions. So you prepare in advance to spend eight hundred billion dollars rebuilding the shacks it cost you seven hundred billion dollars to burn down. And the first step in your rock-head, long-range planning is to start stock-piling lumber. Hell, George, by the time you see Winnipeg again you'll be wearing a kimono and you'll have grown-up geisha girls for daughters."

In the morning the O.C. stepped out of the chapel and briefed the whole company while the men went on with their breakfast porridge and sausage. "As most of you heard over the B.B.C. news last night the enemy has attacked. He's made some gains. The situation is now under control. The company will carry on with its duties. I've just had a detailed sitrep from the First Army L.O. A few tanks got through about nine miles ahead of here late yesterday afternoon. At least three were destroyed and the rest were driven off by our regular and antitank artillery. That was what you heard off and on yesterday and through the early part of the night. There's been no air activity on either side. If the fog and cloud and snow keep up—and mets says it will keep up indefinitely—there won't be any. Until further notice all details, milling, cutting, and headquarters, will carry rifles and small arms at all times. Any questions?"

"One, sir." The Red Finn put down his porridge spoon and rose to attention, assuming the chronic disturber's camouflage as the Perfect Soldier. "Does Private Swanson still get his Canada leave?"

The O.C. glared. "All leaves are temporarily canceled," he said between his teeth.

"Thank you, sir." The Finn sat down. "Rocks," he said behind his hand as he lifted his spoon again.

Later the O.C. had a longer, quieter session with M. Gladu, the Belgian forester, and by nightfall the company was producing ten-by-ten and ten-by-twelve bridge pilings at two-thirds capacity. The warlike noises within their earshot were again sporadic and remote.

The next day a runner crunched through the snow to the stand of spruce on which George and Haig were working together on a bucksaw and told George to report to the orderly room.

The adjutant was waiting for him beside one of the company's two jeeps. "Come on, Ballantyne, you're demoted back to driver. Let's go see if we can find the Dirk and Sporran again."

"Lightning won't strike twice," George lamented, remembering Ben-y-Gloe and the unexpected gusher of Dewar's.

"Well, get in anyway. Let's see what we *can* find."

They drove toward the east. Before they had gone a mile the adjutant abandoned his air of playful mystery.

"The O.C.'s been coming to a slow boil for two days," he confided. "The L.O. from army keeps telling us nothing's happening at all. Corps won't tell us anything. We can't get any kind of contact from the divisions that are supposed to be in this area. Half an hour ago a truckload of GI's went rattling through on the road to Liège as if it was being chased by the very hounds of hell. The O.C. was walking across the square. He tried to wave it down, but the driver just bore down on the horn and barreled right through. He nearly ran the major down."

"Maybe *they* know where the Dirk and Sporran is," George suggested.

"They weren't hurrying *to,* they were hurrying *away.* And then a little while afterward, six GI's straggled in on foot. Only one of them had a rifle left and none of them had any kit at all, not even a blanket or a spare pair of socks. They said they were the only survivors of a whole battalion."

The adjutant waved George down a side road. "Not too fast. They were deserters of course. Probably from that skirmish with the tanks. The O.C. couldn't get anything out of them but a lot of hysterical gibberish. It was just like a little-theater production of *Journey's End.* Keep off the verges, Ballantyne; I'm not sure whether this road has been cleared for mines or not. The O.C. put the whole bloody bunch of them under arrest and messaged corps for instructions about their disposal and also asking for a new sitrep. Corps's only answer was an order to stop clogging the wire

264

with nonessential messages. The O.C. blew his stack and gave me a written order to proceed"—the adjutant consulted a typewritten paper—"on an immediate reconnaissance in the direction of the Rhine and not report back until I have (a) personally established contact with at least one U.S. line unit of battalion or lesser strength and (b) come personally within the zone of fire of at least one enemy weapon of light field artillery or lesser caliber. The O.C., Ballantyne, does not question my bulldog courage, but he does, alas, have some reservations about my brain."

George attempted to strike the same note as the adjutant, a mixture of comradely nervousness and amusement. "I preferred Scotland myself."

"I don't know how good this map is but there should be a five-way traffic junction six kilos ahead and just beyond that there might just be a church. That Yankee L.O. keeps nattering about the ghost front. If the ghosts are walking we might see something from the spire."

They drove on in silence. The walls of pine and spruce, marbled with snow, were like tall slabs of green and white onyx. Occasionally an empty field and an empty farmhouse broke in on the looming sameness. They passed what had once been a big plantation of evergreens. Now it lay dead, an uprooted graveyard of shattered stumps and splintered limbs and black, fleshless trunks eaten to the bone by flames and shrapnel in some random convulsion of some earlier battle. He thought of Haig's description of the furious little Belgian with the blackthorn stick. "*Ssss! Sssss! Ssss! Burn! Burn! Burn! Crash! Crash! Crash!*"

The adjutant's memory must have been prodded too. "What a senseless bloody massacre!"

At the five-way junction a single peeled tree trunk sprouted direction markers as thick as thorns. The signs, some old and Belgian, some middle-aged and German, some brand-new and American, beckoned to all the points of the compass, all the other crossroads in the world. But like all the small-scale signposts and all the large-scale maps by which all soldiers of a rank below full general must take their bearings, they did not deal in the higher truths or the nobler goals and aspirations. They did not say bravely New York 5507 miles or London 421 miles or Toronto 5630 miles or Berlin 612 miles or Paris 361 miles or even Chattanooga, Tenn., 6235 miles or Oswaldtwistle, Lancs., 640 miles or Moose Jaw, Sask., 7796 miles. They said, instead, cautious, mocking, miserly, promising nothing, demanding everything: Malmédy 12 km.; Krinkelt 40 km.; Stavelot 8 km.; Spa 30 km.; Trois Ponts 13 km.; Vielsalm 35 km.; Ligneville 18 km.; Houffalize 70 km.; Bastogne 110 km.

The MP walked over to the jeep with his Tommy gun cradled and his finger at but not inside the trigger guard. "Oranges and lemons."

"St. Clements," the adjutant replied.

"Jesus, it worked!"

"I'm looking for a battalion headquarters," the adjutant said. "What battalion?"

"Well—any battalion."

"Any battalion." The disgust of the traffic cop for the helpless motorist was universal. Then with a trace of friendliness, "You another of those warcos? Hey, I could give you a pretty good story about me and my buddy and a couple of Kraut parachutists that tried to get through here yesterday." For the first time he really noticed their basin helmets. "Oh hell, you're Limeys. Your story wouldn't go to Milwaukee anyway."

"Canadians. Anyway we're not correspondents." The adjutant explained their mission.

"You want to find the front?" The GI suddenly exuded the generosity of a seasoned tourist showing off his knowledge to a stranger just off the boat. "Go on over to the church and climb the tower. My buddy's up there now."

"Anything doing?"

"Anything doing? *Brother!*" The GI slapped his hands on his flanks and did a little jig for warmth. "You know like the fishing guides say in Wisconsin? You shoulda been here yesterday. You'll see the valley when you get up in the tower. Two of our divisions got tangled up there, one highballing out and the other highballing in and the Krauts hit them from the slope. What a fuck-up! The Krauts had some mortars and what looked like eighty-eights and some heavier stuff coming in from farther back and then they come in with maybe ten, a dozen Panthers, four-five Tigers, a couple of hundred infantry, and then, by Jesus! if it ain't fucked up enough already they poured in half a dozen Shermans. Shermans! How do you like that! Me and my buddy had the glasses on them. You could even pick out the white stars on them."

"What about the two paratroops?"

"They're hanging up by their harness over there in the tree if you're interested. But it's strictly a Milwaukee-Eau Claire story.

266

My buddy's from Eau Claire. I already forgot. You're not warcos anyway." The GI blinked his red watery eyes. "Do I sound as if I'm babbling incoherently?" he asked. "I been waiting for my buddy to start babbling incoherently so I could put him in the sidecar and evacuate him. But the son-of-a-bitch keeps saying he's gonna outwait me and then *he'll* evacuate *me*. It was a real fuck-up they had down there anyway. The division that was coming out kept coming and the division that was going in kept going and by the time they got sorted out they both got chopped up real good. It was the Three Eight Seven going in and the Three Four Three coming out. The Three Eight Seven finally got a good antitank screen set up around dark and the Krauts either pulled back or decided to try going around. We had stragglers from Three Four Three limping through here all night but since morning there's been nobody but civilians."

"Thanks." The adjutant nodded to George and they drove away to the church.

"Hey, if you go up the tower," the MP called after them, "ask my buddy how he'd like a nice hot bath. Tell him they always give the exhaustion cases a hot bath and all the whisky they can drink. Tell him I'm still waiting."

They climbed a ladder to the bell tower. Another pair of red watery eyes peered down at them when they were still several rungs below the hatchway, and another high voice, bowstring tight with a mixture of weariness and excitement, demanded and received the password.

"Come on in, Captain. Come on in, pal. I'm Barney Edwards from Eau Claire, Wis. Foresters? That sounds like a cushy deal. I spent a summer on a logging gang back home. Hey, did you see old Jackie-boy back there at the junction? How'd he look? He look a little edgy? How'd he talk? Did it strike you like he was talking funny? I got a hunch old Jackie-boy's just about had it. What do you think, Captain?"

"Nuh." The adjutant stepped across to the far side of the tower and looked into the valley below. Except for one big sloping field, the single roadway, and the bed of a frozen stream, it was a solid mass of snow-dappled evergreens. George picked out half a dozen burned-out tanks in the field, and trucks lay black and shattered along the whole visible length of the roadway. When the adjutant handed him the binoculars George picked out bodies thrown here and there in the lavish careless pattern of hand-sown seeds. Most of the bodies were in olive drab, but a few were in white parachute silk or what looked like ordinary bed sheets. They were inextricably mingled among the hulks of metal and among each other, joined and overlapped in spent intimacy and final longing.

"The white ones are Krauts," Barney Edwards explained unnecessarily. "Jesus, they were really *up* for it. Some of the GI's who went back through here swore the Kraut dog-faces were doped or drunk or both. I believe it. It must be a good mile but every time there was a gap in the fire from the tanks or artillery we could hear the whooping and hollering all the way up here."

From farther away, beyond the valley, two columns of thin dark smoke rose above the arc of the treetops and flattened and dispensed against the low slate sky. "One's what's left of a gas depot and the other's the cinders from an ammo dump. You should have been here yesterday."

"Whose were they?"

"Who else but our next Olympic team, good old Three Four Three. At least they didn't leave it for the Krauts. I guess they figured they wouldn't be able to get it back to New Orleans or San Francisco or wherever the Christ it was they were planning to bivouac next."

"They're a new division, aren't they?" the adjutant asked. George felt an impulse to come to the absentee division's defense too, if only for the ones lying in the snow and churned-up mud below.

"Yes," Barney Edwards said more softly. "They just landed a week or so ago and came all the way across France and Belgium soaking wet in open trucks. One guy told me half his platoon had trench feet before they even got dried off. And if you look at it sensibly there *is* a lot to be said for Frisco that you can't say for this place."

It needed several interruptions before the adjutant elicited the approximate estimated whereabouts of the nearest command post. "Three Eight Seven is dug in all along the left of the trees. I mean *in*. They were either awful good at camouflage or they learned awful fast. But just after dawn there was some GI movement around that farmhouse just back of the second clearing. If they're still there you could make it on foot. I wouldn't take the jeep. The Krauts must have left something on the other hill."

As the adjutant started down the ladder, the GI held George back. "Them God-damn' officers are *all* slow on the uptake. Old

Jackie-boy's in a bad way. A *real* bad way. Tell him I'm ready to take him out whenever he says the word."

It was hard tramping through the trees, but in less than an hour George and the adjutant were drinking coffee with the acting commander of a battalion from St. Louis. The acting commander was willing to be as helpful as he could. "The division's trying to make a ninety-degree turn and hold the northern flank. This was our front last night, but now it's the rear, but if the Krauts come down into the valley again this is the front again. You follow me, Captain?"

"Yes, thanks, Major."

"More coffee? We're not surrounded yet but we're playing a very deep left field. There's nobody in center now that Three Four Three's gone."

Suddenly there was a high wailing overhead, a siren-like call without the siren's undulations, a swelling monotone. George had heard the sound only on one day of his life and that day more than two years in the past, but the special reflex had not been worn away. He hit the floor flat, rolled under the heavy pine kitchen table, slammed his thighs up over his groin and his knees against his chest, threw his arms around his head, and counted the jarring whacks. Each one shook the table a little and the third was close enough to fling a spray of plaster down from the roof. The cycle was repeated five more times with just sufficient interval for counting. He waited for the silence and then took his arms away. He found it curiously gratifying to see the American major in exactly the same attitude beneath the other side of the table. A GI corporal who had been fiddling with a radio set in the corner was rising from behind a massive chest of drawers. The adjutant, however, had not left his feet. He was standing erect in a corner, and when George and the major were on their feet the adjutant displayed a weakness fairly common to men emerging from their first experience under fire. He was under the embarrassing impression that he had behaved with singular bravery while the others had been too quickly and too soon afraid. He pretended not to notice George and the major getting up from beneath the table or the radio operator squirming out from his place of concealment, if not of refuge.

"So that," he said casually, "is the famous *Nebelwerfer*."

"*Nebelwerfer*. Screaming Meemie. Moaning Minnie." The major sat down and poured more coffee with an almost ostentatiously steady hand. "If they stick to their schedule there won't be another one for another hour. If there is, Captain, I'd advise you to hit the deck like the rest of the poor people."

The adjutant looked hurt, clearly deeming himself to be the object of petty envy. "Sorry we can't stay, sir," he said stiffly. "I've got to report back now. But many thanks."

"Sure. Sure. Anytime at all. What did you say your outfit was again?"

The adjutant told him.

"Forestry. That's a new one on me. And you say we're the first outfit you've seen since you left your own headquarters?"

"Yes, sir. We've seen two bushed MPs and you."

"Well, Captain." The major was suddenly aggressive and sarcastic. "Why don't you ask me?"

"Ask you what, sir?"

"You better ask me, Captain, if you want to know."

"I don't know what you're driving at, Major."

"You know all right, Captain. We're all that's between your outfit and the Krauts. They sent you up to make book on us, didn't they? They sent you up to get the morning line."

"Damn it, Major, you have no cause to put it that way. We haven't had any information for two days. No information at all!"

"All right, all right, Captain. Don't ask if you'd feel better. I'll ask for you. Can we hold this road if they come at us again?" The major took another mouthful of coffee and spoke across the room to the radio man. "You getting any reaction at all, Corporal?"

"Still just that Kraut that keeps cutting in."

"We got a good signal going out," the major explained, "but nothing's coming back." He hesitated. "To put it briefly, Captain, the answer is no. We can't. I'm down to two officers and forty-seven enlisted men, a third of what I had three days ago. We can't. That's it and that's all of it. We can't." He lifted his tin mug again, holding it up deliberately and removing his elbow from the steadying table. The cup trembled. The major put it down again and looked around quickly to see if anyone else had noticed. He caught George's eye turning shamefacedly away. "I have to ask you to go now, Captain," the major said distantly. "You've found out what you came to find out. Now I've got things to attend to."

It was another hour before they were back at the road junction. A needle-like sleet was driving down now and the lonely MP Jackie-boy had found what shelter he could beneath the top of their jeep. He got out, his joy at having company again balanced by a vague air of disappointment.

"Well, I be go to hell! I thought you were gone for good. Hey! You know how close you come to losing this jeep? If my buddy had hauled his ass down out of that steeple and let me evacuate him there wouldn't be no jeep left for you."

George and the adjutant climbed in.

"Of course we'da left you our bike and carrier," Jackie-boy said reassuringly. "We wouldn't leave you up the crick. But I saw you come out of the church and start over the hill and then when that cluster of mortars come in I figured they'd pin-pointed you and—anyway you made it. What you find down there?"

The adjutant told him there was a company position immediately below and most of a division scattered in the woods. The MP was listening with only half his mind. "How did my buddy look to you up there, Captain? I bet he's real spooky by now. He's been up there alone for fourteen, fifteen hours. I been alone down here but at least I get somebody to talk to now and then. While you were away some Belgian civilians came through, an old man, an old lady and two kids and a dogcart. The old man used to be a baker in the Bronx but he's forgot most of his English. They got bombed out in the big shoot the other day, but they don't know any more about what's going on up there now than I do. Hey, Captain, would you watch things here while I go up and talk to my buddy? I'd like to get him out while he's got at least some of his marbles left."

The adjutant pleaded that he was already nearly two hours late and Jackie-boy let them go with a reproachful wave.

The O.C. received the adjutant's summary with a grunt of satisfaction. "Good, Earnshaw!" Then he embarked on an exasperated monologue. "I managed to get through to corps and to the area supply commander. They both told me I was free to act on my own initiative and information until further notice. In other words they passed the buck. If we dig in and get pranged it's my fault. If we pull out and the Germans don't keep coming it could be a court-martial. Corps did say that in view of our shortage of weapons, ammunition, weapons training and support my first responsibility is to protect my personnel and my equipment. The area bloke told me 'for my information'"—the major's accent grew more sardonic here—"'for my information' he was taking his headquarters back to Brussels. And then the son-of-a-bitch said, and I know he had somebody right beside him taking it down, my decision need not be influenced by his unless—oh hell!"

The adjutant offered no comment. "We'll get ready to move," the O.C. said. "Dismantle all but personal weapons."

"All but personal weapons, sir? I don't think—"

"Didn't we have a spigot mortar?" the major demanded coldly.

"Oh yes, sir. That."

"Dismantle the spigot mortar. Immobilize all vehicles except those needed to transport the full personnel of the company plus records, plus kitchen gear, and one day's rations. Prepare all surplus stores for demolition, including petrol and ammunition. Have all ranks strip their personal kit to heavy marching order and be ready to move off on thirty minutes' notice. You got all that, Earnshaw?" For all the crispness of his words there was still something tentative in the O.C.'s manner.

"Sir."

"I don't want too much hurry. We may not move at all. I still want to try making contact with our own HQ."

The company's second-in-command appeared in the doorway. "Pardon, Hobey. Quite a few more stragglers just arrived on the outskirts. What shall we do with them?"

"Are they armed? Is there an officer in charge?"

"No officer." The second-in-command stepped inside, removed a hand-knit red and khaki toque from his bald head, and wiped the melting snow from his bushy badger's eyebrows. Like the O.C., he had an earlier and in some ways less complicated war behind him. He gave the impression that if the situation now at hand could only be made clearer he might begin enjoying it. As it was he conveyed nothing more dramatic than a baffled calm. "They seem to come from at least two different divisions and at least three regiments. There are twenty-three in all. Four or five have rifles or Tommy guns. About half them say they were given orders to retreat, every man for himself, when their units were overrun. The other half say they were cut off from their units, which have been wiped out anyway."

"Do you believe it?"

"*They* believe it, Hobey. Or they think they do. I had the M.O. look them over. He says there are at least five genuine cases of battle fatigue and as many more fakes. Two have superficial shell wounds and nine've got trench feet. One poor son-of-a-bitch has got all three—shell shock, shrapnel, *and* trench feet. He keeps yelling over and over again, 'Is this the way to the escape gap?' "

"What have you done with them?"

"Right now they're in quarter stores. I ordered some hot tea and bully beef for them. Shall I arrest them or what, Hobey? There isn't room for them in the building where we're holding the gang that came in earlier."

The O.C. went over to the wall and peered at the crayoned anachronisms covering his battle map. "All I can figure out for sure is it's a long way from Port Arthur. What would you do, Billy?"

"I'm just a bushwhacker too, Hobey."

"Oh, Christ, let them go. Let the other ones go too." The O.C. turned to the adjutant again. "All right, Earnshaw, carry on. I want the company embussed by sixteen hundred hours." He looked around the chapel. Until now George hadn't remembered that the O.C. was really a much older man, well into his fifties at least and perhaps, as some who had known him in the logging camps back home insisted, already well past sixty. "The last time I did this," he sighed, "was at Ypres. But at least at Ypres you could smell the bloody gas. You didn't have to be a bloody swami."

The light had begun to fade when the desolate little convoy moved off toward the main road to Liège. The snowfall had thickened and it was growing colder again. The abandoned trucks and tractors, stripped of their timers and carburetors, huddled bleakly in the village square under the orange reflection of the burning gasoline stores in the open field nearby. Everything else was in order. With barely a day's output behind them there wasn't enough sawdust to bury the blades and generators from the sawmill, but a quick search of the immediate countryside had yielded a sufficiency of haystacks. The few cases of reserve small-arms ammunition had gone into an abandoned well and expired in a tiny, stuttered requiem for the company's never-robust hopes of military glory. As Yuri Wuorio swung over the tailboard of the second last vehicle in the convoy, he came close to expressing the general mood. "Retreat from Moscow!" he growled, half grateful, half furious. "Rocks!"

The last vehicle was the jeep bearing George and the adjutant. The first hour of the journey was a wearing but uneventful series of small mishaps and frustrations encountered in a thickening tangle of traffic. It was slow going over the ice and grabbing mud of the side roads, but after the convoy had elbowed and snarled and literally crashed its way, one vehicle at a time, onto the jammed hard-top to and from Liège, it grew infinitely worse. Now they were not on a road at all. They were in a black, half-stagnant whirlpool, a centrifugal machine in slow motion. They were in the long, slow-writhing belly of some sluggish but hard-dying reptile. The reptile sucked the vehicles in from the lonely forest trails, engorged their flesh and metal and spewed them out again with brutish aimlessness.

The main heave and instinct of the traffic—it had nothing so steady as a flow—was toward the front, but a large part of it was inching painfully and profanely to the rear and the pattern was the same on each new side road, where trucks and tanks and wheel-mounted guns and sometimes men on foot struggled in from the lonely menace of the forest and others struggled outward into its lonely shelter. The gas-reeking air was jammed with a thousand permutations of blasphemy, obscenity, and imprecation. The treads and tires of the vehicles clanged and shrieked and flailed with the same enraged futility as the shouting voices. The great reptile groaned in fearful agony and then quivered and lay still.

Sometime after midnight, when they had been at an absolute standstill for nearly half an hour, the adjutant ordered George to dismount and walk ahead to see how far they'd dropped behind the O.C.'s leading jeep. As George trudged down the muddy shoulder of the road, the men stalled in the forward traffic peered out numbly from their lorries yelling new questions and affronts.

"You lost, soldier?"

"Hey, boy, let's see your pass."

"Hey, you yellow son-of-a-bitch, don't you know they shoot deserters?"

He passed two ambulances and half a dozen empty ammunition trucks before he found the first of their own vehicles. Three or four men had descended and were stamping up and down behind. The rest sat silent on the floor boards.

He looked over the tail gate to see if he could find Haig. But most of the men were either asleep or huddled and dormant against the cold and he did not speak. He trudged past a truckload of silent German prisoners of war, an apparently undamaged Sherman tank, a few more empty supply trucks, and five more Forestry Corps trucks, and then an enormous Meccano set of bridging equipment hopelessly out of gas and hopelessly left in the middle of the road, and finally he found the O.C.'s jeep a mile from where he'd started.

The O.C. was a few yards off the road at the edge of a field. A fire of earth soaked in coal oil was burning fitfully in a small steel barrel and a cluster of other soldiers were gathered around it. The westbound half of the road was covered by a tank hull-down in the ditch, and an officer and a sergeant were standing in the middle of the road, holding the traffic at bay with their drawn pistols and the implied authority of the tank's machine guns and point-blank cannon. George slid through the ditch to where the O.C. was standing, blew on his right hand through the damp woolen glove, and raised it stiffly to his helmet. The O.C. peered at him out of the guttering flames.

"Ballantyne? Where's Captain Earnshaw?"

"He asked me—"

"Not now." The O.C. turned to a tall, lean figure standing nearby and frowning alternately at a sheaf of papers and a map board. This other man had pushed his helmet liner up from his high Gary Cooper forehead. A long green scarf was wrapped several times around his neck and the ends dangled down in front of his camouflage jacket almost to his knees.

"Well, Major," he said at last, "if you're a spy you're the oldest one since Mata Hari. Don't take offense. I'm the oldest general since Custer. I honest to God can't figure what either of us is doing here."

"I have no trouble in that regard, sir."

"Oh, for God's sake don't get shirty. I won't insult you by asking who is Shirley Temple or where's the capital of Wisconsin. Who was Black Jack? Where's Vimy?"

"General Pershing, Vimy's not far."

"It was sure a lousy war, wasn't it? These damned kids try to tell me this one's bad. Frankly the only thing that troubles me now is my prostate gland. Well, you've got to get moving. Forestry Corps."

The general called a sergeant to his side. "Give this officer a pass." Then he said to the O.C., "This is the last check point you'll hit before Liège. You should make better time from here." The O.C. led George back down the road in the direction from which they had come. When they reached the first of their company's trucks, he banged on the doorway of the cab. The head of the second-in-command appeared at the window, recognizable by the shape of the close-fitting, tufted woolen toque. He opened the door and dismounted.

"What's up, Hobey?"

"Nothing much. They're turning a lot of stragglers around just up ahead. But I've finally got an order—I *guess* it's an order; anyway it came from a major general. High-Pockets Harry Sullivan himself—to proceed as planned. But I'm changing the plan a little, Billy."

"Yes, Hobey?"

"High-Pockets says the traffic's going to get better before it gets worse. I'm going back to see if I can get the rest of our vehicles and the Diesel plant and the mill equipment. I want you to stop the main convoy in a field you'll find about half a mile ahead. Turn around one truck with twenty volunteers, at least half them qualified drivers. Put Captain Gundarson in charge and tell him to meet me back in the monastery as soon as he can. I'm going with Ballantyne here to pick up the adjutant. We'll try to get turned around on one of the side roads and go on first. As soon as you've got Gundarson and his salvage crew on the road you keep on to Brussels with the main column. Johnny Carling's still got Number 39 Company working the Royal Forest Park just south of the city on that Chaussé Waterloo. I'll see you there by suppertime. Tell Johnny Carling we'll be ready to start cutting in the morning."

"Then it *was*—" The second-in-command's voice fell bleakly and died altogether.

"No, Billy, it wasn't a false alarm. The stuff is flying back there all right. Just what and just where, High-Pockets either didn't know or wasn't saying. But I won't feel right till I have a go at saving the mill."

"You're the boss, Hobey. Just one question. Do you really want me to ask for volunteers? Why don't I just send a detail?"

"Because it's not a job that *has* to be done. It's just one old buzzard's whim or pride or whatever you like to call it. It's not the kind of job I'd *order* men to do."

"All right, Hobey. But when I ask for volunteers what do I tell them?"

"Just that it's ten to one nothing's involved for certain except a few more hours of somewhat sorer asses than they've got already. But there might conceivably be—not likely but conceivably—some risk of enemy action. No Thin Red Line crap now, Billy. Just tell them the company's going back to get its rusty old tools and get on with its rusty old job." The O.C. nodded a dismissal to his deputy commander and looked inquiringly at George.

"You don't have to come, Ballantyne," he said.

George had been thinking of Haig again. But Haig would have no need of him in the Royal Forest Park on the Chaussé Waterloo, wouldn't even have time to miss him before they were back together anyway. "That's a pretty balky jeep, sir," he said. He did not have to pretend casualness, for casualness was all he felt. The worst thing was the prospect of four or five more hours imprisoned in the cold black belly of the reptile, but you could and did get used to anything.

The return trip was much faster. The eastbound lane thinned. The westbound lane still heaved and grappled and flung back warnings and fresh-minted epitaphs. To the axis of retreat the axis of advance was a raw and monstrously unjust insult, the gibing knife thrust of ignorance and false pride; it was not fair that those too wise and soldierly to die as useless suicides should be mocked by those not yet even tested or informed. "Turn around, you smartass s.o.b.'s! The Krauts up there are thick as lice!" "It was murder! Christly murder!" "The whole outfit bought it!" "They mowed the whole friggin' company down like friggin' cattle!" "Don't go *up there!* You haven't got a chance!" "Don't go *up there!* The only Yanks you'll find are stiffs."

There was a new exhortation, a new plea or protest every time they stopped. Their O.C. paid no attention. As the pace moved up to a steady crawl, the guns and tanks and supply vehicles and the lorry loads of hunched-up infantry reinforcements began peeling off the blacktop and spreading out among the lesser roads into the woods and sloping, snow-deep fields. At last they began to recover some volition and control and to assume the shape of fighting units and subunits, of batteries and battalions and of little *ad hoc* battle groups made up of many remnants, leavings, and spare parts not quite finished. The panic was not yet over, but it had begun to isolate itself.

It was still early in the morning—not later than 0300—when they came to the hill leading down toward their village. The road in both directions was clear, but a small U.S. recon patrol had gone on ahead only ten or fifteen minutes earlier. An isolated copse of firs was blazing fitfully at the edge of the field where they'd left their petrol burning. The squat hulk of the monastery lay quiet in the fluttering reflection. There was no sign of any human inhabitant.

"We'll wait here for Captain Gundarson and the salvage crew," the O.C. said. "As soon as we go down we'll reactivate the R.A.S.C. trucks. We'll load the Diesel first, then the heavy blades and other stuff from the mill, then the handsaws and axes."

The truck arrived in less than half an hour. As the men spilled out into the snow, the adjutant began jogging down the slope toward the village square. George slung his rifle on his shoulder and jogged on after him. The new arrivals fell in behind, crunching in single file, half numb already, obsessed with the single purpose of getting in and getting out and getting back to some place where it was warm. "Rocks!" a disgusted voice behind George muttered.

George stopped and waited for Yuri Wuorio to catch up. "What are *you* doing here?" he asked, partly puzzled, partly amused.

"A typical frig-up," the Red Finn growled. "The convoy was at a standstill and I went sound asleep. Then I woke up needing a piss so bad I could taste it. I fell over the tail gate just as the friggin' second-in-command was calling for volunteers. Tonight even I got rocks."

The hurrying file was strung out halfway across the square toward the cluster of trucks and tractors. The enemy machine guns opened up from the second story of the village inn. Insulated by the thick, unbroken walls, the guns set up a metallic, Twenty-Fourth-of-May, firecrackers-under-a-tin-can clatter, and for a second the line of startled men froze, trying to remember. And then there was the crack of smashing bone, the thwack of imploding flesh, and the wild, gull-like scream of a man fresh-gutted and left one single instant to distill the agony of all life and the terror of all eternity.

"DOWN!" The O.C.'s bellow from the rear of the column was the first recognizable word. "DOWN AND SPREAD OUT!"

"DOWN AND SPREAD OUT!" half a dozen other voices shouted, grasping for the reassurance of unity. As the column fell apart, sprawling and floundering and squirming for cover, the machine gun fired at random, no longer focused on defined targets. A mortar shell lobbed in and smothered itself harmlessly against the hood of a truck. The machine gun found another firm aiming point behind another truck and another badly hurt man cried out. Then, from one of the near, low roof tops a sniper began picking them off with august, ceremonial deliberateness. The sniper was invisible, but his presence overshadowed the square like some cloaked majesty on a balcony. He was taking his sweet and certain time. He had some kind of communication with the mortar and the machine gun, or perhaps they were working to a prearranged plan, for now the machine gun was merely curtaining the roadway into the square and the mortar was blasting steadily at the roadway out while the sniper—or perhaps it was two or three snipers or even more—staked out the targets one man at a time, one bullet at a time, no haste at all, no waste at all.

George crawled inside one truck, darted aimlessly around another, and stumbled in behind a tractor. He could count eight bodies sprawled on the naked cobblestones and there were two others right beside him by the tractor. For a moment he thought he was the only one left alive, but then the stocky little figure of the O.C. burst out of a shadowed doorway, dropped on one knee, raised a pistol in two hands, and then toppled forward into the shallow gutter. George stuck his rifle across the hood of the tractor and fired toward the window he guessed the O.C. had meant to fire at. But there was nothing there, not even the glass was left. He saw a better-looking piece of cover behind a Bren-gun carrier and crawled off again in the shadow of the tractor.

A hand reached out and seized him from beneath. It seemed to come from below the pavement. He flung himself away and grabbed his rifle by the barrel, swinging it backward like a club. The hand held on and dragged him down a narrow stairway. His rifle butt caught on the narrow opening, and before he could strike with it he heard the angry voice of Yuri Wuorio. "Down here! Down here!" He was at the bottom of a tiny stairway, hardly more than a crevice in the cobblestones. A narrow door was open and the Finn shoved him through and sprawled in on top of him.

Another hand pulled him up again. "This way!" It was the adjutant. They groped across a low cellar to a small, empty window opening. The window led to a small square manhole. The adjutant went through first and in a minute there were four of them crouched behind a pile of straw on the outer edge of the village. At first George's only curiosity was for the ground ahead of them. The field was as white and bare and silent as a shroud, but beyond it lay the tall, solid palisade of the forest. "Spread out," the adjutant whispered. It was not until they were on the other side that George had the slightest curiosity to know who the fourth man

279

was. As he fell down just inside the border of the trees he spoke for the first time in almost an hour. "Who's that?"

"It's me, George."

"Oh!" he whispered back. He had grown too weary for thinking, and after the long, savage bludgeoning even his instincts and reflexes barely stirred. The message lay there, so to speak, unopened, but it still clamored for attention. When he recognized it, he still could not tell whether he felt better or worse. One of his last fully controlled and fully obedient thoughts, just before he'd hurried down the hill into the dark, expectant village, had been that his brother Haig was now a hundred miles away, not perhaps yet safe from terror but safe at least from the terror of his terror. He could not reach a conclusion. He wished with all his heart that his brother Haig was truly somewhere else, but he rejoiced with all his heart that his brother Haig was also here beside him in the snow at the edge of the beckoning woods.

CHAPTER TEN

This time we are a thousand times better off than you at home. You cannot imagine what glorious hours and days we are experiencing now. It looks as if the Americans cannot withstand our important push. Today we overtook a fleeing column and finished it. We overtook it by taking a back-road through the woods to the retreat lane of the American vehicles; then, just like on maneuvers, we pulled up along the road with sixty Panthers. And then came the endless convoy driving in two columns, side by side, hub on hub, filled to the brim with soldiers. And then a concentrated fire from sixty guns and one hundred and twenty machine guns. It was a glorious blood bath, vengeance for our destroyed homeland. Our soldiers still have the old zip. Always advancing and smashing everything. The snow must turn red with American blood. Victory was never as close as it is now. . . . If we are to preserve all tender and beautiful aspects of our lives, we cannot be too brutal in the deciding moments of this struggle.—

German officer's letter to his wife; from G-2 report, 101 U. S. Airborne Division.

The following report was received today from Headquarters, V Corps:

The Commanding General desires all commanders to notify their men of the following incident.

On 17 Dec. 1944, at 1500 hrs., near MALMÉDY, German Panzer troops, after capturing 200 American soldiers, lined them up in a field, disarmed them, robbed them and then mowed them down with machine guns, firing from tanks passing by at a distance of from 50 to 100 yards. The few men who escaped fell to the ground and played dead.—Journal of a U.S. infantry division.

We shall probably not have another Christmas here at the front since it is absolutely certain that the American is going to get something he did not under any circumstances reckon with. For the "Ami" as we call him, expected that he would celebrate Christmas in Berlin, as I gather from his letters. Even I, as a poor private, can easily tell it won't be much longer until the Ami will throw away his weapons. For if he sees that everybody is retreating he runs away and cannot be stopped any more. He is also warweary as I myself learned from prisoners.—German private's letter home, from Twenty-First Army Group Psychological Warfare Summary.

At 180100 the Battalion was ordered to withdraw at first light or whenever the Battalion behind was in position. At first light the enemy renewed its tank-infantry attacks with about 12 tanks and the usual platoon of infantry with each tank. Normal barrages were fired by the Artillery and the enemy attack was again halted.

At 180800 enemy tanks completely overran the front-line companies. The infantry accompanying the tanks fanned out and in the melee following enemy tanks came to within 20 feet of the U.S. infantry and the fighting resolved into hand-to-hand fighting and grenade battles.

At this time the only communication with "B" Company was by runner. The left platoon of B had been out of A Tank Ammunition. Six or seven men from that platoon broke and started to run to the rear. The Colonel stopped them personally and sent them back.

At 0900 hours "A" Company Commander reported his Company completely overrun by tanks and infantry. The Company Commander said all his men had holes and that he wanted artillery poured on his own position because it was hopeless anyway. This was the last ever heard of the Company Commander. With the concentration called for, an Artillery Battalion for 30 minutes, the German attack in that sector was stopped. Twelve men from "A's" machine gun squad were all that got to the American lines from that Company.—After-action report, an infantry battalion of the U. S. First Army.

No rest or sleep at all . . . but we are on the way again. The main thing is that the Americans are on the run. . . . We cleared an American supply dump. Everybody took things he wanted most. I took only chocolate. I have all my pockets full of it. I eat chocolate all the time, in order to sweeten somewhat this wretched life. . . . Don't worry about me. The worst is behind me. Now this is just a hunt.—German soldier's letter to his wife; from First Canadian Army Intelligence Summary.

Please, God, not another bed check. Not another roll call tonight. Please, please, God, let him wait till morning, tell him he can't do anything tonight. He's had two counts already and nothing's changed except the figures. And changing the figures won't change ANYthing. AnyTHING. NOTHING can be altered now, everyTHING that has happened has happened. Fiddling with a pencil and a little book will never bring anybody back. Please, God, giver of all mercy, dispenser of all pain, regent of the eternal palace, keeper of the lake of fire, let him wait till morning. Please, God, bid Thy servant accept Thy will.

David Kyle sat upright, stared around him, saw nothing that his open eyes could recognize, and then sank down again, stretched full on the stone floor, and closed his eyes. The hot meal—was it hot stew? hot hash? hot sausage? No matter; it had been hot—still lay warm and heavy on his stomach. The battalion's place of refuge—was it a school, a church, another barn? No matter; it bore a solid roof above a solid floor—had the aspect of a hospital ward, with night lights standing guard at the edges of the soothing dark. It also had the aspect of a massive, communal tomb, a multitude of holy, secret silences.

No, there would be no more interruptions of the sacred, desperate quiet. They would be left alone—the lucky ones in oblivion. There wouldn't be another roll call. The notion that there would must have been part of the dream that woke him up. He closed his eyes more tightly. The undersides of the lids, at first two separate white wells, melted together in a flow of changing colors and became an empty screen. Then, though dreams were not supposed to repeat, the same unsteady, pool-like images appeared, the same faces floating across and above and beneath each other, drifting in and out, and drowning in each other's cold translucent wash.

By far the most dependable and unflagging image was the image of Henry Whelan in the instant of pronouncing his death curse. The words of the curse were already lost in the scalding well of his memory, but the face was secure forever. It was a *Panzerfaust* that got Henry Whelan; a graze that left him just enough time to hurl forth his death curse and then subside, at last and irrevocably triumphant over all contradictions, rebuttals, and dissents. *Pray the whole praying universe!* That was what Henry's eyes cried that his voice meant to cry in the instant of dying, and perhaps he had succeeded, but Dave was certain only of the intent.

The other faces that appeared with some regularity were those of his father, Samuel Kyle, of his colonel, John P. Barnstable, and of God. Once he had caught a flash of Mary Egan, radiant and belligerent, and once of Jack Kennebec minus his sergeant's stripes and without his officer's bars, not only cheated of his promotion but treacherously busted right down to private. Once of Carmen (the Hood) Ruiz driving through a blackened snowbank with a plump blond woman at his side and a captured Schmeisser going rat-tat-tat. But the last three were transients. Besides Henry Whelan, only his father and the colonel and God were permanent occupants. Sometimes his father's face, staring inconsolably out of the drifting pool, would disappear beneath a black bucket helmet and merge with the red and eyeless shattered face of a German soldier, shattered by his own son's hand.

His father's curse, unlike Henry Whelan's, was full of charity, and therefore far more terrible. And unlike Henry Whelan's curse he remembered his father's curse down to its last syllable, down to its last pleading inflection.

"While we thus cheerfully render unto Caesar the things which the Scriptures show to be his, we are compelled to decline all participation in acts of war and bloodshed, as being inconsistent with the duties enjoined upon us by our divine Master toward our enemies and toward all mankind."

And "This is Romans. 'Recompense to no man evil for evil. Provide things honest in the sight of all men. Live peaceably with all men. Dearly beloved, avenge not yourselves, but rather give place unto wrath: for it is written Vengeance is mine; I will repay, saith the Lord. Therefore if thine enemy hunger, feed him; if he thirst, give him drink: for in so doing thou shalt heap coals of fire upon his head. Be not overcome of evil, but overcome evil with good.'"

There had been two of the Germans on the *Panzerfaust*, a pipe-like instrument very much like the bazooka, a member of the bludgeon family, meant to do its work on machines, not men. The *Panzerfaust* had gone against nature in aiming its tank-size rocket at a target so trivial and unworthy of its strength as an individual soldier of the infantry, but just before its fatal lapse nudged half of Henry Whelan's right chest aside, Henry perceived what it was up to. Though he tried to throw himself away, slamming Dave to one side with the heel of his fist and diving to the other side with the recoil, the *Panzerfaust*, after all, was no farther away than the length of a burning half-track. Henry started his dying curse before it hit him, and finished it as he spun away. *Pray the whole praying universe!* The last two words were the only ones Dave caught for certain, but the others fitted, fitted what Henry had tried to be and seem before, fitted his last, unyielding fury.

Henry did take one of the two *Panzerfaust* men with him, and Dave had taken the other one with the butt of his M-1 smashed between the eyes and a bullet fired so close the muzzle came back dripping.

Now, despite the solid roof above, the solid floor below, and the food still warm and heavy in his stomach, the restless procession had been set in motion once more. The faces were not contesting against each other; on the contrary they reinforced and backed each other up. The man who killed Henry Whelan had become a part of Henry Whelan and the two of them were in alliance, demanding of Dave Kyle whether in slaying the man who slew Henry Whelan he had not in part slain Henry too. The face of the murdered murderer of Henry Whelan was also the murdered face of David's father, Samuel Kyle, and Samuel Kyle's face in its turn was the face of the colonel, John P. Barnstable, and in its turn the murdered face of God. . . . *Then shall thou receive the mark of the Beast.*

It was too late for undoing or redoing anything whatever. If John P. Barnstable could only perceive even this much of it—could only accept this irreducible minimum of their common fate—then they could all of them, if only for a little while, cease their pointless chorus of lament and accusation and perhaps, just barely and just perhaps, go back to sleep.

Carmen's voice was right beside his ear. "Jesus Christ!" Carmen groaned. "The son-of-a-bitch is at it again."

He had forgotten that Carmen Ruiz's presence was not, like Henry's, limited to the drifting pool of light on the underside of his eyelids.

"He's going to do it again," Carmen said. "I think I'll go down to the other floor."

"I think I'll stay here. Where's Kennebec?"

"He's O.K. He's flaked out real good."

"How long have we been here?"

"Five hours. The son-of-a-bitch is at it again. I'm going down to the other floor. Come on."

"I don't think I could make it." It had been a mistake, after all, to throw their blankets so close to the fireplace. At the time, when they had stumbled in, it had looked like a piece of really stupendous fortune to find room so near the fire. The fire was already lighted and two of the cooks, miraculously spared with one whole truckload of food and pots and pans, and left by a further miracle with a remnant of strength and will, had begun their preparations. Carmen, whose instinct for the small, essential advantages was usually dependable, had dropped a few feet away and urged Dave and Kennebec to do the same.

But as Carmen would have foreseen if a similar situation had been presented sixty-two hours earlier, the area near the fire was the very worst place for rest or refuge. It became the battalion's command post as well as its cookhouse, aid station, and most densely populated dormitory. In fairness, it had to be recognized that the colonel did not order anyone away. All he asked for himself was space enough for a few ammunition boxes, two to serve as chairs for him and the executive officer, and four others for a table on which to get on with his immediate tasks. A radio man set up his 630 set nearby, but was not for the time being allowed to use it. The colonel studied his maps while he ate, exchanging remarks and observations with the executive officer between mouthfuls. Dave, eating too, watched the colonel eating and marveled that any man of this battalion, of this room, of this place and time, could be so fully in control. Halfway through the meal the colonel took a couple of pills. "Benzedrine," Carmen Ruiz guessed, grateful to have an explanation for the colonel's being so alert and wide awake while he himself was drifting off like a school-boy drowning in hot Ovaltine.

It might have been an hour later or it might have been a day later that they took the third roll call. Dave had not been sleeping heavily or continuously on account of the faces, and the change in the colonel's voice had brought him, startled, all the way to his haunches before he sank back again and resumed his contemplation of the drifting pool beneath his eyes.

"Now wait. Now wait a *minute!* Give it to me again." There was as yet no absolute sign that the colonel's control was slipping away, but his voice was greatly changed. It was not a voice of alarm, but rather a voice of indulgent disbelief.

"The over-all, sir? Or the breakdown? The reply came from the other ammunition-box chair.

"Well, both."

"Battalion strength four officers, one hundred sixty-seven en-listed men. Total all ranks one hundred seventy-one."

"We were under strength anyway." The colonel spoke more soberly, as though he were answering a charge. "Let's not forget that."

"Yes, sir. Quite a bit. Total strength, December fifteen was— I have it here—five ninety-eight."

"They promised full replacements by the twelfth. Well, never mind. Give me the breakdown again."

"Yes, sir. Company A ninety-six."

"Company A ninety-six."

"Company B fifty-nine."

"Company B fifty-nine."

"Company C none."

"I want that repeated, Captain," the colonel said slowly.

"Company C none."

"We'll come back to that, Captain." The colonel's voice was now both slow and hard. "You've got it wrong but we'll come back to it. Don't think you're getting away with anything—we'll come back to it. What was the battalion total again?"

"One seventy-one, sir."

"All right. Now give me Company C again. Give me Charlie Company."

"Charlie Company none, sir."

"You checked that personally?"

"Yes, sir."

"I mean you personally—I'm a patient man, Captain, but make sure you understand the question because I don't want any more wrong answers—I mean you personally checked everybody in this building personally?"

"Yes, sir."

"Including the wounded?"

"Yes, sir. Only three wounded got back, sir."

"I know. I KNOW." There was a period of silence. Finally it was broken by the executive officer.

"Sir?"

"Well?"

"By personally did you mean—"

"I meant personally. Did every man in this building answer the roll personally, personally to you in person? Did he personally give you the name of his company?"

"Well, sir, there were a few I just couldn't wake. I had the corporal try but it couldn't be done. In every case there was somebody awake nearby and I let the man who was awake answer for the man who was asleep."

"That's what I THOUGHT, God damn you, you lying bastard! That's what I KNEW! I could have you court-martialed, you lying bastard!" The colonel's voice contrasted grotesquely with his words; it was half a sob, half an anthem of praise; it was the voice of a man pumping another's hand, slapping another's back, hugging the bearer of stupendous good news. "I KNEW it!" The colonel laughed unsteadily. "O.K., Captain, O.K. We'll let it pass. You're tired, I'm tired, the men are tired. But I've still got to have the right count on Charlie Company."

"I'm sure it's right, sir."

"Now see here, Captain Osborne. This is my command. It's not your command. I don't expect you to feel the way I do. This is my battalion. It may not be yours, I don't pretend to know. How long have you been with us?"

"Ten days, sir. But if I may say so, sir, that wasn't called for. I consider it very much my—"

"Yes. Yes. Of course you do. Let's not quibble, Osborne. My

battalion—our battalion has been hurt. We took a beating, Osborne, but we didn't quit. We made a retrograde movement to straighten out the division front but we did it under orders. We withdrew but we didn't retreat. That's what everything will show, Osborne, and you know it as well as I do. That's what the logs and journals and after-action reports will show all the way down, right through corps and division and regiment, right down to battalion right here. If it hadn't been for the hundred and seventy-one men in this building and the three-hundred plus others who didn't make it here this whole sector might have folded. Maybe you don't understand that, Osborne. I'm damned proud of this battalion. I hope you are too."

"I am, sir. I'm very proud."

"All right. Then how dare you tell me, Osborne, that this battalion let a whole company disappear without a trace? How can you stand there and tell me that, Osborne?"

"Truly, sir—"

"Don't truly-sir me, Osborne. Why do you think I sent you back to check your first count, Osborne? Why? Why, God damn it! Why?"

"I—I didn't really know, sir. You didn't say why you didn't trust the first count."

"Well, now you do know. I didn't trust your first count because it was a God-damn' LIE! And I don't trust your second count because it's a God-damn' LIE too!"

"All right, sir, I'll check it again."

"You're damn' right you'll check it again. And you'll do it right. I'll only tell you once more. I know it's not a pleasant job and not an easy job. I know some of these men haven't had any rest for three days and waking them up again won't give you, or them, much happiness. But you've got to do it because I've got to know what happened to Charlie Company. Sooner or later we'll have contact again with regiment or division. I'll have to report the state of this battalion. And I'm not going to turn in a false report that I've got a whole company missing—missing to the last man—just because my executive officer is too squeamish to do his duty. I'VE GOT TO FIND OUT ABOUT CHARLIE COMPANY!"

Suddenly the room was silent. When he spoke again the executive's low voice was like a small whisper in a cave. "Come on, Corporal. We'll start on the lower floor and work back up here."

Two sets of footsteps receded from the fireplace toward the stairway at the far end of the long, dim room.

This time there were no dreams. When next Dave found himself struggling for his bearings the images were gone, replaced again by a noisy, all too substantial reality. Its focal point was not this time the anguished, rasping colonel, but an exploding Carmen Ruiz. Carmen's explosion was clearly homicidal in its purpose, but for all that it had a gentle, wary, almost furtive quality; except for the accident that, in one of its first convulsions, one of Carmen's hard boots accidentally lashed out against Dave's temple, Dave might have remained unconscious throughout the whole remarkable event. Carmen was struggling and panting on the floor beside him, grunting methodically and swearing under his breath, attempting with a quiet, terrifying intensity to choke the life out of a gasping second man while a third man tugged at Carmen's collar and tried to tear him loose. The struggle was made all the more deadly by the apparent acceptance by the other two of an understanding that it must remain private. It was not only Carmen who was ruled by a compulsion to stealth. His adversaries were straining and grunting and clawing and pummeling and scrabbling and scraping with a concentration as deadly and all-devouring as his, but they too held their oaths and threats and other declarations to the pitch of hoarse, spat-out whispers.

Though Carmen was not in trouble, it was plain he soon would be. The man he was choking was much taller than Carmen and almost as thick, and the other man was at least of average size. Dave thrust himself like a wedge between Carmen and the upper man and grabbed one of Carmen's wrists and tugged it loose from the throat of the lower man.

"It's Dave," he whispered, making it as persuasive as he could, but instinctively respecting the convention of stealth.

"Dave?" Carmen panted, and then suddenly relaxed. The taller man rolled away and pulled himself to one knee, rubbing his neck. It was the executive officer. The officer took a few moments to get his wind and then said, *sotto voce* and with an astonishing lack of feeling, "Is this your buddy, soldier?"

"Yes, sir." Dave had his arm around Carmen's heaving shoulders. Carmen was still a little shaky, but, if it had been a seizure he was in, he was now out of it. His head and shoulders had begun to droop.

"Tell him to tell me his name," the executive officer said to Dave. "Tell him to tell me his name and his company."

"Yes, sir," Dave said.

"Or if he doesn't want to tell me, he can tell the corporal here," the officer said. "It doesn't matter. But he's got to give his name and company."

"I already gave it twice tonight, I won't give it again." Carmen's voice was flat, not in the least impassioned, but Dave knew it came from behind a wall of stubbornness that nothing would dent or shake. "They woke me up twice, Dave. The second time they woke me up I said I'd kill them if they did it again."

"I know, Carmen. They woke me up twice too, but I guess they had to. We've been all cut up to hell, Carmen, and they're just trying to get it straightened out where we're at. We really got cut up, Carmen. Even worse than it looked."

"You praying right we did." Carmen's shoulders coiled again and he started to shake. "We praying well got the praying Jesus prayed right out of us." It was the first time anyone else had used Henry Whelan's private surrogate Word. There was no guessing whether Carmen's use of it was some eerie reflex or a planned, thought-out pledge of fealty and remembrance. "Now you tell the praying captain and the praying corporal here to pray off and praying well stop bothering me. I said I'd praying kill them and it's still not too praying late."

The corporal spoke to Dave. "Your buddy could be in real bad trouble. The captain's took about as much as any man would take. Your buddy would be in it up to his ears by now only the captain didn't want the colonel to hear. We're trying to give your buddy a break."

"Just tell him to give me his name and company," the executive officer said. "And we'll write it off."

"Can't I speak for him?" Carmen had put his head down again. His arms were hugged around his ears. Dave bent as low as he could, trying to inspect Carmen's eyes in the scant light from the fireplace. "I think he's gone, sir."

"You look, Corporal," the officer ordered.

The corporal knelt beside Dave. "He's out, sir. His eyes are open, but he's out."

"All right, who is he? What's his company?"

"PFC Ruiz, Carmen. Able Company."

"And yours?"

Dave told him.

The captain's shoulders slumped. "All right, Corporal, that's it."

Dave watched them move across to the pile of ammunition boxes. The dark shape of the colonel, much smaller than it had been before, hugged the top of the improvised table like a half-full sandbag. The executive stood over them for a moment, deliberating. Then he said to the corporal, "We'll let him sleep. See to the sentries and then hit the sack yourself."

The fecund magic of the sack was one of war's unfailing mysteries. For eight hours, overseen and protected only by a few dozing pickets, the battalion lay pressed against the sack like a spent and fallen Hercules on the bosom of the earth. But as the dark, unseen night dragged on into a gray morning and then crept on through morning until almost noon, the sack's annealing warmth flowed up and forth like a fountain of plasma. The signs of revival were sporadic and undramatic, but they were not to be mistaken. A man belched, at first in his sleep, and then, the belch having awakened him, repeated it deliberately, quietly rejoicing in the simple power of decision. Another man left his sack to urinate in a corner where a dozen others had urinated, unremarked, the night before. Two or three of his immediate neighbors now growled in protest. Others began drifting outside. Someone produced an almost new pack of Camels. The saintly resilient cooks stoked up the fire and ringed it with a vat of stew and a boilerful of K-ration coffee. The company's most expert sniper came upstairs with his helmet full of snow, put it near the fire, and unrolled a half bar of Lifebuoy soap, a toothbrush, and a Gillette razor from a soiled but still gaily colored flower-patterned towel. His performance had the foolish grandeur of bugle call at Khartoum, or on the sands of Sidi-el-bab or at the battlements of the Alamo.

Some, but by no means all, of the talk concerned the last three days. It was not obsessive or theatrical talk, not even talk of the kind that is remembered. "Well, for Christ's sake, Jonesy, nice going! Hey, Pete! Jonesy hung onto his Christmas parcel after all. And he still ain't opened the son-of-a-bitch." "Was somebody asking for Baldy? Hertz? He got a piece of eighty-eight over by that haystack at the red farm. A farmer came right out and pulled him in the house. It didn't look too bad, Baldy was holding the top part of his leg but it looked as if it would be O.K." "Hey Buczyk, how'd you finally make out over that stream?" "The sonabitchin' ice broke like you said it would. It was just nicely up to my balls."

"Hey, do you suppose the rest of the Christmas mail will still get up? I ain't had as much as a God-damn' postcard." "Well, you can't tell. There's still six days to go. That's hardly long enough for them bastards back at the depot to steal it *all*."

Dave and Carmen ate in silence. Carmen's wild and glassy look was gone. How much of the night had stayed with him Dave saw no point in trying to guess. He'd have liked to talk about Henry Whelan for a while, but something told him that to do so might be asking for more complications. His own troubles were too various and tangled to unload on Carmen, even with the help of their common feeling for Henry, and Carmen's problems almost certainly were as large and hard to budge. But Carmen finally made a move.

"That was quite a show I put on, Dave," he said. "I wonder what Henry would have thought."

"You were kind of gone," Dave said cautiously. "I wasn't sure you'd remember it."

"Oh, I knew what was going on. I didn't have charge of it, I couldn't stop it, I wasn't *kind* of gone, I was absolutely gone—but I still knew what I was doing."

Dave could think of no comment.

"The hell of it was I knew it wasn't the exec's fault. Just before I went to sleep for the third time I heard him arguing with the colonel about another roll call. The exec didn't want any part of it. But when the exec and that lousy corporal burst in on me again it didn't matter who sent them. I was geared up for them. I had both barrels cocked and the good Lord Jesus Christ himself couldn't have stopped them going off."

There was something strange and solitary in the way Carmen spoke. It was as if Carmen had some merciless need to explain some offense deeper and harder to bear than the one that had been witnessed.

"Everybody's forgotten it by now," Dave said. "It wasn't such a big thing."

"For some people no," Carmen acknowledged sadly. "But for old Carmen yes. You know, Dave, there was just one thing I wanted to be in the Army. Do you know what that was?"

Dave waited.

"A square. You know why?"

"In a way," Dave said doubtfully.

"No, you don't. That's because you're a square yourself. Henry was a square too, no matter how hard he tried not to be. I guess it's something you're either born or you aren't born."

Dave's face still showed his puzzlement.

"Except when I had that tryout for the ball club and that fat has-been of a batting pitcher made such a horse's ass of me, except for that one summer I never did a square thing in my whole life. I was hustling and heisting and running errands for bootleggers, books, and the numbers game before I was out of grade school. And I didn't mind, Dave. I wasn't exactly proud of it, not proud the way some of the other kids in the neighborhood would have been, but I wasn't ashamed, either. It was just a choice I'd happened to make, the same choice other kids made when they decided to be lawyers instead of doctors or doctors instead of cops. My old lady used to work on me pretty hard to go in for a trade or see about getting a job on the lake boats, and one summer she damned near nagged me into going over to Ontario and picking tobacco. But I always had the edge on her because, well, in the first place my old man was a bum and it didn't get anybody anyplace trying to hold *him* up to me and well, in the second place I always had this knowledge in the back of my mind that if I *wanted* to be a square I could *be* one and, this was the thing that mattered, a very successful one. Maybe a big-shot square, maybe a contractor or a banker or the owner of a chain of delicatessens or a taxi business. I used to toy with the idea, as easy as bouncing an India rubber ball, of getting married to somebody halfway between Mary Pickford and Clara Bow and living in a house with thirty rooms. I didn't think anybody, square or not, had a bit more talent than me. I could be what I wanted and if I wanted to be a hood it didn't mean that was the only thing I could be any good at. By the time I was grown up my old lady had stopped bellyaching and it was only when that God-damn' spik ran out on my sister and went in for a priest that I got this screwy idea of turning into a square and showing them all, my old lady *and* my sister *and* the spik priest *and* the older priest who used to take me in confession until we gave up on each other, *and* the Wop women up the street whose dopey kids went from the Boy Scouts to technical school to jobs as streetcar conductors, got this idea I'd show them all just once, and now that I look back on it show myself that it had never been anything but a free choice between being one thing and another. Does that make sense, Dave?"

"Yes," Dave said. "I've spent a lot of time proving and improving things too."

"I told you and Henry that I joined up because I got stoned and lost my judgment. In a sense that's right. But I never made it clear what the exact order was. When this mealymouthed spik ran out on my sister they all tried to blame it on me, my old lady blamed it on me, the old priest blamed it on me when I went crawling back to him trying to find somebody that would see my side of it. He didn't put it quite as daffy as my old lady and my sister but it added up to the same thing. 'Look at the picture right in the paper! Look at what the paper comes right out and calls him,' the old lady kept squalling at me. 'Carmen the Hood Ruiz, minor Buffalo Racketeer Picked Up Yesterday in State Vice Probe. No wonder! What chance has the poor girl got for a decent husband?' I didn't mind so much if it was the only way to give my sister an out. But then my sister yelled, 'And only a *minor* racketeer at that!' I really loved that girl but what the hell! The old priest wasn't any better. Well, we'd just got in the war and I got this big idea about showing them all. I'd march away to the war as square as Richard Barthelmess and then I'd come marching back an officer and a hero with a chest full of ribbons and a curly little forgiving smile for the whole lousy bunch of them. I had to get stoned before I could actually go through with it but it wasn't on account of getting stoned that I decided to join the Army, it was the other way around."

"You decided to be a square, then." Dave tried to offer consolation. "But you've succeeded at it and that's what you said you'd do."

"Until last night." Carmen pursued his demon relentlessly. "Oh, I'd given up on the medals and the officer deal. I was satisfied just to be a good average country dog-face. Oh, maybe a little better than most, but why not? I was shot at at least three times before I even heard of Hitler. So as far as that part of it went, I never worried much, not as much as I should have, I guess. That part of it, the Full-Speed-Ahead-and-Damn-the-Torpedoes crap, I'd already had some practice at, I was less worried about how I'd get along with the Krauts than how I'd get along with Uncle Sam. I put myself on the side of the Law because I had to make this big point of mine. Maybe you don't know it, Dave, but in all the time I've been in the Army I've never had a charge laid against me, never had a reprimand. I haven't brown-nosed anybody but I've tried to show

Respect. And what's the upshot, what's the payoff? I end up in the middle of the night trying to strangle the Law. Trying to muscle an officer. A nice officer at that. Hell, even back in Buffalo I was never a cop killer."

"Well, Carmen"—Dave wasn't sure whether the hint of banter was in order or not—"at least you've got a highly developed conscience."

"Conscience!" Carmen banged his empty mess tin on the stone floor. "Conscience hasn't got a damned thing to do with it. It's not conscience, it's disgust. If I've got to buck the Law forever, why in a crummy place like this, at these crummy rates? Why didn't I stay in Buffalo? With the shortage of booze and half the girls working in factories, a guy who knows the way to the cache could end up with all the dough west of Albany."

Dave had been watching for an opportunity to deflect the conversation toward the study of his own special predicament. But Kennebec appeared from the direction of the piled ammo boxes.

"Well," Kennebec announced, "I don't know whether it will stick or not, but the colonel just made me an officer."

"That's great, Jack!" Carmen said.

"Promotion in the field!" Dave was genuinely impressed and for Kennebec's sake he sounded absolutely awed. "That's twice as good as the ordinary kind."

"Well"—Kennebec, pleased but embarrassed, invited their forgiving raillery—"I hate to think what young Henry would have said."

"Now do we get to call you sir?" Dave asked.

Kennebec looked properly uncomfortable. "Not till I get my bars up. And then only when there are strangers around."

Kennebec started away but Ruiz held him with a question. "You were talking to the colonel long?"

"A while," Kennebec apologized. "I'm the only—uh—commissioned officer in our company and he made me the—uh—acting company commander." He started away again. There was something nervous and uncomfortable about him. Something more serious than his new responsibilities was rattling Kennebec, and the businesslike, unimaginative sergeant didn't rattle easily.

"It gets better all the time," Carmen said.

"I guess so." Kennebec's tone was dry and still uneasy. "I guess it does. Anyway"—he hesitated between the temptation to stay and talk some more and the knowledge that he was already talking too much—"anyway the colonel just gave me an important job to do."

"Like what, Jack?" It was Carmen who spoke again, but Dave looked up with new curiosity too.

"Like finding Company C."

"Oh, God almighty, Jack! He's not back onto that!" Carmen struck his head with his own closed fist. "Did you hear him last night?"

"Just at first. Thank God my sack was shatterproof once I got into it. The duty corporal told me you guys had some kind of a dust-up over Company C. The colonel didn't mention it."

"No, he wouldn't. He got himself hopped up with benny till he couldn't think of a God-damn' praying thing but Charlie Company and another praying roll call. Then he dropped his praying bombs and hit the praying sack himself. How do you mean *you* got to find Charlie Company?"

"Not me personally. Our company. We were the last to lose contact with them. The colonel says we're going to find them."

"He's lost his marbles, Jack. There's no Charlie Company."

"The colonel says there is. Charlie was dug in better than any of the other companies, on that ridge near the little river. Had good ammo, good rations, a hundred and sixty men on strength, only twenty short. After the main attack came in, after the tanks got through and the wires went out, there wasn't any sign of Charlie at all. A little shooting from over that way but not as much as there should have been. Then nothing—not a thing."

"So there isn't any Charlie Company. There damned near isn't any praying battalion, either."

"In the colonel's book there's still a battalion and it's still got a Company C. I've got to find it."

"Well, good luck, Lieutenant. You know damn' well what happened to Charlie Company. They just prayed off. They just had a better place to go than the other companies and a better way to get there and they just prayed off."

"I don't think Charlie Company took off on us," Dave interrupted. And after a moment he added, "Maybe we took off on them."

"Maybe." Kennebec looked around. "That's what the colonel's wondering. He's outside walking around all alone in the snow and that's exactly what he's wondering."

"How could that be?" Carmen demanded. "I don't know how

far we ran, but I know every little hill I climbed or every creek I waded or every bush I fell through some son-of-a-bitch was on my tail and he was shooting and every time I got a chance I was shooting back."

"We didn't retreat," Kennebec said. "We withdrew. Six miles, according to the map they just gave me."

"Why don't you say it, then?" Carmen had grown blackly despondent. "Charlie Company never moved. Charlie Company never had a chance to move. They didn't even know *we* were moving. The colonel nailed Charlie to the cross and now he's had a chance to think it over he's got himself nailed to the cross."

"Maybe. He's in a bad state. He's just arrested the executive officer for insubordination." Kennebec, obviously hating himself for his unofficerly disloyalty, went on in a total surrender to his desperate need of friends. "You're right, you know, Carmen. The poor bastard *has* lost his marbles. And they'll stay lost till we find Charlie Company."

"So what happens?" Dave asked.

"Nothing. Until we find Charlie Company or get some word of Charlie Company nothing happens."

"You mean we're not even going to haul-ass out of here?" Carmen asked.

"We don't move back. We don't move up. We stay here. The colonel says we can't break radio silence because the Krauts are all around us. The fact is he's not half as scared of finding the Krauts as of finding the regiment or the division."

"Oh, come on, Jack. Now you're starting to lose *your* marbles."

"I guess I have or I wouldn't be talking like this. O.K., I'll give it all to you. The duty corporal was there when the exec was arrested this morning. The colonel started to chew the exec out about Charlie and the roll call again. The exec as good as accused the colonel of ordering a withdrawal without making sure the order ever got to Charlie. One thing led to another and then the exec said what's more there never was an order from regiment to withdraw, Charlie Company or no Charlie Company. The exec showed him the log and there was no order there. The colonel accused the exec of tampering with the log. Then he tried to make some kind of a deal; he tried to persuade the exec the Krauts must have broken in on the wire with a phony message. That would have let the colonel off the hook, but the exec had taken such a beating he was in a worse state than the colonel. He wouldn't buy it. He as good as called the colonel a liar and a coward and now he's relieved of duty."

"Well, you wanted to be an officer." Carmen wanted it to be pure sarcasm, but he was full of helpless anger. "So what are we going to do?"

"I don't know just yet."

"Where were you going just now?"

"Just out. There's lots of snow left out there for walking around in. I thought if I tried it I might get some kind of an idea."

Carmen fumbled in his trousers pocket, pulled out a handkerchief, and extracted a half-length cigarette butt. Kennebec held out his lighter.

"Let me go take a look for Charlie," Carmen said. "I got as good a chance of finding them as anybody."

"No," Kennebec said. He spoke with such quick resolution that it wasn't hard to see the suggestion had not come as a complete surprise. "I don't want to send anybody looking for Charlie."

"You got some better way? You got carrier pigeons stowed away? You got to send a runner or a scout or a patrol. Whatever it is you got to send somebody. Who? Who you got, Jack? Green young punks still wondering when the next USO show goes on, which way to the PX, how come they ran out of Cokes and Hershey Bars so soon. I'm not knocking the replacements, Jack. But this is no place for a green hand. You saw that young Colhurst get it and plenty like him the same way. Find Charlie Company? Even in this praying jungle they couldn't find a tree to piss behind."

"Let me go with him," Dave said suddenly.

"No. I already decided to take it from the duty roster. We're working on the B's right now. There's a Blanchard, a kid from Texas, got up a week ago, and a Bryers, an older man from a little place in Ohio, used to be a foreman in a cannery. I just talked to them to size things up. They've both had some map training. They came through this last thing in better shape than some."

"Jack, don't do me any favors," Carmen said. "You think it's a privilege to sit here waiting till your crazy colonel hollers for help? Or till he finds a new pill to give him back his guts? Or till the Krauts come and get us? Jack, you're an officer now. Let old Carmen go and find old Charlie."

"Why not, Jack? Let me go with Carmen." Beneath the tug of excitement Dave knew he'd never know for certain what he was really seeking now. Atonement of some kind, some new system of reckoning up a badly blotted ledger. Or perhaps just his own form of retrograde movement. Nothing as straightforward as a retreat. Only a cunning little hedge bet on the forsaken, seedy, ludicrous, insane, but still terrifying faith of his fathers; a stand-by foxhole in case by some wild fantasy the lake of fire turned out to be the well of truth.

Even Samuel Kyle could not call this a warlike errand. It was a mission of rescue and expiation. If the hand of Samuel Kyle was not yet on his shoulder, it trembled very near. The face of Samuel Kyle was far less implacable and tragic then than it had been in the throbbing night. The faces of God and Colonel John P. Barnstable were not ready to withdraw their accusations, and Henry Whelan and the shattered blood-red German were unrelenting still. But Dave's blood quickened with a shiver of strange hopefulness. He'd had his cake of going off in splendid errantry to the wars; perhaps there was still a chance to eat the cake of redemption and forgiveness.

"You sure you want to, Dave?" Kennebec was asking. "I wasn't even going to tell you guys about it. You sure, Carmen?"

They both nodded gravely.

"All right," Kennebec said. "Check your ammo. There's some left down on the next floor. The cooks have a few hard rations left. Take at least two days' supply each. There's a few pairs of extra socks and some new blankets in stores—that's downstairs too—I'll go and rustle up some maps and we'll go over them in a few minutes. I'll see if the colonel wants to talk to you himself."

As it happened the colonel did want to talk to them. He was still outside, pacing up and down alone in the snow, when Kennebec led them to him.

The colonel somehow had retained possession of his dress overcoat, which he was wearing now above his combat clothing. The coat still bore the memory of its last pressing, in someplace far away and sometime long ago. He had dispensed with the liner of his helmet and had stuffed an extra scarf into the gaps between the lower edge of the helmet proper and the arc of his forehead and temples. One end of the scarf drooped down a little over one gray, stubbled cheek. Imprisoned between the slovenly headgear and the residual nattiness of the overcoat, the colonel's eyes burned with the gallantry of a down-at-the-heels but undismayed guerrilla king. The wonderful therapy of the sack had bestowed its blessing on him too. Though his voice was still excited, it was much firmer. He smiled and put a hand on Dave's shoulder and then on Carmen's and then stepped back a pace or two, inspecting them with grave approval.

"By God, Lootenant!" he said, "you said you were giving me the two best men in the battalion and I believe you. Let me have those names again. Here, put them in my book"—he groped beneath his outer finery and held out a notebook and a pencil—"write the names down for me. Ah, good. Kyle. Ruiz. Good! Good! I don't mind telling you that after this little hassle is over there's going to be a little new hardware spread around this battalion. If I had my way, Kennebec, every man jack of them would get at least a Silver Star. But that's hoping for too much. One thing we *can* do, by God, and that's make sure any hardware that's going gets to the men who've done most to earn it."

Carmen's expression glittered briefly at the hint of medals. Dave was disappointed to see it, but then he turned away from Carmen because he was afraid the same perverse, unworthy, unwanted flicker might have crossed his own face too.

"No task ever given to anybody in this battalion is as important as the task I'm giving you two men." The colonel glanced at Kennebec and paused like an orator slowing down for the shorthand reporters. "You know you're going out there to find Company C. Just where I don't know, you don't know, Lootenant Kennebec doesn't know. All I can do is get you started. How and where you finish is going to depend on your own guts, your own brains, your own endurance, your own sense of duty to the hundred and seventy men here with the battalion and the hundred and sixty men somewhere out there with Charlie Company. You know we've come through a tight spot now, we may be in an even tighter spot in the next hour, the next day, the next week. *You know that?*"

Dave lifted his shoulders. He had to believe in the word of Jack Kennebec, he had to believe in his own eyes and ears, he had to believe in the worldly intuitions of Carmen Ruiz. But at the same time he had to believe in the colonel. His need to believe in the colonel was, indeed, no less fierce than the colonel's need to believe in him.

"Yes, sir," Dave said. "Yes, sir," Carmen said too, without even waiting to hear whether Dave had spoken or not.

"All right now, I had these passes made out to you." He handed each a slip of paper. "All they say is you're soldiers of this battalion on a special mission and you're to be given every facility and co-operation. There's nothing in there about what the mission is. If you're captured—I'm going to level with you men because I know you're going to level with me; you *will be* in danger of being captured—if there's a chance of being captured destroy these papers. If you get through to Company C—and I say you *will* get through, that's where my money rides—this is your message. Tell the officer commanding, whoever he is by now, to give you his map reference and strength and get you started back here with it as soon as you've got it memorized. Then tell him he's to get his company moving over here too and on the double. If due to enemy dispositions that's absolutely impossible—and make it clear I said both absolutely and impossible—I want his explanation for failing to comply with his orders and taking part in the retrograde movement ordered by regiment to battalion and battalion to companies at twenty-thirty hours December sixteen nineteen forty-four. Repeat that."

Dave and Carmen paraphrased the message in turn. The colonel had to correct each of them once on the hour of the withdrawal, but that was all. Yet something still troubled him.

He kicked a chunk of ice across a snowdrift like a boy dribbling a ball. "It's not just the survival of the whole battalion and the survival of Company C," he said, almost as if he were pleading. "It's the battalion's good name, the good name of every man jack of us. If you men—oh hell! you couldn't—if I were forced to send two ordinary men on this mission and they goofed off, if they just took a long walk, well, God, men, we'd never hear the end of it, would we? I mean, Jesus, men! A whole God-damn' company!"

"We won't goof off, sir," Dave said.

"Just keep them praying Krauts away," Carmen exhorted the colonel. "We'll be back and so will Charlie Company."

The colonel's spirits were now in a state of manic heartiness. "That's the God-damn' talk I like to hear! Jesus, men, with six hundred men like you—" A new idea stopped him. "Now look. This is even more important than what I said before. Even if Company C can't get back over here I want this from them. I want a written acknowledgment that they received notice the battalion was making a retrograde movement at twenty-thirty hours on December sixteen nineteen forty-four. I want a written statement from the officer commanding or the acting officer commanding that the company duly received an order to participate in said retrograde movement."

Dave got the substance of it to the colonel's satisfaction. Carmen said more tersely, trying but not hard enough to conceal his distaste, "They're supposed to say they got the word we were pulling out on them."

The colonel's moment of exuberance was gone. He took a step forward. Between the vestigially dapper coat collar and the scarecrow helmet his eyes blazed threateningly.

"By Jesus, man!" He started it as a bellow. Carmen looked back at him with quiet attentiveness—a loyal subject of the Law, the stolid embodiment of Respect, a very paragon among Squares. The colonel decided not to press it. He put out his hand to each of them in turn and strode back toward the big stone building, an end of his scarf trailing down beneath the helmet across his tailored shoulder.

Two hundred yards from the building they were stopped by one of their own sentries, a half-frozen replacement whose uniform and combat boots still showed traces of their pristine gloss through a layer of sodden mud and sludge.

"Armor."

"Knight."

"I wonder who makes those games up, anyway?" The sentry sat down wearily on a splintered fir tree. "Either you guys got a cigarette?" He looked curiously at the rolled blankets slung behind them, their canteens and spare rations, their extra ammunition pouches. "You going on a hike or something?" he asked suspiciously. "Hey!" The tone of bleak disgust turned suddenly to alarm. "The outfit's not pulling out again, is it?" He started to scramble to his feet. "It's God-damn'-well time. Wait. I'm coming too."

It took a good minute to dissuade him and Dave succeeded only after showing the paper from the colonel. After that they made good time, traveling partly on a compass bearing and partly with the help of a distant hill that occasionally came in sight when a break in the trees moved the horizon back a little. The hill showed on their maps as two miles away, although it looked closer under the heavy slate sky. According to the maps there would be a gorge containing a small mountain stream beyond the hill, and beyond the stream a flat stretch of wood broken only by a twisting cart trail and an intersecting firebreak. And then, a total of six miles from where they had started, the ridge where Company C had been dug in when last seen and heard from.

The country was ludicrously peaceful. New snow had obliterated most of the tracks left behind by the battalion itself, but their blaze marks still lay here and there among the clutching firs, discarded cans and ration boxes. A Browning automatic rifle on its side. A shallow little scar in the forest floor where someone had tried to scrape a foxhole. A few improvised sleeping tents of branches. A defiant little training-manual breastwork of thick, fresh-cut tree trunks, conceived and coaxed into being by some intensely, obdurately, pathetically soldierly young squad leader. Then a lone straggler dead and frozen stiff.

There had been no close fighting here at all. It was here that the battalion, after the first two days and nights—sometimes with its face to the enemy, sometimes with its back to the enemy —had funneled back in from an impossibly wide front of six hundred men to an impossibly narrow front of one hundred seventy-one; here that it had gathered what was left of its will to live; here that it had discovered itself alone, the enemy gone as swiftly and unbelievably as he had first appeared behind the now ancient rain of cannon fire.

Dave stumbled on a snow-covered root and plunged heavily to one knee. Carmen helped swab away the blood from his skinned left hand. Carmen was sympathetic but relieved. "Don't race me, Dave, you got longer legs and better wind. Old Carmen is forty-one and aching. How old are you, Dave?"

"Twenty-four and clumsy. You go ahead, Carmen."

"Try not to run over me, Dave."

Those were the last words either of them spoke until nightfall. A little farther along their compass route they came on an old logging trail that led in approximately their direction, the direction of the hill, the gorge, the stream, the ridge, and Company C. Carmen paused only long enough for the most perfunctory and fatalistic inspection of their new channel in the frozen surf of green and white; it wasn't really an inspection at all but a statement of credo, a shrug: if the praying bastards are there they're there and pray them all but six. Nevertheless he hesitated a few extra seconds, waiting for Dave to hurry up and make him turn away from the easy, careless invitation of the trail and return to the safer tangle of the forest. But Dave stopped, turning meanly away from the whole delicate business, glad to follow on the softer route and equally glad to be free of any provable part in choosing it. Carmen threw him the look of a man too proud to bargain with his betrayer and slouched off at the low-stepping gait of the infantry, the soldier's gait, which is the exact antithesis of the military gait.

By a benevolent coincidence, the ambush was bungled as unforgivably as the manner of their falling into it. An overeager or overapprehensive German fired a rifle grenade far sooner than he needed to, and Dave and Carmen escaped unscathed and as it turned out unpursued. They never knew for certain whether they'd bumped six men or sixty. Dave saw the floundering shadows of at least four and judged from the wild splatter of Mausers and Schmeissers that there were as many more better hidden. He caught up with Carmen in a clump of underbrush, and they waited silently for the stalkers who never came. Then, just before the early dusk, still without a word exchanged, Carmen got up and set his compass and started out again through the forest's blackening heart and Dave waited until Carmen was twenty or thirty yards ahead and started out after his long shuffling footprints. Now they made their mistakes on the side of caution, as much ashamed as frightened. It took them more than two hours to cover the next two miles, and when they came in sight of the little woodcutter's hut in which they finally made their bivouac, they spent an hour more watching it and making a slow, belly-scraping three-hundred-sixty-degree reconnaissance for marks of recent habitation.

Carmen finally spoke after they had a fire going in the iron brazier and coffee warming in their mess tins to go with their cheese, canned pork, and biscuits. The single window was tightly boarded, buttoning the hut as tightly as the night outside. Neither of them thought of putting out a watch. What they needed most now was rest and warmth. This was a professional calculation, and after the folly and unspoken accusations of the logging trail it made them both feel easier.

"We still got enough grub for two days," Carmen said.

"Sure. And we could get lucky. We could find a chicken or some eggs."

They spread one blanket on the floor and lay on it together and pulled the other blanket over them. The brazier glowed securely and Dave's watch said there was still a good four hours till midnight and another six or so till dawn.

After a while Carmen said, not making an issue of it, not reproving anyone, but merely calling attention to a significant fact, "We already got lucky, Dave."

"I know. Let's write that one off."

"How much luck are we entitled to?" Carmen was not looking for an argument, but it was plain that he was being nagged.

"As much as comes," Dave said.

"I guess so. Around the crap table it's always a new roll. The dice aren't supposed to average out. Say you make the hard four, that doesn't hurt your price on the hard eight next time. Always a new roll. I can't believe it. Assuming honest dice, I mean."

"You're superstitious, Carmen, aren't you?"

Carmen lifted himself on an elbow. In the glow of the fire his expression was eager and very shrewd. "You mean religious, don't you, Dave?"

"No, I don't." It began almost as a cry of alarm, but Dave brought it short. "Well, have it your way."

"Feel this." Carmen fumbled under his shirt and held out a piece of metal on a chain. "My St. Christopher's medal. For travelers. Superstition? Religion? Who knows? I had one son-of-a-bitch of a holt on the medal back there in the bushes."

Carmen put the medal back. "I never even showed it to Henry. You know who gave it to me? It was a joint present from my old lady and my sister. When they found out what they'd done the two of them and this son-of-a-bitchin' spik that left my sister standing practically naked in the aisle—when they found out I'd joined the Army they suddenly wanted everybody to let bygones be bygones but by then the bloody bygones were the hell-and-gone over the fence and out of the park and all they could think of was to turn the whole problem over to St. Christopher. If that doesn't work there's always the candles."

"Yes, there's always the candles," Dave said.

"But you're not superstitious." In spite of the overlying mixture of exasperation and yearning, Carmen's voice still had the note of shrewdness. "Not superstitious or religious."

Dave would have liked to be as frank with Carmen as Carmen had tried to be with him. But there were no words direct or concrete enough. He had no talisman to hoard against the final test, no vision of purifying tapers to fall back on when other hopes were lost. All he had was Company C. Carmen had Company C too, but he had the other things as well.

"I'm not sure, Carmen," he said. "But I believe in luck all right. We had good luck on the last roll and needed it. Maybe we'll need more. Anyway I've got to find Charlie Company."

"Don't worry, Dave," Carmen said with a trace of jealousy. "So do I." It had after all been his idea in the first place.

Just after what passed for sunrise on that wet, slate-colored morning, they fell in with Hectorforce. The personnel of Hectorforce consisted of one Corley Hector, a squat thick silo of an infantry captain from Wyoming, another captain, from the Medical Corps, two artillery lieutenants, a dozen sergeants and corporals, and nearly a hundred private soldiers of assorted backgrounds and local military affiliations. Its equipment was an average of one rifle, pistol, Tommy gun, or carbine and twenty rounds of ammunition for every two men; two light mortars, one thirty-seven-millimeter antitank gun in good working order and in charge of a corporal cook; two Sherman tanks, both with trained drivers but only one with a trained gunner, three Browning automatic rifles, a small hoard of gasoline in small portable jerricans, and a little notions heap of hand grenades, bottles already made up into Molotov cocktails, axes, spades, signal flares, and mines.

They found Hectorforce on the reverse slope of their landmark hill, identified themselves to a laconic and incurious picket, and were escorted, still being allowed the dignity of their rifles, into the presence of the commander. Captain Hector was eating his breakfast in a kind of hobo jungle set inside a roofless pillbox of tree trunks. There was a fire in the center of the pillbox and a dozen men sat around it staring at a square biscuit tin that simmered with odds and ends of other rations from other tins. All the men were dirty, wet, and bearded.

Captain Hector greeted the newcomers with stern warmth. "As our Limey friends would say—no names, no pack drill."

One of the men at the fire looked up out of malevolent red eyes. The line apparently was already old and growing less humorous with age. "Grab some chow and then get over to the dugout on our left and report to Lieutenant Clancy. In"—he looked at his watch—"thirty-six minutes from now we're attacking across the brow of the hill. Lieutenant Clancy will give you the details."

"Ride 'im, cowboy!" The soldier who had looked up muttered venomously and then looked down again.

Captain Hector was cleaning out his mess tins with a handful of snow and spruce twigs. When he had finished he pulled a long, well-tooled Italian commando dagger from his canvas belt, sharpened another twig, and began picking his teeth. His amiable blue eyes wandered without haste among the hunched-down soldiers.

"This may be the last time," he said conversationally. "I'm not promising, just saying how it looks to me. We could make it all the way."

No one said anything in response. "Well, Jesus." The captain wasn't pleading or even reasoning. Just from the steady, unhurried way he looked around and held his thick, low, hard fullback's body it could be told that his authority needed no asserting. He wasn't coaxing anybody, he was just being consoling and kind. "Well, Jesus, we're halfway there already, aren't we?"

"Why not?" One of the seated men put it in the captain's own lazy campfire tone. "We always have been."

The captain laughed and got to his feet, rotating his thick competent arms like an athlete unlimbering.

"Twenty minutes now. Any questions?" He laughed again, more quietly. "I mean sensible questions. No? Well, all right then. Just remember it's all in the point of view. I was up there a couple of hours ago. You men think you're groggy. Christ, I walked over at least six Krauts who were out so cold I could have taken the fillings from their teeth. We've got all the edge. They don't know we're still here. We know they're still there."

"You know what, Captain?" one of the men asked spiritlessly. "I don't think they *care* where we are. I don't think they give one good God damn. We bumped them three times in the last two days and now we're halfway up the friggin' hill and they're dug in on the other side. They're up there like the New York Yankees and we're down here with our friggin' record of oh-for-three. Why the hell *should* we interfere with their friggin' rest?"

"Could I ask a question, sir?" another man asked. "How much of the big stuff have they still got?"

"It wasn't that easy. I couldn't make a count. But we know we got one of the SP-eighty-eights and one of the Panthers and two of the tank destroyers yesterday afternoon."

"So they've still got maybe six tanks and four or five guns. Is that correct, sir?"

"Likely. But remember it's the point of view. They think they've finally licked us. Now all they've got to do is outwait the poor bastards in the valley or starve 'em out or smoke 'em out or chop

307

'em up a little at a time. They think they've got our guys down there in the bag. I think we've got *them* in the bag."

"Like the friggin' canary's got the cat."

The captain laughed again but then turned persuasive. "Don't forget there's several thousand good Yanks in that valley and over a hundred more here. In between there's less than a thousand Krauts. Sure they've got the drop. Sure they've got the road. But what will happen when we come barging up their ass? The guys below will come barging down their throat. So who's in the bag now?"

It would have been interesting to know what Captain Hector did in civvy life. Perhaps, except for the lapses in his language, a Y.M.C.A. secretary or the coach of a not very talented high-school football team. There was something forced and phony about his optimism, but this only made it the more difficult to resist. By a kind of intellectual bum's rush, the captain had expelled logic from his forum and made innocence and absurdity the yardsticks of truth and reason. The sad little cluster of faces glittered faintly in the firelight. "Those bastards will never know what hit them," the captain said.

Dave had momentarily forgotten Company C. Now he walked around the fire. It seemed ridiculous to salute in this preposterous hobo jungle behind the nondescript breastwork of logs piled in lopsided haste, beside the square blackened can of C-ration stew on the dying hearth of pine root, amid the beggared bandits waiting at their junk pile of dirty, insufficient guns, old bottles, old cans, and rusty ammunition cases. But when his eyes met the stubbornly unadmitting, unconceding old-young eyes of the captain he knew that here was a man to be saluted in any climate or any setting. He was sorry he had approached the captain at all. He sensed at once that he was going to be misunderstood but it was too late to turn back.

He held out the paper that the colonel had given him.

The captain handed it back. He laughed again, but this time with an edge of hardness.

"Soldier," he said, just above his breath, "I guess I didn't make myself plain enough when you first came in. No names, no pack drill. A lot of things have happened to a lot of U.S. soldiers in the last three days that are better forgotten. You've noticed I didn't even ask you for the number of your unit. I see it's here on this paper and I see you're on a special mission. There are a hundred and seven officers and enlisted men of the U.S. Army in this position and all but, I'd say, eighteen or nineteen of them landed in this vicinity from various directions with special missions just like you. They didn't all have it in writing, but they were all going somewhere else. Now there's only one place they're going. That's up to the top of this hill: Do you have any trouble with my meaning?"

"No, sir," Dave said. "I just wanted to ask if you'd heard anything about Company C, First Battalion, Nine Five Seven Infantry."

"If I had heard I wouldn't believe it," the captain said firmly. "At this moment there are only two military formations I recognize by name or number. One is the German Army. The other is the United States formation designated as Hectorforce, which is the force you have just joined and from which you will take your orders until further notice."

"Yes, sir." Dave was grateful to the captain for keeping his voice low. Thank God no one else could hear, not even Carmen, who he saw was watching.

"Let me give you one last word." Captain Hector was not angry, not even contemptuous. "Except in the eighteen or nineteen cases I mentioned before, every last man in Hectorforce arrived in this area under the impression that somebody had ordered him to retreat or that his unit had been wiped out and that he therefore had no personal choice left but to retreat. There has been an awful lot of retreating in the United States Army in the last three days. There will be no retreating by Hectorforce. Do not, under any circumstances, mistake any order you get here for an order to retreat. Do not, no matter what seems to be happening in the next few hours, fall into the error of believing that Hectorforce has been wiped out and that you as its sole survivor are therefore free to retreat alone. Hectorforce is not going to be wiped out and it is not going to retreat. Now pick up your buddy and get the hell over there and report for duty to Lieutenant Clancy."

"What was that all about?" Carmen muttered as they followed a footpath through the snow in search of Lieutenant Clancy.

"I just asked if he knew anything about Company C. He didn't know but said they might be down there with the rest of the men in the valley."

"Does he really think we can spring them?"

"Yes."

"Do you?"

"Yes."

They found Lieutenant Clancy in a long, deep secondhand dugout covered with fir trunks against air-burst and treetop shrapnel. There was a fire going at each end of the dugout. A dozen soldiers stood along the walls, those who had guns checking their magazines, those who hadn't loading up with anything else that might prove useful until—the calculation was unavoidable—one of the guns might lose its present owner and become available for reallocation. Some of the weaponless men had gathered up boxes of small-arms ammunition, and others were stuffing ration cases into sacks made up of camouflage netting and odds and ends of rope. Two men had made a stretcher of new-cut spruce poles and a couple of rainproof ponchos. No one was talking.

The officer was recognizable as an officer only because he stood a little apart. There was no undercurrent of hostility from or rejection by the others; it was more a matter of self-consciousness than anything else. Considering that no one knew anyone else, the atmosphere between the officer and the men was surprisingly loose.

It was Dave who broke the quiet. "Lieutenant Clancy, sir? The captain sent us over."

"First-rate. First-rate." The lieutenant took a step in their direction and stopped, an unfinished response to some old tribal instinct. He was a wiry little man, much slighter and younger than Captain Hector, and much less accustomed to command, but he was not backing away from the necessity of command.

"You've got rifles. First-rate. Lots of ammo? First-rate. Where have you been?"

"Well, sir—"

The lieutenant broke in quickly, as though heading off a social blunder. "I don't mean the last few days. I mean generally. What experience have you had? That is, you're infantry, aren't you?"

"Yes."

"We're looking for one of our companies." Carmen would not be happy with anything less than a full declaration. "The colonel told us—"

"Yes. First-rate," the lieutenant interjected again. "No need to go into it now. We move in four minutes. I'm a gunner, so you probably know more about this kind of thing than I do. Needless to say there'll be no artillery support. Even if we had it we wouldn't use it. Any tanks you hear at first will be theirs. We've got two Shermans that will come up in support but they won't even start their motors until we've made foot contact. Don't make any latrine stops. If you get pinned down get up and unpin yourself. Captain Hector and his squad are going to take care of the Panthers and their other heavy stuff. We're guarding his flank. The only other thing is watch for the other GI's coming up from below."

Considering the disparity in their ages and natural airs of authority, Clancy had given a surprisingly good imitation of Captain Hector. He had imparted to the dugout something of the impalpable, paradoxical quality of the wooden fortress just behind: a melancholy that was deep and settled but that still stopped short of despair. The men were not willing to enter into the officer's enthusiasm, for they could not be deceived by it. Yet they felt the need to humor him a little—a need as much their own as his—even while they let him know they weren't taken in.

"Oh yes. Watch out for *Schu* mines after the first half mile."

"*Schu* mines?" One of the other men threw in a falsetto Ed Wynn giggle. "I stepped on a *Schu* mine once, Lieutenant, and I haven't noticed a damned thing since."

"Well." The lieutenant was puzzled but felt the need of making some response. "They don't look like much but they're pretty nasty. They're liable to"—he got it too late to do anything except flounder, but he did it well enough—"oh hell! Mother warned me I'd never be anything but a straight man." Given a fair chance, Clancy had the makings of a good officer.

Now a few small scraps of conversation eddied back and forth. Nothing big. Nothing heroic. Nothing at all original. Two men exchanged addresses and discovered that they'd once had dates with the same girl on the same lake in Minnesota. One man got some advice on treating trench feet, which he was certain, despite the criminal indifference of the U. S. Army Medical Corps, he had had since early in the Huertgen Forest. Another tried to get off a new joke about two whores in Tennessee, but someone else horned in and spoiled the ending.

"Ninety seconds now," the lieutenant said. "Don't forget the five yards." He knew better than to offer oratory, but his sense of occasion called for something at least. "Remember those Krauts are mighty pissed-off too. My outfit picked up a PW on the day they first attacked and even before the attack went in he'd been on a forced march of sixteen hours. No matter how long we've been going they've been going a day longer. And get this: this PW said they hadn't had any mail, not one bloody bit of mail, for five weeks before they started. No ordinary mail. No Christmas mail. No mail period. Their morale's all shot to hell."

"Mine's great," someone muttered. "Just great. I got morale coming out of my ears."

Clancy ignored it. "O.K. Here we go. Don't bunch up."

Dave was fourth out of the dugout. The lieutenant was in front, then a corporal wearing steel-rimmed spectacles, dramatizing the fact that he was really a clerk. Then Carmen. After the fire the air was colder than he'd remembered it, but it was also strong and bracing. There was still no hint of sun, but as they moved up the slope the trees were a little less dense and the light was better than it had been in nearly a week. The line fanned out to the left, each man keeping approximate dress on the movement to his right. They moved slowly and carefully, with the stretcher men and the ammunition and rations men falling a little back where they wouldn't be in the way at first, where if the need should come they could drop their cargoes and move up to take the idle guns.

No mail, the lieutenant had said. No ordinary mail. No Christmas mail. No mail period. It was a bitter thing to imagine happening to anybody. Again the stricken vision of the German falling away just after Henry Whelan. Was he one of the mailless ones, unshriven, stripped of grace, remembered best and last by the executioner? With what inflection had he carried the mourning for his absent mail through the portals of eternity? Was he forgiving, even after it was too late to make his forgiveness known? *They always wrote before. It can't be their fault.* Or condemned, with no hope of remission, to an everlast of hating? *Oh, the bitch! The evil bitch! I knew it all the time.*

Somewhere during the first—withdrawal? retreat? retrograde movement? redeployment? collapse? honest, unavoidable defeat? Why did everybody make so much of the choice of words?—somewhere behind a tangle of shell-wrecked trees the ashes of Dave's own last mail lay safely burned. A few men had ignored the order, but to him and, he sensed, to Carmen and to Henry, who was still there then, it had seemed as reassuring and sensible as an order to fasten seat belts before landing. It was in earnest that sound, coherent orders were still being thought out and given; that someone was still in control; that the line still held back through platoon and company and battalion and army right back to the corner post-office box in Battle Creek. Mary's last letter, which had seemed a little stiff and chatty when it first arrived, had gained new tenderness and feeling in the instant of being committed to the flames. He saw her small, soft, competent hand dropping it in the green box, saw her walk off again with her red head dancing beneath the elms like the last unconquered leaf of autumn, saw her firm hips swinging just a little under the skirt that met the letter of Sister White's specifications without in the least neglecting the warning against false prudence and mock modesty. "A spectacle to the world, to angels and to men."

He stopped thinking about Mary, Mrs. White, and the hemline and concentrated on the demands and probabilities of the minutes straight and close ahead. He realized that he had begun to feel better. It was never good to be going into battle, the men who talked of the joy of the battle must be either maniacs or liars, but if it had to be done it was done best this way, attacking toward a concrete goal beside men that you could see with your own eyes. Carmen was moving steadily and carefully on his right, well abreast of the bespectacled corporal and his full five yards away. Occasionally the little figure of Lieutenant Clancy drifted in and out of sight beyond the corporal. Clancy stopped now and then, waiting for them to stop in turn. Then he'd glance to *his* right, making sure of their squad's firm contact with the rest of Hectorforce. On Dave's left the lanky *Schu*-mine man was gliding through the trees with the expertise of an Iroquois scout in the movies. He was smiling blissfully, lost in admiration of some far-off boy in some farther forest. Once he caught Dave catching him out in a particularly fancy little "Look, guys!" side step. He was only momentarily abashed. Then he grinned and lifted his hand, confessing that he knew he'd been detected.

The line stopped and froze so competently that the stretcher team, coming up behind, almost caught up before it froze too. Clancy had brought his hand up. Whatever he was listening for did not repeat itself. They moved on and then halted and froze again and this time the sound was there.

In one of his few loquacious interludes Sergeant—now Lieutenant—Kennebec had dealt with the theory, by no means an original one, that certain men were naturally allergic to certain sounds and certain other men were naturally immune. Heredity and instinct were somehow involved. A man who'd never heard, say, the throb of the exotic new buzz bomb or the unheralded smash of the new V-2 might be absolutely paralyzed by it; this same man, who had perhaps been in a dozen barrages of eighty-eights or ten or twenty mortar stonks, could still, while by no means unfearful of the eighty-eights and mortars themselves, remain relatively unmoved by their special noises.

No doubt it had something to do with pitch or decibels, like those special dog whistles. Some sounds automatically got to some men and some didn't. No one was expected to take the theory seriously, except as a basis for argument. In any case so far as Dave was concerned, it had already been shot to pieces. Before this attack began, the sound of tanks, in so far as it had had any special accent or intimations, had been for him a rather friendly and sporting sound. A moving tank always gave warning. You could tell where it was, how much company it had, how far away it was. It seldom fired blind, so if you took reasonable care not to let it see you it was much less apt than the undiscriminating cannons, rockets, bombs, mines, and fixed-line machine guns to destroy you by mistake.

In Normandy and in the thrust through the plains of France and Belgium, Dave hadn't minded tank motors. But now, still less than four days old, the memory of their Panther back at the big Fort Knox foxhole had become a part of his blood stream and his guts, of the very sea water in his very veins. He could not tell whether it was one motor calling or two, or many—the captain had admitted there were several of them around. But something was calling, and as he stood there waiting for someone to make a move the notion clutched at him that it was calling him, David Kyle, by name. It couldn't be the same tank that had crushed young Colhurst and then sniffed around on its dripping belly and panted back to get the other three. It couldn't be that one, because that was the one Jack Kennebec had slaughtered and left roasting in its own rank juices. But this tank could be that one's mate as well as not. There had been more than one at first, the place was not so far away, and whatever front there was had not moved so systematically . . .

Clancy waved them on toward the sound. The corporal in the spectacles looked around and reached out and threw an arm around the trunk of a fire-barked pine. Carmen walked over, ignoring the spacing, and said something to him. The corporal took off his glasses, wiped them on an end of his scarf, and then, as though everything had been explained, pushed at the tree for leverage and stumbled forward.

Ahead it grew much lighter. Nakedly light. Lieutenant Clancy had paused at the edge of a firebreak. He stood behind the best tree he could find, and the others dressed up to him and tried to merge with other trees. It was as stiff and formal as a high-school pageant when everybody, astoundingly, has found the right chalk mark on the floor and is looking in disbelief and consternation toward the prompter.

It was a wide firebreak. It stretched between two solid lines of trees in a bald slash and went up and over the crown of the hill. At the horizon it met the tanks coming down, two abreast and three deep.

Clancy and his squad still stood like a ceremonial guard, each man welded to his tree. The tanks had not yet seen them but had somehow sniffed their presence out, and now they were making their solemn march the pageant's final scene. The tanks had dealt with this seedy, sorry nuisance three times already and had nothing to fear including fear itself. They had not yet opened fire. Their engines and the clanking tracks beneath them still made the only sound.

The tanks were close enough that it could be seen a man was standing erect in the open turret of one of the foremost ones, looking carefully ahead to the fringes of the wood, holding a microphone to his mouth, and talking steadily as he searched.

The infantrymen supporting and supported by the tanks were shrouded in white helmets and parachute silk and bed sheets. They had none of the operatic flourish of the dragon-crossed centaur at their head. They crept in and out of the shelter of the tanks like wary white ferrets. They held their bodies low and the barrels of their Mausers and Schmeissers high and kept coming on, full of guile and stealth and readiness. There were fifteen or twenty of them behind or at the flanks of each of the six Panthers.

The mechanical, dirge-like lament of the deep-pitched motors had grown so near that Clancy, still undetected, had to shout. "Don't aim at the tanks! Take the men on the ground! Fire when I fire!"

Someone else fired just ahead of him, from just across the slashed-out roadway. The top half of the dragon-centaur in the leading tank toppled forward, but the half beneath crawled on. The turret of the flanking Panther swiveled toward the side and its long gun roared out a thunderous bay of wrath and vengeance. Then all six tanks were firing into the trees, raking wildly with their cannons and machine guns while the white foot soldiers fell on their bellies, searching for targets, not at first finding them but firing anyway. The trees crashed and snapped and split apart like overripe, August-hot seed pods, but the belly-down infantry and the hull-down tanks were all firing high and, as an extra dispensation from the gods of Hectorforce, the tanks were using nonfragmenting AP shells.

Hectorforce was firing back from four different positions, two on each side of the road. Dave was down, partly hidden by a pine stump, propped on one elbow and sighting into the white billow of the German infantry. His mind was perfectly clear. He even took an extra two or three seconds after getting off the first round to reset his range for a hundred yards. But his hand was not so steady. He found he could not hold a target. He aimed just for the left of the first of the leading tanks, where the black approaching wall of metal met the white swirl of snow and camouflage cloth. The fire was even and steady from the other three segments of Hectorforce. For a moment all the Germans stopped, even the tanks. Another helmeted figure appeared in the turret of the second forward tank. Another hand came up with another microphone, and the human half of another cross-bred centaur toppled down on the dragon undershell.

From across the firebreak there was a high, bubbling shriek of "Medic!" Incredibly, beyond all reason, the two stretcher men of the Clancy squad ran past Dave, dragging their tatter of spruce poles and furled ponchos, ran into the open clearing, and ran across untouched. They might have been the first GI's the Germans actually saw, for the momentary inertia was broken and the tanks came on again, the infantry still darting in and out behind. Suddenly someone in the German infantry began shouting, a weird and piercing bardic cry that seemed to strike against the sounds of the shells and bullets and engines and echo back from them like a death wail from a dungeon. The cry was picked up and in a moment half the German infantry were on their feet running crazily ahead of the tanks, some with bayonets fixed to their thrust-out rifles, some firing as wildly as they ran and yelled, but all coming on. There was no time to wonder if this was another of their tricks, no time to speculate whether, as it had often been said of the cheating bastards before, the Krauts were drunk or doped.

There was now only time—and very little of that—to go out and meet them, to show them what they were up against, to stop them in the open or be engulfed by their insane weight of numbers. The bespectacled corporal, not even waiting to get back to his feet, knee-walked out into the clearing, waddling and staggering like a wounded duck, firing his Tommy gun until something hit him in the chest and left him balanced briefly on his forelegs before he folded over on his side.

Carmen was out in the clearing and so were Lieutenant Clancy, the *Schu*-mine man, and one of the spare-ammo bearers, now in place behind the surplus Tommy gun. Dave squirmed over beside Carmen, firing into the general mass, briskly but not hastily, his mind still clear enough to tell him that when his magazine was empty there would be no chance to load it up again. Flecks and gobs of red appeared against the mass of white ahead. The general yelling of the Germans ceased, yielding to scattered cries of private pain and terror.

For the second time the Germans stopped, the closest of them now hardly a hundred yards away. The tanks, grown cautious, made no attempt to catch up with the reckless infantry. The forward lines of Hectorforce scrambled back to cover and for a few eternal instants there was a weird three-way impasse, the German infantry stopped, the German tanks unwilling to move until the infantry recovered, the astonished survivors of Hectorforce unwilling to dispute or disrupt a miracle.

And then one of the white figures in the foreground raised an arm, signaling back to the tanks. The idling motors grunted into gear and the black column inched on again, the cannon trained just above the shallow drift of foot soldiers, the painted iron crosses bold against the monstrous blackened slabs of armor.

Still no one reopened fire. The gap between the grinding tanks and the waiting infantry shrank in careful, hinching, almost apologetic fits and starts. The tanks seemed to be trying, in their massive, clumsy fashion, to maintain the general pretense that whatever violence had been afoot before the violence was ended now. But they kept coming on.

There were two separate points of concentration. For the Germans the focal point was the edges of the roadway, a point-blank cannon shot, a short-range Mauser burst ahead. For the waiting men of Hectorforce it was the narrowing gap between the two merging shapes of their enemy, the patch of unoccupied roadway

317

between the stationary German infantry and the moving Panthers. The concentration everywhere was so perfect that when the thick short bulk of Captain Hector emerged at the side of the roadway the Germans did not see him at all, and at first he made no more impression on his own watching comrades than if he had been a discreet stagehand stealing quickly out from and back into the wings.

The captain would have been recognizable, nevertheless, if only for the dark, silo-like silhouette bent low under the periscopes of the tanks but still well above the white billow of the infantry now less than an alley's width ahead of him. Around his shoulders were strung two dark leaden leis of mines. The nature of these adornments was as unmistakable as the innocent, dogged faith in which the captain bore them out into the uncovered narrows between the front of the tanks and the rear of the soldiers on the ground.

"Holy Christ!" Dave heard Carmen gasp from behind the adjoining tree. "The loony son-of-a-bitch has got two daisy chains."

The captain bent down a little lower, shrugged one of his two heavy necklaces loose, and carefully spread it out in the path of the right-hand tank in front. He took an extra two or three seconds to pull it straight, fussing with it until the six mines in the chain were approximately level. Then he moved, still full of faith, still with no more than a corner of his eye to spare for the machine itself, into the path of the second tank and spread the second string of mines in the same way. By the time he was fully satisfied the tanks were no more than thirty feet away. Captain Hector turned and loped back into the trees, a little more hastily now, but not sufficiently so to risk attracting attention.

The tanks hit the mines almost together. Their treads jarred upward, rising only slightly and half smothering the bursting mines, drowning the quick tattoo in metallic pings, like big, rock-weighted lard pails muffling a nickel's worth of firecrackers. But they had both suffered grave internal wounds. On one a part of one tread dangled loose and broken and its cannon drooped and swung half-circle, the power controls gone. From the turret of the other the semblance of a man appeared, trying to hold together a red and broken face and declare surrender with the same wet hands. "I'll take him!" Carmen yelled, but someone from the other side of the road got in first.

Both the leading tanks began to smoke. The four other tanks behind, the route ahead now hopelessly blocked, were trying to turn in their own length on the suddenly chaotic roadway and get back to where they could move or see. A knot of German infantrymen started a charge, yelling again, but when the first two men pitched forward in the snow the others ran back behind the shelter of the smoking Panthers.

Captain Hector raced back into sight, this time helping a GI with the long tube of a bazooka. A third tank stopped and sent forth a tendril of flame.

"Come on!" Clancy yelled. GI's spilled out from both sides of the roadway, now shouting as fiercely and incoherently as the Germans had shouted before. The last three tanks had got turned around and crashed off to the right under cover of a dried-up creek bed. The only Germans in sight were a score of dead and a dozen or so of quiet wounded, the stronger ones dabbing furtively at themselves with swabs and bandages and tourniquets torn from their stained camouflage clothing and the weaker ones wanly absorbed in their various terminal symptoms. The field belonged solely and completely to Hectorforce.

The paradoxical Captain Hector, who had greeted the dismal circumstances of an hour before with such enthusiasm and rearranged them with such staggering bravery, was now an indecisive hulk. The GI's—there were still eighty or ninety of the first one hundred seven—rushed and milled around him, leaving the rules of war where their leader had just deposited them, in a state of absolute suspension, a condition of blissful nothingness. The soldier who had been so obdurately funny back in the timber pillbox slapped the captain's wide, low shoulders and shouted, "Jesus, boss, you broke the God-damn' bank!" Their own two Shermans, freed from their seal of silence when the shooting began, clattered into sight with their turrets unbuttoned and their commanders waving boisterously as soon as they had comprehended what they saw.

"Keep moving!" Hector yelled at everyone. "Keep moving, God damn it! Where are the other Yanks? Why didn't they come up from the other side? Keep moving, God damn you!"

"Where, sir?" Hurt by the rebuff but willing now to forgive anything, the retired gag man shouted respectfully on behalf of them all.

"Where?" Hector shouted back at him. "Where? What do you mean where?"

Lieutenant Clancy fought his way through. "What do we do, Captain? Consolidate or pursue?"

"You've lost your God-damn' mind!" the captain yelled accusingly. "Consolidate what, for Jesus' sake? Pursue who, for Jesus? We've gotta get out of here!"

"Come on now, men," Clancy shouted. "Get moving!"

"Where? Where, for God's sake!" A single mortar burst fell in just behind.

"Another God-damn' trap!" the gag man bawled.

"Where are the bastards from the valley?" Captain Hector stepped up to Lieutenant Clancy and yelled right down his throat.

"I don't know, Captain," Clancy said defensively. "Am I supposed to know?"

"Somebody around here should know something." Hector reinforced his helplessness with synthetic fury. "The bastards never made a move, did they? Did anybody fire the signals?"

"What signals, Captain?"

"Never mind! Get these men moving!"

"Where, sir?"

"The only place there's left, God damn it. Over that hill and down where the other Yanks are. Come on, now, men! Come on! Do you want to stay here and get crucified?" He led them at a spread-out trot up the last hundred yards of the roadway and once more into the thick depth of the forest. In twenty minutes Hectorforce was safely united with the larger force it had sallied forth to rescue.

No one knew the exact American military population of the Schoenen und Einsamen Berge and its wooded concourse of draws, glens, and small plateaus. The remnant of one whole division was there plus—to use the harshest terms that anyone who had held his ground against the first numbing onslaught was in a hurry to apply to anyone who had not—some of the stragglers and breakaways of two others.

The only coherent center of command was at the divisional headquarters in a largish town fourteen miles away, on the other side of the German siege lines. From the late evening of December 16 to this midmorning of December 19 the divisional command's radio messages had been competing, with only occasional success, against the steady jamming of German marching music, German news reports of a complete and total victory in the Ardennes, now more familiarly known as the Bulge, and German invitations to come and join all the other happy GI's in the warm and well-fed prisoner compounds. However large or small their number might be, the men of the Schoenen und Einsamen Berge (which translated as the Beautiful and Lonely Mountains) were reminded that they had not been forgotten. Their requests for heavy air support had been received and given the highest priority by SHAEF itself. As soon as the weather made it possible—and better weather was continually imminent—the German guns and tanks that held the heights above the Beautiful and Lonely Mountains and controlled the exits to the south and west would be subjected to mass bombardment by every available bomber, fighter-bomber, and rocket plane. Transport planes would drop vast supplies of food, winter clothing, ammunition, and medical supplies to the hungry, the hurt, and the frozen. Moreover, their local commanders were assured that another "powerful friend" named Bulldozer was on the way to join them by land. Since the Germans had already intercepted the crudely coded signal and fed it into the radio band to the solemn strains of *"Deutschland über alles,"* the local American commanders saw no reason to keep its contents secret. They let it be known that the famous Nineteenth Armored Division was pushing steadily eastward while the Typhoons and Thunderbolts, and Mustangs, the Mosquitoes and Lancasters and Flying Fortresses stood by already loaded on runways stretching all the way from Brussels and Luxembourg to Yorkshire and East Sussex, waiting only for the clouds to part above the Beautiful and Lonely Mountains. The men for whom this rescue was designed were reminded that, until rescue arrived, they stood athwart the Siegfried Line itself, that they and another garrison of Americans surrounded but unyielding at another place called Bastogne had become a symbol and a beacon to free men everywhere.

Hopeful as its future was deemed to be, the present circumstances were appallingly gloomy. The mountains were less a military position than a patchwork of targets and burrows jammed into four or five square miles of forest, snow, icy hillside, and valley bottom. Despite the close proximity of the several thousand men who had found a flimsy, shivering refuge in its ditches, dugouts, foxholes, frozen stream beds, and sparse shacks, barns, and cellars, they had no effective central direction and no central plan except to hang on. Two of the division's three infantry regiments were spread over the two highest hills, but their only real contact with each other had occurred when, during the first confused night of their encirclement, they met in the gorge between their hills and fought a brief pitched battle under an impartial barrage of German artillery fire. As communication became more difficult and movement of any kind more dangerous the regiments themselves and the stragglers and breakaways who gravitated to their blood-caked banners fragmented into small units and subunits united only by their common misery and their common hope. Their one piece of good fortune was that they had ceased to be a threat to the enemy or even a very serious inconvenience. The German spearheads, the American last ditches, and the shifting no man's land were five, ten, as much as forty miles beyond the mountains. The Germans sealed off the roads, left an adequate force of tanks, artillery, and infantry on guard, and contented themselves with the painless, inexpensive uses of attrition. Every day their carefully rationed artillery stonks claimed new victims. Every day the five thousand—six thousand? seven thousand? eight thousand?—residents of the Beautiful and Lonely Mountains looked toward the sky for the promised Forts and Thunderbolts, listened across the bleak, hostile hill crests for the promised Shermans, looked and listened and grew less numerous.

Though the exact conditions varied from dugout to dugout and foxhole to foxhole and the lack of co-ordination made accurate calculation impossible, there was perhaps enough ammunition left in the whole U.S. encampment to sustain perhaps one battalion through a half day's serious skirmishing. There was no blood plasma for the wounded anywhere, no penicillin, and no bandages. The only reliable statistic on rations was that some individual soldiers and some groups of soldiers had some food left and some had none at all.

The arrival of Hectorforce caused only a momentary excitement. The sorely disappointed Captain Hector recovered his spirits and his presence of mind halfway down the slope, pulled a white cotton pillow slip from inside his combat jacket and led his panting comrades in unmenaced by friend or foe. At first the GI's below mistook them for the spearhead of the long-awaited armored division and greeted them with a ragged but heartfelt cheer. The amenities were soon over. An American major came halfway out of a timbered dugout and wrestled Captain Hector to the ground, pummeling him with Old-Grad fervor. Hector got up again with difficulty. The men behind him simply dropped and lay in the snow, only half listening. It was some time before it became apparent that it was all another tremendous balls-up. Gradually it came home to the principals and to their audience of old residents and newcomers that the captain and the major were not carrying on a conversation at all. They were speaking lines, appealing to an audience, begging judgment, demanding expiation, pleading for release from self-doubt. Long after they had begun to understand each other they still sought the understanding and favor of the men around them. Their voices grew louder, their lines more simple and woodenly functional.

"But, Captain, if you're not from the Nineteenth Armored—"

"I told you, Major. We're an *ad hoc* force of American soldiers. We're just these men you see here."

"Whose orders have you been acting under, Captain?"

"Well, Major, just the general orders any American soldier acts under in an emergency. We knew there were some enemy troops and guns and armored vehicles on that height of ground back there and we knew there were some American troops on this ground below and—may I ask a question, Major?"

"Certainly, Captain. You go ahead and ask your question."

"When you heard it start, Major, why didn't your men come up the hill?"

"Captain, too many men have tried going up that hill."

"Well, no offense, Major. It was probably easier going up from the other side. But my men got there. And we had an escape route open if someone had just come up to help us keep it open."

"Captain, even if I'd been fool enough to send my men up there, I don't have the authority. I'd have needed the authority of my battalion commander and he'd have needed the authority of our regimental commander."

"I see, Major. Could I ask if the situation was reported to your battalion or regimental commander?"

"Certainly, Captain. You go ahead and ask anything. In the foregoing instance the answer is no. Would you like to know why the answer is no?"

"Yes, Major, I would like to know why no attempt was made to support and take advantage of the attempt of my men to relieve the position of your men."

"Well, the reasons are manifold, Captain. One. When the racket started up there I had, lacking divine guidance or special occult powers, no means whatever of ascertaining either its cause or its intention. Two. The only contact I have with my battalion or my regiment is *vie-ya* runner *vie-ya* an observed route that can only be used at night. Three. My men have been through an ordeal which, to judge from the comparatively fresh condition of yourself and your men, you could not at present be reasonably expected to comprehend. My men are exhausted. Moreover their supply of ammunition is, for all offensive purposes, exhausted also. Four. The situation here is scheduled to be properly and adequately corrected at the earliest possible hour by Allied forces much better equipped for the task than those at either your disposal or mine. If there is no further unauthorized interference with the authorized plan this position will shortly be relieved by a very large force of Allied aircraft and armor."

"Thank you, Major. I see now that it was the duty of my men not to attack the enemy, but to retreat."

"You are too hard on yourself, Captain. I did not wish to suggest that you and your men can be blamed in any way for the confusing state of our army's intelligence. It is my impression that they and you have conducted yourselves with singular gallantry. It is my advice that you make yourselves as comfortable and secure as you can until we are relieved. My men will be glad to loan their trenching tools to those of you who are without them."

"Thank you, Major. Lieutenant Clancy, have Hectorforce dig in."

"Oh, and Captain. I wouldn't take too long. The next stonk is due in forty minutes. That is, unless recent events have so upset the enemy that he may move his schedule forward."

Dave and Carmen had a sufficient foxhole ready for the first stonk. By the time the second one arrived, just after nightfall, they had enlarged it enough to accommodate both their stretched-out bodies, with room for a good floor and insulating walls of fir. Later on Carmen borrowed an ax and chopped enough logs for a roof. Around midnight a totally unexpected windfall arrived, a ration party with a generous ladleful of almost warm stew and a can of bully beef for each of them. "Here, showboat!" a man grunted. "Compliments of General Custer."

"What do you mean, showboat, you bastard!" Carmen growled. But his heart wasn't in it.

"They say this is the last of it." The man outside wasn't nursing grudges. "Better save some in case. But hey! You know what? A runner just came in from regiment and you know what? They had Army-Notre Dame weather on all the English airstrips yesterday. It broke around Brussels too. It's due to break here tomorrow morning. Christ, we'll be knee-deep in porterhouse steaks by noon. They got a definite fix on the Nineteenth Armored, too. It's nine miles away and barreling right through."

But the day brought only more snow. The Germans moved a sound truck onto the far hillside and with their usual methodicalness turned it on every hour on the hour. With the backdrop of snow-blanketed trees and the walls of the valley to work against, the acoustics were remarkably good.

Sometimes they played noisy, very much overdone sound tracks of artillery barrages and moving tanks interspersed with the cries of what were intended to be taken for wounded men. These were a distinct annoyance and they were not entirely without tactical significance. Heard alone, the sound tracks were distorted and scratchy and gave themselves away, but when they overlapped one of the real barrages they were highly dangerous. The first time this happened one of the men of Hectorforce had been walking from his foxhole to visit a new acquaintance from among the old originals. Several men, half standing up in other foxholes merely for the sake of not sitting down, saw him clutch his stomach and fall, writhing to the ground. His movements were so exaggerated and theatrical that everyone took it that he was mocking the phoniness of the phony sound track. When they pulled him in he was genuinely dead from a genuine piece of air-burst shrapnel, and from then on, phony or not, the recorded battle noises kept them down as firmly as the real ones. More so if anything. By now most of them, particularly those who had been there since the beginning, were parties to the unarticulated but well understood convention that a man who tried out his luck in a real barrage, knowing it to be real, was pursuing his own private business in his own private way, testing his horoscope or his saints or his devils when his private timetable said he must. However it came out for him, he deserved respect. But there was nothing to respect about plain blundering.

At other times various Germans came on live, big Jesse Crawford-at-the-mighty-console voices floating in from nowhere, booming in from everywhere. Somebody shouting back from one of the foxholes nicknamed this part of the broadcasts Major Bowes' Amateur Hour, and it did seem as if the Krauts must have had some sort of a talent contest going to see who had the best mike personality. Or maybe they were running tours for their congressmen. *"They don't have congressmen, you jerk."* There were a new voice and a new routine every time. "Hello, fellow soldiers. My name is Kurt Messinger. My home town is a town called Koblenz, probably very much like your home town. I am what you would call an ordinary GI. Choe, just another dog-face, and I'd like . . ." "*Give him the hook!*" "Good morning, brave Americans. I mean that sincerely and humbly. All Germany, like all the world, is deep in admiration today for your brave and valiant defense. That is why the German people again offer you the hand of friendship to go with the praise of the world and the prayers of your loved ones back home and once more invite you as honorable soldiers . . ." "*Bring back the trapeze act!*" "This is the adjutant of *Kampfgruppe Weiser*. I bring the American commanders and their soldiers official and solemn notice that if your useless and criminal continuation of this senseless and suicidal . . ." "*Where does it hurt most, Bud? Your head or your ass?*" "Good evening. They tell me over here that you boys over there may be finding these little greetings too serious. That's the whole trouble with this damned war. Everybody takes it too seriously. That reminds me . . ," "*Holy Jesus, not Bob Hope AGAIN!*"

They saved the music until night. "*I want to buy a paper doll that I can call my own . . .*"

"*Jesus, the Mills Brothers!*" Nearly everybody sang with the Mills Brothers the first time.

"*A doll that other fellows cannot steal . . .*"

There were Glenn Miller and Benny Goodman. "Bugle Call Rag" and "Tuxedo Junction." Bob Crosby's Bobcats and "Can't We Be Friends." "That's Eddie Miller on the tenor sax. THE Eddie Miller."

"*If I had my way dear, you'd never grow old . . .*"

By the middle of the second night no one joined. The weather was still socked in, although the reports continued to be hopeful. During the forty-eight hours there had been three more meals. Hunger was not the chief of their enemies, nor was the cold, nor —although the casualties still grew steadily if unspectacularly— was the shelling. The greatest enemy was time. Time had lost all its refinements and subtleties, all its individual veins and arteries and pores and cells, all its varieties of shade and mood and texture. And yet time was not completely dead. Time still held whatever seed of life and change was left. It will be better when it's dark. It will be better when it's light. But the seed, the only seed, was barren. Time began to lose even the shape of dread. It will be the same when it's dark. It will be the same when it's light.

Two German fighter planes swept in low. "If they can get through, why can't ours?" They left more propaganda leaflets.

"THE DRAFT-DODGERS AT HOME EXPECT
EVERY JOE TO DO HIS DUTY."
"COME BACK, DADDY. I'M SO AFRAID."

There was a special midnight broadcast. "Fellow soldiers, we're all conscious that Christmas is now—how many days away? Have you kept track? In the warmest spirit of comradeship we play you now a song you all love. The words are in German. You all know the tune. . . ."

Then on a tinny, distorted honky-tonk sound track:

"*Stille Nacht, heilige Nacht! Alles schäft, einsam—*"

"Drop dead, you bastards!" A lonely GI voice sobbed a lonely cry of anguish and despair toward the hidden hillside and by some weirdly providential accident the sound track at that instant broke down.

"Carmen?"

"Yes."

"You know that tall soldier that was on the other side of me when we came over the hill?"

"Yes."

"I ran into him when I went to the can. He's talking about trying to get out."

"Uh-huh."

"What do you think?"

"I don't know, Dave. This God-damn' weather can't—"

"I was wondering about Charlie Company."

"Oh hell now, Dave."

"Even if the weather does break I don't see how—"

"You're forgetting the Nineteenth Armored."

"No. I just don't see how—anyway I don't think Charlie Company's even here."

Carmen was silent for a long while.

> And then those flirty-flirty guys
> With their flirty-flirty eyes
> Will have to dance with dollies that are real . . .

327

When Carmen spoke again it was in the lowest of whispers, so low he might have been hoping not to be heard.

"You still awake?"

"Yes."

"You know something?"

"What?"

"I think old Carmen's finally had it."

"I'll believe it when I see it."

"It's a young man's war, Dave. You've got fifteen years on me."

"I still can't keep up to you."

"You won't listen, will you, Dave? I've got trench feet."

Dave breathed more easily. "They don't come on that fast. I've got a spare pair of dry socks."

"On me they come on very fast."

"How do your feet *feel*, Carmen?"

"You like to make it rough, don't you? The truth is, Dave, my feet feel fine."

"Oh."

"Yes, oh."

It was socked in again. "Good morning. My name is Klaus Webber. My home town is a town called Essen, probably very much like your home town . . . Usually we play the music only at night, but since Christmas is so near . . ."

"Stille Nacht, heilige Nacht . . ."

It was not long after the 0800 hours barrage that the senior officer's party arrived. There wouldn't be another stonk before 1100 now. This was always the most active part of the day. Heads popped up everywhere from the little gopher village and a steady trickle of bodies followed them. There was a brisk traffic to and from the latrines that all but the wounded and the totally hopeless cases of shell stupor still made use of. Captain Hector rounded up a burial party for the two men whose trench had been hit in the stonk at 0400. A few men foraged for dry wood and tried to coax fire in or at the edges of their burrows. Here and there a man just got out and walked around for a few minutes, stretching and getting the feel of the morning, or went over to visit with a neighbor.

Although he made it from the eminence of one of the two highest of the hills, the senior officer's entrance was not in itself impressive. Setting an example, he came across the valley at a careful crouching gait and crouched down at the hub of the lopsided wheel of foxholes. He had, of course, removed his officer's insignia and only a few of the men here had ever seen him before, so that the only immediate evidence of his authority was the fact that the two lesser officers who accompanied him followed and imitated his movements and knelt down a little to the rear of him when he knelt and started to speak.

"All right, men," he called out to the gopher village. "Get back in your holes and stay there but come up enough so that you can hear me."

One of his companions bellowed for attention. "This is your commanding officer, men. He has something important to say to you. Colonel Walling, men."

"No, no!" the colonel shouted. "Not commanding officer, men. Senior officer, men. I'm commanding officer of my own regiment. I'm senior officer in this position." His tone was as ambiguous as the words. It was hard to tell whether he meant to rally them to a banner or to disown them.

"Colonel Walling, men! Your senior officer."

"I may have more important news for you before the morning is over," the senior officer called to them. Every foxhole was occupied by at least one head. "What I have to tell you now is that effective this moment, there will be a total cease-fire. In seven minutes a party of not more than four enemy personnel will arrive here, unarmed, under a flag of truce. We have confirmed this by radio contact. That is all I have to say now. Your present order is 'Cease fire!'"

"Cease fire!" the officer who had introduced the colonel shouted more loudly.

Someone threw a helmet high in the air. Someone else began pounding the frozen earth with a mess tin and another waved a gaudy new home-knit scarf. One man tore up a letter and threw its pieces into the murky air, like confetti. There was a scatter of wordless yells.

"Silence!" the colonel shouted.

"Silence!" the other officer shouted.

"There will be absolutely no demonstrations. Either now or later. No demonstrations of any kind. That's an order, men. Any violation will call for very extreme punishment."

"Well, God, Colonel!" someone shouted. "Aren't you even going to tell us who's quitting?"

"That will do!" the colonel shouted.

The Mills Brothers returned, forestalling further speculation.

"It must have been moon glow, way up in the blue . . ."

The Germans marched in two ahead and two behind, very brisk, very correct, their map cases and brief cases as stiff as corset stays. Not looking around, not taking advantage of the opportunity to gather information. The one who carried the white flag had even less expression than the one who was in command. There was just no way of guessing whether the Germans were preparing to surrender or to be surrendered to.

One of the Hectorforce men could not, nevertheless, resist trying. "Yellah sonsabitches!" he called after them across the ground to Dave and Carmen. "They're licked and they know it."

"It's the Nineteenth Armored that did it," another neighbor speculated. "They must have showed up in the night."

"No. It's the air. It's the Forts. Even the Krauts know this weather can't last forever. They know they're on borrowed time."

"You got it, boy! Say what you like, the sonsabitches may be yellah but they're awful smart. They want to do their dealing while they're still alive."

The colonel and his two accompanying officers went back with the Germans. The senior officer and the senior German had saluted simultaneously, offering no hint of which one was on top. As they walked away they were chatting as politely and casually as two professors strolling across a campus. The American, of course, was extremely beat and dirty and the German was so starched and glossy that even he was embarrassed, and slouched a little in sympathy. If anything the difference in their attitudes was somewhat in favor of the American.

When the truce party had disappeared into the woods, the first aborted current of excitement swelled up again. Captain Hector and the major who had greeted Hectorforce at first strolled around the foxholes together, making a point of being on good terms, and reminded the men that there was to be no undue noise but suggested they get out and move around while the moving was good.

"What's up, Major Barker? Can't you tell us anything?"

"Honestly, men, I haven't got a clue."

"What's the score, Captain? Who's doing what to who?"

"You guess, soldier."

Nothing happened for an hour. Then two hours. A medical officer came in from one of the two main hills with three parties of stretcher-bearers, rewound the damp and dirty bandages of the walking wounded, and carried two stomach cases back toward the hill. "Hey, what's it like over there?" someone asked one of the stretcher men. "You got buildings? You got beds or something?"

"You ever been in the Palmer House in Chicago?" the stretcher man said. "No? Well, then there's no use me trying to describe our setup then."

"That's good, Mac. Maybe you could get a spot with that medicine show the Krauts are running. They got lots of talent, but they need fresh material."

The sound equipment was silent throughout the long morning. This in itself was held to be a favorable omen. "The way I see it," a new acquaintance assured Carmen, "if we got the Mills Brothers licked the rest is easy." Captain Hector and the major tried exhorting some of the men to use the chance to improve their foxholes, but no one was buying. In one way or another they were all sure they'd be moving out by nightfall. The only question left was how and where and in aid of what.

At last the senior officer and the two other Americans came back alone, now bearing the white flag themselves. They had been away a long time and they had been very tired when they started out. It was natural for them to return even more dragged out than when they'd gone. Colonel Walling waved the waiting soldiers to come in and stand around him. There was no rushing. They closed in almost shyly. Dave caught Carmen studying the colonel's black, expressionless face for some hint of what was coming. When Carmen saw he was observed he dropped his gaze. He was as flustered as if he'd been caught peeking through a keyhole.

At last the soldiers who were movable—there were closer to three hundred than to two hundred, Dave guessed—were ready to hear.

"Well, men," the senior officer said, "I have no speech to make. I'm surrendering this entire position to the enemy at fifteen hundred hours." He did not wait and it wasn't necessary to wait, for there was no answering sound.

"I've just been on a conducted tour of the German emplacements. I don't know, of course, if they showed me all their guns and other armaments but I do know they showed me a very great deal. A very great deal more than we have now or can—uh—expect by any rational guess or calculation. So far, the German commander assured me, he has been under instructions only to contain this position and neutralize it. He now has new instructions. To liquidate it as of fifteen hundred hours today. You are a small portion only of the American forces isolated in these mountains. There are between seven and eight thousand of you altogether. You know your own situation with regard to rations, ammunition and medical supplies. It is no better and no worse than the situation of your comrades. I wish I had better news for you, men, but I haven't. You will be accorded all the rights and protection of prisoners of war under the recognized articles of war. You should know what your captors have a right to demand of you and what you have a right to demand of them. If you are in any doubt your own officers can help you. That is all I have to say. My deputy, Lieutenant Colonel Karpuck, will take over with the further arrangements. That is all I have to say, men, except, well, except"—the senior officer stiffened and looked to his front—"except God bless you all and God bless America."

Someone tried to start a cheer for the senior officer, for America, for themselves, for the end of their war no matter how sorry an end it had turned out to be. The cheer didn't work out.

The senior officer's chief companion remained behind while the senior officer turned and started back toward the hill.

"You will destroy your personal weapons at once. Break up your rifles and other small arms, bury the bolts and other removable parts along with any unexpended ammunition. Get your gear in order and be ready to march at fourteen thirty hours."

"Ahhh. How do you say 'hurry up and wait' in German?"

The assembly began to disperse under cover of nervous jokes and sullen protests. A man held up his rifle and shook his head. "And they told me you were my best friend!" He took the barrel in his two hands, whirled it around his head, and smashed the butt against the nearest tree.

The lieutenant colonel called them back. "One minute, men. One of your officers has asked whether you're ordered to surrender. No, you're not. Any of you who want to try breaking out on your own between now and thirteen hundred hours, an hour and a half before the—uh—take-over, men, are at liberty to do so. Those who choose to do so may keep their weapons and ammunition or take anyone else's weapons or ammunition. It's a long risk and I don't advise it. Neither does Colonel Walling. Your chances of making it are very slim and if you're caught—well, I think most of you know the difference between an orderly arranged take-over and, well, the same thing in the middle of a pitched fight. Most of you have heard what happened at Malmédy. In any case if any of you are going you'd better go at once and in groups of not more than four or five. By the way, I'm going."

Carmen and Dave sat together on the edge of their foxhole, dangling their feet inside. It was a restful position, a good change from the cramped and aching contortions of the last three days and nights. Now that everything had been settled, a mist of grateful laziness had settled in. Carmen looked down the barrel of his rifle. "Look at that, Dave," he said proudly. "By God, I'll bet there's not a cleaner rifle between here and Washington, D.C."

"You always were good about your rifle," Dave said generously.

"Well, here goes." Carmen stood up. "You want me to get rid of yours too, Dave?"

"Not right now. Not for a few minutes."

"Well, O.K. I don't mind waiting." Carmen sat down again and let his feet droop into the trench. "Dave, you're not thinking—" It was the same slow, hesitant tone he had used in their last long talk, as if he had been driven against his will to start saying something and was stalling as long as he could before finishing, hoping that something would stop him. "Dave, we've talked a lot of crap between us in the last few days. Me more than you. Let's forget the crap. You're not going to find Charlie Company. I'm not going to find Charlie Company. It was a good idea. Now it's a lousy idea."

"I'm scared to stay here, Carmen." Before he was finished Dave knew it had been precisely the wrong thing to say.

"Don't go phony on me, Dave. I know which one of us is scared."

Dave felt an almost irresistible urge to hand his rifle across the foxhole and end this lewd peering back and forth between his soul and the soul of Carmen Ruiz. He'd have given anything, now that it was too late, if he had only made some real attempt, a really deep and honest attempt, to explain how his own permutations of terror had coalesced and run together; how his father and God and Colonel John P. Barnstable in his dress overcoat and Henry Whelan and Henry's and his dead German and, yes, even to some more delicate degree Mary Egan had closed their ranks again and repeated their accusation in unison, still defying him to find an answer. Now the quest for Charlie Company was the only possible answer left. "I'm going to try to break out, Carmen," he said.

"Then what are you waiting for?"

333

"Well, I wanted to say good-by."

"All right. Good-by."

"Carmen, it's got nothing to do with you. What makes sense for me wouldn't make sense for you."

"Stick around, Dave. Stick around and rub it in. Why don't you read me back my earlier speeches? About old Carmen the Square and how he was going to wow them back in Buffalo. My old lady and my rotten little whore of a sister and the lousy spik priest and my St. Christopher medal and the girl with the Lifebuoy soap and the parade they nearly had when old Carmen came marching home. Stick around, Dave, and get your money's worth. You're going to pick up the tab, aren't you?"

"I guess I might as well get moving, then, Carmen."

"I guess you might as well." Carmen grabbed his rifle by the sling, letting it drag deliberately in the muddy snow, and without looking back again moved heavily toward the edge of the woods, to the impromptu dump where other soldiers had begun breaking up other rifles already.

A few men who had made the other choice were starting out, making what farewells they had to make as quietly and unobtrusively as possible. The wall of doubt, envy, shapeless recrimination, and unspoken pledges invisibly violated was as real and palpable as the wall between the outer foxholes and the solid mass of the forest. The partings were laden not so much with anguish as with embarrassment and they were soon over.

Dave hurried, with his head bent low. He had lost his map somewhere during the strange charge of Hectorforce, but the essential information was still fixed in his mind. Jack Kennebec had given him a compass at the last minute before their departure from the battalion. He remembered it now for the first time, dug it out of a trouser pocket, and found that when he unlocked it the needle moved freely, apparently in good order. The putative dwelling place of Charlie Company was almost straight southwest, as promising a direction to take as any. As he passed out of sight of the settlement of foxholes, he crossed a small lateral firebreak, a backstop for the one on the other hill. He started to climb downward and away from the Beautiful and Lonely Mountains. He guessed that he was going parallel to and a little away from the German lines. Now that the surrender was so close, he guessed also that there was neither time nor any immediate need for much caution. He went as fast as the clinging snow would let him.

Not more than a dozen men had gone ahead of them, some like himself all alone, the others in twos or threes, and they had all melted out of sight. He picked up a single set of fresh footprints and without exactly meaning to follow them kept them in view, telling himself this made the going a little easier. He had had some ill-defined feeling that by remaining entirely on his own he might make some sort of atonement for whatever injustice he had done to Carmen, but at the same time the desire to catch up with whoever it was that was ahead grew with the growing forest darkness.

Then, waiting for him behind a screen of spruce branches was Captain Hector—also altogether alone. The captain did not recognize him. "Want to team up, soldier?" he asked without enthusiasm when Dave was within whispering range.

"I came down the hill with you three days ago," Dave whispered.

"Oh. Then in that case." Hector shrugged his thick shoulders and started to move away.

"Wait a minute, sir."

"Sir?" Hector stopped and glared out of the growing shadow. "You trying to start something, boy? This isn't a very good place."

"I'm not trying to start anything. I wouldn't mind teaming up."

"You know what you're asking for?" Hector was still on the defensive but he was less belligerent. "This doesn't seem to be my lucky war."

"Well," Dave said, consoling them both, "if they'd come up the hill to meet you—"

"Us," the other interjected generously. "I remember you now. You were one of the ones that came in just before we started. You had a piece of paper."

Dave tried to explain about Charlie Company and how important it was to go on looking. But as courteously as the captain listened, it became flabby and without point. Without going all the way back to Battle Creek and Ann Arbor he was in the same position he'd been in with Carmen. And he didn't have the eloquence to set it perfectly straight even for himself. "Captain, I'd like to go with you again."

"Well, as far as heading for that ridge, that part's O.K." Hector looked at him more closely. "How would you like to take over?"

"Not me, sir."

"I told you not to sir me. I'm not sir. I got rid of my bars. Since you're picking the route you better be the brass. I'm sick of being the brass. I'm bad news. I had a hundred and seven men start up over that one hill and they kept going. Every time I looked behind there they were and every time they looked ahead there I was. There they were and there I was and then there was everybody in the God-damn' bag. I didn't get them there by acting like some ordinary, everyday heel. No, I did it big and different. Like some clown out of a two-reel movie. My bars. I threw them in a fire. You be the brass. You've got the paper."

Dave waited. Finally Captain Hector shrugged his thick, low shoulders and started walking again. Dave fell in beside him.

Hector stopped and faced him. "Let's have a little spacing, shall we?" He pondered silently for a few moments. "You really aren't sore at me? About that balls-up back on the hill?"

"The balls-up wasn't yours, Captain," Dave assured him.

"Or ours. Maybe you're right. Frankly I never thought there was much to that God-damned major but pure chicken. But you know something? You're the first man who came down that hill with me who's said a word to me since. Voluntarily, I mean."

"There hasn't been much chance for conversation," Dave reminded him.

"You think some of the other guys thought I was O.K.?"

"I think they all did."

"Well, what the hell, let's get going. Watch your space, O.K.?"

The optimist began taking over again. "In the long run, you know, any Krauts in this sector are just as much surrounded as we are. I figure all we got to do is find a place to sleep tonight and maybe—what the hell, there'll be a farm left somewhere, maybe something to eat—and by this time tomorrow . . . How far do you figure it was to where the guys from your outfit are supposed to be?"

"I checked the map. It was about five miles from there."

"All right. Six miles from here." The captain slapped a woolen-gloved hand against a pine trunk. "Christ, soldier, we got it made."

"You damn' right, sir." Dave knocked on the wood of his rifle.

"You don't have to call me sir," the captain said. "At least not now. Maybe when there's another officer around. But for now you might as well call me Corley. What's your name, by the way?"

"Dave Kyle."

"O.K., Dave. Let's get hauling. Only three more shopping days till Christmas."

CHAPTER ELEVEN

Christmas was approaching too on the other side of the ocean—although, due to the time zones, it was not yet quite so near. There too a multitude of things, some without precedent, demanded to be thought about in the crowded days and dreamed of in the lengthening nights.

"He'll have his parcel by now," a million women told themselves. "This will be the last one."

"Would you rather go to the Astor or the Music Hall? The Astor's got Mickey Rooney and a new young girl called Elizabeth Taylor. The Music Hall's got Judy Garland in *Meet Me in St. Louis*. The stage show is The Nativity. They always do The Nativity so beautifully."

"I see Eddie Cantor's got Nora Martin as his special guest."

A senator from Dakota claimed that within the next twenty, "perhaps ten," years the States would be at war with Russia. Gimbel's had reduced the $3.98 blouses to $2.98 and a wide selection of $7.95 blouses to $5.95. A heavy snow fell on New York and the sanitation commissioner explained that his staff had been cut from 11,000 to 8,700 and he had trouble getting spare parts and new tires for his trucks. The new war-bond drive, however, went six billion dollars over the top; as the Bloomingdale ads said they were after all offering $100 at a low and behold U. S. Government price of $75. The butchers of New York proposed to stage a mass strike against the Office of Price Administration and the War Food Administration, claiming that 90 to 100 per cent of their meat found its way into the black market through "5,000 pages of completely unworkable regulations." On the positive side, however, the makers of Walker's gin took large newspaper ads to proclaim that between Repeal and Pearl Harbor Americans bought more Walker gin than any other kind and that, thanks to prudent stockpiling through their contacts in China, Czechoslovakia, Italy, Saxony, Spain and "other sources of top-grade aromatic botanicals essential for fine gin," the Walker people were well prepared for peace. The stock market hit another high. Sugar Stamp 40 was declared valid through February 28, 1945.

There were girls everywhere that year, prancing girls, plodding girls, happy girls, tearful girls, desperate girls, cheerful girls, brave girls, cowardly girls, fat girls, thin girls, lovely girls, ugly girls, sinful girls, virtuous girls, hunting girls, hunted girls, generous girls, greedy girls, German girls, Japanese girls, English girls, Canadian girls, Stateside girls, and only the tiniest percentage of them with their names on marquees or in the radio listings or in the ads for war loans.

One of them, a redheaded one and very comely, walked down a snow-drifted street in a small city in Michigan. She had just come out of church and she went alone at the side of the roadway, not on the sidewalk because the sidewalk was still blocked with last night's snow. She went up the street and then turned and went another block and knocked at a wooden russet-colored door. The people inside were still taking off their things. "I wondered if you might have had a letter yesterday. It's more than two weeks now for me."

"Here, Mary, let me take your coat," the man said.

"No, Mr. Kyle, I have to get back to work. The paper says it's very serious. One of the writers over there says it's the greatest battle in American history. We can't get our planes up, either. I just wondered if you'd heard."

"God will decide about David. David's already decided about God."

The older woman looked up. "You shouldn't have said that, Samuel."

"I didn't mean it in that way, Mary," the man said gently. "He's my son."

The younger one sat down on a big plush chair. "Could I have a glass of water, please? Would you like to see my dress? I made it for him and he was fond of it and I decided to put it on and go to church today."

In a newspaper office in Winnipeg another girl brushed back her green celluloid visor, glared indignantly at a male colleague helping her lean over a teletype machine, and announced severely, "You should be ashamed of yourself."

"I—oh God, Vera, George is one of my best friends. If you'd

get rid of that bloody soap or perfume or that heaven-sent body maybe old buzzards wouldn't be carried away."

"I was looking for the communiqués."

"So, in a manner of speaking, was I. Here's the German one. I don't think we'll use it. It looks as if they're whistling in the dark as usual."

He handed across a sheet of teletype copy.

"Strong German forces, after short but tremendous artillery preparations, launched an offensive from the west wall at 5:30 A.M. and have overrun in the first assault American forward positions between Hohe Venn and the northern part of Luxembourg. The great offensive is taking a favorable course. Details will be announced only later in order not to give information to the enemy, who has been taken completely by surprise."

"What does ours say?"

"The SHAEF one. Wait a minute." He rummaged in a tall cardboard basket. "That damned copy boy threw it away again. Here it is. 'Fighting has increased in the Monschau area,' et cetera et cetera."

"Do you know where Monschau is?"

"Well, not exactly. If it meant anything they'd have censored it anyway."

"What does the *Times* summary say?" Her face was like a marble carving, Aegean, Balkan, white, and full of ancient trouble.

"The *Times* summary is on the floor too. That copy boy is the greatest editor this paper ever had."

"I'll find it."

"No, I will. Here. It says they've gone twenty miles. It says they're a surprisingly strong force. For God's sake quit worrying."

"Could I have the rest of the day off, Mr. Smith? I'm pretty well caught up, there's just a phone check or two—"

"If you want to go somewhere and brood the answer's no."

"No, I want to see someone."

"All right, Vera."

The Parthenon Restaurant had been remodeled and renamed many more times, and now, as Aunt Emmeline's Tea Room, it had replaced the chrome and plastic with chintz and still no customers. "Say vat you vill about Aunt Emmeline," the gentleman opposite sighed, sniffing at his cup, "she serves a wery vigorous brand of tea."

"Have you heard anything at all? If I could only get something in the mail—even if it didn't, even if it doesn't—"

"Wera, stop it now. Aunt Emmeline, a cup of the special for the young lady. Yes, I know where Hazel is. Hosay found her. It took some time but when I told Dorothea that Hosay had to find her he did. In San Diego."

"How long ago, Mr. Massinov?"

"Last week. It didn't make sanse to tell you, Wera, and it won't make sanse for you to tell Geortchie."

"What is she like? You might as well tell me."

"An old beat-up tramp. Just an old beat-up tramp. Do you want to tell him that?"

"Oh, Mr. Massinov. Why do the best men gravitate to the worst causes? He's got poor Hazel and poor Haig and the way I feel now poor me. He bled for Joe Wilson and my poor jailbird father and his own dead father and Sylvia and old Mount Rushmore and for that matter Dorothea and whoever was playing third base for the Winnipeg Maroons and was having bad luck with his batting average—"

"Yes, Wera. And me." The gentleman turned a vast Easter Island face to the teacup, and then he lifted it and gazed out of a pair of ancient brown eyes. "But we both might as well stop vorrying, Wera. You think Geortchie's too good to live. Also it might be he's too good to die. It happens that way sometimes too."

It was a long walk up the tenement stairs, but Gretchen Waldeck was always glad to make it. Frank's mother was always pleased to see her and even his uncle Otto had mellowed with the years. Since the outlawing of the Bund and the conspiracy trials Otto had decided there might be other sides to the question. Perhaps the Führer had forced his hand too much and perhaps the Bund itself had been trapped into errors by the Jews and the communists.

Through those first years they had speculated endlessly. At first Otto had said, "Franz is sure to be in the Wehrmacht. Look how they ran through Poland, look how they ran through Holland and Belgium." Then when America came in and the indictments against the Bund mounted with every week Otto said his nephew must be in a concentration camp. His nephew might have made a few youthful errors, but he'd never fight against America even if they tried to force him at gun point. The FBI questioned Otto two or three times but finally seemed to lose interest in him.

There had been no direct word at all, of course. Letters by the hundred went unanswered or came back unopened.

Gretchen brushed a little melted snow from her cheek.

"Gracie, that's the first time in two years. You promised you wouldn't cry if I wouldn't and—well, you mustn't."

"Jumping Jesus, Hattie, it's Christmas. Let her cry in peace."

Gretchen tried a little laugh and straightened up her snow-brushed curls.

"Hans Boeselager's back from Japan. On special leave. He's had seventy combat missions. He's got, I think it's seven medals."

"Hans was always a fine boy," Otto said.

"He—Hans—Hans has asked me to marry him."

"Oh, Gracie, how marvelous!" Frank's mother came across the little room and embraced her. "When will it be?"

"I don't know. Perhaps not at all. You see I told Frank, and Frank told me—I know it was a long time ago—"

"A very long time, Gracie. Time you forgot him, dear. Not altogether. But in that way."

"I've been reading about this new attack in Belgium."

Otto went to the stove and poured a cup of coffee. His hand shook a little and when he came back his small blue eyes glinted with excitement. "*Ach*, did you ever hear such a thing! One day they're beaten to their knees—the next they're storming back to the Channel! *Ach*, say what you will about Hitler. Say what you will about the German Army—when it starts to march it's mighty hard to stop. I wonder if after all, that young Franz—"

"Otto!" Hattie's admonition was so sudden and ominous that Otto almost dropped the coffeecup. He glanced toward the doorway in alarm, as though expecting spies to burst in.

"But they'll soon see!" he declaimed quickly. "They'll soon see what they're up against! When Uncle Sam makes up his mind to fight—they'll soon see," he finished lamely.

The two women had withdrawn their attention from him already.

"Marry Hans," Mrs. Koerner said.

"If it were only that easy. If I only knew where Franz is, or what he's doing, or what they've done to him. If only—oh, Mrs. Koerner, I said I'd be his girl until he told me I wasn't. He hasn't told me yet."

CHAPTER TWELVE

A new snow was lashing in. They would have to get off the road soon. They'd have been run down already except for a piece of outright luck; the Sherman just behind had broken a tread on a Teller mine. Franz Koerner held his hands close together at the top of the steering wheel, ready to yank suddenly either way.

He hadn't given up yet and he had no intention of giving up. They were at the moment going away from the Meuse, imprisoned in the sluggish heave of the U. S. Army inside which they had successfully lost themselves. But nothing could alter the fact that they had reached the Meuse once and been no more than one blown bridge-piling from getting across and might conceivably if not probably make it back for another try.

The main direction of the Ami traffic, and thus their own, had been reversed and was now from west to east. The chief spearheads of the three German armies had either been thrown back or contained and forced to probe for new gaps and chinks through which to recover their first momentum. Wherever the new attacks and counterattacks led, they were slower and clumsier than in the first days, with none of the dash or excitement or the wild, plunging force. All you could sense in the motion of this Yankee column was the floundering of some dogged beast blinded and impaled and turning in its tracks, determined to die, if dying was needed, with its face toward the slayers. For now at least on this road there was only one way to go and that was where the wounded beast was going. Dangerously, perversely, Franz felt a kind of admiration for this rebellious prey. In a sense these were still his people, and though it was tragic and stupid that they had chosen or been required to die, it was good to see how well they died.

In the first days, when their collapse seemed so complete and abject, he had found himself more than once on the verge of defending the stricken Amis to his two companions. It was well he hadn't. Tannenbaum, who had been growing more disgusted and pessimistic by the hour, could not possibly have profited from any sign of sympathy for the enemy. Lemmering, who had been growing more fierce and silent, burning with impatience and a mounting hate, might have confused sympathy—even the simple uncritical sympathy of one soldier for another—with treason. It was wonderfully reassuring to have another SS man riding in the seat behind him, but it was anything but relaxing.

In the meantime it was neither Tannenbaum's nor Lemmering's mood, but the enemy's, that had become most disturbing. The Sherman that had almost run them down had not been suspicious; it had been something more dangerous than that—impervious to reason. There was no question of checking or arguing over credentials; to the obsessed and red-eyed soldier in the hatch the one point at issue was that there wasn't room on the narrow road for the jeep creeping west and the tank raging east and the tank wasn't turning around or stopping for anyone, friend or foe. For all the Yankee sergeant cared the password could have been "Heil Hitler!" and the counter "Long Live Hirohito!" and the third baseman of the Brooklyn Dodgers might have been Shirley Temple. "Get out of the way!" he'd yelled and gunned his motor and except for the accident of the Teller mine he'd have gone right over them. It was then that Franz had turned around for the second time. There'd be another side road and he'd go around and back and get in behind again. The Meuse was still not so far away.

He made another mental summary of the record they'd have ended with if the mine hadn't given them another of their several reprieves. Their record wasn't sensational, he had to admit, but it wasn't bad, either. In several other taverns, cafés, and village squares they had found and used other opportunities, not unlike the first one back on the first morning, to add to the confusion, apprehension, and divided loyalties of the civilian population. They'd had two more fairly serious skirmishes with small groups of moderately—but not sufficiently—suspicious Americans. The additional casualties to the enemy had not been numerous, but they had been as numerous as they had to be.

They had in addition intercepted and identified a dispatch rider attached to Operation Greif and given him the map reference of a very large American gasoline dump to try smuggling back to their own lines. They had cut a lot of American communications wire. One fortunate morning Franz had stopped at a temporarily unoccupied crossroad, turned the direction signs around, and then, just in time to meet an advancing U.S. division, had put on his MP's gear and stood in the roadway routing the traffic across and away from the direction in which it was meant to go.

Their arrival at the Meuse just as the U.S. engineers blew their bridge had been a disappointment but not a disaster. They might conceivably have slammed across and earned some selfish little niche in the pantheon of heroes, but they could never have held on; by then the Panzers were hung up miles away, and consolidating a bridgehead—on that particular afternoon and that particular crossing—was out of the question. Adding everything together, it hadn't been a bad performance. At the moment, with the Amis climbing up their heels, he hadn't any specific ideas for improving on or adding to it. But at the very least they ought to be able to find some more wire to cut before nightfall and perhaps start back for another try at the Meuse.

"Oh damn!" Now they couldn't move either way, either toward the Meuse or back toward Germany. Ahead of them a troop-carrying truck was half on and half off the road, hub-deep in heavy mud. Two or three GI's walked back from it. Even in the fading light there was an unreal newness to them, an aura of recent shaves and dental cream and Cokes and Doublemint Gum. They strode back so new and fresh that the inside legs of their pants still creaked and swished; they weren't even waterlogged or well pissed upon.

"Having fun?" Franz asked. There wasn't much immediate chance of getting any further message back, but he started fishing just from habit. In a moment he'd have more information than he knew what to do with.

"Fun? Oh, sure." The boy who spoke was full of wise, old-soldier boredom. Very soon they'd tell him the name of their division, which would likely turn out to be the Invincible Eagles or the Crimson Lions and whose number would be forthcoming soon afterward. The sad thing was that if they were Eagles they wouldn't yet have learned that nobody is really Invincible and if they were Lions they wouldn't know that Crimson is not solely the color of flags but is also the color of blood and sometimes very stained and dirty.

"You been up there?" Another of the GI's looked at Franz's shoulder. "Sir?"

"Yes."

"They claim"—like the first one, this boy didn't sound concerned or even particularly cold or miserable; he was still full of ignorance and K rations—"they claim there's some shooting going on."

Erich Tannenbaum had been listening. "That's what they claim," he interrupted with the smallest trace of weary sarcasm, the tiniest hint of vengeful warning. "That's what they claim," he repeated. "They claim there's more shooting up there than you can shake a stick at. They claim several persons have been injured."

Lemmering stirred and grunted. For the last two days he had tensed perceptibly almost every time Erich spoke.

"That will do, Sergeant Foster," Franz said.

"We ain't aiming to shake a stick at it," one of the GI's said. "Hey, it looks like they got our wagon unstuck again." He handed Erich a half pack of Luckies. "Good luck, smart guy."

"Good luck," Erich called after him, stung by an imperceptible pity and remorse for the things they had in common. "I really mean that!" he called again.

One of the GI's stopped and looked at him. He shrugged in puzzlement and walked off to his truck.

Imprisoned in the convoy of bigger, slower vehicles, Franz groped for another hour to find a trail leading out. The snow had let up, but it was now almost completely dark. He decided the only thing that made sense was to stop for the night and wait to see what morning offered. A few hundred yards along the trail, near a shelled-out farmhouse they found a two-stall cowshed. They ran the jeep in behind it, collected some fir branches for sleeping on, and some dry wood for fuel, improvised a fireplace with rubble from the farmhouse, and soon were warm and almost cheerful.

Food had ceased to be an acute problem, thanks partly to the fine talent for scrounging that Erich had developed during his career as steward at the officers' clubs in Paris and Berlin. In the first days the reeling Amis had been, along with their more serious punishments, on the verge of starving, and one of the penalties of their own queer existence—in Erich's rueful phrase—was that when the God-damn' Trojans ran out of grub so did the poor God-damn' horse. But once—as, in one of his rare moments of optimism, Erich predicted they would—the Amis got their messing arrangements under better control, eating became, like politics, the art of the possible. Tonight they ate canned sausage and cheese and slabs of sweet chocolate, courtesy of a well-provided and generous assault-gun crew from Richmond, Virginia.

Despite their almost incredibly high state of comfort, Lemmering was more saturnine and baleful than he'd ever been. Franz asked him once if his Russian wounds were hurting.

"No, sir," Lemmering said. There was nothing wrong with the sir, but the possibility that any Ami could have strayed within hearing of their wilderness bivouac simply did not exist and they all knew it. All the sir did was emphasize the fact that all through the meal Sergeant Foster had been calling the captain Franz and the captain not only had not rebuked him but had called the sergeant Erich. At least, Franz reminded himself guiltily, they hadn't been talking German. Nevertheless the next time Erich spoke to him he said stiffly, "I think, now that this relaxing little interlude is over, we will resume the correct forms of address."

"Yes, sir," Erich said without inflection.

In a while Lemmering asked if he might make a request. Franz said he might. Lemmering's thin, scarred face was without expression as he asked permission to walk back to the border of the main road and observe the convoy for an hour or two. It was a maddening proposal, for there was no really sound reason for making it, and no really sound grounds for refusing it. Behind it was still another reproachful implication—the unspoken charge that here they were, three healthy soldiers of the Third Reich, lying within half a kilometer of an important enemy military formation and preparing only to spend the night digesting an excellent meal beside an excellent fire. For Franz to have protested that it was just as vital to practice adequate military maintenance on their bodies as on their weapons and their jeep would have been to admit that some occasion had arisen for defending his actions to a subordinate. Nor would it have been a satisfactory answer to tell Lemmering bluntly that it was plain damned silly to spy on the convoy by night when they could much more safely ride with it by day. There was always a chance, however remote, of picking up something big. And to suggest that there was any danger Lemmering would betray himself, or them, would have been unfair; Lemmering was perhaps the most efficient and single-minded soldier Franz had ever known, excluding only his former divisional commander of the 12th SS, Standartenführer Paul Raubal. Lemmering just wasn't the kind of soldier who got caught hiding in the trees.

"Let's all go out and do a *Jungvolk* exercise," Tannenbaum

interjected sardonically. "Or let's do something real big and take a few pot shots at the truck drivers."

"When your comment is needed, Sergeant Foster, it will be asked for," Franz said coldly. Lemmering had thrown the merest glance toward Tannenbaum.

"Of course you may go, Corporal Christianson," Franz said to Lemmering. "Be back in no more than an hour and a half. I don't need to tell you that until we find a reasonably important target, plus a reasonably good chance of success, we will do nothing to jeopardize our mission."

"Thank you, sir." Lemmering stood at attention. "I will do nothing to jeopardize our mission."

"What a man!" Erich didn't speak until a whole minute after Lemmering's departure. He was unable to disguise either his distaste or his respect or to conceal a certain shakiness.

"Yes," Franz said, less coldly than before, "he's quite a man."

"Not for instance, like me, sir."

Franz ignored the heavy sir. "What's the use of fooling? He's the guy who's winning the war."

"*If* it's being won."

"It's being won. And it's him that's winning it. Not you. Not me either."

"Oh, come off it. What's the Yankee phrase? Must keep up with the latest, kitchen-tested U.S.A. slang, you know. Brown job? Yes. Come off it, Franz. You don't need a brown job from me. But I can be big. If that's what you want to be told let me be the first to tell you. You're a better soldier than Lemmering ever was."

In Normandy, when he was five months younger, it would have been true. Here—

"What's more, Franz, I might as well do the whole job at once. I think you're even a better German."

Franz looked away into the fire. Erich waited for him to reply and then asked, with the curious hint of solicitude he sometimes displayed at the most unlikely times, "Did I say something wrong?"

"No. I suppose not." For a moment other matters, far-off and highly irrelevant, rushed in on Franz's thoughts. What a strange mixture they made and, even after all these years, what a strong mixture. The crazy but rocklike slant of P.S. 77 leaning down from Eighty-fifth Street to Eighty-sixth. The calm warm slant of Miss Margaret Kelly's green cross-eyes. The dancing blue eyes of Hattie Koerner, not yet troubled, while he plunged down the

347

five flights of wooden stairs to begin another day. "You be a good boy, Frankie." "You bet I will." The Berlin Hofbrau and the Bavarian Bakery and "Frankie, you're at bat!" "I pledge allegiance to the flag of the United States of America and to the Republic for which it stands, one nation indivisible, with liberty and justice for all." "Jumping Jesus, Hattie! The Bund intends to combat all atheistic teachings and all abuses of the pulpit designed to undermine the morals, ethics, or patriotism of Americans. Jumping Jesus, Franz! The Bund exists so that dictatorship of a small, racially and ethnically alien Jewish minority, to which the mind of the entire nation is being rapidly subjected may be broken . . . I tell you, Hattie, the best Germans and the best Americans stand for exactly the same things. Frankie's found it out." I pledge allegiance to Gretchen Waldeck. "Hey, do you think it would be all right to kiss you, Gracie? I mean in front of all the people?" "I think it would be all right, Frankie. As long as you don't make it too long."

Erich Tannenbaum broke in on him, still in the solicitous tone he'd used before. "I'm sorry. I *shouldn't* have said it."

"What the hell are you talking about?" It was a pure reflex, and a savage one, the reflex of a man who has caught a trusted friend snooping in his diary. "Honest to God, Tannenbaum, it's no wonder Lemmering gets so fed up with your half-assed nattering."

Tannenbaum looked away. His refusal to strike back heightened Franz's savage need to strike at him again. He stood up, dark, solid, and menacing, every inch the Hauptscharführer of the elite Schutzstaffel. Erich stood up too, pale and rigid. He too was having difficulty keeping control.

"I don't care how much trouble your clever old-school tongue gets *you* into, Tannenbaum. It's not getting me into trouble if I can help it. It's nearly done it two or three times, you know."

"I believe," Tannenbaum said, "the phrase you've used before is 'jeopardize our mission.' I was interested to hear that you and Lemmering returned to it just now. I recall that the phrase was also current not long before Gotthold Preysing met his—ah, accident."

Franz caught his eyes and held them. Tannenbaum had to look up but his eyes were steady too.

"You're really not much use to this army," Franz said. "I hope you're not quite useless enough to fall on your own bayonet."

"I haven't got a bayonet. Is it all right if I go to bed now?"

"Yes." *I haven't got a bayonet. Why, the cocky little bastard!*

The war might scare Erich to death, but it would never quite tame him. Franz sat down and stared into the fire, waiting for Lemmering. Why did everything, not just some things, but everything, have to turn to ugliness or failure? But no, he argued stubbornly back, not everything, and nothing permanently. Once they got across the Meuse the wounds would all begin to heal. FREE AMERICA! *SIEG HEIL!* FREE AMERICA! *SIEG HEIL!* FREE AMERICA! *SIEG HEIL!* FREE AMERICA! If you want a woman I'm the woman. If you need a woman I'm—I'm not afraid. Gretchen, if you knew how beautiful you are—beautiful in all the time past and all the time ahead—I'll be back and soon. It will all come clear to everybody when we get to Antwerp and Antwerp's where we're going because Antwerp's where we must.

Lemmering came in and said that nothing new was happening on the road. His duty no longer compelled Franz Koerner to remain awake. It was nevertheless still some hours before he slept.

In the morning their hopeful side road disclosed its true identity as a dead-end logging trail, and there was nothing to do but return to the highway and sidle back into the main stream of the American traffic. The night had done little to change its pace, which still reminded Franz more of the last reflex of the quarry at bay than of the headlong coursing of the hunter. The thin metaling of the road surface was now chewed to a total ruin, and along the shoulders the mud was sometimes too thick and holding even for the tanks to manage without help from the engineers. And for every ten or twelve machines that groaned and cried for traction in the mud and ice at least two or three others were dead and black and silent on the verges, wrestled there and left there out of gas, out of petrol, out of benzy, out of Otto, out of essence, out.

By being both quick and patient and skidding, slithering, or bulling through whatever scraps of daylight he could find, Franz kept the jeep going somehow. His map told him there was an honest side road five kilos away and he hoped to make it by noon and have another try at circling back as deeply as he could into the enemy's headquarters, communications, and supply areas. His guess was that they'd be able to change direction again by noon.

The road was heavily policed now, and the only traffic allowed to move against the almost stagnant main stream was a trickle of motorcyclists, a very occasional jeep carrying the stars of at least a major general, and a few grievously toiling ambulances. Franz saw a motorcycle coming back around the fender of a stalled gun-tractor and looking for gangway on a strip of improvised corduroy in the ditch. He thought he would get there first and jammed his foot to the floor. The two vehicles slid to a halt with the motorcycle leaning against the jeep and Franz's chin no more than an inch away from a khaki shoulder. To his only mild dismay he perceived that the shoulder bore the mudstained gold leaf of a major.

"Bloody idiot!"

"Sorry, sir." Nobody was paying much attention to the amenities, but it was better to be safe. "Hope there's no damage. We'll have you out in a jiffy. All right, Sergeant, give the major a hand."

It was only when the motorcyclist had dismounted that Franz got a look at his face. The shock was so stupefying that at first his only reaction was to repeat himself. "Sorry, sir. Hope there's no damage. Hurry up now, Sergeant, and give the major a hand."

A few helpful GI's, passengers in a stalled truck nearby, were already beginning to manhandle the jeep in one direction and the motorcycle in another.

"Hold on a second, boys," the major said. "This is the Goddamnedest coincidence you ever heard of." The major broke into a suddenly familiar guffaw, smoothed his scarf of blue parachute silk, and began fastening one of the top buttons of his combat jacket. "She's a funny war, all right. I was actually looking for you, Captain. Got some new orders for you." Franz was still trying to erase his gape. "Something wrong with you, Captain?" Another guffaw. "You get banged up? Memory hazy? Don't worry. It's happened to a few others. McNair. Remember now? McNair? Joe McNair."

He remembered everything, of course—at first too much to reassemble. The long night at the other roadside, waiting for the guns to start—how far away? how long since? Fifty miles away—no, it had been shrunk again, now back to twenty perhaps. A week ago? Yes, only a week. McNair. Major Joseph McNair of Omaha, Nebraska. Oberst Werner Ziegler of the Wehrmacht, Ziegler-McNair, his final briefing officer and bidder of Godspeed.

"Sorry, sir," Franz mumbled, raising his voice for the benefit of the adjacent GI's. "We did take a bitch of a pasting the first two days. I've been so slow on the uptake I'd have trouble recognizing my own mother." It wasn't a good recovery but it was good enough. "What do you want us to do, Major?" one of the helpful GI's asked patiently.

Ziegler-McNair finished fastening the second top button of his jacket and tucked the blue scarf inside. Franz cursed himself for having made the *Oberst* use the clumsy—and by now perhaps even dangerous—recognition signals. Now he remembered something else: their brief, whimsical dismissal, back on that other roadside, of the third recognition signal. "Rap twice on my helmet?" "On the theory"—Ziegler-McNair's guffaw again—"that you'll be mistaken for a woodpecker."

"Look, Captain." Ziegler-McNair began wrestling his bike around. "If there was any traffic we'd be holding it up. There's a junction about two kilos ahead. When I came past it twenty minutes ago, it was fairly clear. My orders for you are oral and a little complicated so I'd better meet you there. If your driving improves"—guffaw—"I'll see you for a spot of lunch."

Ziegler-McNair was waiting at the rendezvous. He led them down the almost empty side road and across a large logged-off clearing.

"Alone at last!" he guffawed, and then insisted on being introduced socially to each of Franz's companions, both by the *nom de guerre* and the real name. He took off his helmet and put it on the hood of the jeep. "I suggest we all forget our rank for the next hour," he said jovially. "We've got to take time to eat and I've got some things to tell you so we might as well be comfortable."

Lemmering was already hacking down some evergreens to sit on. Erich spread a few cans of rations on the jeep beside the *Oberst's* helmet and began making a fire on the ground nearby. The *Oberst* leaned back against a fender, offered Franz a Chesterfield, and lighted one himself.

"Now, my dear Captain from Manhattan—you don't remember that, do you? You do? I'm flattered. I was rather proud of it, considering the acoustics—give an account of yourself."

Franz ran through a day-by-day summary. He kept it as impersonal and undramatic as he could, less through modesty than a desire to see how an objective report, objectively rendered, would strike an objective audience. The *Oberst* nodded approvingly from time to time, up to the point when Franz said, "We were able to reach the approach to the bridge but their engineers demolished the near piling before we could attempt a crossing."

"*Sieg Heil!*" The *Oberst* made it half a salutation and half a shout of outright glee. "Then by God! Operation Greif *did* get to the Meuse!"

He put both arms around Franz and, in the same vein of military respect mixed with boyish ebullience, kissed him on both cheeks.

"Wait!" he cried. He went over to the saddlebags of his motorcycle and returned holding aloft a bottle of Four Roses whisky. "My most treasured battle trophy. I've been saving it for a great occasion. There will be greater occasions still, but we can't let this one pass." He poured half its contents into a big aluminum cup. And now he was wholly solemn. Lemmering sprang to attention and even Erich stood up. "To the first soldiers of the German armies to reach the River Meuse during the victorious winter offensive of 1944! *Heil Hitler!*"

"*Heil Hitler!*" As the *Oberst* passed the cup, Franz's blood rushed through his every cell and corpuscle in a bursting flame of pride and pure devotion. The *Oberst* clapped him on the shoulder, took the cup away, and handed it to Tannenbaum. When Erich and Lemmering had finished drinking the *Oberst* returned them all to the easier mood of the barracks-town *bierstube*.

"Now I'll give *my* news."

"You have some fresh orders for us?" Franz reminded him.

"Keep your shirt on, *Scharf*. Or I should say Sarge? Aren't you interested in the larger picture?"

Lemmering and Erich had gathered in, their faces as intent as Franz's.

"I see you are. Enough of this loff-making"—guffaw—"but that's another story. It will keep too. The news is good. Sensationally good."

The *Oberst* waited. "I know, I know. You want to ask, 'Then why the hell aren't we in Antwerp?' Well at the risk of losing my head—if good prewar Four Roses can't buy loyalty any more, life isn't worth living anyway—well, I'll tell you why we're not in Antwerp. We're not in Antwerp on account of that fat pig-butcher Sepp Dietrich."

Everybody knew, of course, that Oberstgruppenführer Dietrich, commander in chief of the Sixth Panzer Army, had indeed served behind a meat counter before he emerged—cleaver still in hand, his detractors insisted—to rise through the ranks of the Brown Shirts to a place of eminence in the SS. Everybody knew it, but not many said it, certainly not in the presence of other SS men. Franz intercepted Lemmering's hard stare and asked quickly, deliberately emphasizing the rank, "Did Oberstgruppenführer Dietrich run into unexpected difficulty?"

Ziegler-McNair either missed the hint or didn't care to take it. "Dietrich's difficulty"—this time he was content with a chortle— "is that the ability to make *knockwurst* is not a substitute for military genius. Although he got his attack started on schedule, he was unable to keep dragging his own overstuffed gut, much less an entire army, at the rate the Führer's initial plan required. To be fair to poor old Seppy, the Yanks have been behaving abominably. At first it looked as though Seppy had them completely crushed and overrun on the northern flank. After I saw you on the road I had to go back to headquarters and for a few hours everyone was dead certain we *would* be in Antwerp either on the first or second day. But the Yanks—oh, let's really be kind to Seppy, he'll need kindness from now on—the Yanks and the lousy roads slowed him down just enough to stop us making the coast in that first great bound. And they blew up one huge gasoline dump that Seppy had been counting on capturing and one of Seppy's reconnaissance patrols missed another through plain lousy map reading. And so we didn't get to Antwerp after all on that first wild Saturday. A detail, a detail."

Franz thought he might as well get it over now—get everything over and forget everything. "Then we're licked after all?"

"Licked! Licked! Good God, no! How stupid of me! I'd forgotten how far you've been away from the big picture. I tell you the whole operation has been a sensational success."

There was no trace of jocularity now. "Damn it all, I've been at headquarters right through until yesterday. I've been seeing our own reports, hundreds of American reports—their communications are so fouled up we get their orders and intelligence faster than half their own outfits get them. I've been listening to the B.B.C. and the American overseas broadcasts, reading summaries of what the Allied press itself is saying. Even Eisenhower's communiqués admit at least obliquely that they've taken a stupendous defeat and are still taking it. Oh, they're talking now of successful defense and even counterattacks and all that nonsense. They have to. But I tell you the only essential difference between what the Allies themselves are saying and what the High Command is saying from Berlin is that we say this victory is decisive and they don't go quite that far."

"How decisive?" Franz asked stubbornly.

"Here. Pass the bottle. There's enough for one more toast. You'll remember, my dear Captain from Manhattan, I told you exactly seven days ago that you'd be home for the Fourth of July. I also told you that before the war I was for many years a newspaper correspondent in Washington and New York. Here's to our next drink then. We'll have it in New York. Let's be conservative and make it Thanksgiving Day, and I don't mean some Thanksgiving Day, I mean next Thanksgiving Day, Thanksgiving Day 1945. Where shall it be? Let's combine it with a little sight-seeing and make it Jack Dempsey's on Broadway. A firm date, Captain. No, no"—it was Tannenbaum he was looking at now— "I'm not insane, *Unteroffizier*. I don't expect a complete surrender by the Allies. But this victory gives us back our very vitals—it gives us time! Time to remind the West that Germany is still unconquered and unconquerable. Time above all to remind the so-called democracies that their real enemy is over there on the east. Time to wring an honest and honorable settlement from people who are as sick of the bloodletting as the people of the Reich themselves."

"But none of this works unless we get to Antwerp."

"*Himmel!* What a collection of—here's a new one to use on your next Yank MP—sad sacks! We will get to Antwerp in spite of the slight delay. Even if we don't, all we need to do is hold the gains we've made, force a stalemate through the winter on this front, move a few divisions to the east, hand the Russians a similar haymaker with the other fist, and—"

"I believe you!" Tannenbaum sounded dazed. "By God, sir, even I believe you."

"Oh, if there were only time to tell you all the good news. But we've all got to get back on the road soon, so I can give you only the highlights. But I will hold nothing back. You deserve to hear it all. You reached the Meuse. You three men—by the way there were four men in all the crews."

"Shrapnel," Franz said.

"Ah. Let us toast the gallant absent one. His name?"

Tannenbaum's eyes went from Lemmering to Franz. Neither turned away. "His name was Gotthold Preysing," Tannenbaum said. "As I remember it those were the last words he spoke. 'My name is Gotthold Preysing.'"

"To Gotthold Preysing, then." The *Oberst* resumed his feet.

The others repeated the toast as they drank in turn. Franz felt no twinge of guilt or hypocrisy. They had done what they had to do and for all his self-righteous pretensions Tannenbaum

354

damned well knew it. Franz watched Lemmering drink. For the first time in all their weeks together, a shadow of emotion, a little flicker of something very near to human feeling, crossed the other SS man's lean, scarred face. Again he came to attention. "To Grenadier Gotthold Preysing." For a second the four men stood absolutely silent in the clearing beneath the snow-covered evergreens.

Once again the *Oberst* broke the spell. "How can you possibly doubt that we've got them on the run? Who knows better than you do? Haven't you, yourselves, been roaming among them at your pleasure, devouring them wholesale and sampling their blood like eagles loosed among fat squawking pullets?" The *Oberst* allowed the guffaw full rein for the first time in half an hour. "You must forgive my purple prose, Captain. I told you I'm a journalist by trade; got to keep my hand in, you know. Let's, however, forget my exaggerations and the evidence of your own eyes. Let's say, for the sake of argument, that at this level here, the level of man against man and tank against tank, we have been temporarily checked. Let's go back to the seats of the mighty. The Allied command has been split wide open already. Montgomery, whom the Americans detest, has been brought down from the north to take over the operational control of Bradley's armies. Leaving aside the military mess this has created it's the worst blow for Anglo-American relations since the Boston Tea Party.

"Ah, those poor American generals." The *Oberst* chuckled. "Their country does not provide overnight headache cures for its unlucky military figures. Poor General Bradley. Poor General Patton."

The *Oberst* looked at his watch.

"I must take an extra minute to tell you about poor General Patton. He was forced to break off his attack in the Saar to come to Bradley's rescue up here. A tragic blow to his hopes of immortality; they say he had planned to end the war singlehanded in his Saar offensive. But this is not the most affecting thing about the recent career of General Patton."

The *Oberst* fished into his pocket. "This is so priceless I had a copy made. It was picked up a couple of days ago on a prisoner from Patton's army at a town called Wiltz, a hundred kilos or so south of here. It seems that just as our offensive began Patton had concluded that God wasn't pulling His weight for the Amis. So he issued a typical instruction: a special prayer circulated to

355

every member of the U. S. Third Army with firm orders to pass it on to God, like a letter to his congressman."

The *Oberst*, grinning hugely, read from the paper: "*Almighty and most merciful Father, we humbly beseech thee, of Thy great goodness, to restrain these immoderate rains with which we have had to contend. Grant us fair weather for Battle. Graciously hearken to us as soldiers who call upon Thee that, armed with Thy power, we may advance from victory to victory, and crush the oppression and wickedness of our enemies, and establish Thy justice among men and nations.*"

Tannenbaum seemed almost as pleased as the *Oberst*. "In Eisenhower we trust," he chuckled, "but let's keep Jehovah warmed up just in case."

"Eisenhower! Now there *is* a tragic case. Thanks to a few calculated security leaks, the word got back to SHAEF just before the kickoff that Oberst Skorzeny was preparing another of his famous private parties. The notion was allowed to trickle through that the target this time was nothing so trivial as a Mussolini or a Horthy. It was Ike himself! Well, you can imagine the flap behind the Yankee lines when honest young tourists—like yourselves—from the Wehrmacht and the SS began floating down from the sky in Yank uniforms and driving through in Yank jeeps and opening up their guns from Yankee tanks. Our agents in Paris tell us the bodyguard around Ike these days is so thick he needs a second bodyguard to clear the way to the latrine."

"The Arimaspian!" Tannenbaum's ejaculation was a cry of pure joy. He grinned at Franz, willing to forget anything in the exuberant, crazy memory. "'As when a gryphon thro' the wilderness, with wingèd course, o'er hill or moory dale, pursues the Arimaspian.' Sorry, sir."

The *Oberst* had been caught quite off guard. "Some other time," he muttered. His manic mood had been diluted by the baffling interruption. He looked at his watch once more.

"Well, then, here are your orders. Operation Greif is terminated."

He held up his hand, signaling that rank was once more fully in effect and he wanted no more interruptions. "No. No. Greif has not been a failure. It has accomplished many of the things it set out to do and has succeeded less well in others. If Oberstgruppenführer Dietrich"—the tone now was firmly respectful—"and his gallant Sixth Panzer Army had not run into such stubborn resistance, the main forces of Greif would have vaulted through and seized the crossings of the Meuse, as planned. But that proved impossible. The Skorzeny brigade has been disbanded. It is already being reincorporated into the regular forces."

Franz could not take it all in. After the *Oberst's* heady saga of the last hour this anticlimax had the stunning force of a shell concussion. The *Oberst's* voice went on, but it was nothing like any voice he had ever heard before; it might have been Kobold or a Troll calling from the depth of the forest in the muffled language of incantation.

The *Oberst* listened silently to a long rumble of gunfire not far ahead.

"You will proceed as fast as possible toward our own lines. At the first opportunity you will cut back around the lines, using the infiltration tactics that got you here. Except on and immediately beside the main roads, the division between the armies is still very fluid and uncertain and you should have no more trouble crossing that way than you had in crossing this way. You will surrender to the first German formation you meet. Are you listening, Captain?"

Franz lifted his head.

"You will have no trouble establishing your identity." There was just the hint of a jest again. "If you could persuade the Yanks that you are Yanks you can surely persuade the Germans that you are Germans. You'd better attend carefully, Captain. I have no intention of repeating this."

"Yes, sir." Franz had barely heard the nearby guns, but the *Oberst's* words still left a clubbing echo behind his temples.

"Demand to be taken to the nearest corps headquarters and from there to the nearest army headquarters. You will be reassigned immediately to new duties."

"Yes, sir." The residual shock waves were fading now. There were no Kobolds hidden in the forest, no dark gnomes calling out in mockery. It was not some ghastly trick of imagination. These were real words that he was hearing.

"I must emphasize the need for speed. Every man is needed in his proper place; in addition it no longer suits the general plan to have German soldiers in enemy uniform roaming around inside the enemy lines and subject to the risk of capture. Well, that's about it. I've got to go and see who else I can round up. Most of the other crews are already back and fighting with regular divisions. None of them got as far as you did. None of them did better. Good work and good luck. I'll see you at Jack Dempsey's."

"I'll see you at Jack Dempsey's," Franz said dully.

"Now see here. The German armies can't afford quitters, now above all other times. Snap out of it, Captain!"

"Quitters?" Franz said. "There are no quitters here."

"I know there aren't. I tell you, Captain, it's been a picnic and it's still a picnic. You see that rise of hills right ahead of you? That's where you'll be going. That's where you'll re-enter the German lines. Let me tell you about two little actions that took place there within the first few days. And remember: things like them have been happening, everywhere all along the front, dozens of them, scores of them, every day. The main mass of those hills is called Die Schoenen und Einsamen Berge. In case you're stopped by the Yanks again, the translation they use is the Beautiful and Lonely Mountains. Do you know what happened there the other day? Two whole regiments of Yanks were captured in one single haul. Eight thousand men, according to their own admission. In all the military history of the United States of America there has only been one greater mass surrender—Bataan. That's already admitted by their own newspapers."

Franz wanted desperately to encourage and support the *Oberst* now, but all he could muster was an inane "Of course."

"This is less exciting. I mention it only to show you again how close the Allies have come already to the bottom of the barrel. Just to the left of their position there's a little tucked-in village. A few nights ago a large Allied patrol blundered into the village square right under the guns of our First SS Division. It was, of course, like shooting fish in a barrel. Our boys think one or two might have escaped, more likely none. Here's the significant thing. Do you know who those Allied front-line soldiers turned out to be? Front-line, hell! They were ahead of the front. They were log cutters from somewhere in the Canadian bush!" The *Oberst* essayed an outright laugh. "And even that's not so unusual. To the feeble extent that they've held together at all, half the enemy outfits have been held together by cooks and clerks and drivers, anybody the battalion and company commanders can lay their hands on. A picnic, Captain! Let's get moving again, shall we?"

He held out his hand. Franz did his best to meet the *Oberst's* eyes fully, but his own eyes fell away. There was a new feeling between them; not exactly shame, more like old-fashioned prudery or reticence, as though at an unexpected confrontation of naked-ness. Now it was the other man who hesitated.

"I see."

His voice was sad and there was just the smallest trace of pleading in it. Franz could make no response.

The *Oberst's* voice grew hard and bitter and he spoke this time in German. "You have your orders, *Hauptscharführer*. Carry them out. I have only one last thing to add. You think I've been exag-gerating, romancing, lying. Dangerous occupations all of them, *Hauptscharführer*. When you make your report I would not, if I were you, bother reporting that you reached the Meuse. The fact is that you didn't."

"What—"

"If you had studied your maps more carefully you'd have real-ized it wasn't the Meuse but a tributary called the Salm. An im-portant tributary. But not the Meuse."

Obersteutnant Werner Ziegler of the Wehrmacht, alias Major Joseph McNair of Omaha, Nebraska, turned toward his motor-cycle. "I intend"—he returned to English—"to be in Dempsey's restaurant on Thanksgiving Day. The invitation is still open. Good luck."

Night stopped them again. As they struggled down the main road once more, the density of traffic diminished steadily. All through the late afternoon shells came lobbing in from the hills ahead. It was unorganized fire and wholly undramatic, just enough to bite off a vehicle or two here and there or chop a new crater in the ruined road itself. At dusk a hastily planted but awk-ward field of Tellers covered by a hull-down Panther halted the head of the column entirely, and word came back that forward movement would cease until 0700 hours. The regular units and the jerry-built, *ad hoc* battle groups that hadn't already peeled off to seek more room for deployment on the chancy lateral roads found what shelter they could among the trees.

This time Franz and his crew weren't so fortunate as to find ready-made cover. They did, however, manage to wrestle the jeep well beyond the ditch and throw a lean-to of green boughs against it. They divided their second-last tin of canned pork and stretched out close together, Franz in the middle. Lemmering was asleep at once; if it hadn't been so foreign to his flinty nature he might have been suspected of showing off, of reminding them subtly that until you'd wintered on the Russian front you didn't know what winter meant.

There was no way of amending or repealing what had been said the night before, and nothing was to be gained in trying. If only as a military duty, nevertheless, Franz had to let Tannenbaum know two things. First that he himself had recovered at least partly from their afternoon with the mercurial Ziegler-McNair and was doggedly rebuilding his morale. Second that, whatever harsh things he had blurted out before, he hadn't written Tannenbaum off as a soldier.

"I'll tell Lemmering before we start out again." It was his semi-parade, semifraternal tone. "The Amis are obviously getting ready to mount a full-scale counterattack. If we're going to get back to our lines we've got to get back before it starts. If we're stopped again we won't waste much time arguing. I want an instantaneous signal to open fire. The signal will be when I clear my throat. O.K.?"

"O.K. When you clear your throat we start shooting."

"No questions? We may have a very rough day ahead of us."

"Don't bother, Franz. So far as I'm concerned they've all been rough days. As you so cogently pointed out."

"You know damned well what was eating me last night." That was much further than he should have gone, but he went even further. "If you hadn't known what was eating me I wouldn't have gone berserk."

Tannenbaum did not reply for a moment. Then, without directly changing the subject, he went around its flank.

"That *Oberst!* What a shortchange artist! One minute we were at the Meuse, the next right back on the Rhine. And that son-of-a-bitch Skorzeny! One day the Arimaspian o'er hill and moory dale; the next day"—Tannenbaum huddled into his own corner of the cold and menacing night—"this."

It occurred to Franz that someone might be close enough to hear. But there had been no nearby movement in the surrounding trees and Erich's familiar imitation of the forlorn and betrayed but secretly all-wise clown had a sad appeal that he could not bring himself to reject.

"For a while there, after the second drink, I could actually smell Paris again and I could not only see the lovely Yvette, by God I could *feel* her! And Berlin! And Else! I wonder if the lovely creature ever did let that bloated tub get to her? No. No. God simply would not allow such a thing. Else, of course, did have a somewhat overdeveloped sense of the practical, but no! no!—I must not even think of it."

Erich began half humming, half singing a reprise of the far-off evening in the far-off barracks room. "'*Allons les enfants*—' did I ever tell you about Francine?"

"Yes. The one in Brussels."

"*Le mot juste. The* one. Occasionally, in spite of the disadvantages of your background, you display a nice streak of sensitivity. The bastard made it sound pretty easy, didn't he?"

"What do you mean?"

"In spite of what he said, the mines will be as thick as the pine cones. There'll be one of theirs behind every spruce tree and one of ours behind every fir. And do you know what their united and holy purpose will be? To see that neither the fair Yvette nor the fragrant Else nor the incomparable Francine shall ever again—did I ever tell you about my father?"

"Let's get to sleep, Erich. There's nothing to worry about, we'd better get to sleep."

"A remarkable man. It's unfair to say that *they* destroyed him. They merely supplied the occasion. He destroyed himself. You should have seen him cast a trout fly, though."

Franz reached out and put his hand on Tannenbaum's shoulder. "See you in the morning, Erich."

Erich sighed, even his desolation all used up. "All right, then. See you in the morning, Franz."

Franz tossed restlessly on the evergreen mattress. There was something else he still had to do before morning came, another kind of preparation for another set of circumstances. If he had been able to do this other thing at any time in the last three years, he would have done so, but the command to stop trying to write had not been one to trifle with. To have disobeyed would have been disloyal and moreover dangerous—perhaps as dangerous, almost, to her as to him.

But now the thing he weighed seemed to bear no hazard to anyone—or none beyond the end of wondering and worry. If he were in a position to do so by the next nightfall, by the time he was back inside the German lines, he could tear the letter up and no one would be damaged. If not—well, if not, he himself would be beyond further harm, he would have no power to soil the blood or betray the honor even by accident or by sentimental folly. More important, the letter might help repair or at least conclude any harm she might have suffered through any sentimental folly of her own.

The calculation was made methodically and he put it into effect methodically. He removed his loose-leaf notebook from a jacket pocket, opened it at two blank pages near the back, turned on his small flashlight, and began writing with the U.S.-made pen they'd given him with his original camouflage kit.

On one page he wrote simply:

To Whom It May Concern:
As this is written I have no way of telling whether it will be found by a German soldier or an American soldier. As a soldier I ask that the note on the following page be forwarded by whatever means may be permitted to the address below, although I realize this may not be possible until after hostilities have ended.

It took a moment to remember the street number. He hesitated for a moment, with the Eveready light suspended over the Eversharp pen, wondering whether it would be best to begin "Dear Gretchen" or "Dear Gracie."

In the sludgy dawn an infantry lieutenant from Des Moines stuck his head out of a foxhole and did his best to dissuade them from going on.

"Look at that sky, Captain."

"I don't see anything. It's the same sky."

"No. It's thinner. Away thinner. They've been predicting a break for a week. Today's the day. Today's the day the gallant knights of the wild blue yonder throw away the empties, button up their flies, and get back to work. You wait here, Captain."

"I wish I could. But there's a whole regiment of artillery lined up right behind us and they're too short of ammo to do a map shoot. Until I get an observation post set up they're as useless as the Air Force has been."

"I tell you, Captain, there are still a lot of Krauts in that bush. If that's all you need to know, take my word for it."

"How far away?"

"Maybe a mile. Maybe less. Give the air a chance to clean them out. I hear there's two more infantry divisions moving up right behind us. My battalion got two thousand gallons of gas last night, the first we've seen in a week. We got ten dozen new tires. Give the war a chance, Captain. You don't have to win it by yourself. I don't have to win it by myself. Not any more."

"I know."

"Just wait a couple of hours, Captain. This is the end of the line. The country ahead is theirs. Anybody you see from now on will be either a Kraut or a lost GI."

"Thanks. But I've got a very narrow-minded CO. He likes me to do what he tells me."

"Well, then—Jesus! If I ever make another crack about the gunners! Go get 'em, Captain!"

He had decided to stay with the jeep as long as possible. For one thing it was a valuable piece of equipment; more important, if they moved together, openly, and with no attempt at concealment it might simplify the mechanics of surrender when they reached their own lines again. A narrow but passable loggers' skid road led up the rise ahead toward what he guessed must be the first main slope of the mountains. A quarter of a mile beyond the outpost of the American lieutenant he stopped and draped a square of white silk across the hood.

It was now 0715 hours, still very early in the heavy gray shadow of the forest. A few individual guns were firing a mile or so to the south and east—sniping probably, or ranging in. There was nothing organized, nothing resembling a barrage.

"Do you think it's really going to clear, Franz?" Erich asked. "Do you think their bloody air force will start up again just when we get back home?"

"How the hell should I know?"

Lemmering now asked a question.

"The white flag. If we run into Yanks, will it not confuse them?"

"Probably. Take your safety catches off. And remember your signal."

It was another half mile before they met the Canucks. Franz would have recognized them at once as either Limeys or Canucks from the washbasin shape of their helmets and the droopy cut of their battle-dress trousers. The little round gun their officer held before him like a thank-offering was the first Sten he'd seen since the weeks in front of Caen.

There were four of them, the officer and three others. They emerged together into the center of the trail like black ghosts summoned from a spell and stood there as if still unable to cast the spell aside.

Uncertain men had become a commonplace now. So had men with gaunt cheeks, matted, filthy beards, and staring red eyes, but these four were as spent and beaten as any soldiers Franz had seen since the last days at Falaise. The officer was trying to make some show of assertiveness by maintaining his wavering Sten gun in a position something like the ready. Of the other three men one suddenly sank to his haunches in the snow and put his head between his arms. Of the two who remained standing the taller one supported the shorter with one arm, but each of them kept a grip on his Lee-Enfield, balancing it near the trigger guard. The smaller one had a caked khaki bandage over one eye and he was blinking hopefully with the other eye. The officer remained transfixed and it was the bandaged soldier who spoke at last. When he did so the North American accent was unmistakable.

"Who are they, George? What is it?" His tone was that of a bewildered but trusting child and he lifted his head and blinked again.

The tall soldier made an almost invisible movement with his rifle, sliding his hand an inch toward the trigger guard. "It's all right, Haig. It looks as if we're there. It looks as if we're all right now. They're Yanks."

Franz kept one hand on the wheel and the other on the butt of his Tommy gun, out of sight beside the seat. He did not want to be the first to create any new movement or sound. The officer was still frozen behind his Sten.

The tension was now so great that Franz decided that the lesser risk was in speaking. "My God!" he said, putting as much admiration and pity into it as he could. "And we thought *we'd* had it rough."

At first the officer merely continued to stare and Franz thought he might be incapable of speech. When he did speak the voice, though weary and cracked, contained a wholly unexpected trace of indignation.

"Who are you?"

"Artillery recon. What say we put down that gun?"

"What's the white flag for?"

"I guess you haven't heard. Peace is breaking out all over. Suppose you tell me who *you* are."

"Canadian Forestry Corps. Where are your lines?"

"Just back there, pal. No more than half a mile. You're all fixed up O.K. now. There's a dressing station that will take care of your friend. It's pretty well all over but the shouting."

"Who won?"

"You know damn' well who won. We won. We were always winning."

"Then tell me some more about the flag."

"Now look, Mac. Things are moving pretty fast around here. I just can't stick around to give you the whole story. Suppose you put down that gun and move on back. That boy needs attention. I think you all do."

"You're right there. Let's put my three boys in your jeep and we'll all go back together."

"I would if I could. There's nothing I'd rather do. But I've got a date to keep with a Kraut surrender team. Put the gun down."

"Do me a favor then, will you? Just for my peace of mind. Say this after me. Say this. *Where in the wide world is the western wilderness?*"

"Gladly." Franz felt a great surge of relief. "Why didn't you say you thought we were the Katzenjammer Kids? *Where in the wide world is the western wilderness.* Okay now?"

"Just about." The Canadian officer moved his head in the direction of the back seat, where Lemmering had leaned forward into the gap between Franz and Tannenbaum. "Let's get him to say it now."

Lemmering had never been worth a damn on his *v*'s and *w*'s. Franz looked past the officer to where the taller soldier still held the short one on his feet and they both still gripped their rifles. And then, almost apologetically, as though he were in a drawing room and realized it wasn't quite the thing to do, he began clearing his throat.

CHAPTER THIRTEEN

Just before they met the jeep, Haig had fallen back and stopped and George had gone back to get him.

"I'm tired, George. I think I'll sit down."

"No."

They went a few feet more. Earnshaw was ahead and Wuorio was behind him. Earnshaw fell once more, but as he fell he lifted the Sten over him, free of the snow. Then he put his other hand ahead and pushed himself up.

"I'll just sit down for about ten seconds," Haig said. "Ten seconds, that's all. I'll count. One—two—"

"Haig, I swear to God, I swear that once we get over that rise—"

"I'm going to sit down."

"No, you're not."

George had stopped speculating about the limits of endurance. Once, somewhere around yesterday, he'd thought he himself was done, but some streak of pure malicious pride forced him to take one more step and then two and then he knew he'd go on, if he had to, forever. I'm the best man here, this self-admiring voice lectured him, and if nobody else quits how can I? It was a simple case of mind over matter.

The matter, it had to be admitted, was growing less impressive. Wuorio had always cultivated and paraded his gauntness as an expression of class pride; on one famous occasion back in Scotland the sergeant-cook had turned up three eggs a man for a Sunday breakfast and the Red Finn had refused to eat a single one, attributing his self-denial to Stalingrad. Now he was as lean and bony and dirty and ugly as a fire-charred spruce trunk. Even Captain Earnshaw, who had always had a weight problem, had grown so skinny that his battle dress hung from him like soggy washing. Haig looked even worse. The shell had landed right at his feet and the blast had done something to his eyes. He could see a little out of one, but the other hurt badly even though there was no blood. Earnshaw had put his scarf around it.

"You're O.K.," Earnshaw had assured him.

"Sure," Haig had said, and stumbled on.

That was a very long time ago. They slept when they could, when they had to. They dug holes in the ground and put ever-green branches in them and partook as best they could of the warmth of the earth. They huddled up spoon fashion, as the loggers had done a hundred years ago in the Ottawa Valley.

After the second day they had no food at all. "I have no intention of starving to death," Captain Earnshaw said. "I'm told you can go thirty days. We'll just have to forget about food. We won't talk about it and we won't think about it." Snow was plentiful for drinking.

"Captain Earnshaw," Wuorio the Red Finn said, "have I your permission to make a remark?"

"Yes, Wuorio."

"You've got rocks in your head."

"We'll just postpone the arguments, Wuorio. Keep moving."

"Suppose I don't?"

"It would be a serious violation of King's Regulations and Orders. An extremely serious violation."

In addition to the chancy shot that blinded Haig they ran into one full-scale artillery barrage. A machine gun had them pinned down for one whole day and on another day they hit a patrol of German riflemen as lost as they were themselves. They traded eight or ten shots and the Germans broke it off. It was then that George realized he would go as long as anyone else.

Once they came down a little draw and ran into four men in GI uniforms. Wuorio burst into tears. George put his arms around Haig's cold and trembling shoulders and Earnshaw walked on ahead. Then the other men started shooting. Their aim was no good at all, they were paralyzed with the cold. "They're Krauts!" Earnshaw yelled. George threw Haig to the ground and fired back.

"Where are they, George? Tell me where they are."

"Right there, Haig."

Haig had got to his knees. His scarf was trailing down to his ribs and his rifle was wound up in it. "George, I can't see them. I can't see them at all."

"They're gone anyway."

The sounds of battle kept calling them and then receding. Once they were within two or three hundred yards of a squad of tanks. The tanks were so close they could hear their individual noises.

"Four," Captain Earnshaw said.

"Yes," Wuorio said, "and they're Panthers."

"We'll go and see."

Even Wuorio did not dispute the decision to go and see the tanks. By now the spell of human gravity drew them to any sign of habitation, to any emanation of life or death. But the tanks suddenly broke away from the clutch of the forest and they never found them.

"Haig, are you all right?"

"No, George. I'd like to sit down. I'm tired."

Captain Earnshaw scooped up a handful of snow and then tore some twigs off a fir tree. "Eat them slowly," he said.

"Captain Earnshaw," Wuorio said, "I'd like permission to make another remark."

"That's all right, Wuorio. You can quit talking like a barracks-room lawyer."

"I withdraw my previous remark."

"Your previous remark is already forgotten. Keep moving."

When they heard the jeep Earnshaw signaled them to stand still. Then, when the jeep kept coming down the firebreak he waved them out.

Earnshaw was an unusual man. He shouldn't have been able to hold his gun up at all, but he had it high enough that the men in the jeep at first simply stared. The one in the driver's seat asked him to lower it, but Earnshaw kept it high.

"Who are they, George?" Haig asked.

"They look like Yanks."

Wuorio dropped to the ground and started being sick.

The driver kept asking Earnshaw to put his gun away, but Earnshaw got into an argument about the white flag on the hood of the jeep. Earnshaw had turned out to be a totally different person from the amiably boozy companion of Ben-y-Gloe. He was very hostile; now he launched a long word game with the man in charge of the jeep and George felt for his trigger guard. Halfway through the game he knew for certain that the captain's suspicions were right. He had his man picked out, the thin, mean one in the back seat. Earnshaw, he was sure, would take the one he was talking to. The one in the other half of the front seat would have to wait.

Everything stood still for a second and then the driver coughed and grabbed his gun from beside the seat. Earnshaw fired high and late and the driver's first shot hit him in the chest. In the cold still air the sound was like a breaking tree. George hit the thin mean man just as he hit Wuorio the Red Finn.

The second man in front was only ten feet away but he fired above George's head. George fired back and hit him.

Then his rifle jammed. He had done his best to look after it, but the trigger would not move. The big man who had been driving flung himself out of the jeep and then slowed down and finally stood as still as a statue behind his Tommy gun.

There were only the three of them left of the seven, George and this big man in the U.S. captain's uniform behind the Tommy gun and Haig, standing blind nearby, with his rifle in the snow where he had dropped it in the first eruption of shock and terror.

The dark face was set and angry and the short submachine gun swung a little to the left, preparing to spray across George's chest and then on to Haig in one fluid, foolproof burst.

"Get in behind me!" George yelled at Haig. With a cry of foolish, final defiance he hurled his useless rifle toward the Tommygunner's face and began a useless lunge.

But Haig, who must still have seen their shadows through his blindness or somehow found the line of fire with his ears, was quicker and more unexpected. A microscopic infinity ahead of the quick geometric crack-crack-crack he threw his body between George and the darting muzzle of the gun. The bullets straightened him and drove him back into George's arms and the two went down together.

The gunfire stopped as abruptly as it had begun. George floundered to his knees just in time to see his brother's executioner tear an empty clip away from the Tommy gun, stare at it in resentful disbelief, and then turn and run off into the trees.

He went and knelt for a moment beside the bodies of Haig and Earnshaw and Wuorio and then he went and looked at the two dead Germans sprawled inside the jeep. He realized gratefully that he was acting on pure reflexes; he was conscious of no feeling except an urge to keep all feeling at bay, no thought more profound than the thought that where the destroyer of his brother and his friends had gone he must go too.

He took a few steps down the roadway to where Haig had dropped his rifle. He checked the clip and discovered it was full, fired one shot into the ground to make sure the rifle itself was working and then lurched into the trees, following the footprints at a wavering dogtrot.

CHAPTER FOURTEEN

The last thing Hector spoke to Dave was a warning.
"Don't trust any of them. Don't even trust me."
"No, I think I'll trust you. If I don't, where am I?"

In a while there was a sound of movement close by. Hector signaled Dave to stay where he was and then went on alone.

There was a frozen crack of small-arms fire and after that a tremendous jarring silence. Dave groped through the trees, too sick from the constant presence of disaster to worry about being careful. But he could not find his friend. He lost the footprints in a tangle of alder and underbrush, discovered himself flailing senselessly at a clutching wilderness, then shouted, then put his hand up to stop his shouting.

He went for the rest of the day on a compass bearing, not making any real time at all, not especially caring whether he did or not. He was moving to keep alive, not in the hope of finding friends. At dark he found a little depression in the snow where an animal had slept the night before. There was a deadfall tree above it and he tore some boughs from the nearby pines and went somehow to sleep, with the animal's scent around him like a cloak. When another morning came at last he didn't particularly welcome it and he didn't resent it, either.

With the loss of his religion he had lost the solace of fatalism, but now his fatalism at least returned. This was going to be his last day on earth. The belief had nothing of the occult in it and, so far as he knew, no trace of Christian resignation. It was simply a question of mechanics, of the technical capacities of the instruments that kept him going, the fading heart and the failing muscle. It was all very well to speculate on the x factor of the human will and how it could upset all other speculations, but in the long run —in this case on the last day—it came down to uncomplicated, unavoidable high-school physics and chemistry.

That was really what had stopped Carmen: physics and chemistry, rather than the manifest defects of his manifestly defective soul. If he had been able to hit that batting-practice pitcher, perhaps Carmen, whatever his taints of character, would still be here. If the mix of Captain Hector's genes had impelled him less to recklessness, perhaps he'd be here too. In these reflections Dave felt no virtue and no comfort, just something of fairly minor interest to mull over while he proceeded on his last day.

He still meant to go as long as he could, and as the morning light, the cruelly late light, pointed down among the trees he sat and looked around. Then, not far away, there was another eruption of small-arms fire. Dave started toward it, yielding without question to the tidal pull of another human presence.

He heard the other man crunching through the trees. He watched until the other man was almost on top of him.

He was a tall man, wearing the uniform of an American captain. Dave greeted him joyously, because he was another soldier in trouble, but also with prudent deceitfulness. "*Achtung!*" he yelled. The other man looked in quick bewilderment into the trees, saw nothing, and dropped his gun. "*Kamerad!*" he yelled.

When Dave stepped out the other man laughed. "You're a Yank! My God, when you yelled '*Achtung!*'"

"Yes, I'm a Yank. Who are you?"

"The same. My God, you haven't got a cigarette, have you?"

"Who are you with?"

"Arty recon. It was sure a great reconnaissance. A few miles more and we'd have been in Poland."

"Was that your shooting I just heard?"

"Some of it."

"What happened?"

"We ran into some Krauts. They're all around the place."

"Did you lose anybody?"

"Yes, three."

"Let's go and find them."

"The hell with that. The place is lousy with Krauts."

The big man reached down to pick up his Tommy gun.

"Don't do that," David said.

"Why not? It's empty anyway. Otherwise," there was a note of pride and apology in this, "you don't think I'd have dropped it, do you?"

"I still don't know who you are."

"What do you mean? I don't know who *you* are if this is a debate."

"It's not a debate. Let's go over and see what was left behind by that shooting."

"No, that would be crazy. One of the Krauts got away. He's waiting there."

"Just a minute."

Dave looked upward through the white treetops and for the first time, because the heavy, far-off droning had drawn him there, he noticed that the sky had a new color.

"It's opened up!" he yelled.

He could see them far above, high-flying planes, big ones, Connies, or Forts most likely, wave after wave of them flying in gleaming V's, and behind them and far below a noisy strike of fighter-bombers. He hadn't seen so many planes since the other side of the Seine.

The big ones must have dropped their load almost directly above because the great terrible pounding began not more than three or four miles ahead and although they could not see the stuff the planes were still in sight when they circled back for home. But the bombers alone never won over the infantry or the tanks, Dave reminded himself in affinity with all the desperate men who had to fight on the ground. He was sympathizing with the Germans ahead, whoever they were, even as he rejoiced in their doom.

The other man's dark blue eyes moved from the noisy sky to the gun Dave held pointed at his chest.

"Keep your hands up," Dave said.

"What's wrong with you? Don't you recognize an American officer?"

"There was some shooting over there. I still don't know what it was."

Another massive wave of planes came over. "I guess this will about finish it." The big man's tone was easy and conversational.

"I guess so. Just the same you'd better keep your hands up. You can put them behind your head if you like."

Then there was a noise of movement in the nearby snow and brush and a tall, gaunt soldier in Canadian battle dress floundered into the clearing.

"That's him!" the new man shouted.

"Who are you?" Dave called back, now covering both men with his rifle. The new man had carelessly come into the clearing with his rifle at the trail.

"I'm Canadian Army, George Ballantyne, Canadian Forestry Corps. Your friend here just killed some friends of mine."

"The one who's lying might as well tell the truth." Dave had grown so weak his own voice was hardly audible even in his own ears, but his mind seemed to be full of clarity. "We'll have to go and see what happened over there but if you want you can save us all some time."

The big man looked up again at the throbbing sky and shrugged. "Why not? I'm Hauptscharführer Franz Koerner of the 12th SS Division, presently detached for special duties."

In the last ten minutes an incredible transformation had come over Dave's big prisoner. He had grown younger by ten years and older by a century. His face had softened and still it had become as drawn and haggard as the face of the spent Canadian, Ballantyne. He shook his head and looked up again at the sky far above the trees, a much farther but a much more imperative sky than any of them had seen in much longer than a week. He took one hand from behind his neck and brushed it across his eyes and raised his head toward the sky again.

Whatever rage Dave had wanted to feel had eluded him, and to his surprise and vague disappointment he could find no rage in the face of the newcomer, the exhausted Canadian. For a moment the three men stared at each other, imprisoned in a foolish, futile silence.

At last Dave broke it by asking the only question he could think of. "Where did you get that uniform?"

The big—what was the correct word: spy? traitor? saboteur?—appeared to have heard only partly. "What? Oh, the uniform. It was issued to me as part of my equipment."

"Where are you from, Koerner?"

"Berlin."

"Before that?"

"Before?"

"Yes, before."

"Well, I was from the States."

"I guess it doesn't matter, but do you want to tell us where?"

"Oh, a place called Yorkville. In New York."

"You were in the Bund."

"That's right. I *am* in the Bund."

"Why did you do it, Koerner? Why did you do it?"

"Why did you do what you're doing? Why did"—Koerner nodded at the Canadian—"he? He said I killed some of his friends. What were they doing in my way? I had as much right there and as much reason there." There was little feeling in the big man's voice. It was a voice of inquiry and speculation as much as disputation.

"One of them was my brother," the Canadian said. Again there was the same queer air of judicial gravity and regret, as if anger had grown too small an instrument to serve the needs, demands, and due processes that were now beyond further putting off.

A big flight of C-47 transport planes droned overhead, and another big flight of fighter-bombers reached for the roads and hills.

Dave waited for the sound to die away. "We've got to shoot—" He heard himself speak the first few words and looked in appeal to each of the others in turn. How best to pronounce the sentence? To address the Canadian and put it, "We've got to shoot him?" Or the prisoner in the dock and say more courageously, "We've got to shoot you?"

He began again. "A traitor"—it was not much of a compromise, but it sounded, somehow, more impersonal and less brutal—"has to be shot."

Now the strange silence returned. It was the prisoner who spoke first, his old-young face partly turned away. "All right, then."

"No!" Ballantyne cried out in abrupt alarm, and Dave felt it was he, not the prisoner, who was being offered a reprieve. "No, God damn it, make somebody else do it! Let's take him in with us."

The prisoner had lowered his hands. His old-young face contrived the trace of a smile. "But you see," he said, "I'm not going in with you." The clever bastard, Dave thought. The lousy clever bastard. "I'm going to start walking away into the forest, unarmed, with my back to you. What you do about it is your problem; it's no longer mine." He hesitated. "I warn you of one thing. Don't try to stop me with anything but your guns. I've had better luck these last few days, apparently, than you have, and if it gets down to hand-to-hand I'm strong enough to handle you both."

"What," Dave asked, hating himself for his weakness, "if I don't shoot?"

"That again is largely your problem. I'll try to find another gun in the woods there somewhere and get back into the war."

"But the war's over now." Dave found himself, absurdly, trying to protect the prisoner from himself.

"For you perhaps. Not for me. As you say, a traitor has to be shot."

Koerner nodded toward George Ballantyne and said with what might have been either genuine emotion or another piece of cunning, "I'm sorry about your friends. The other two were friends of mine." Then he turned around and started walking, neither slowly nor with undue haste, into the trees.

"Stop!" Dave cried after him.

"For God's sake stop!" the Canadian cried.

Koerner walked on and Dave raised his gun. Now there was no escape for either of them. Each of them had chosen this moment or had it thrust upon him and there was no going back for either. Dave straightened the gun. Against whom? Against this stranger from his native land? Against his father Samuel Kyle? Against God or Henry Whelan or Carmen Ruiz or Mary Egan—or himself? Was this where damnation became final, when the lake of fire flooded over and became irrevocable and beyond escape? He had wondered enough already, he told himself in this irrevocable, irreplaceable split second, there was no time left for further wondering. He must do what he was compelled to do and hope that at last this high white forest would release him and allow him to make his peace on earth with Samuel Kyle and claim his life on earth with Mary Egan. He corrected his aim.

They reached the body together. "He wouldn't stop," the Canadian said. "There was nothing else to do."

"No, there was nothing else."

The inspection of the body was soon over. "The dog tags don't tell anything. He's supposed to be somebody named Williams, a Catholic and blood type O," the Canadian said. "There's a note here in his notebook. It's meant for a girl back in the States." He looked and handed it on.

Dear Gracie:

This is the first time I've had a chance to write to you in many years. I hope life is going as well with you as it's been going with me. I've been lucky enough to find a lovely girl from Hamburg and because you deserve it so much I know you too have married well and happily.

Please, Gretchen, if this reaches you, give Mother and Uncle Otto my deepest love. It's too bad we all ended up on opposite sides of this strange war. It will be interesting to see who wins it.

Yours sincerely,
FRANZ KOERNER

Without saying anything they hacked some branches loose and placed them on the man below.

David looked more closely at the Canadian. "You're in bad shape."

"I guess you are too."

"Let me give you a hand. The planes dropped their stuff about four miles ahead. That means we can't be very far from our lines. Let's just take it slow."

"Do you know what day this is?"

"I think it's one day or two before Christmas. The attack started a week ago, didn't it? That would make this—what? The twenty-third?"

The Canadian pulled himself wearily to his feet. "Will you come and help me cover up my brother and leave a marker there?"

In an hour, partly guided by the continuing flights of planes and the sound of their rockets, guns, and bombs, they came to a main roadway. Miraculously, a convoy of American tanks and trucks and marching infantry was moving up already in the direction of the massive hills ahead.

There hadn't been any more chance for thinking. As Dave labored across the ground pooling his uncertain strength and balance with the uncertain strength and balance of his new comrade George Ballantyne, he still had no idea where he and it were coming out. To his prime inquisitors—his father, his deserted God, Henry Whelan, John P. Barnstable, Corley Hector, and Carmen (the Hood) Ruiz—had now been added the only man he'd had to know before he'd had to kill him. The big strange man from Yorkville would be no easier to answer than the others, for, like the others, he would not phrase his questions in words that allowed a yes or no. But Dave's conclusion of a while ago was growing, if not precisely steadier, at least worthier of hopeful further thought.

A soldier leaned out the back of one of the slowly moving trucks.

"You boys O.K.?" he shouted anxiously.

"Not bad," David Kyle shouted, half supporting George Ballantyne and half supported by him.

"It's only a little way," the soldier in the truck shouted encouragingly. "There's chow back there. There's even beds. You'd better go faster."

Dave looked up. It was George Ballantyne who spoke for them both. "Can't you see we're going as fast as we can?"